The Nameless Day

"Douglass has again brilliantly blended detailed research with religion and magic to reinterpret actual historical events.... this captivating historical fantasy ranks with the best in the subgenre." —*Publishers Weekly* (starred)

"Captivatingly written, this first installment of a planned trilogy should win fans of fantasy and historical fiction alike."
—*Booklist*

"Her best book yet ... an intricately shaded tale from the black-and-white world of medieval religion."
—*Romantic Times BookClub Magazine*

"Filled with the intricate weave of religious and political history that made up an era when church and state were not yet divided, this powerfully written tale belongs in every fantasy collection and has strong appeal for fans of historical fiction."
—*Library Journal*

The Wounded Hawk

"Douglass puts her Ph.D. in history to good use in skillful attention to period detail and credible medieval action, so that her saga should please fantasy enthusiasts, history buffs, and even fans of the Left Behind series."   —*Booklist*

"Historical fantasy aficionados should not miss this compelling multilayered series."
—*Romantic Times BookClub Magazine* (four stars)

"Douglass seamlessly fuses the period's class struggle for freedom against tyranny with a disturbingly vivid look at the ambiguous battle between good and evil."
—*Publishers Weekly*

by SARA DOUGLASS
from TOM DOHERTY ASSOCIATES

THE
CRIPPLED
ANGEL

THE CRUCIBLE: BOOK THREE

THE
CRIPPLED
ANGEL

THE CRUCIBLE: BOOK THREE

Sara Douglass

TOR®
fantasy

A TOM DOHERTY ASSOCIATES BOOK
NEW YORK

This is a work of fiction. All the characters and events portrayed in this book are either products of the author's imagination or are used fictitiously.

THE CRIPPLED ANGEL: THE CRUCIBLE: BOOK THREE

Copyright © 2002, 2006 by Sara Douglass Enterprises, Pty, Ltd.

Originally published in 2002 by Voyager, an imprint of HarperCollins-Publishers, Sydney.

A Tor Book
Published by Tom Doherty Associates, LLC
175 Fifth Avenue
New York, NY 10010

www.tor.com

Tor® is a registered trademark of Tom Doherty Associates, LLC.

ISBN-13: 978-0-765-34284-3
ISBN-10: 0-765-34284-7

First edition: January 2006
First mass market edition: August 2006

Printed in the United States of America

0 9 8 7 6 5 4 3 2 1

CONTENTS

Europe

Northumberland

Carlisle

England

Sheriff Hutton

York

Ravenspur

Conway Castle

Bramham Moor

Saxbye

Flint Castle

Lincoln

Shrewsbury

Kenilworth

Oxford

The Thames

Halstow Hall

Windsor Castle

London

Barming

Dover

Wales

Ireland

Waterford

Scotland

England

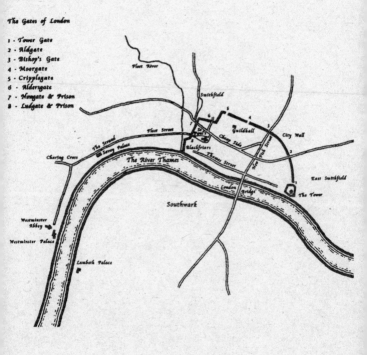

The Gates of London

1 - Tower Gate
2 - Aldgate
3 - Bishop's Gate
4 - Moorgate
5 - Cripplegate
6 - Aldersgate
7 - Newgate & Prison
8 - Ludgate & Prison

The Gates of London

He married his wife on Sunday
Beat her well on Monday,
Bad was she on Tuesday,
Middling was she on Wednesday,
Worse was she on Thursday,
Dead was she on Friday;
Glad was he on Saturday night,
To bury his wife on Sunday,
And take a new wife on Monday,
To beat her on the Tuesday.

—Version one of a
traditional English nursery rhyme

THE
CRIPPLED
ANGEL

THE CRUCIBLE: BOOK THREE

Prologue

Friday 1st March 1381

✠

THE CHAMBER WAS close and warm, its windows closed, its air thick with the scent of herbs.

There was silence, save for the moans of the woman squatting between two midwives before the roaring fire in the hearth.

The woman giving birth was naked; her skin gleamed with sweat, while her unbound hair had soaked into glistening strings clinging to her shoulders and back. The midwives bent over her, holding bunches of soothing herbs close to her nostrils and open mouth, rubbing the small of her back encouragingly.

They did not murmur instructions to her, for Marie was of their own and knew what was happening both to her own body and to the baby it was trying to expel.

Two other women stood half-shadowed on each side of the shuttered windows. To one side stood Catherine of France, daughter of the insane Louis and the adventurous Isabeau de Bavière, her attention as much on her silent companion as on the labouring Marie.

Slightly distanced from her stood Joan of Arc, Maid of France, staring intently at the woman struggling to give birth. Her face, if possible, was even more tortured than that of Marie.

She was terrified of what Marie was about to birth, for she feared the child's father was not of earthly origin.

Joan had spent these past seven months since Charles' crowning at Rheims Cathedral in a fugue of despair. This despair was not caused by Charles' stubborn refusal to move from Rheims, or to do anything that might be construed as even vaguely warlike, but by the swelling of Marie's body. Indeed, Joan's despair had increased in direct proportion to the escalating distention of Marie's belly. Marie might not know how her child had been conceived, or who had put it in her, but Joan had a very good idea, and she knew that if the child confirmed her suspicions then she would have no choice but to abandon her crusade for the Archangel Michael.

How could she serve an angel who so callously used women's sleeping bodies? Who was so inherently flawed? So inherently sinful? And so arrogant in that sinfulness?

"See?" said Catherine conversationally, very well aware of Joan's distress. "The baby is about to be born."

Joan jerked, an almost inaudible moan escaping her mouth. She wished she could tear her eyes from Marie, or run from the room, but she could do neither. She prayed meaninglessly, futilely—for she was not sure to whom she *could* pray—that somehow the actuality of Marie's child would prove the archangel's innocence.

But in Joan's innermost being she knew that was impossible.

In her innermost being, Joan knew that the archangel had put that child inside Marie.

And in her very few, most painfully honest moments, Joan knew that the archangel had lied and abused and manipulated her even more grossly than he had Marie.

All Marie had to do was endure the agony necessary to birth his child.

All Joan had to do was die. To die for the cause of a sin-crippled angel.

How could that *cause be good, and just?*

Marie was struggling even more now, moaning as she

bore down on the child. One of the midwives moved in preparation to catch the baby as it slithered from Marie's body; the other rubbed even more vigorously at Marie's back.

Catherine moved her eyes from Marie, looking at Joan.

There was no venom, or even triumph, in her gaze. Once she'd hated and loathed Joan, but now she realised that the struggle taking place within Joan was even worse than that which consumed Marie.

Of all people, a child of the angels herself, Catherine was one who empathised with those the angels used and manipulated. She also knew that, riven by her doubts, Joan was no longer such a terrible threat to the cause of Catherine and her fellows.

She wondered again, as she had so many times over the past few months, why the angels believed they could afford to alienate Joan.

Was Thomas Neville now so much their man?

Catherine frowned slightly. The small amount of news she'd managed to glean about Thomas Neville over the past few months indicated anything but that. He'd abandoned his vows and married Margaret Rivers, half sister to the Demon-King himself, Hal Bolingbroke. Surely Neville was **more** in the Bolingbroke camp than in that of the angels?

A particularly intense moan from Marie—more of effort than pain—made Catherine turn back to the woman. The midwife waiting to catch the child had moved forward now, her hands held ready, her eyes intent. Marie threw back her head, bearing down with every ounce of strength that she had.

She gave a sudden wail, almost of surprise, and Catherine saw the baby slither forth.

"'Tis a girl!" cried the midwife, who laid the baby on the waiting linens and was securing the cord as Marie herself sank down to the floor.

Catherine looked back to Joan.

The girl was staring unblinkingly at the scene before

her, her eyes round, almost starting from her head. Beads of sweat glistened on her forehead and cheeks, and Catherine thought them less a product of the chamber's warmth than the intense emotion within Joan herself.

Catherine saw that the cord binding Marie and the baby had now been cut, and the child was wrapped securely in some linens.

She walked over, and took the child from the midwife. "I will bring her back momentarily," she said at Marie's murmured protests, then walked slowly back over to Joan.

"See this child?" she said, half-holding the baby out to Joan, even though she knew Joan would not take her.

Joan stared down at it, her form trembling slightly.

She was a beautiful child.

Angelic.

And . . . something else.

"Can you feel *what* she is?" Catherine said softly, so that neither Marie nor the two midwives could hear.

Joan's mouth half opened, and her tongue flickered over her lips. Her lips moved, but no sound came forth.

She was still staring at the child.

"Can you feel what she is?" Catherine said, more forcefully, but still low.

She is a demon, Joan. You can sense that, can't you?

Joan's face twisted in agony, and she finally managed to tear her eyes from the child to Catherine's face.

The lack of malice—worse, the *understanding*—that Joan saw there appeared to distress her even more.

"Can you now see," Catherine said, "how 'demons' come into this world? How is it that we are hated and vile creatures, Joan, when our only sin has been to be abandoned and loathed by our fathers? Who is the more hateful, Joan? The child . . . or the *father*?"

"I don't . . . I can't . . ." Joan said, then she shuddered so violently that Catherine took some pity on her.

"Go now," she said. "I will come to you later, and speak with you honestly."

Joan stared at her, blinked, looked once more at the child, then fled the chamber.

JOAN STUMBLED as if blinded through the passages and hallways of Charles' palace in Rheims. She managed to gain her small chamber having fallen only twice, and immediately groped her way across the darkened room to a small altar in the corner.

"Saint Michael?" she whispered. "Blessed saint?"

Even now, even though Joan's mind *knew* the corruption of the angels, she refused to accept it. She wanted the archangel to appear and reassure her. She needed him to demonstrate to her how she'd been misled, how she'd misunderstood, and how there was a reasoned explanation for all she'd just witnessed.

After all, surely the ways of the angels were strange to the poor minds of mortal men and women?

"Saint Michael? Blessed saint . . . *please* . . . I need to hear your—"

What? My explanation?

Joan's head jerked up from where it had been bowed over her clasped hands, but there was no physical sign of the archangel. No light, no glowing form, nothing but a heavy coldness that felt as if it had stepped all the way down from heaven.

I owe you nothing, Joan. I care not what you choose to believe. You have proved yourself fragile and useless. I cannot believe that I ever had faith in you.

"Saint Michael, please—"

Please what? *Do you expect me to explain myself to you? I have finished with you. Done.*

"The child. *Tell me about the child!*"

The cold intensified, and Joan gasped with pain as it wrapped itself about her.

You have been as nothing. We had thought once to have need of you, but you have proved yourself a passing fool-

ishness on our part. You no longer please us, and we rescind our favour.

The cold, impossibly, grew more intense, and Joan shrieked as iciness enveloped her lower body.

We return you to your normal womanly self, Joan, and leave in place of our favour all the loathing for your kind that we bear. We have no longer any need for you, Joan, and, not needing you, we choose to despise you.

And with that, the icy grip of the archangel gave one final, agonising clench, and then it, as the archangel's presence, vanished, leaving Joan collapsed and weeping on the floor.

There she lay for long moments, unable to cope with the weight of the archangel's loathing and betrayal on top of witnessing the birth of Marie's child.

She suddenly lurched to her feet, her face twisted and wet with tears, and tore from the wall where they hung the sword and banner of the Archangels Michael and Gabriel.

She took the banner, and tore it first in two, then each of those two pieces into many more, shrieking and panting in her anger and sense of betrayal.

How could she have been so credulous, so naive, as to let herself be used by such corrupted beings as the angels?

The banner shredded easily, almost as if it too recognised the lies with which it had been constructed, and Joan only paused in her maddened destruction when the banner lay in pieces at her feet.

Then she reached for the sword.

She held it for a moment, staring wild-eyed at it, her sense of betrayal growing even stronger with every second that passed. Then she took it and dashed the blade against the heavy stone sill on the window.

The blade shattered into three jagged sections.

Joan screamed, allowing the useless hilt to fall clattering to the floor.

How could she have made herself the instrument of evil? What if her entire life had been a lie? A cruel hoax, and she the only one not to realise it? Had all of France, all of Christendom, been laughing at her?

She should have stayed home and tended her father's sheep. That, at least, would have occasioned no laughter.

Perhaps she should go home ... tend her father's sheep ...

But what if her father also now despised her? Laughed at her?

In this past hour, and particularly in these past moments, Joan's entire faith, her entire reason for *being*, had been stripped away in so cruel a manner that had her sword still been intact Joan would undoubtedly have fallen upon it.

She started to shake, her tremors becoming so violent that she fell to the cold stone floor. She moaned and cried out, wishing that death would simply come to take her in this moment of despair.

"Joan," came a voice so deep and comforting that Joan believed it merely a dream. "Joan, you are so greatly loved that my eyes run with tears for you. Joan, see ... see how I weep with love for you."

Joan blinked, still curled in a tight ball on the floor. Was this a phantasm? Or the archangel come back to torment her?

Another voice spoke, a woman's this time. "Joan, will you see? Will you raise your eyes and see how much your lord loves you?"

It was the woman's voice, rather than the man's, that made Joan raise her face from the stone flagging and stare before her.

She gasped, hardly crediting what her eyes told her.

The chamber had disappeared. Instead Joan lay on the top of a low hill. Before her a woman knelt at the foot of a cross.

Not daring to believe, Joan raised her eyes still further.

An almost naked man gazed down at her from the cross. He had been vilely nailed to the wood through his wrists and ankles, and a crown of thorns hung askew on his bleeding brow. His loincloth was darkly soiled with the blood that had crept down his body.

Yet, even so cruelly pinned, the man smiled down on Joan with such infinite love that her despair vanished as if it had been swept away in a great wind.

"Lord Jesu?" she whispered.

"Joan," he said, and she could see how much each word cost him. His chest and shoulders were contorted in agony, his every breath an agonised nightmare.

"Joan, will you trust me?"

Joan's gaze slipped to the woman. She was young and pregnant, and very beautiful, with translucent skin, deep blue eyes and dark hair.

She was also sad, weeping, but somehow serene and strong in that sadness.

"Have you been vilely treated by the angels as well?" Joan asked the woman.

"Aye," she said, "as has my lord. Joan, we would give you a purpose back into your life, and a gift also."

"A purpose and a gift?"

"Both with all our love," the woman said, and Joan realised that she spoke for both herself *and* Christ, who hung in such agony on his cross that he found speech difficult.

"Your purpose shall be France," said the woman, and as she spoke she raised her right hand and made with it a sweeping gesture.

A dark vista opened up before Joan's eyes. It was France, but a France devastated and murdered. Fields lay burning, houses and castles lay toppled, clouds of smoke and ash billowed over the countryside.

Out of this horrid cloud rode a man on a dark horse: a man Joan had never seen before, but one she instinctively knew was the Demon-King. A handsome face under silver-gilt hair, pale grey eyes, a warrior's body and a warrior's bearing.

He rode his stallion over the broken bodies of French

men and women and children, and they screamed and wailed and bled as he progressed.

Not once did he look down and pity them. Instead, his face was swollen with glory and victory.

His stallion strode forth, and more bones cracked, and more children died.

"I know him," said Joan.

"Aye," said the woman. Her hands were now to her face, and she wept as if her heart broke.

Turning her eyes back to the woman, Joan wondered if she wept for France, or for the Demon-King.

"If Charles does not rise against him," the woman continued, gaining some control over her weeping, "then this is France's destiny."

"Charles is a lost cause," said Joan. "I have given him my all. I have begged and pleaded and threatened. I have spoken prophecies and wrought him miracles, but still he sits here in Rheims and weeps and wrings his hands. France needs a king to lead it, and what it has is a pile of useless excrement. I cannot change him."

"Yes, you *can* change him," said Christ, groaning with the effort of speaking. "See."

The vista changed so that France became a land of sundrenched meadows and laughing children. In this new France the Demon-King still stood, but his sword hung useless at his side, his shoulders had slumped, his form was thin and tremulous, and his feet had sunk to their ankles in a pool of bubbling black mud. Dread suffused the Demon-King's face, and his mouth hung slack with dismay. He stared towards a horizon where appeared a great and mighty king on a snowy war stallion. It was Charles, but a Charles Joan did not think existed.

Behind him rode a shining army—an army of a united and strong France.

The Demon-King whimpered, trembled violently, then sank into the bubbling pool of black mud until he had completely vanished.

"How can this be so?" Joan said.

"All you have to do," said the woman, now leaning forward and taking one of Joan's hands in hers, "is to tend your sheep."

Joan frowned. "I do not understand."

The woman smiled, and kissed Joan very softly on the mouth. She began to speak, and she spoke without interruption for many minutes.

At first Joan's face twisted with horror, then it relaxed, and assumed a radiance born both of wonder and of hope.

"*I* can do this?"

"You are the Saviour of France," said Christ, and he smiled with such tenderness and love through the haze of his own torment that Joan's heart overflowed with the strength of her love and joy. "The path ahead of you shall be tiresome and often painful. You will doubt. But I—"

"And I," put in the woman.

"—will always be there. We will not forget you. When you are at your darkest, *then we will be there for you.*"

MUCH LATER Catherine came to Joan's chamber, thinking to talk more of Marie's child, and to use its birth to ensure Joan's total alienation from the angels.

What she found astounded her.

Joan knelt before her window, which she had opened to admit the dawn light. About her lay strewn the fragments of what Catherine recognised as Joan's sword and angelic banner.

"Joan?" Catherine said. "Are you well?"

Joan lowered her hands, which she'd had clasped before her. She rose and turned to face Catherine.

For an instant, Catherine thought that the girl had tripped entirely into the murky waters of insanity, impelled by the truth she'd been forced to witness last night. But then she realised that Joan's face was infused not with madness, or even with her previous obsessive devotion, but with a peace so profound that Catherine's eyes widened in wonder.

"What has happened?" she said.

Joan smiled secretively, although not in a sly manner. "I have found myself," she said.

Catherine indicated a small stool. "May I sit?"

"Oh, yes. Forgive me. I should have asked you myself."

Then Joan, who sat on the edge of her narrow bed, tilted her head and regarded Catherine with a modicum of curiosity. "You have not come to gloat, have you?"

Catherine shook her head, wondering what it was that had caused this great change in the girl over only a few short hours. When Joan had run from Marie's birthing chamber, Catherine thought her close to breaking.

"I had wondered," Catherine said carefully, "if you might need someone to talk to."

"That was kind of you," said Joan, knowing that was not quite the reason Catherine had come to her.

Catherine hesitated, not sure what to say next. This was not the Joan she had expected to find.

Joan spoke again, filling the uncomfortable silence. "How is Marie, and her daughter?"

"They are well," Catherine said.

"For the moment," said Joan, "but how will Marie venture forth into the world, an unmarried woman with a bastard child? I worry for her, and feel guilt, knowing how I deserted her when she needed me most."

"I have arranged for her a place as housekeeper in a small convent in Amiens. The sisters will be pleased to receive her, and both Marie and her daughter will be nurtured."

Joan's mouth twitched. "If only they knew *what* they nurture," she said, and then the amusement died from her face. "Tell me of the angels, Catherine, and of the misery they have visited on you, and on mankind."

And so Catherine took a deep breath and, as Hal Bolingbroke and Margaret had once talked to Thomas Neville, told Joan all she knew. For millennia the angels of heaven had descended in spirit upon sleeping mortal women and made them pregnant. The angels had violated these women, for they were unknowing of their angelic visitations, and unconsenting. These women became pregnant, and birthed remarkable children who became leaders in their societies, adding greatly to that society's culture and store of knowledge. One day God Himself had visited a mortal woman, and made her pregnant, and the resulting offspring, Jesus, like all angel-children, became a remarkable leader within his society, save that he preached of love and freedom from Heaven's clutches.

Jesus opened the angels' eyes to how dangerous it was to allow their children to live freely within human society. Having trapped Jesus within Heaven, the angels then ensnared humankind within the Church, which taught that all angel-children were "demons," inhabitants of hell, in an effort to negate their influence.

When she had finished Joan looked sorrowful, but still composed. "We have all been grossly misused and abused," she said.

Catherine nodded, satisfied. "What will you do now?"

Joan smiled, beatifically, as if at an inner vision, and Catherine wondered if she'd slipped back into her previous blind and obsessive piety.

But the expression passed, and Joan spoke calmly and reasonably. "I had thought to return to my parents' home," she said. "I thought to devote myself to the tending of my father's sheep."

"That's a wonderful—"

"But I have changed my mind," Joan said, grinning slightly at the expression on Catherine's face. "Oh, do not worry, Catherine. I have no doubt that I shall end my days watching over my father's sheep in some blessed meadow, but there is still one small task left for me to do here first."

"And that is?"

"To fit Charles for his rightful place, as King of France."

"You cannot *still* mean to accomplish that! Charles is a hopeless imbecile who—"

"He will not always be so," Joan said. "He merely needs an infusion of strength. I am that strength."

"Then we are still at odds."

Joan took Catherine's hand. "Yes. We are. Indeed, our positions have hardly changed. You fight to replace Charles with . . . well, with whomever. And I fight to give him France. What has changed is that I now understand you, and in understanding you, I have come to a realisation."

"And that is . . . ?"

"I think that one day we will be friends. Even, I dare to venture, that we will fight for the same end."

Catherine opened her mouth to speak, but Joan continued quickly. "Am I not a prophetess? Then hear me out. In the end, I think we will both do what is right for France, and I think that we will both take the path that *love* demands of us, not those paths that previous blind allegiances have shown us."

Catherine chewed her lip, then nodded. "Should we still spat in public, Joan? Should I pull your hair every time you pass?"

"Oh, indeed! Otherwise your mother will think the world has come to an end!"

They both laughed, then Catherine rose, aiding Joan to rise at the same time. She kissed Joan's cheek.

"Be well, Joan."

"Aye," Joan said. "I think I will be, now."

PART ONE

Windsor

In the meane time . . . certain malicious and cruel
persons enuiyng and malignyng in their heartes . . .
blased abrode and noised dayly amongest the vul-
gare people that kyng Richard . . . was yet liuyng
and desired aide of the common people to repos-
sesse his realme and roiall dignitie. And to the fur-
theraunce of this fantastical inuencion partly
moued with indignacion, partely incensed with furious malencolie, set vpon postes and caste aboute
the stretes railyng rimes, malicious meters and
tauntyng verses against king Henry . . . He being
netteled with these uncurteous ye unuertuous
prickes & thornes, serched out the authors . . .

—*Edward Hall,* Chronicle, *1548*

Chapter I

✠

LORD THOMAS NEVILLE walked slowly through the gardens of Windsor Castle, heading for the entrance to the King's Cloister. He narrowed his eyes slightly against the mid-morning brightness of the sun, enjoying its welcome warmth even though its glare made his eyes ache.

Windsor Castle had long been favoured by the English kings, but since his coronation seven months ago, Bolingbroke had made it his main residence. He'd not wanted to reside in Westminster, which he thought cold and uncomfortable; the Savoy was still in ruins; Lambeth Palace was unavailable now that the new Archbishop of Canterbury had moved in; and the only other truly regal palace in London was the Tower, which needed another few months' worth of renovations before it could be suitable to use as Bolingbroke's royal residence. So Bolingbroke had moved his court to Windsor, a solid day's ride west from London.

Neville raised his face slightly, staring towards the silvery stone walls of the castle, looking for the tall, graceful, second-level windows of the Great Chamber. Ah . . . there they were, so afire with the glare of the sun that no outsider would be able to peer through and intrude upon the privacy of the chamber's occupants. Neville had no doubt that by this time of the day Bolingbroke would be settled with his advisers and secretaries and counsellors.

And here Neville was in the gardens.

"My Lord Neville! Morning's greetings to you!"

Neville jumped, silently cursing the sudden thudding of his heart. He squinted against the sun, then relaxed, nodding to the man striding down the garden path towards him.

"My Lord Mayor," he said, extending a hand. "My congratulations on your recent election."

Dick Whittington took Neville's hand in a firm grasp, then indicated a nearby bench. "If you're in no hurry, my lord?"

Neville sat with Whittington on the bench, wondering what the Lord Mayor could want to say to him.

"I am pleased to have this chance to speak with you, my lord, that I might ask after your lovely wife and children."

"Margaret? Why, she is well, as are Rosalind and Bohun," Neville responded, surprised at the enquiry. Whittington hardly knew Margaret . . .

"I have just come from the Great Chamber," Whittington said, after a slight hesitation, "and an audience with our king—you know of his edicts regarding education, and clocks?"

Neville nodded. Over the past months Hal had instructed that science and the new humanities were to receive a greater weight in schools at the expense of religion, while clock hours were to replace church hours of prayer in people's daily lives.

It was all, Neville knew, part of Hal's not-so-subtle turning of his subjects' hearts and minds away from the religious to the secular.

"Aye, well," Whittington continued, "I needed to consult with His Grace over some of the details of the new school curricula, and the appropriate fees the clockmaker's guild can charge for the installation of clocks in all London's gates and major steeples."

Neville shifted impatiently, wondering why Whittington was subjecting him to this pointless conversation.

"My lord," Whittington said, his eyes narrowing in what might have been amusement, "I am keeping you from your duties, and for that I apologise, but—"

Ah, Neville thought, *now we reach the heart of the matter.*

"—I admit to some curiosity, even some concern, over the fact that His Grace now conducts his morning's counsel . . . and you are not there to advise him. I remember the dark days of Richard's reign, and his cruel edicts and taxes which set England's peasants into rebellion, and to their destructive march on London. I remember you and Hal as confidants, brothers almost, in the desperate quest to discover a means to end Richard's cruel reign. I remember how you *fought* together, in England's name, to put Hal on the throne and Richard in close prison."

Then I did not know that Hal was the Demon-King, Neville thought, keeping the expression on his face a mixture of the vaguely pleasant and the vaguely impatient. *Then I did not know the extent of his manipulations and his lies. We were close then, but now I know what truly he is, and how he used me, our "brotherhood" is at an end.* Neville simply did not know anymore whether Hal had seized the throne for the good of England . . . or if Hal wished to use the English throne as a base from which to launch a campaign of European (if not world) conquest. Should Neville believe Hal's protestations of wanting to work for the good of all men and women, or should he listen to his doubts, which whispered that Hal was interested in only one thing—using demonic power to enslave mankind?

As a result of his doubts, and because he simply no longer trusted Hal, Neville had distanced himself from his once close friend.

"Hal is now king," Neville said. "He has great lords

and Privy Councillors; and even," he allowed himself a small smile, "Lord Mayors to advise him. He does not need me so much."

"And the friendship has died along with Hal's elevation to the throne? I ask," Whittington hurried on, noting the surprise in Neville's face, "because I care deeply for Hal, and I cannot think that he is the better man for the loss of your friendship."

"He has not lost my friendship," Neville said, noting Whittington's easy use of Bolingbroke's Christian name. "We have merely grown distant with circumstances." He did not say that what Bolingbroke had lost was Neville's complete trust once he'd realised the depth of Bolingbroke's lies and manipulations.

"Hal did what he needed to gain the throne," Whittington said very quietly. "England is the better land for his actions."

Now Neville stared outright at Whittington. What did he allude to? Bolingbroke's rebellion against Richard, or the series of well-planned murders that ensured Bolingbroke was the only Plantagenet left to succeed to the throne?

And if Whittington alluded to the murders . . . then what did that make the Lord Mayor? Man, or demon?

"Who are you?" Whittington said, his voice still quiet. "Hal's man, or the angels'?"

With that question Whittington displayed an understanding that only a demon could have known: that Neville was the angels' chosen champion against the demons. Since discovering Hal's true nature, as well that "demons" were in fact the result of angels' liaisons with human women, Neville had retreated from his original fanatical support of the Church, but he had yet to choose whether he would fight for the angels or for the demons. Both sides curried his favour, but as yet Neville was highly reluctant to make his decision. There was so much as stake.

Neville abruptly stood, knowing now on which side the

Lord Mayor fought. "I am my own man, my Lord Mayor," he said, knowing that would be the answer Bolingbroke most feared, and knowing Whittington would certainly report it back to the king. "And now, *I* will detain you no longer. I am sure London needs its Lord Mayor more than I do."

And with that he turned and strode away.

As Neville disappeared into the building, Whittington looked to the windows of the Great Chamber, and shook his head slightly.

BOLINGBROKE LOOKED down from the window of the Great Chamber, catching the shake of Whittington's head.

His face hardened, his suspicions confirmed.

Behind him droned on the voices of his advisers, debating the merits of raising the passport application fee yet again, but Bolingbroke heard none of it.

Instead, his thoughts were full of Neville.

Why was Archangel Michael so confident of Neville? How could he be so sure of him?

"What is your secret, Tom?" Bolingbroke murmured. *"What is your secret?"*

NEVILLE BLINKED as he walked under the stone arch into the shaded walks of the King's Cloister. There were a few people about enjoying the early spring air, but it was still relatively quiet.

Neville nodded to two young lords whom he knew, then ducked into the stairwell that led to the royal apartments on the second level.

He emerged in the upper gallery, but turned away from the door leading to the Great Chamber and to Bolingbroke. Neither did Neville so much as glance at the open door of the beautiful chapel that ran along the upper gallery at right angles to the Great Chamber.

Instead, Neville walked purposefully towards the Queen's apartments and the loveliest chamber in the entire castle complex—the Rose Tower.

He paused at the door, nodding to the two guards standing outside, then walked through without any announcement . . . apart from Bolingbroke, Neville was the only person in the royal court (*in the entire kingdom*) permitted so to do by the lady within.

Neville paused just inside the door, hearing it close softly behind him, and looked about.

There were several ladies in the chamber, all grouped about the hearth, spinning and gossiping softly.

Margaret was not among them, and Neville supposed his wife was still in their apartment with their two children.

Mary lay on a couch set by the windows so that the morning light could fall upon her, and so that her gaze could in turn fall upon the awakening springtime outside.

Neville smiled, knowing Mary regarded him from under her downcast eyelashes, and walked towards her. As he did so, he once more admired the beauty of this chamber, as he did every time he entered it.

Bolingbroke's grandfather, Edward III, had redeveloped and redecorated much of Windsor Castle, and the pride of his refurbishing was the Rose Tower chamber, which Edward had made his inner sanctum. The walls and domed ceiling were painted deep crimson, and covered with scattered stars. At regular intervals across this bloodied, starry night were brilliant green enamelled cartouches, each holding within its gilded border a single delicate rose. Now Edward was dead, as was his successor Richard, and Bolingbroke was king, but it was Bolingbroke's wife, Mary, who had taken this most beautiful of chambers as her inner sanctum, and that, Neville thought as he knelt on one knee beside her couch, was only as it should be.

"My lady queen," he murmured, kissing her hand. "How do you this fine morning?"

"The better for your presence, Lord Neville," Mary replied, and smiled.

Neville's eyes sparkled with merriment. "My lady queen," he said, continuing their playful formality, "may I beg your indulgence to rise from my poor knee, and perchance—"

"Sit at the end of my couch," Mary said, laughing now, "where, Jesu willing, you might cease your groaning."

Neville did as she bade, careful not to disturb the silken wrap about her, or to place any pressure near the delicate bones of her ankles and feet. For a minute he did not speak, studying her face.

Mary watched him unquestioningly, for this moment of silent regard was a normal part of their morning greeting ritual.

"You have slept well," Neville said finally.

"Aye. My physician, Culpeper, has formulated a new liquor which allows me to forget my aches and moans for an hour more each night."

Neville's merriment faded at Mary's mention of her illness. Ever since her marriage to Bolingbroke, Mary had been wasting away from a growth in her womb. Sometimes she had a period of wellness that lasted as long as three or four weeks; more often she lay as she did this day, pale-skinned with dark pouches under eyes shadowed with pain.

And yet never did she complain, or moan about the injustice of life.

Silently, Neville reached out a hand and took hers. If his relationship with Bolingbroke had slid from deep friendship into wary politeness, then his relationship with Mary had taken the opposite path. Neville spent several hours each day with Mary—no doubt occasioning much gossip in court—talking, playing chess or, as now, merely sitting with her as he held her hand.

Her condition had stabilised somewhat over the past five or six months. From what both Mary and Margaret had told him, Neville knew that the mass in her womb had stopped actively growing and had instead shrunk to a small, hard lump; Mary no longer exhibited signs of pregnancy, nor expelled blackened spongy portions of the growth. Nevertheless, it continued to suck at Mary's vitality, and often to cause her great pain and discomfort.

But not to any mortal extent.

Neville wondered what Bolingbroke thought about this.

Bolingbroke and Mary no longer shared the same bed, both claiming that her illness made it impossible for Bolingbroke to sleep well. Bolingbroke had moved to chambers in a distant corner of the royal apartments, where he made no secret of occasionally sharing his nights with an accommodating lady of the court. Mary shrugged away her husband's unfaithfulness, and from the few words she'd said to him about it, Neville knew that she was secretly glad to escape the burden of her husband's sexual demands. She was not bitter, nor angry, and spoke of and to her husband with the greatest respect and good humour.

Neville thought her a saint, but he was unsure about how Bolingbroke regarded Mary's continuing grip on life. As a man (as a man-demon), Bolingbroke loved and lusted for another woman, Catherine of France. As a king, he lusted for the day he could hold a male heir in his arms.

Mary stood in the way of both lusts, and showed no sign of moving into the waiting pit of her grave any time in the near future.

Mary's hand tightened very slightly around his, and Neville wondered if she somehow not only could read his thoughts, but thought also to offer him comfort instead of asking it for herself.

Then the door to the chamber opened, breaking the spell between them.

A guard entered. "The Lady Margaret Neville," he said, bowing in Mary's direction, "with her children."

Mary let Neville's hand go, then smiled. "Let her enter," she said, and the guard bowed once again and opened the door wide.

* * *

MARGARET WALKED through the door, her seven-month-old son, Bohun, nestled in her arms. Directly behind Margaret was her maid, Agnes, with Margaret's two-year-old daughter, Rosalind, tugging at one of Agnes' hands as she looked curiously about her.

Both Margaret and Agnes sank into deep curtsies. Then Margaret took Rosalind and walked to where Mary and Neville sat. Agnes retired to a stool in a corner by the hearth to await her mistress' pleasure.

Margaret glanced at her husband as she approached, then smiled warmly at Mary. "How do you this day, madam?"

"Well, thank you, Margaret. I think that perhaps you and I can walk a little about the gardens this afternoon. It shall be a beautiful day."

"Gladly, madam." She started to say more, but then Rosalind broke free from her grip and scampered over to Mary, clambering up on the couch and cuddling in close to the woman. Margaret half reached out to grab her away, then saw the expression on Mary's face and dropped her hand.

"Do not let her hurt you, madam," Margaret said.

Mary's face had lit up as Rosalind snuggled into her body, and now she lifted her eyes to Margaret, and laughed a little. "What? This child? Hurt me? Nay, how can love hurt?"

Again Margaret felt her eyes sliding towards Neville, who she knew was regarding her steadily.

"You are so blessed in your children," Mary said in a half-whisper. One of her hands slowly stroked Rosalind's shining dark curls. Then she looked at Margaret again. "And in your husband."

Now Margaret could not help but look at Neville. He smiled slightly, but she could not entirely read the expression in his eyes, and so she looked away again.

* * *

WHEN THEY left the Rose Tower Margaret handed the two children into Agnes' care and asked Neville if he would walk awhile with her in the cloisters.

He linked an arm with hers, and together, slowly, they strolled about the sunlit flower beds, their bodies moving in unison, their hips occasionally bumping through the thick folds of their clothes.

"Mary seems well," Margaret eventually said.

"Well enough for a dying woman," Neville responded, his eyes once more on the glittering windows of the Great Chamber.

"Tom . . ."

Neville pulled her to a halt, and turned her so that their eyes could meet. "What is troubling you, Margaret?"

She gave a harsh laugh. "How can you ask that? My fate rests in your hands; the fate of my kind, and of humankind, where you decide to gift your soul. Of course I am troubled, for I do not think I know you anymore."

He studied her a moment. "And?"

"And?" Margaret took a deep breath. "And . . . you once said you loved me, but now I do not know. You spend so much time with Mary—"

"You think that I love Mary? No, do not answer that, for of course I love Mary."

Margaret's eyes suddenly filled with tears.

"I do not covet her flesh as a man is wont to covet a woman's flesh," Neville continued, "for I am lost in my covetousness of *your* flesh." He ran the fingers of one hand gently down her neck, and his eyes down the sweet curves of her body. "And I do not love her in a courtly fashion, for I could not imagine composing verse to any love but you. I love her as goodness personified—I do not think there can be any person living as good as Mary. And I love her because she is trust personified."

"Trust personified?"

Neville's hands were on Margaret's shoulders, firm

and resolute. "I trust Mary as I trust no one else," he said. "For of all people walking on this earth, I think she is one of the few who cannot be anything but what she appears. Mary has no secrets, and no secret plans."

Margaret lowered her gaze. "You have not yet forgiven me for what I—"

"And Hal," Neville put in.

"—did to you . . . with Richard."

Neville's expression tightened at the memory of how Hal and Margaret had stage-managed her rape by Richard, then coldly manipulated Neville's guilt to force him to admit his love of her. "I have forgiven you, Margaret," he said, and his hands loosened their grip on her shoulders. "And I still swear my love for you, and for our children. But I walk with open eyes now, and, yes, that makes a difference to how I see you . . . and all yours."

He does not trust me, Margaret thought, wishing not for the first time that she hadn't agreed to Hal's plan. "I am your wife, Tom," she said, reminding him of the promise she'd made to him the day Bohun had been born. "Not Hal's sister."

Margaret lived in terror that she might lose her husband completely. She had never thought she would love him so much, or feel so great a dread at the thought that he might walk away from her. She wished she had never tried to manipulate him, wished she'd been honest with him sooner, wished she'd never given him cause to mistrust her. *Believe me, Tom,* she pleaded, *please.*

Neville smiled gently, and touched a thumb to her cheek, wiping away the tear that had spilled there.

"Of course," he said.

Chapter II

Friday 3rd May 1381

☩

THE GREAT HALL at Windsor was not so grand or so large as the great hall at Westminster, but it was imposing enough and, when it was lit with thousands of candles and torches as it was this night, it shimmered with a delightful fairy light all its own. May had arrived with all its attendant ritual and games and seasonal joy, and Bolingbroke had organised tonight's feast to mark the commencement of his spring court. Thick sprigs of early spring flowers hung about pillars and beams, the scent of the flowers combining with that of the freshly laid rush floor to delight the senses of the guests. Servants had erected trestle tables in a long rectangle down the centre of the hall, and now they groaned under the weight of their linens, their gold, silver and pewter ware, and the initial dishes of the feast. The entwined harmony of lively chatter and music from the musicians walking up and down the aisles wound its way to the roof beams and then back down again, echoing about the hall.

The feast was proving an auspicious start to the weekend of tourneying that lay ahead.

Neville and Margaret sat with his uncle Ralph Neville's wife, Joan, and her mother, Katherine, the Dowager Duchess of Lancaster, on the first table to the right of the High Table. Their placement was an indication of the king's high esteem. As Baron Raby and Earl of Westmorland, Ralph Neville himself sat with the king and queen at the High Table on the dais. Sharing the High Table with Bolingbroke, Mary, and Raby sat the Abbot of Westminster, Henry Percy Earl of Northumberland, and John Holland Duke of Exeter and Earl of Huntingdon.

The abbot's presence at High Table was no surprise. Not only was he the senior ranked churchman present, but the Abbot of Westminster was the man who'd crowned Bolingbroke as King Henry of England. To *not* seat him at High Table would have been a grave insult to both man and Church.

As the abbot's presence was no surprise, neither was that of Ralph Neville, the Earl of Westmorland, and Henry Percy, the Earl of Northumberland. The combination of the power and influence of both these northern nobles had been pivotal in allowing Bolingbroke to raise the army needed to wrest the throne from Richard. But while Raby was an old family friend, taking as his second wife Bolingbroke's half sister Joan, the Percy family's loyalty had once been with Richard. Northumberland's allegiance to Bolingbroke was still relatively new, and thus relatively fragile—and made the more fragile because Northumberland's son, Hotspur, had yet to swear allegiance to Bolingbroke. Bolingbroke had gone out of his way these past months to keep Northumberland happy, and to heap upon him (as Raby) those preferments both men deserved for their part in bringing Bolingbroke to the throne.

Bolingbroke had not ascended the throne via the smooth transition of father to son. Instead, Bolingbroke had wrested the throne from his cousin, Richard, taking England to the very brink of civil war in so doing. For long months England's nobles had been divided between those who'd supported Richard's right to hold the throne, and those who'd supported Bolingbroke's right to take it from Richard. In the end, Bolingbroke's faction had prevailed, but the wounds were still open, particularly since the December reports of Richard's untimely death due to a sudden fever while incarcerated at Pontefract Castle.

Thus the inclusion of John Holland Duke of Exeter and Earl of Huntingdon at High Table. Exeter had not only been one of Richard's closest supporters, he was also Richard's older half brother: Richard and Exeter shared a mother, the beautiful (and sexually adventurous) Joan of Kent, who had been married to Sir Thomas Holland before the Black Prince seized her (she'd also had a bigamous marriage to William Montague, but fortunately there'd been no children from that union). Over the past six months Bolingbroke had worked assiduously to gain the acceptance and eventual support of those nobles who'd originally supported Richard. Bolingbroke had ostracised none of them, and had presented many of them with good preferments, appointments, and, on occasion, an advantageous marriage.

Yet Bolingbroke still sat the throne uneasily. Only rarely could allegiances be changed overnight, and Bolingbroke never knew what the smile on a courtier's face truly meant: allegiance, or hidden treachery.

Tonight, however, any concern about allegiances was well hidden behind smiles and courtly conversations. Mary was looking better than she had for several weeks. Her face was still pallid, but her eyes shone brightly, and her thin hands were steady as she accepted delicacies from the plates of her husband, on her left, and Raby, to her right. Bolingbroke engaged her from time to time in courtly conversation, but most of his attention was given to Northumberland, Exeter and the Abbot, who were all seated to his left.

Those whose allegiance he was most unsure of received his most gracious smiles.

Thomas Neville, watching the interplay from his spot close to the High Table, smiled himself at Bolingbroke's efforts. *Doubtless he thinks to ensure the country behind him before he embarks on his campaign of the world conquest,* he thought, and his smile faded a little.

It was a pity for Bolingbroke that Richard had died under such shadowy circumstances—and Neville had no doubt that Richard's death had been an expeditious murder rather than an unfortunate fever—and not nobly in the course of battle. Neville remembered how Bolingbroke had won the support of Richard's army outside Flint Castle with golden words rather than with bloodshed, and now he wondered if perhaps Bolingbroke hadn't miscalculated. Perhaps he should not have called a halt to what brief battle there had been before Richard had taken a blade in the throat. Perhaps . . .

"Your thoughts must be all-consuming," said a voice to Neville's right, "for they have surely taken your attention from the feast spread before us. And *such* a feast!"

"Forgive me," Neville said, smiling as he turned to face his dining companion, John Montagu Earl of Salisbury (and relative of the William who had bigamously bedded Richard's mother, Joan). Montagu was another noble who had backed Richard—the damn hall was packed with them!—and doubtless Bolingbroke was hoping that Neville could charm Montagu as the king was doubtless charming Holland. "I was merely wondering what had so caught the abbot's attention."

Montagu glanced at the High Table: the Abbot of Westminster, Bolingbroke, and Holland and Northumberland had engaged in a lively conversation that had the Abbot's cheeks a bright red with excitement.

"Our king's plans for Westminster, perhaps," Montagu said.

"Aye. Rumour has it that the abbot is excited at the thought of Parliament finally moving out of Westminster Abbey's chapter house!"

Montagu laughed easily, although the fingers of his right hand toyed nervously with his knife. "Your Hal has wasted no time making his mark upon the land," he said.

Neville's smile did not slip at Montagu's usage of "your Hal." "Parliament needed somewhere new to sit," he said. "The chapter house was too crowded, and the abbot had spent the past fifteen years complaining of the rowdiness of both Lords and Commons." He broadened his smile with a little effort. "He claims his meal times to have been quite ruined."

"But to give Parliament the use of Westminster Palace . . ." Montagu said. His knife was now making irritating rattling sounds as it jiggled against the side of his pewter plate.

Neville shrugged. "The palace was cold and draughty, and of little use for the family that Bolingbroke hopes to have surround him."

"And faint hopes of *that*," Montagu said in an undertone, shooting a glance towards Mary.

"It is understandable, perhaps," Neville continued, "that he should want to refurbish the Tower instead, and make of it not only a palace fit for a king, but a warm home as well."

"But to give Saint Stephen's to *Commons!*" Montagu said, and his hand finally stopped playing with his knife as he fixed his dark eyes on Neville.

Ah, Neville thought, *the crux of the matter.* Parliament would now sit in Westminster Palace and, for the first time, the Houses of Lords and Commons would be permanently divided. The new home of the House of Commons was to be the supremely beautiful St Stephen's Chapel, where Lancaster had married his Katherine, but Lords . . . Lords . . . Neville's smile finally lost its forced thinness and blossomed into a mischievous grin.

"Commons is the much larger house," he said, "and Saint Stephen's can accommodate them easily."

Montagu remained silent, now staring at his knife.

Neville fought to stop himself from laughing. "But of course, I can understand that many among the lords might be, ah, disgruntled, that they shall from henceforth sit in . . . the kitchens."

It was the merriment of the nation. Although Westminster Palace had several large halls, most were currently entirely unsuitable for permanent habitation by the

House of Lords. The Painted Chamber's floor was almost rotted through, and needed replacing, while its foundations were dank with rising damp. Repairs were desperately needed. White Hall had, for over fifty years, been divided up into sundry chambers for clerks and officials of the Chancery, and it would take a generation not only for all the brick partitions to be pulled down, but for suitable storage space to be found for all the rolls and deeds of government bureaucracy, not to mention all the grumpy Chancery officials. The Great Hall of Westminster was reserved for ceremonial occasions and the daily activities of the King's Bench, as various other legal courts.

That left the kitchens which were, in actual fact, a good choice. The great hall of the kitchen was of a similar size to the Painted Chamber, was solidly built, well lit, and, by virtue of being a kitchen, was well heated with five great hearths; and now that the palace was no longer to be used as a residence, the huge kitchen complex would no longer be needed. Once the cooks, dairy maids and butchers were moved out and the hall scrubbed, it would actually make a very good home for the House of Lords.

It was just that it was a former *kitchen!* While many lords accepted it in good humour—their new home would be far more commodious and comfortable than the cramped chapter house—many grumbled about it, feeling the location a slur. The beautiful St Stephen's went to Commons, while the lords got the kitchens. . . .

At least the people on the streets of London and, presumably, the fields of England, have something to smile about, Neville thought.

Then, before he could speak again, the Abbot of Westminster rose to his feet, his cheeks now a deep-hued crimson (although whether with excitement or drink, Neville could not tell), and called a toast to their handsome young king, and all in the hall rose, and raised goblets towards Bolingbroke.

* * *

MUCH LATER, Bolingbroke rose, extending his arm to Mary. She rose herself, but her action was decidedly unsteady, and Bolingbroke's eyes flew to Margaret at Neville's side.

Margaret murmured in concern, and moved about the tables towards Mary in order to help her.

Bolingbroke's eyes locked with Neville's, and he tilted his head slightly.

Neville nodded, understanding. Making his apologies to both Montagu and to Katherine, Lancaster's widow, he moved quickly and silently into the pillared aisles behind the tables.

"MORE WINE, Tom? Surely you cannot have yet drunk yourself into stupidity."

"Thank you, sire," Neville said, taking the goblet that Bolingbroke extended.

"Hal," the king said. "Call me Hal, Tom, when we are in private like this."

Neville had left the hall and walked quickly to Bolingbroke's private apartments as Bolingbroke said his good nights to both his guests and to Mary. He'd waited almost half an hour in the antechamber to Bolingbroke's suite before the king had entered, dismissed all his attendants with an impatient wave of his hand, and nodded Neville through into the inner bedchamber.

Now Bolingbroke sat in a chair before the fire, stretching out his legs and sighing. "Come, sit down, Tom. It is rare enough that we have this chance to so enjoy privacy, and there is no need for you to stand on ceremonial deference."

Neville's mouth twitched as he sat in a chair opposite Bolingbroke's. Bolingbroke could pretend all he liked that it was ceremony and the business of the nation that had kept them from their former close friendship, but

Neville would have none of it. He would no longer tolerate the lies that had once characterised their friendship.

"We are not the friends we once were, Hal." Neville raised his goblet in a silent toast to Bolingbroke, but smiled, taking any potential sting from his words.

"Aye," Bolingbroke said, looking down to his own goblet. "Well . . . that we are not."

Then he looked directly back to Neville, the firelight glinting in his silver-gilt hair and lighting his pale grey eyes. "I no longer know you, Tom. And that terrifies me."

"Why? Because you think to have lost a friend, or because you think to have lost control of me?"

Or because you fear I will not hand my soul to Margaret when the time comes? Neville's soul was to be the battleground between demons and angels. It had been foretold three years ago that if Neville chose love over the angels' wishes, if he chose to hand his soul on a platter to a woman he loved, then the demons would triumph. But if he chose against love, then the angels in heaven would prevail. Neville once again thanked Christ that he'd had the strength to refuse to watch Margaret transform herself into her true being while birthing Bohun. In that single refusal, Neville had, he hoped, given himself more room to manoeuvre.

Bolingbroke's mouth twisted. "You were ever blunt with your words, Tom." He paused, his eyes not faltering as they gazed at Neville. "I am terrified for both those reasons."

"I thank you for your honesty," Neville said. "If you had said anything else . . ."

Bolingbroke managed a slight laugh. "What? You would have raised a rebellion?"

Neville took a sip of wine, and decided to be bold. "I can do far worse to you, Hal, should I have a mind to." *I can choose for the angels, Hal.*

All amusement left Bolingbroke's face, and he leaned forward. "Do not threaten me!"

Neville leaned forward himself, taking Bolingbroke's fury full on. "Then promise never to lie to me again!"

Bolingbroke stared a moment or two longer at Neville, then gradually the fury faded from his face and he leaned back in his chair. "I cannot afford to, can I?"

Neville also sat back, one part of his mind thinking that he and Bolingbroke were engaged in some bizarre seated dance. "Nay. Not after all the lies you have told me in the past."

They were both silent for long minutes, thinking of the web of deception Bolingbroke, and Margaret, had spun about Neville.

It was Neville who finally broke the silence, his mouth lifting in a wry grin. "Who would have thought, Hal, that such a once intensely devout friar would sit so comfortably with the king of demons?"

"Such are the strange twists that life takes, Tom."

Again there was a silence, and again it was Neville who broke it.

"You have been honest with me," he said, "and so I shall be honest with you. Do you remember that moment during your coronation when the abbot asked if there were any reason you should not take the throne? If there were any man who disputed it?"

"How can I forget it."

"You looked at me, knowing that if I spoke, I could yet ruin your triumph."

Bolingbroke did not speak, waiting for Neville to continue.

"That moment stretched on and on," Neville said very softly, "as I thought."

"And of *what* did you think?"

"I thought of you that day you rode your white stallion into the centre of Richard's army outside Flint castle. I thought of what you promised them: freedom."

"A better life," Bolingbroke murmured, "for themselves and their families."

"I made myself a vow in that moment," Neville said. "I vowed that whatever your birth blood, your *demonry*, if you worked tirelessly and truthfully to ensure the freedom of the commons of England, those men and women who have ever loved you, then I would condemn heaven into hell if it might help you."

Bolingbroke's eyes widened, and he sat up slightly.

"But if," Neville continued, "I thought that you had lied to those men and women and to England, then I would do everything I could to ensure that you were thrust down into hell."

Bolingbroke stared, then spoke. "I did not lie, Tom. I would die if I thought it in the best interests of England's common men and women."

Neville shrugged and drained his goblet. He stood up, moving to the nearby table to refill it, turning to refill Bolingbroke's as well.

"Our friendship will never be what it once was, Hal. Not now."

"But we can still work together? For England?"

"Aye," Neville said, and raised his goblet. "For England."

There was an uncomfortable silence as both men drank, then Neville spoke again. "Talking of England, I am assuming that it was for unity's sake that you turned so much of your fabled charm on Exeter this evening?"

"I did my best, Tom. I did my best. At the least he laughed cheerily at my poor jests."

Ah, thought Neville. *Then Exeter is a dangerous man and undoubtedly thinking to raise a rebellion.*

"And what words passed between you and Montagu?" Bolingbroke enquired.

"General charm, but some sourness over the new home for the House of Lords. Hal, be careful. There is yet unrest."

"A kitchen has never caused a revolution yet, my friend. I shall have that kitchen decked out in fine emeralds and scarlets, and much gold gilding, and once the lords remember that the wine cellars lie directly beneath the former kitchen, well . . ."

"I have also heard whispers—no, not from Montagu, but in the streets and stables—about Richard. Hal, some say he is not dead."

Bolingbroke's mouth thinned. "Trust me, he *is* dead."

"Oh, I trust that you would not have him left alive to niggle at your legitimacy. But Richard's name is powerful whether he is dead or not. A single rumour that he escaped Pontefract Castle and waits in the marches for all true Englishmen to gather at his side would be enough to destabilise your seat on that throne."

"Richard is dead!"

"But he may still haunt you," Neville said. "Be careful. You may be beloved of the commons, but there are many who would not weep to see you dead on the cobbles with a knife between your ribs. Richard's name is the one they will use to thrust that knife home."

Bolingbroke waved a hand. "I will prevail."

"And I hope that you do," Neville said, "for of all things I do **not** want another Richard to take your place."

Bolingbroke smiled, and the atmosphere between them eased a little further. "You have taken good care of Mary," he said. "You and Margaret. For that I thank you."

"She is a treasure, Hal. The people on the street adore her almost as much as they do you."

"I have been lucky in my wife," Bolingbroke said.

"But not as lucky as you had hoped?" Neville said.

Bolingbroke sent him a sharp look. "What do you mean by that?"

"Mary will never bear you an heir. Have you thought about setting her aside?"

"That is a brutal remark, coming from one who claims that my wife is a treasure."

"Then I ask you as a king, not as a man. As a king, you need an heir. How does the king answer my question?"

"I can never set Mary aside," Bolingbroke said. "And that is the answer of the king."

Neville nodded, turning to stare into the flames as he thought. No, the king could not set Mary aside, and certainly not for the woman Bolingbroke truly wanted, Catherine of France. The commons adored Mary, and would loathe Catherine. It might be the end of Bolingbroke's kingship if he set Mary aside.

So Bolingbroke the king was going to wait for Mary the queen to die.

Neville wondered very much what Bolingbroke might do if Mary did *not* die. A crippled, barren wife was second only to a successful rebellion as the worst lot in life that fate could deal a king.

"And France?" Neville said.

Bolingbroke hesitated. "France? You know I will turn my attention to France sooner or later, Tom."

"Aye." *For there lies Catherine . . . and untold wealth and land.* "Take care you do not become another King Arthur, Hal. So caught by his glorious dreams of conquering the entire civilised world he neglected his own family where waited his doom. Remember what happened to Arthur's dream of Camelot."

Bolingbroke shot Neville an unreadable look, then took a deep breath. "I *must* to France, but not merely for the 'glory'. France waits for me, and for you."

"Waits for *me?*"

"Aye. It will be in France that the angels, no doubt using their mouthpiece Joan of Arc, will ask you for your decision, Tom. My road, as yours, will lead to France."

Neville thought a moment, then nodded. Of course. Doubtless, Joan would present the choice on behalf of the angels. "Arthur's dreams ended in France," he said.

Bolingbroke stared at Neville. "Then I pray to our sweet Lord Jesus that France shall not prove the end of mine."

Chapter III

Saturday 4th May 1381

— i —

✠

IT WAS STILL dark, but Mary could hear the world stir outside her chamber windows. There was a faint, distant clattering interspersed with the low growl of men's voices: grooms readying the horses for the day's entertainment. There was another clatter, closer, and this noise was interspersed with more feminine voices: women in the kitchen courtyard, darting to and fro between kitchen and great hall, carting pails and dishes, readying the morning's breakfast. And faintly, so very faintly, came the morning song of the birds: the pigeons and doves of the stables, and the wilder, lovelier melodies of the meadow birds.

Mary kept her eyes closed, her hands clenching at her sides under the light coverlets, and bent her entire will to concentrate on the sound of the birds. But it was no use. The world of stables and of kitchens kept intruding, destroying the peace of the birdsong, and soon Mary knew the world of the court and of her responsibilities as queen would also intrude in the guise of the careful voices and hands of her waiting women.

Reluctantly, she opened her eyes. Just a slit, a glance

under her lashes, for Mary did not want anyone who might be watching to know she was awake. Still dark, it appeared that there was, as yet, no one up and moving about the chamber, but now Mary could hear the altered breathing of the two women who slept on pallets at the foot of her bed. Mary realised they were awake, steeling themselves to rise in the cold air of the chamber. Once they had gathered their bravery, and risen to pull on some clothes, they would stoke the fire in the hearth, air Mary's clothes before it, and fetch warm water and a dish of soft white bread soaked in warm, watered wine from the kitchens. When all this was done, they would turn their attention to Mary, and ask her gently if she felt well enough to rise against the day; if she felt well enough to take some bread and wine.

Did she?

Mary closed her eyes again and concentrated on her body's aches and pains. The great hard lump in her lower belly sat as rocklike and as unforgiving as it did every day. If she tried to move slightly in her bed, then Mary knew her flesh would drag and catch about the unmoving mass as if it were seaweed caught at a shoreline by a great rock. But at least today the lump did not send lancing fingers of pain throughout her flesh, and for that Mary was grateful.

On the days that the lump woke, and raged, she could hardly bear to live.

But if the lump lay quiescent, then the great bones of her legs, and those of her lower back, ached abominably. This was a new discomfort, and Mary wondered at it. She had not ventured far beyond her chamber in the past weeks: on most evenings to the great hall for evening supper, and sometimes to the courtyard if it were sunny and warm enough, and even then Thomas Neville generally carried her, so Mary knew there was no reason her bones should be complaining. Had they grown tired of their enforced resting?

Or was this some new manifestation of her illness?

Tears formed behind Mary's closed eyelids, and she fought to keep her breathing steady and slow, lest she alert her waiting women to her distress.

No, sweet Jesu, let not this affliction have struck my bones as well.

Had she not prayed enough? Confessed her every evil thought? Had sweet Jesu found her wanting in some way that now she was to be further punished?

Mary had spent the past year trying her best not to complain and not to fear, knowing that her illness was a test sent by God. She would not fail.

But, oh sweet Jesu! It was so hard! So hard.

It was not the pain that distressed Mary, but her ever increasing sense of complete failure. She'd failed as a woman, as a wife, and as a queen. As a woman she had shrunk from her husband's attentions, as a wife she had not been able to bear her husband a living child, and as a queen, she had not only failed in her duty to provide the realm with an heir, but she had not been able to perform those duties that a queen should—as a helpmeet to her husband the king, so that he could the better shoulder the onerous duties of office.

Every time that Bolingbroke held her hand most gently, and told her with an even greater gentleness that she was not to fret about it, Mary felt even worse, and even more the failure.

And on those days when she saw the calculation lurking behind the superficial kindness in his eyes . . .

Mary's breath almost caught audibly in her throat, and she froze, wondering if her women had heard her. But, no, they still continued to lie, dozing perhaps, and not listening too closely for a sign that their mistress was awake.

For the moment, Mary did not want to give them that sign. Not just yet. A few minutes more, and then she would be prepared mentally to start her day.

Bolingbroke. Mary's feelings for her husband ranged between the fearful and the thankful, neither of which gave her much peace. Fearful, because she well knew her husband's lust and desire for Catherine of France, and also knew her husband enough to know he was both impatient and angry at her ill health. Her increasing, but not yet fatal, illness made Bolingbroke chafe all the more for the moment when he could publicly pursue Catherine.

Thankful, because Bolingbroke continued to be so gentle and tolerant of her in public when he might well have been dismissive, if not angry. Thankful, because Bolingbroke kept her at his side—a living part of his court—when he might have discarded her into some dank, out-of-the-way castle or manor house while he enjoyed (more openly) the comforts and company of women more suited to his needs.

Once, and not so long ago, Mary had thought to have some power over him. The English adored her when she knew they would loathe Catherine, and Mary had thought this might have stayed Bolingbroke's hand against her.

But after what had happened to Richard . . . if Bolingbroke could so easily dispose of a king, then what would he do with an unwanted wife? How much longer would he tolerate her? How long did she have before—?

"What? Still abed? Women, to your feet. Pleasure awaits!"

Mary heard the two women at the foot of her bed spring to their feet, stumbling over the blankets as they did so. But she did not start, or even, for the moment, open her eyes.

Instead, her mouth curved in a small smile of joy. Had he known that she would be lying here in the pre-dawn dark, a prisoner of both her failing flesh and her terrified thoughts?

She heard him move to the side of her bed, smelt his manly fragrance, and finally she opened her eyes, and allowed her mouth to stretch into a full smile.

"Tom, what do you here in my chamber so early?"

There was a faint light from the windows now, enough to catch the flash of Neville's smile within the blackness of his well-clipped beard.

"Come to rouse you for the tournament, lady. Myself and," he glanced over his shoulder, "my lovely wife."

Now Margaret's form rose behind that of her husband, and Mary's smile stretched even wider. She looked back to Neville, still grinning at her.

"You shall cause great gossip, my lord, coming so unannounced into my chamber."

Margaret laughed, and walked around Neville to sit on the side of Mary's bed, gently, so as not to jolt her. "He has me as a chaperone, madam. His jealous wife shall make sure he gets up to no mischief."

Mary's eyes filled with tears again, but tears of gratefulness rather than despondency or pain. Their jesting did for her what no amount of solicitous words and gestures could do—make her feel worthwhile, as both a woman and a friend.

"I come merely because my wife thought that she might need a loud voice with which to rouse you," Neville said. He'd taken a step closer to the bed, and now stood behind Margaret, one hand resting on her shoulder. "I shall not stay, for I know these first hours of a queen's day are dominated by her women, and do not allow the presence of a man. But," he found his voice had lost its jesting tone, "how do you feel, my lady queen? Does the thought of a day at the tournament cheer you, or cause you distress?"

Mary smiled at Neville, and then at Margaret. "It cheers me," she said, "for I think I shall enjoy watching full grown men beating each other about the ears with lances and clubs."

Neville nodded. "Then I shall leave you to the attention of your ladies, madam," he said, "and will instead go to ensure that your litter, comfortably cushioned and screened, is waiting for you after your breakfast."

He bent, kissed Mary's forehead familiarly, then kissed Margaret's mouth, and with a bow and a flourish, left the chamber, flashing a grin at the two women standing by the hearth as they watched with curious eyes the group about their queen's bed.

BY MID-MORNING it had become apparent to all concerned that the great tournament at Windsor would be held under fine and warm skies. A great omen, whispered some among the ten thousand strong crowd that had gathered, for the bright dawning of the new reign. Many had made the journey from London to the tourneying fields a mile beyond Windsor over the previous days, others from the countryside nearer the castle that very morning. Some were there only to watch the jousting of the nobles, some to partake in the wrestling matches and other games scheduled to entertain the throng, others to set up stalls to cater to the thirst and hunger of the spectators and participants alike. Still others were there to feed off the crowd itself: cutpurses and thieves, and grim-faced friars determined to convince as many as possible that the Devil Himself lurked among the fun and frivolities scheduled for the day.

Trenches, recently erected wooden picket fences and lines of determined pikemen kept the commoners at a respectful distance from the tents and horse lines of the nobles and knights—numbering some seven thousand if all their retainers were counted. The tents, with their gaily flapping pennants, flags and ribbons, stretched over almost fifteen acres of meadowland. Horse lines divided the grouped tents of households and loyalties—double lines of snorting, stamping, rolling-eyed destriers, kicking at their grooms as one means of tempering their impatience for the battles ahead.

Almost precisely between the tent city of the nobles and their retainers and the throng horde of onlookers and merchants lay the tourneying field. It covered almost four acres: the green-grassed tourney field itself, flanked on two sides by the three-storey timber stands for the wives and families of nobles; and spaces for the common crowd at either end and in a narrow, fenced area directly before the stands. Pennants and ribbons fluttered here as they did among the tents, while jugglers, sword dancers and musicians with lutes, harps and bagpipes wandered up and down the jousting lanes of the tourney field, entertaining the gathering crowds until the fun and bloodshed should get under way in earnest.

By midday the spectators had gathered tight about the timber stands, which were packed with the families of the combatants. Jingling and clanking from the tents and horse lines suggested that both men and beasts were readying themselves for the fray, and a murmuring rose from the crowds.

Just as the restlessness edged towards the potentially uncontrollable, a shout went up, and the crowds roared as one (even if most had no idea what was going on). Two columns of richly attired and liveried horsemen rode onto the field, an escort for a horse litter of unparalleled magnificence.

"The queen!" the shout went up. "The queen! Hurrah for Mary, sweet Mary!"

Neville, riding his skittering stallion close to Mary's litter, leaned down and grabbed a handful of the rich silky stuff that made up the hangings.

"With your permission, madam," he said.

"Of course, my lord," Mary's voice said. "I would show them my gratefulness."

Neville grasped the hanging more tightly, then lifted it and threw the material across the top of the litter, nodding to his squire, Robert Courtenay, who rode as escort on the other side, to do the same. Within moments both men had exposed Mary and her waiting women inside the litter to the full view of the crowds, and the roar rose to a thunder as Mary leaned forward and waved to the gathered people, smiling sweetly. She looked thin and pale, but her thinness and pallor was counterbalanced by her patent merriness and joy at the reception of the commons.

The thunder, if possible, grew louder, and people waved hats and scarves above their heads, acknowledging their queen.

But within the litter, Margaret saw how Mary's hand trembled, and how her lips pressed too tightly together.

"Madam," she murmured, leaning close, "do not tire yourself."

Mary continued waving. "I cannot disappoint them," she said. "A little ache here and there is a small enough price."

Margaret's eyes narrowed. Mary was suffering more than a "little ache here and there." When Margaret had aided Mary in her morning ablutions, and helped her to dress, she'd noted with concern how the queen had winced and, on several occasions, bit her lip to keep from crying out. And when she'd brought Mary her bowl of bread sops, Mary had hardly been able to swallow more than five mouthfuls.

If nothing else, Mary was likely to faint from hunger, if not her pain, within ten minutes.

Carefully, and as surreptitiously as she could, Margaret moved close enough to Mary to pack in some more supporting cushions about her back and hips.

"I do thank you," Mary whispered as she continued to smile and wave, and the sheer gratefulness in her tone brought tears to Margaret's eyes.

"When we are settled in the stand," Margaret said quietly, "I shall give you a few drops of Doctor Culpeper's liquor, which I have in my waist pouch. It will deaden some of the pain."

Margaret saw that Mary was about to object, and hastened on: "You shall be of no use to anyone if you cry out and faint from pain and weakness, my lady. A few drops will ease the pain, but allow you to remain alert."

To Margaret's relief, Mary nodded slightly, and Margaret looked to see Thomas watching, and she inclined her head and watched the relief spread over his face as well.

The acclaim of the crowds only grew louder when the

litter drew to a halt before the grandstand at the head of the field. Thomas Neville jumped down from his horse, and bowed before Mary in the litter. She nodded, and he leaned forward and gathered her into his arms, gently adjusting her weight so that he did not jolt her.

"There are ten thousand men here today who would give their lives for you," he whispered.

"I do not deserve their—"

"You deserve the reverence of the sun and that of the moon as well, my lady," he said. "That of ten thousand men is the very least of what you are owed."

And with that he strode to the stand, climbing the stairs to the royal box and resting his queen gently onto the pile of cushions waiting there for her.

Margaret and the three other accompanying ladies moved to their places behind and about Mary as Neville bowed deeply one more time and took his leave with a smile.

At the bottom of the stand he spoke softly and urgently to Courtenay, his eyes jerking over the crowd as he spoke. "Robert, I do not like the feel of this day. Bolingbroke was a damned fool to organise this tournament in the first instance, let alone when rumours of Richard are feeding more fires than all the chopped wood in England."

Courtenay nodded, his own gaze wandering over the crowd. The majority of kings in the past hundred years had banned tournaments, not only because the violence of the tourney field tended to get out of control and spill into the crowds, but because very few kings liked being surrounded with the private armies of the nobles.

Times like these, ambitious nobles tended to get ideas.

"At the least," Courtenay replied, "Hotspur is not here."

Neville grunted. Hotspur, once the close friend of both Neville and Bolingbroke, was still lurking in the north, "attending", as he communicated to Bolingbroke in the occasional letter, to the Scots.

He had yet to offer his allegiance to Bolingbroke, and

Neville did not think he ever would; not with Hotspur's ambitions, and not with the army he could raise in the north whenever he needed. If Bolingbroke ever wanted to leave England to fight for France, he was going to have to "attend" to Hotspur first.

"If Hotspur and his army had been here, Bolingbroke would most certainly never have consented to the tournament," Neville said, then managed a tight grin. "Damn Hotspur. Why is he never here when we need him?"

A movement to the side caught both men's eyes. Men with horns had moved into ranks either side of the field.

"Bolingbroke is about to arrive," Neville said. "Robert, I would be better to spend my time moving among the combatants than here. At least for the time being. Will you—?"

"No need to voice the command, my lord. I will guard Mary, the lady Margaret and the other ladies with my life."

"Good. I will send a company of men to assist you. Robert—"

"With my *life,* my lord!"

Neville nodded, clapped a hand briefly on Courtenay's shoulder, then melted into the crowds behind them.

BOLINGBROKE ARRIVED in much greater splendour than his wife, but to no less acclaim. He cantered onto the field atop a great, white dancing stallion caparisoned in crimson and emerald green silks and tassels. Atop Bolingbroke's brow rested a glinting golden crown, resplendent with gems, and about his shoulders hung a purple velvet cloak, trimmed with ermine. His tunic and leggings were all of cloth of gold, richly embroidered and thickly crusted with pearls and silver threads. His face was confident and joyous, and he stood in the stirrups, waving to the crowd, and shouting to them his well wishes and his love for them.

It was fine theatre.

At the head of the field Bolingbroke reined in his stallion, sinking back into the saddle. He raised his glorious face, staring directly at Mary. As she nodded, he smiled, and bowed in the saddle to her, making humble obeisance to his wife.

The crowd adored it.

"He should have been an actor on the stage," Mary whispered to Margaret.

"He would not dare not to love you," Margaret replied. "Not here. Not now."

Mary gave a very small nod, then smiled the greater at her husband, now rising from his bow, and waved at him with her hand to join her in the royal box.

"We are all actors in this great drama," she said, and then she turned her head to Margaret and looked her full in the eye. "But sometimes I think there is more to this plot than my ladies will tell me."

Before a startled Margaret could think of a response, Mary had turned back to Bolingbroke, now dismounting from his stallion, composing her face into a smile of proper wifely love and respect.

"Best give me your vial of Culpeper's liquor now, Margaret," Mary murmured, "so that I may the better play my part."

Chapter IV

Saturday 4th May 1381

— ii —

✠

THE TOURNAMENT BEGAN immediately Bolingbroke had taken his place beside Mary and nodded his readiness to the officials.

Within ten minutes the grinding, bloody, sweaty, bone-breaking, heart-stopping action had begun. Having agreed to the tournament itself, Bolingbroke had nevertheless drawn the line at allowing the traditional melee of several hundred knights drawn up into two opposing forces that charged down the field to engage in several hours of hacking, clouting and cursing until only a few men (and horses) were left standing. Instead, the action began with something only a little less spectacular.

The tourney field had been divided into twenty-five jousting lanes, and at the drop of the official's flag, fifty knights lowered their lances and kicked their stallions into motion. The thunder of the great horses' hooves as they crashed down the lanes was outdone only by the screams of the crowd and the eventual grinding and screeching as lances struck or glanced off the breastplates and shields of opponents. Some knights managed to hold their seats, others were unhorsed on their first pass and left to flounder on the turf, hoping the momentum of their fall and the weight of their armour wouldn't roll them into the path of an oncoming destrier.

Destriers were bred for their density and thickness of muscle, their strength and their weight: they were not renowned for their ability to jump anything larger than a mouse or dodge anything in less than a gentle quarter-mile curve.

One man died and two were crippled when the huge, sharpened hooves of galloping destriers cut right through their armour and the bones and flesh beneath.

The horses trampled on, almost unaware of the men they had cut to ribbons beneath their hooves.

The unhorsed knights who managed to roll to their feet rather than under the oncoming death of destriers steadied themselves and drew their swords. Those knights who made it to the other end of the jousting lanes still on their horses now dismounted and drew their own swords, striding as best they could in their enveloping armour back down the jousting lanes to meet their opponents in true chivalric fashion, one on one, sword to sword. Blades clattered against heads and necks, trying to find that sweet opening between helmet and shoulder and breast armour.

Opponents rested after each swing, gathering their strength to once again raise the massive blades with arms made heavy by their encasing armour and strike again.

Blood seeped out from joints in armour, and trailed in apologetic rivulets down breast and thigh plates. Breathing became harsh, and was intermixed with curses and shouted entreaties for aid to sundry saints. Some men pissed or shat themselves, either with fear or exertion, and the stink of urine and faeces added itself to the other manly odours of battle.

The crowd went wild. Men surged against barriers, each individual shouting encouragement to the knights of his choice, and curses against their opponents. Some spectators threw rocks and other missiles into the arena.

Some turned against their neighbours and sent fists crashing into cheekbones and chins in the excitement of the moment.

The behaviour of the noble families and wives in the stands was scarcely better. Women leaped to their feet, waving streamers of their household colours, urging their menfolk on to greater efforts with voices shrill with battle lust. Young pages and valets, beside themselves with sorrow that they should not be on the field themselves, punched fists into the air, and shouted wagers into the din, sure that *their* lord would be the one to prevail.

And amid all this, the valets and pages of the fallen darted among the warriors on the field, litters dragging and bumping behind them, searching out their masters that they might attempt to roll them onto the litters and get them to the dubious safety of the surgeons' tents.

Bolingbroke leaned forward eagerly, one fist clenched, his eyes straining to take in all the action.

"Surely this death and maiming is not so exciting?" Mary murmured, sickened at the sight before her.

"I need to know on whom I can rely on the battlefield," Bolingbroke replied, not lifting his eyes from the tournament. Then he relaxed a little, and leaned back. "There? See? It is all but done. Some knights have conceded, while others have won outright."

He stood and clapped his approval of the actions of the men below, and the crowds roared with him. The fighting was done now, and some knights strutted off the field, having triumphed against their opponents; later they would receive tokens from the king to mark their victory. Others slumped wearily, shamed. And others, twisted, moaning or worse, lay still on the grass waiting for the final scurrying pages to come by with their litters.

And when all was finally cleared, men darted out with baskets of sawdust to dry out the patches of clotting red so that the next two lines of jousters would not slip and fall on the blood of their predecessors.

The day proceeded.

* * *

NEVILLE WANDERED through the barely controlled chaos amid the tents and horse lines of the nobles. Several rounds of jousting had now taken place, and soon the tournament would move into its most exciting stage: the great nobles, men who had fought and lived through a score of battles, would joust one on one.

No doubt there shall be a few scores settled this day, thought Neville as he pushed his way through the crowds, seeking his uncle Ralph Neville's tent. Ah, there, the standard of Westmorland. He nodded to the guards outside the tent's entrance, then ducked inside.

His uncle was standing in the centre of the space, almost fully armoured, his face a mask of impatience as two of his squires tugged at buckle straps, and twisted plates into place. The earl grimaced at Neville's entrance, and Neville was not sure if that was because one of the squires had tugged too tightly, or because his uncle was not happy to see him.

"You're not going to fight?" Raby asked. "You have decided to play the part of the spectator?"

Ah, no wonder his uncle had grimaced at him. Raby had never been the one to pass a fight without adding his sword to it.

"There will be battle enough in the coming months," Neville said. "Today I will wander the encampment, the better to understand the strength of various houses."

"Humph," Raby grunted. "First a warrior, then a priest, now a courtier. Will there never be an end to your incarnations, Tom?"

"I am just Tom," Neville said, "choosing to reveal myself in different ways." He walked closer to his uncle, and the squires, their task done, melted away. "Will you have some wine before you enter the lists, Uncle?"

"Aye. It will steady my hand."

Neville walked to a small table, poured out two goblets

of wine from a ewer, and handed one of them to his uncle. "And who is your opponent?"

Raby hesitated. Then . . . "Exeter."

Neville halted with his goblet halfway to his mouth, stunned. "Exeter? John Holland?" *Richard's half brother against his uncle, the man responsible for garnering support for Bolingbroke, who then supplanted and then murdered Exeter's brother?*

"The very same."

"And who arranged this?"

"Exeter himself, I believe," Raby said, and drained his goblet. "I heard he specifically asked to be set against me."

Neville took the empty goblet from his uncle's hand and set it, together with his untouched one, to one side.

"Uncle . . . be careful. Exeter is dangerous."

"And I'm not?"

"I didn't mean dangerous as in skilled with a weapon, Uncle. I meant dangerous in the use of treachery. Do you think he will allow his brother's death to go unchallenged? Unrevenged?"

"If he knows what is best for him . . . yes."

Neville turned away, fingering Raby's mail gloves, which lay on the table. "The Hollands are a powerful family," he said.

Raby walked up beside Neville and took the mail gloves, pulling them on. "They wouldn't dare. They are not that powerful. No doubt Exeter grumbles in private, as do most of the Holland family. But to take on Hal? No. They wouldn't dare. Tom, they *wouldn't*."

That's what Richard and de Vere believed about Bolingbroke, Neville thought, *and that mistake killed them.*

He forced a smile to his face. "Then I wish you good luck in your joust, Uncle. I hope your lance bounces off his balls and bruises them so badly he shall not sire any more sons."

Raby guffawed loudly. "I shall aim with intent," he said. "England could do with a few less Hollands. Now, where are those damn squires? I need my helmet!"

* * *

WHEN HE'D left his uncle, Neville wandered as close as he could to Exeter's tents without attracting unwanted attention. Sundry knights and nobles scurried about, most in full battle armour, all with tense expressions and narrowed eyes that darted this way and that.

Neville stood behind the tent of a minor noble and chewed at his lip in thought. How many men did Exeter and his fellow Hollands have with them? Two or three hundred, no more. They wouldn't have been able to bring any more without attracting undue attention.

So, Exeter's allies, then. Who were they likely to be? Northumberland? Northumberland had ever had his disagreements with Bolingbroke and his father, the Duke of Lancaster, and particularly with Neville's own family. But Northumberland had too much to lose by turning against Bolingbroke, and far more to gain by standing at his side.

So Northumberland was unlikely to ally himself with Exeter, and Hotspur, Northumberland's son, who may very well have supported an Exeter bid to topple Bolingbroke, was still far in the north.

There were, of course, a slew of lesser nobles who might support Exeter—Neville well knew that the wounds caused by Bolingbroke's extraordinary rise to power had not yet healed—but Neville simply couldn't see how they could hope to form a force strong enough to defeat Bolingbroke's allies who *were* here in force; Raby and Northumberland, in particular, had huge escorts of men at the tournament.

A movement to his left caught Neville's eye and he turned, then frowned slightly at what he saw.

None other than the Abbot of Westminster, striding out of Exeter's tent and looking guilty enough to confess to Christ's murder if someone should put a knife to his throat and ask him to say the words.

The abbot disappeared down a narrow alley between rows of tents, and Neville hurried after him.

After five minutes the abbot paused, looked about—causing Neville to duck behind a saddled destrier—then entered a small tent. In an instant he was out again, and a few heartbeats after his exit five Dominican friars hurried out, split up, and merged into the crowds.

What was the abbot doing, consorting first with Exeter, then with Dominicans, of all people?

Neville hesitated, then followed one of the Dominicans. The man's hooded black figure made him easy to track at a safe distance in the otherwise gaudy multitude.

The friar led Neville back towards the hordes of common folk who had come to watch the tournament. Now and then he would stop, catch the attention of a small group of men and women, whisper something, then move on.

Neville's disquiet grew, especially since the people the friar talked to remained agitated after the friar had moved on, and turned to talk to others within the crowd. He watched the Dominican work his way through the throng, thought about continuing his pursuit of him, then decided to ask some of the people what they'd been told by the friar.

"My good man," Neville said quietly to one man standing in a group of five or six others, "what did the friar tell you?"

The man glanced at his fellows, licking his lips nervously, then looked back at this lord who had addressed him.

"He said—" The man hesitated. "—he said that Richard our king is not dead, and that he will be riding to London within the week to reclaim his throne."

"*What?*"

"It's what he said."

"It's not true, dammit! Man, believe me, Richard is *dead!*"

But the group stared at Neville, shaking their heads, and looked about uncertainly.

"Perhaps he still is alive," one man said. "Why shouldn't he be? Perhaps these stories of his death were false."

Neville opened his mouth to refute the lie one more time, then shut it as he suddenly realised what Exeter was going to do.

"My God," Neville whispered, and hurried off.

MARY SHIFTED a little on her cushions, trying to ease the agony coursing up and down her spine. Her face twisted, and she gasped.

"Madam?" Margaret whispered, shocked by the whiteness of Mary's face. She grabbed at Mary's hand, then looked to Bolingbroke.

He was already staring at Mary, and had taken her other hand. "Mary," he said, "how bad is it?"

"Bad enough," Mary whispered.

Margaret locked eyes with Bolingbroke. The fact that Mary had admitted her pain told her a great deal: Mary was in absolute agony. Nothing else would drive her to actually admitting discomfort.

"Do something," Bolingbroke hissed to Margaret, then turned to smile and wave at the people whose heads had turned to watch what was happening in the royal box. *She is tired, no more.*

Margaret hesitated. "I have no more of the liquor," she said.

Mary tried to smile, and failed dismally. "I have been too greedy," she said. "It is my fault."

Again Margaret locked eyes with Bolingbroke. *I can do for her what I did for Lancaster in his final hours. Ease her pain.*

No! She will know that you are other than what you present yourself!

And would that be so bad?

Meg, do not go against my will. We will be finished here soon enough.

Margaret dropped her eyes. *I hope it is not your fate to die a lingering, painful death, Hal.*

"I will be well enough once we leave this place," Mary said. "Do not fear for me, Margaret."

"It is difficult to avoid fearing for those whom you love dearly," Margaret said, and her eyes filmed with tears.

"I am suffering no more than those poor men below who have been trampled beneath horses' hooves," Mary said, patting at Margaret's hand. Then she lowered her voice to a whisper. "Thank you for caring, Margaret."

Margaret took one of Mary's hands in both of hers, and very, very gently rubbed its back with her thumbs. With Mary, as she had done with Lancaster, she should dig her thumbs in deeply to give the relief required for such pain, but if she did that, and eased Mary's pain to a remarkable degree, then Mary would indeed suspect something.

So Margaret gently rubbed, and the continual movement, with the slight power she put into it, managed to take the edge off Mary's pain. It happened so gradually that Mary herself did not connect the very slight easing of her pain with Margaret's rubbing.

She merely thought the ease was due to Margaret's love . . . which, in a sense, it was.

After a few minutes Mary straightened her back a little, and lifted her head, suddenly becoming aware of the concerned looks being sent her way.

Mary smiled, then waved her hand a little. "A bad moment, my good people," she said. "Nothing else. See, I am quite well now."

And gradually those staring smiled, nodded, and returned their eyes to the tourney field before them.

Once their attention was back on the field, Mary turned to Margaret, and kissed her cheek. "Thank you for your love," she said. "It means so much."

Margaret blinked back her tears, and smiled, and would have spoken save that Bolingbroke leaned over and hushed them.

"Quiet! The joust of the tournament begins."

Mary turned her head back to the field—its grass now all but torn up where it wasn't littered with congealing pink mounds of sawdust. All but one jousting lane had been cleared away, and at either end of this single remaining lane sat two great warriors on their destriers: Exeter and Raby.

Both men and their mounts were fully armoured: Raby in black armour emblazoned with the Neville device across breastplate and helm; Exeter in gleaming white armour, similarly emblazoned with his own heraldic devices.

An official shouted an instruction, and both men slowly lowered their lances.

Their destriers bunched beneath them, knowing that at any instant they would be sent thundering towards their opponent.

A flag dropped, the crowd roared, and the destriers lumbered into movement.

Bolingbroke leaned forward in his chair, his face tense, one fist clenched. "Do me proud, Ralph," he muttered. "Do me proud."

Raby and Exeter pounded towards each other, their bodies hunched over lance and shield, their heads swaying with the violent movement of their horses.

They met in a grinding of metal in the centre of the field: sparks flew, horses grunted, but both lances slid off their opponent's shield harmlessly as each passed the other, trying to pull up their destriers with hands laden with shield and weapon.

Squires leapt to their masters' aid, catching the destriers and turning them about.

The crowd's roar grew louder.

Bolingbroke turned to say something to Mary, then stopped, his eyes fixed on Thomas Neville, who had climbed the stairs into the stand and was now fast approaching the royal box.

"Tom?" Bolingbroke said.

Neville reached him, glancing at Margaret and Mary,

and then to where Robert Courtenay stood with a group of armed men in the back of the stand, before bending down to Bolingbroke.

"Treachery, sire," he whispered. "I think Exeter means to—"

He got no further, for just then Exeter and Raby met again in a clash of metal and horseflesh in the centre of the field. The grinding and screeching of lance against shield grew to almost unbearable levels, and then Raby's shield toppled to one side, dragging its owner over with it.

Exeter managed to drop his lance, grabbing a club that hung at his side. In a heartbeat he'd raised it on high, then smashed it into Raby's helm.

Neville's uncle slid unceremoniously to the ground in a clatter of armour and a flailing of legs and arms. His horse skittered off, rolling its eyes.

"Ralph!" Margaret whispered, half-rising. She had been Raby's lover once, and had never ceased caring for him.

"Hal!" Neville said, equally as urgently. "You are in danger—"

Exeter ignored Raby struggling ignobly in his heavy armour on the ground, dropping the club and grabbing at his sword to wave it about his head. He turned to the gates that marked the entry and exit point of the tourney field, the vigour of his sword-waving doubling.

Horsed and heavily armed men flooded into the tourney field—a thousand at the least—some liveried in the devices of Exeter, others in the devices of various other members of the extended Holland clan, and more yet in the liveries of the Earl of Rutland and the Earl of Salisbury.

"Sweet Jesu!" Bolingbroke said, lurching to his feet as the seriousness of the moment suddenly hit him. Already other men—those of Bolingbroke's personal guard, nobles and retainers of Northumberland and Raby and other noble houses allied with them—were rushing towards the tourney field. Sporadic fighting started where the two groups met, but the crowds of commoners, now lurching this way and that in terror, were so thick that it was hard for the king's defenders to get close to the rebels.

"Hear me!" Exeter screamed, turning his destrier about in tight circles as he addressed the crowd, and still waving his sword about his head. "Hear me! I come on behalf of Richard the King. Yes! Richard! He still lives. *Richard lives and will be in London within the week to remove this monster from the throne!*"

The crowd's noise swelled. Richard lived? Then several people shouted out: "Yes! Richard lives! We have heard it from men of God. Richard lives."

And then another shout, coming so fast upon those of Exeter and the crowd that Bolingbroke had not had a chance of speaking himself.

The Abbot of Westminster, standing up from his place in one of the side stands: "Richard lives and shall come home to London to claim his rightful seat on the throne within the week. Believe me. The Church stands behind Richard!"

The crowd pushed forward, shouting and screaming, the hours of high excitement now turned into a rebellious surge.

"Give us Richard!" several people yelled, and soon the refrain was taken up by all around. "Give us Richard!"

"Stupid yokels," Bolingbroke said under his breath, his face bright red with fury. "Give them a refrain to yell, *anything,* and they'll shout it from the rooftops until they are silenced only by the sword!"

"Hal—" Mary said, trying to grasp his arm, but he twisted it away from her.

"You must get out of here," Neville said, checking to make sure that Courtenay and the score of armed men with him were now making their way towards the royal box. If they moved quickly, Bolingbroke and Mary still had a chance to move—

"Seize him!" Exeter shouted, now waving his sword towards Bolingbroke.

"Richard is dead!" Bolingbroke shouted. "Dead! How can you shout for him now when only months before you shouted *my* name in Westminster Abbey?"

"He has misled you," shouted the abbot and Exeter together. "Richard lives, and will shortly return to reclaim his—"

"My good people," said a soft voice, and, miraculously, all heard it.

Mary was rising unbalanced and shaking from her chair. Both Margaret and Neville reached out hands to steady her, exchanging a shocked glance as they did so.

"My good people," Mary said again, extending her hands outwards, palms up as if in supplication. "Will you listen to me?"

The crowd quieted, although murmuring still swelled up and down its length. Faces turned to Mary.

"I am so distressed that you should be told such lies by those who have no respect for you," Mary said, and tears ran down her cheeks.

Now even the murmuring quieted, and the entire tourney field and its surrounds, packed with over fifteen thousand people, stared at their queen.

"Richard *is* dead," she whispered, and amazingly that whisper reached every corner. "Did I not weep over his still white corpse? Did I not swaddle him in his shroud as his mother once swaddled him as a babe?"

Bolingbroke stared at her, incredulous. Mary had never seen Richard's corpse, let alone spent hours weeping over it or swaddling it.

But the crowd was staring at her enthralled—even Exeter and his band—and so Bolingbroke held both his tongue and his incredulity in check.

"I think perhaps my Lords of Exeter and Westminster have been mistaken," she said, gracing both men with a sweet smile. "Perhaps what they meant to say was that my beloved husband," and now she smiled almost beatifically at a still incredulous Bolingbroke, "has arranged for Richard's poor corpse to make its way in solemn procession back to London, to lie in state in Saint Paul's, so that all Englanders may have a chance to say their farewells to their beloved boy-king."

She turned back to Exeter, who was staring at her from under the raised visor of his helm, then to the Abbot of Westminster, who was licking his lips and, patently, thinking furiously. "Is that not so, my lords?" Mary said. She folded her hands before her.

The abbot glanced at Exeter. "Um, well," he stumbled. "Perhaps we might have been mistaken—"

"She lies!" Exeter screamed, now standing in his stirrups and brandishing his sword towards Mary. "She mouths nothing but foul lies! Richard lives, and he—"

"Will you listen to this man befoul your beloved queen?" shouted Raby. He'd struggled to his feet when all attention had been turned towards Mary, and now he stood at Exeter's stirrup. "How can any deny the beauty and truth of what our adored queen says?"

As quickly as it had been engaged and manipulated by Westminster and Essex, the mood of the crowd now swung again.

"Mary!" they screamed. "Mary!"

"Fool," Raby said under the screams of the crowd and, so quickly that none of Exeter's close companions could stop him, slid the unscabbarded blade of his sword up into the gap between Exeter's abdominal and hip plates.

Exeter twisted, but it was too late. Raby leaned all his strength behind his thrust, and the sword tore through the stiffened leather beneath the plate armour and deep into Exeter's lower belly.

The duke grunted, dropped his sword, then slid off his horse—and further onto Raby's sword.

Instantly, his supporters started to back away.

Mary, who had not failed to notice Raby's actions, clapped her hands, keeping the crowd's attention on her. "My husband assures me Richard's corpse will be back in London within the fortnight," she said, "where you may all have the chance to view it and say your farewells. May sweet Jesu bless you all."

And yet again the crowd roared in acclaim, and did not notice Northumberland's and Raby's men moving through the rebels, seizing the nobles who had thought to topple Bolingbroke.

Mary stood, waving and smiling, until order had been achieved. Then she said, "Beloved people, will you excuse me if I sit? I am so tired—"

She got no further, for suddenly she sank down, her entire frame shaking with pain, and Margaret wrapped her arms about Mary's shoulders, concerned.

"Hal—" Neville said urgently.

Bolingbroke turned to address the crowd. "I must take my wife home," he said, "for she has been greatly distressed by the treachery Exeter forced her to witness. Will you perchance excuse your king and queen?"

There were shouts of goodwill, then the crowd began to disperse.

Neville finally relaxed. "Hal, you would be dead now if it were not for Mary."

Bolingbroke held Neville's eyes, sharing both his shock and relief at the turn of events. Then, as one, both men looked down at Mary.

She had fainted dead away, and Margaret and one of her other women were rubbing her hands and wiping her forehead with a soft cloth.

"Sire," Margaret said, "she must be returned to Windsor. *Now!*"

Bolingbroke nodded, but it was Neville who spoke.

"I will take care of it," he said, then looked at Bolingbroke. "I think that you, sire, ought to make plans forthwith to bring Richard's 'poor corpse' back from whatever pit you had it thrown in."

Bolingbroke's mouth twisted. "Not before I have had a chance to deal with Exeter—if he still lives—and our trusty friend the abbot," he said. "I hope you took good note of who else had taken Exeter's part, Tom."

"Aye," Neville said. "And they were many more than I know you would like to think, Hal."

Then he bent down, and, with Margaret and the other ladies fussing about, gathered Mary into his arms.

Chapter V

Saturday 4th May 1381

— iii —

✣

"WELL?" SAID BOLINGBROKE, turning to face his chief advisers.

They stood in the cool evening light in Bolingbroke's private chamber: the king had allowed no servants in to light either the fire or the lamps.

"Exeter will be dead by dawn," Raby said. He was slumped wearily in a chair, still in the sweat-stained garments he'd worn under his armour. His face was drawn, sallow now rather than swarthy, and a dark bruise ran up one cheek. "His wound is bad."

Bolingbroke grunted. "And for that you have my thanks indeed. Westminster?"

"Huddled praying in the chapel," Neville said. "Surrounded by fifteen men-at-arms and enclosed by locked doors."

"You cannot have him killed," the Earl of Northumberland said. "He is a churchman."

Bolingbroke's face left them in no doubt what he thought of all "churchmen." He turned abruptly, and strode away a few paces. "Then he shall rue the day he ever thought to raise his shrill little voice against me," he said. "He's finished."

Behind him, Neville, Northumberland, Raby and the other three men present—Bolingbroke's Chancellor, John Scarle, and Sir John Norbury and Lord Owen Tudor, members of Bolingbroke's household—exchanged glances. Bolingbroke's mood had been vicious ever since they returned from the aborted tournament. Armed guards now surrounded and infiltrated every part of Windsor, and more were stationed in the fields beyond. Bolingbroke was taking no chances.

And no one blamed him for that. Exeter's plan, born of desperation, would have stood a very good chance of succeeding, had it not been for Mary's quiet words . . . and the respect the crowd had for her. The cry that Richard still lived, appealing as it did to the English crowd's sense of drama and intrigue, could have rallied the entire ten thousand behind him. Once the crowd was behind him, shouting his cause, then seeds of doubt would have grown in everyone else present. *Was Richard still alive? Was he planning a return to London?*

Exeter had used the very same tactics against Bolingbroke that Bolingbroke had employed against Richard: the manipulation of dramatic words to turn loyalties. His voice wasn't as sweet, nor his words as seductive, as Bolingbroke's had been to Richard's army outside Flint Castle, but still . . .

No matter that the very-dead Richard would never stage a return to London—at least not alive. All Exeter would have needed to do was manage to place Bolingbroke under armed guard, and very soon Bolingbroke would have been as dead as Richard, and Exeter's faction in control of England.

"Rutland?" Bolingbroke said, still with his back to the group watching him. "Salisbury? And every other of the damned Hollands that thought to join with their cousin Exeter?"

"In prison," Raby said. "Under guard."

Bolingbroke spun about to face them. "They will hang in the morning."

"Sire—" Neville said.

"Nay, do not try and dissuade me, Tom," Bolingbroke said. "I cannot let them live. You know that. I need to send a message to anyone else—" He paused. "—out there who might harbour the same plans and ambitions as Exeter." No one said a word. All knew to whom he was referring. *Hotspur.* "As for Exeter's retainers," Bolingbroke continued, "and those of the other rebel lords, well . . . they shall receive pardons as evidence of my true mercy. I will not murder all of England in spite."

Neville shot Bolingbroke an unreadable look, but Bolingbroke chose to ignore it.

"My friends," Bolingbroke continued, "your advice, if I may. Who else do I need to fear? Who else should I guard my throne and England's stability against?"

Everyone studiously avoided looking at Northumberland.

"The Dominicans," Neville said. "There were several within the crowd this afternoon spreading word that Richard still lives. They were Exeter's allies."

"So," Bolingbroke said, looking at Neville with some speculation. "The Dominicans do not like me, and would like to unseat me. Can you tell me why, Tom?"

Because you are a demon, Hal, and because they suspect it.

"Many within the Church distrust you," Neville replied, "especially since you directed that religious studies receive less emphasis in schools and universities in favour of the new secular humanism. And your reforms of the calendar . . . many priests view that as a turning away from God."

Bolingbroke shrugged. He picked up a piece of fruit from a bowl, and bit into it, keeping his eyes on Neville.

"But you—we—have one bad enemy within the Dominicans. Prior General Richard Thorseby," Bolingbroke said, spitting out a seed and tossing it into the grate.

Years ago Neville had joined the Dominicans in order to assuage his guilt over his lover's suicide. Thorseby, who headed the Dominican order in England, had never liked Neville, and had distrusted the men's motives for joining the order. Thorseby's dislike and distrust slid into open hostility when Neville abandoned his Dominican vows in order to marry Margaret. Thorseby was a bad enemy; as the Dominican Prior General in England he had the influence, as also the friends and allies, to create havoc for those he hated.

"Aye. No one has seen or heard from him since June last year when the rebels torched Blackfriars. I do not like that."

"Well," Bolingbroke said, "no doubt he will turn up sooner or later, and no doubt with a renewed plan to see you incarcerated, Tom. But for the moment, I do not think the Dominican whispers are the worst—"

"But these whispers that Richard is still alive?" Raby said.

"I will return to those in a moment," Bolingbroke said. "There is one worse potential traitor in England that I think we all need to discuss. Here. Now."

Northumberland slowly rose to his feet. His face was grave, his eyes hard. "You refer to my son, sire. Why do you not say it aloud?"

Bolingbroke faced the earl, his own eyes as flinty as Northumberland's. "He has refused to swear allegiance to me. He sits in the north with an army of twenty thousand behind him—and the ability to raise another twenty thousand—that he claims to need against the Scots. He looks south, and hungers. Combine all those facts, my lord, and I see a very real threat."

"He has done nothing wrong!" Northumberland said.

"Save refuse to swear me allegiance and collect swords about his person in numbers the Scots do not warrant!" Bolingbroke shouted.

"Sire," Raby said softly, rising to place a cautionary hand on Bolingbroke's arm.

Bolingbroke shot Raby a furious look, then turned his gaze back to Northumberland. "Will you swear me Hotspur's allegiance, my lord? Will you swear to me that your son will remain a good and faithful subject?"

"Hal!" Raby barked. "That is enough. Northumberland saw you to your throne. Do not ask this of him now when—"

"I am not a stable boy for you to so rebuke me," Bolingbroke said, swinging back to Raby. "Remember who it is you address."

Then he spoke to Northumberland again. "Your aid has proved invaluable to me, Northumberland," he said, "but do you have any idea how quickly my love and support of your house will fade if your son leads an army south?"

"Why did I support you against Richard if I thought to then throw my son against you?" Northumberland said.

"Perhaps," Bolingbroke said, his voice very low, his eyes furious, "you supported me against Richard so that eventually your son might have an easier path to the throne."

"Sire—" Northumberland growled, taking a step forwards.

"This has gone far enough," Neville said, and nodded to John Scarle, the Chancellor, who laid a hand on Northumberland's arm and whispered something in his ear.

"Northumberland cannot swear Hotspur's allegiance," Neville said to Bolingbroke. "He *cannot!* Hotspur is a man grown, and must do it himself. Do not visit the son's sin of omission on the father who has proved such a valuable ally to you."

Bolingbroke stared at Neville, then nodded, the muscles about his face and neck visibly relaxing. He looked to Northumberland, still standing, still staring furiously.

"My lord, forgive me. This afternoon's treachery has proved a great trial, and has made me snap at those I should trust before all others."

Northumberland waited a few heartbeats, then inclined his head, accepting the apology. Scarle tugged a little at his arm, and Northumberland sighed, and sat down.

Gradually, the other men resumed their seats, and Bolingbroke took a sumptuously carved chair close by the unlit grate.

"I must bring Richard's body back to London," he said. "Mary was right. The people must view it."

"Is it," Raby said carefully, "in a state *fit* to be viewed?"

Bolingbroke raised his eyebrows, assuming an innocent expression. "In a state fit to be viewed, Raby? Whatever do you mean? Richard died of a fever, not a vicious clubbing or a tearing to bits by dogs. Of course it is fit to be viewed. As fit as any six-month-dead corpse can be, of course."

He sighed. "No doubt the royal purse shall have to bear the cost of the candles placed about the coffer, and the mourning robes for the official wailers and weepers. Richard has ever been an expensive burden to England."

Chapter VI

Saturday 4th May 1381

— iv —

✝

SHE DREAMED, AND yet it felt unlike any dream she'd been lost in before, for in this dream she was both witness and participant.

She dreamed of a woman, a woman on her knees atop a dusty, stony hill swept by a warm, fragrant wind. Above pressed a heavy, depressing sky; the atmosphere was hot and humid, and full of noiseless lament. In the distance was a walled city dressed in pale stone, and a roadway lined with people leading from the city gates to the hill where she knelt.

The woman's world had turned to grief. Her tears ran down her cheeks and dripped into the neckline of her white linen robe. Dark hair lay unbound down her back and clung in dampened wisps about her face. A cloak of sky blue lay to one side.

Several yards away lay her husband, still and dead, his corpse battered and bloodied. He had been sprawled across a rock for the vultures to feast on.

She reached out a hand towards him, wordlessly, now too exhausted and emotionally devastated to weep any more than she already had.

How could it have ended like this? Why had people hated him so much?

"Take her!" came a shout, and she jerked her head up at the same moment her hands slipped about her swollen belly.

People—soldiers, several priests and a crowd of ordinary men and women—surged towards her, and she started to rise. But her foot caught on the hemline of her robe, and she tripped and sprawled on the dusty earth.

She tried to rise again, desperate, knowing they meant her death, but she was too late.

Hands seized her by the shoulder of her robe and by her hair, and dragged her to her feet.

"Whore!" someone cried, and the entire crowd took up the accusation. "Whore! Whore! Whore!"

"I am not," she said, but her words were lost in the roar of the crowd. "I am not!"

I am not a whore, but a queen, she wanted to say, not understanding *why* it was she thought that.

But delusions were not going to help her or her unborn baby now.

They dragged her forth, ignoring her pitiful cries for mercy, to where a long-dry well had been covered over. Men tore away the wooden beams that closed the well, exposing a thirty-foot drop.

Then, still roaring their hatred, they threw her down.

They stopped roaring soon enough to hear her body hit the rocks at the bottom of the well.

A minute passed, then one of the priests grunted as he saw her limbs move slightly in their agony.

"She lives still," he said, bending and picking up a rock.

All about him, those closest to the rim of the well bent down, and picked up their own rocks.

Then they began, one by one, to pitch them down towards the woman.

It took them most of the remaining hours of the afternoon to kill her completely, and before they were done they'd broken every bone in her body.

* * *

MARGARET SAT by Mary's bed, watching the woman's chest rise and fall in shallow, slow breaths. Mary had been moaning in agony by the time Neville had carried her back to her chamber, and Culpeper, the castle physician, alerted to her need by runners who had come ahead, had been ready at hand. He'd given Mary a powerful infusion of monkshood, wild mushroom and opium poppy, which had eased Mary's pain within minutes.

It had also caused her mind to drift, and for almost an hour Margaret had sat holding Mary's hand as the queen talked of things she could never have seen, and people she could never have met.

Now, Margaret hoped, Mary had finally settled into a deep sleep.

But just as Margaret was about to rise and go to her own bed, Mary's eyes flew open.

"Meg?" she whispered in a cracked voice. "Meg? Are you here?"

"I'm right beside you, my sweet lady. I have never left."

"Where am I, Meg?"

"Why, you are in your chamber in the Rose Tower, my lady."

Mary's head slowly rolled back and forth and her eyes searched. "No, no. I cannot be. What is that wind? And that scent of sweet spice upon it?"

"Madam—"

"And why do I weep? Why do I feel such loss?"

Margaret leaned closer and saw that, indeed, Mary did weep. Great tears rolled down her cheeks.

Mary stared ahead, as if looking at someone. "Is he dead? Is he?"

"Madam!" Margaret grabbed Mary's hand between both of hers, and squeezed as tightly as she dared.

Mary continued to stare ahead, then she gasped, and cried out softly. "No! No!"

"Mary!" Margaret was beside herself, wondering what to do. Had the potion been too strong? Was it murdering Mary instead of aiding her? She half turned, meaning to wake the women who slept at the foot of Mary's bed, but just then Mary whipped her head about on the pillow and stared at Margaret.

"You are not all you would have me believe, are you, Margaret?"

Margaret opened her mouth, not knowing what to say.

Mary's mouth grimaced in a frightful rictus, her breath odorous due to the potion she'd imbibed and the dryness of her tongue.

"Margaret," she whispered, "why do so many people lie to me?"

And then, suddenly, she was asleep, and breathing easy. Her hand relaxed away from Margaret's.

Chapter VII

Friday 17th May 1381

✠

"WHAT CLEARER SIGN could you hope to have, my lord, than that of Exeter's revolt?"

The son of the Earl of Northumberland, Sir Henry Percy, commonly called Hotspur, slouched in the chair, staring at Prior General Richard Thorseby with dark, unreadable eyes. The Prior General had joined his household six months ago, just after Bolingbroke had himself crowned. And for six months the Prior General had been whispering and arguing and pleading: King Henry was an evil man who had murdered Richard and who would drive England into the mud of ignominy should he be allowed to keep the throne.

And who else was to act if not Hotspur?

"Exeter's revolt lasted an afternoon, Prior General," Hotspur said, "and ended in his death and those of his allies. I do not call that a 'clear sign.' "

"People resent Bolingbroke! The country will rise up against him if *you* lead!"

Hotspur sprang out of his chair, snatching a pike from a surprised man-at-arms guarding the doorway of the chamber, and threw it down at Thorseby's feet. "If you think the country so ready to rise, then lead it yourself!"

Thorseby took a deep breath and composed his face.

He folded his hands inside the voluminous sleeves of his habit and affected a righteous air, not realising that it only antagonised Hotspur further.

"Bolingbroke must be overthrown. He is the devil's spawn."

Trying to keep his temper, Hotspur strode to a shuttered window, unlatched one of the shutters, and drew it open. Outside there was nothing but cold, grey fog, with here and there the bare black branches of wind-blasted trees reaching into the low sky like the skeletal fingers of a corpse.

Lord God, Hotspur thought, *I do not know which I hate more—the damp climes of these northern lands, or the ever-whining voice of the Prior General.*

He stood a few minutes, allowing the still grey landscape outside to calm him, then he closed the shutter and turned back to Thorseby.

"I can understand your dislike of Thomas Neville," Hotspur said, "but why your sudden hatred of Bolingbroke? Do you profess to hate him, and thus beg me to dislodge him from the throne, only so you can once more claim Neville?"

Thorseby took his time in answering. In truth, he *did* loathe Bolingbroke because of his protection of Neville . . . but that was not all. Sometimes, over these past few months, he'd had strange visitations from shadowy, cloaked figures who had whispered that they were the messengers of the angels, and it was heaven's wish that Bolingbroke be torn down and destroyed. In his more lucid moments, Thorseby feared these shadowy, whispering visitors were but figments of his imagination. But these moments were few and far between, and generally Thorseby *knew* he had God, the angels and all of heaven behind him on this issue.

Bolingbroke must go. Neville must be brought to justice. And Hotspur was the most logical instrument of God's will.

"Bolingbroke is an ungodly man," Thorseby said, ensuring his face and voice remained calm and reasonable. "He murdered Richard and unjustly usurped his throne. He *must* be brought to justice. If my words do not persuade you, then be prepared. Soon God shall make His will clear with an unmistakable sign. You might not believe me, my lord, but you shall surely believe God."

"Oh, and what shall God do?" said Hotspur. "Send a plague of frogs? Turn the Thames red with blood? Strike dead the firstborn son in every family?"

"I should hope not the latter, my lord, if only for your sake."

Hotspur grunted.

"I counsel you, my lord, to prepare your way now. Speak closely and secretly with those who will support you. Exeter was rash, stupid. He deserved to fail. But if you—"

"Do *not* tell me how to wage a war, Thorseby."

Thorseby closed his mouth, raising his eyebrows slightly as if a schoolmaster rebuking his wayward pupil.

Hotspur picked up a letter that he'd been reading before Thorseby had come in. It was from his father, Northumberland, now back in his northern stronghold, and it contained many interesting statements and yet more interesting suggestions and promises. Hotspur's father had grown somewhat tired of Bolingbroke, it seemed, especially since Bolingbroke had proved himself so willing to doubt Northumberland after Exeter's attempted rebellion. A word here, a frown there, and so easily did allegiance shift. Hotspur pretended to peruse the letter for a few minutes, then he folded it carefully, and put it down again.

"If any man wishes to challenge Bolingbroke," he said, "he will need more than swords behind him."

Thorseby smiled, small and cold. "I am a powerful man in my own right," he said. "The Dominican family will stand behind you. Already my friars have been whispering, preparing the way for God's will as expressed through you."

Thorseby's Dominican 'family'? More like a murder-

ous flock of black crows, thought Hotspur, and shivered slightly at the thought of the great winged beasts swooping down on him through the cold, grey mists.

"If God sends me a sign," Hotspur said, "then I will move. Until then, I merely watch."

"And plan."

Hotspur hesitated, but only slightly. "And plan. Begone, Thorseby, for I think to warm this chamber with your absence."

PART TWO

Dog of Pestilence

Lady Mary stood all skin and
    bone,
Sure such a lady was never
    known:
This lady went to church one
    day,
She went to church for all to
    pray.

And when she came to the
    church stile,
She sat to rest a little while.
When she came to the
    church-yard,
There the bells so loud she
    heard.

When she came to the church
    door,
She stopt to rest a little more;
When she came the church
    within,
The parson pray'd 'gainst
    pride and sin.

On looking up, on looking
    down,
She saw a dead man on the
    ground;
And from his nose unto his
    chin,
The worms crawl'd out, the
    worms crawl'd in.

Then she unto the parson
    said,
Shall I be so when I am
    dead?
Oh yes! oh yes! the parson
    said,
You will be so when you are
    dead.

—Traditional English nursery rhyme

Dog of Pestilence

Chapter I

Tuesday 21st May 1381

— i —

✠

THE NAVE OF St Paul's in London was crowded with people but, strangely, nevertheless completely hushed. Many had queued patiently in the courtyard since many hours before dawn, hoping to be among the first admitted inside.

To see.

Two days ago King Richard's corpse had arrived in London from Pontefract Castle in West Yorkshire. One hundred men-at-arms had accompanied the coffin on its black-draped bier, protecting it from the curious, subdued, close-pressed crowds. Behind the men-at-arms came nineteen hessian-wrapped and ash-painted professional mourners, one for each year of Richard's life. They had accompanied the corpse to St Paul's, where six of the men-at-arms had carried it inside, the cathedral's doors closing promptly behind them.

The dean and his monks had spent two days preparing both display and corpse. That amount of time had set tongues a-wagging all the faster. Why did they need so long? Was it proving hard to stitch up the dagger holes?

Or to smooth his poison-ravaged face with flesh-coloured wax?

But now St Paul's and Richard's remains were thrown open to the inspection of the curious, and the Londoners had flocked to the occasion in their thousands.

Richard lay in an open, solid oaken coffin, its joints well sealed with wax and other substances, set on its bier before the altar. Candles and incense surrounded the bier save for a space directly before the coffin where a single person could step close for a quick viewing.

To one side stood an ever-changing guard of several priests and friars, there to ensure that the individual's viewing *was* only quick, and that he or she did not attempt to snatch a lock of the dead king's hair, or a scraping from under his fingernails to sell at a local relic market.

Dick Whittington stood in line with everyone else, and was as curious as everyone else. Whittington was no fool, and had understood very well that Bolingbroke could not have allowed the former king to survive as a lodestone for every disaffected person in the kingdom. Nevertheless, he thought, it *was* a shame that Bolingbroke couldn't have arranged for Richard to fall off a horse in front of a score of impartial witnesses, or arrange his drowning in a swollen river as Richard and his party were attempting to cross. The rumours sweeping London ever since news of Richard's death had ranged from the bizarre to the almost certainly correct: Lancaster's ghost had so terrified Richard one dark night he had fallen down dead (or Lancaster's ghost had set fire to Richard, or flayed him, or torn off his genitals and eaten them, leaving Richard to bleed to death); a band of Scottish soldiers had infiltrated Pontefract Castle in an attempt to kidnap Richard and make him *their* king, but had mistaken Richard for a guard, killed him, and then kidnapped the guard and installed him on the Scottish throne; Richard had choked to death on a frog which had taken up residence in the damp castle; Richard had pined to death over his lover, Robert de Vere; Bolingbroke had sent a band of assassins to Pontefract to murder Richard by means most foul.

Worse were the rumours that Richard was not dead at all, and that news of his death was only an official attempt to disguise the truth—that Richard had escaped Pontefract and was even now riding on London with an avenging army of tens of thousands behind him.

God had anointed Richard, therefore would God allow Richard to be so destroyed? And if Richard were truly murdered, would God allow his murder to go unpunished?

The truth, Whittington thought, as he slowly shuffled forward a few places in the queue, was that the Londoners, as many other among the English, were starting to feel a trifle guilty about their role in Richard's downfall. They had abandoned Richard with an indecent haste, supporting "fair Prince Hal's" counterclaim to the throne. While Richard had been festering in Pontefract, awaiting his murder, they'd been crowding about Westminster Abbey, shouting Bolingbroke's name as if it were a charm against evil.

Now they were here in their droves, impelled not only by curiosity but also by guilt.

Starting to get impatient, and finding that his joints ached greatly in the chill damp of the cathedral's nave, Whittington craned his head, trying to see how much longer he might have to wait. The queue appeared to stretch for some thirty or forty persons before him, but the priests standing about the coffin were making sure that people were moving briskly, and not loitering too long over Richard's open casket.

No one showed any signs of wanting to loiter, however. Perhaps, Whittington surmised, the stench was putting off even the most guilty or ardent of viewers.

Loiter they might not, but Whittington noticed that every man and woman who turned aside from the coffin had pale faces as they crossed themselves, halting briefly for the blessings of the priest. And they were quiet as they walked away, not pausing to whisper or gossip.

Some drew their wraps tighter about themselves, and looked nervously over their shoulders with darting eyes.

All left the cathedral as quickly as they could.

Whittington's curiosity grew, and he fidgeted impatiently.

The queue ahead of him was moving very quickly now. Perhaps only some four or five stood between Whittington and his turn at a viewing, and Whittington's head craned all the more. He could see a little into the open coffin over the shoulders before him—there was a heavy drape of a richly embroidered material over most of Richard's body. Whittington could see a pale blur of a face, and it appeared that Richard's skeletal arms and hands were crossed over his chest, clutching a gold crucifix.

He shivered suddenly, feeling as if a winter frost had dug deep into his bones.

The people ahead of him visibly shivered, too, and hurried the faster, bending only briefly over the coffin.

Then, finally, it was Dick Whittington's turn, and he stepped forward. A priest murmured in his ear, "Hurry! Hurry!", and the stench of hot incense and cold decaying flesh assaulted his nostrils, making his stomach roil.

He stepped up to the coffin, and peered in.

Richard's remains were horrible to behold. His flesh had shrunk close to his bones, his skull was sparsely dotted with a few clumps of dry hair, his eyelids had gummed closed over sunken eyeballs. His nose was a thin ridge only barely covered with the remnants of flesh—in one spot cartilage had poked its way free.

His desiccated lips were frozen into a horrible rictus, showing yellowed, slimy teeth. Behind them loomed something huge and horrid—his swollen, blackened tongue.

Whittington tore his eyes away from Richard's face and looked to where his skeletal hands clutched a crucifix. The fingers were clasped so tightly about the cross that in places the flesh of Richard's hands had rotted into the chain, and then reformed about it; the crucifix had become part of Richard's flesh.

"Move on!" came the whisper from a close attendant priest, and Whittington looked one last time at Richard's face . . .

. . . and screeched in terror. Richard's eyes had opened, revealing black, glistening orbs. They rolled in Whittington's direction, and, as the Lord Mayor stared, horrified, the dead king's lips moved: *Murderer! Murderer!*

Whittington tried to move, but couldn't. Richard's eyes held him locked in place.

Murderer! Murderer!

There was a clink, and Whittington realised that Richard's finger bones had clicked as his hands moved about the crucifix.

Whittington, Whittington, what do you think? Shall I rise from my grave to my throne again?

Whittington's face contorted, and he physically wrenched himself away from Richard's rolling eyes. He stumbled back, almost falling, then turned about, his breath coming in great, gasping gulps.

He realised no one was looking at him—*Why? Why? Had no one seen what he had? Had no one wondered at his strange reaction? Had his guilt made him imagine the entire episode?*—then realised that everyone was staring at a richly cloaked and garbed man walking slowly up the clear space of the centre of the nave.

Gold glinted about his brow.

Bolingbroke.

Whittington stumbled farther away from the coffin, staring at Bolingbroke.

Bolingbroke had no eyes for anything but the coffin. He strode forth slowly but purposefully, his eyes fixed on the bier and what lay on it.

Don't go near it! Whittington's mind screamed. *Don't go near—*

"Sire!" he gasped as Bolingbroke approached. "Sire!"

Bolingbroke ignored him. His steps quickened, the heels of his boots ringing across the flagstones, the hem of his cloak fluttering out behind him.

Every eye in the cathedral followed Bolingbroke up to the coffin, to this meeting of kings.

Bolingbroke stepped up to the bier, put his hands firmly on the edge of the coffin, and peered inside.

The only indication of what he saw within was a very faint tightening of the muscles along his jawline.

Whittington could *feel* the corpse roiling about within, *feel* the hate and injustice and vengeance reaching up to seize Bolingbroke by the throat. He wanted to rush to Bolingbroke's side and tear him away, but he couldn't move, couldn't so much as twitch a muscle.

This was between Bolingbroke and Richard alone.

Something spattered on the stones beneath the bier, and Whittington's eyes looked down, as did everyone else's in the cathedral save Bolingbroke's, who kept his eyes firmly on whatever was happening within the coffin.

Fat drops of thick, black blood oozed from the joints of the coffin, soaked into the material covering the bier, then dripped onto the flagstones where it pooled in a mess of foulness.

The entire cathedral took a great breath of mixed fear and awe.

The corpse bled in the presence of its murderer.

Bolingbroke's face twisted, and he lifted his hands and stepped away from the coffin.

He looked to the priests standing frozen to one side. "Take this coffin and its contents and burn it," he said. "Richard was ever adept at fouling up the realm."

He started to say something else, to address the crowds present, but as he opened his mouth, a low, vicious growl interrupted him.

Everyone's eyes, now including Bolingbroke's, swept to the open doors of the cathedral, from where the sound emanated.

There stood a hound of such vast size that most instantly assumed it was of a supernatural origin.

Richard's soul, perhaps, come to exact its vengeance.

The hound stalked forward, its legs stiff with fury, its hair raised along its shoulders and spine. It was entirely black, its body covered with weeping sores. Its head it kept low, its yellow, unblinking eyes fixed on Bolingbroke, fetid strings of foam dripping to the floor from its snarling snout.

Bolingbroke moved his cloak slightly away from the sword he wore at his hip, but made no other movement.

The hound's snarling increased both in volume and in viciousness. As it progressed up the centre of the nave, the very path Bolingbroke had just walked, the hound lowered its body until its belly almost scraped the flagstones, creeping now, rather than stalking.

Its eyes shifted slightly from Bolingbroke to the coffin behind him.

Bolingbroke stepped to one side.

All down the nave, as the hound crept past, people shrank back, making both the sign of the cross and the sign against evil. Many clutched charms, some whispered hasty prayers, all wished they had chosen some other time to view Richard's corpse.

The hound was now close to Bolingbroke.

The king took another step away. The hound ignored his movement. Its attention was all on the coffin, and on the spreading pool of black, clotting blood beneath it.

Slowly, slowly it crept closer, growling all the while, until its head was under the bier.

Then, suddenly, it lowered itself completely to the floor, gave a small yelp, and lapped at the blood.

As it did so, the sores that covered its body swelled and then burst, scattering great gouts of pus over the floor.

Someone in the crowd screamed: *"It is the black Dog of Pestilence!"* There was a shocked silence, then someone else screamed, formlessly, terrified, and suddenly there was panic as people stampeded for the doors.

The Dog continued to lick at the pool of blood, and its sores continued to swell and burst.

Whittington forced himself forward, and grasped Bolingbroke's arm.

"Sire. We must away. *Get away from the Dog!*"

"It is already too late," Bolingbroke said softly, and Whittington was not surprised to see tears rolling down his cheeks. "Too late."

He turned and looked Whittington directly in the face. "The pestilence has returned. Sweet Jesus Christ help us all."

Then he pulled away from Whittington's grip and walked down the nave and out the doors.

The Dog of Pestilence continued to lap.

Chapter II

Tuesday 21st May 1381

— ii —

✠

MARGERY HARWOOD LIVED with her husband, William, and their three children in a comfortable house on Ironmonger Lane off Bishopsgate Street. Margery was proud of her house—she spent an inordinate amount of time polishing, sweeping, washing and straightening— but her pride in her house formed only one part of her general satisfaction with life. She and William had emigrated to London when they were just married, and Margery pregnant with her first child. They'd come from a small village just east of Gravesend, where there was little prospect for an ironworker of William's calibre. So to London they had come, and if the first years establishing William's business were hard, then all the effort had been worthwhile. Now Margery was in charge of a house of ten rooms, a pantry, cellar and wine store that was stocked with far more goods than those of her neighbours, and three servants and a cook. William not only had a thriving business, but he also had five apprentices, as well as two guildsmen, working under him. Margery and William's children—three sons, praise be to God!— were healthy, and well ahead of their classmates at the guild school in learning their sums and letters. Their future was assured. Life was good.

Margery was in the kitchen at five of the clock that afternoon when everything fell apart. She'd been busy all day, supervising her servants as they cleaned out the cellar in preparation for the crates of spring-fresh vegetables that would soon fill it, consulting with the cook about that evening's fare, and then helping her to strip the eels and baste the vegetables for William's favourite pie, and thus Margery had enjoyed no free time at all in which to stand in her doorway and gossip with the neighbours.

She had no idea of what had happened at St Paul's that day, and, by virtue of the fact that her home was tucked right at the end of Ironmonger Lane, a reasonable distance from Bishopsgate Street, which was itself on the far side of London from St Paul's, she'd heard none of the fuss that had carried up and down most of the city's main thoroughfares. Both William and her sons had yet to come home, and in any case, Margery wasn't expecting them for another hour or so.

So when the scraping at the kitchen door came, Margery merely muttered her displeasure at the interruption, told the cook and the kitchen girl that she'd see what was about outside, wiped her hands on her apron, and walked to the door that opened into the kitchen courtyard.

Ironmonger Lane was a quiet part of London, rarely visited by the beggars and criminals seen in so many other streets, and so Margery had no hesitation in throwing open the door.

A massive black dog stood not three feet away, staring at Margery with yellow eyes, snarling so viciously that ropes of saliva spattered across Margery's apron.

Margery gave a small shriek, and slammed the door closed.

"Mistress?" asked the cook, staring up from the table where she'd been rolling out pastry.

Margery took a deep breath. "A dog. A stray," she said. "Nothing to be concerned about." And she walked back to the table to her duties, resolving to ask William to speak to the local alderman about the problem of stray dogs.

At that moment she heard their front door open, then, after the shortest of intervals, slam closed. Footsteps thudded down the corridor towards the kitchen.

William, their three sons, and two of his apprentices. William's face was shiny with sweat, his pale blue eyes wide and panicked.

"Lock the doors," he said, his voice hoarse and breathless. "Shutter the windows!"

"William—"

He ignored her, brushing past the cook and the kitchen girl to bolt closed the shutter over the kitchen windows. "Harry!" he said, looking at his eldest son. "Upstairs— the windows!"

Harry nodded, and darted away towards the stairs.

"William, *what is going on?*"

"Pestilence," William said, staring about wildly as if looking for something else to shutter closed.

Margery drew in a deep breath. "But we haven't suffered from the pestilence in—"

"How long it has been doesn't matter," William said, and directed his middle son into the front rooms of the house to shutter the windows. "What matters is that the pestilence is back *now.* Have you opened the door to anyone this day? Any beggars, anyone who has touched you?"

Margery stared at him, then very slowly looked down at her apron. Wordlessly she tore it off, then bundled it into the coals in the hearth.

IT WAS too late. By evening one of the apprentices, the cook, two of Margery's sons, and William himself were fighting raging fevers. Huge swellings appeared in their armpits, at the bases of their necks, and in their groins.

They were tight and agonising, filled almost to bursting point with black blood and pus.

Margery did what she could—and she was left on her

own to do it, because the two still-healthy servants had fled the house at the first signs of sickness—but that was little enough. She moved from bed to bed, wiping faces and hands with cloths wrung out in cool, herbed water. When her youngest son and one of the apprentices began to soil themselves with great clotting black messes, she changed their linens, her heart almost failing at their screams of agony as she rolled them over.

In the dark of early morning, as she was trying to change the linens under the apprentice, three of his buboes burst, and he bled to death, screaming, in under ten minutes.

And the nightmare had only just begun.

By dawn, William was dead, drowned in the mass of blood and pus that had collected in his lungs. The child and the apprentice who had so far escaped were tossing with fever, and Margery, in emptying out a bucket of blood and pus-stained rags into the courtyard refuse heap, suddenly realised that her arms were aching, and difficult to move.

There were hard lumps in both of her armpits.

Margery stood there for long minutes, the bucket at her feet, staring sightlessly at the refuse heap before her.

She moved her arms, very slightly, and again felt the painful swellings in her armpits.

Margery began to weep, great sobbing gulps, full of exhaustion and terror. She remembered how only a day ago her life had been so good, how the future shone so bright, how she and William had done so well for themselves from such humble beginnings.

Now?

Now it was all gone. Gone in less than a day.

Margery slowly sank to the cold cobbles, lay down, and waited to die, staring up at the grey sky with her weeping eyes.

Much later, dogs began to feed on her almost dead body.

Chapter III

Tuesday 21st May 1381

— iii —

✞

BOLINGBROKE STRETCHED TIRED neck and shoulder muscles, and looked one more time at the plans and documents that Dick Whittington had spread on the table. He lifted a candle—even though dawn light now shone through the windows, it was still not strong—and peered more closely at the plan of London spread before him.

He and the Lord Mayor, as also Bolingbroke's Chancellor, the Bishop of London, and several other clerks and secretaries, stood in one of the upper chambers of the Tower of London Keep. Most of the palace was still undergoing renovation, but at least this chamber was finished, and warmed by a fire roaring in the grate.

Someone—Bolingbroke had forgotten who—had thrown rosemary and rue on the fire, and now the sweet scent of the herbs infused the chamber.

Bolingbroke didn't think the herbs would have much effect in keeping the pestilence at bay.

The door to the chamber opened, and a man dressed in the livery of the Grocers' Company hurried in. He bowed perfunctorily to Bolingbroke, then whispered in Whittington's ear before hurriedly quitting the chamber.

"Well?" Bolingbroke said.

"Over a hundred and twenty more deaths," Whittington said, his shoulders slumping. "Sire, the pestilence has now touched most parts of London."

Bolingbroke nodded. "That black Dog has done its work well."

Several of the men in the room exchanged glances, their eyes filled with superstitious fear. Reports of the Dog of Pestilence had come in all night, appearing first here, then there, then somewhere else. No one could catch it, for whenever a band of men closed about it, the Dog merely seemed to vanish into the night air.

"A hound from hell," the Bishop of London whispered, and crossed himself.

"Not from hell," Bolingbroke said, sending the bishop a sharp glance, "but from heaven. This is *God's* retributive work."

"God's work it may be," Whittington said, forcing a brisk, businesslike tone into his voice, "but it will be man's work to deal with it. Unless," he gave the bishop an enquiring look, "the bishop knows some prayers that will drive the pestilence from among us?"

There was a silence. Then the bishop folded his hands before his corpulent belly, looked down, and muttered: "Prayers will be said in churches, of course, but if this is God's work, then it is His way of punishing sinners and there is little that we—"

"Don't tell me that this pestilence is God's means of carrying off sinners," Bolingbroke snapped. "The innocent are dying as readily as anyone else. Besides, if this pestilence was meant to carry away only the sinners amongst us . . . then why are most of London's damned priests and friars still alive?"

There was a twitter of laughter, quickly subdued, and the bishop flushed.

Bolingbroke stared at the bishop a moment longer, then turned back to Whittington. "Well? What *can* we do?"

"We can do some things to make life safer for those

still well," Whittington said. "Already I have sent orders to set up pest houses here," his finger stabbed at the map, "and here, and here."

"Good," Bolingbroke said. "They are well beyond the city walls. But should people be moving their infected through the streets?"

Whittington shook his head. "The pest houses will be used for people travelling into London, or those trying to leave, to isolate them until we are sure they are not infected. For those families already suffering within the city walls . . . well, men are even now moving through the streets, hanging bundles of straw from the windows of infected houses, and daubing their front doors with red paint."

Bolingbroke flinched. "Cursed by a daub of red paint and a bundle of straw."

"No one is allowed to leave or enter those houses," Whittington continued. "Not even to deliver food."

"Then pray this pestilence passes quickly," one of the clerks muttered, "or else people will starve within their homes."

"What else?" said Bolingbroke. He waved towards the fire. "Should we . . . ?"

"Already done," Whittington said. "Great bonfires salted with brimstone and saltpetre have been set up in all major intersections. With sweet Jesu's aid they will burn the pestilence from the air. Anyone who has to walk the streets, and they are precious few—the watch, those carting away the dead, and physicians and their apprentices—have been given nosegays of herbs and waxed cloaks to help the pestilence slide away from their persons."

None of which will protect them against God's black hound, thought Bolingbroke, but he did not speak his thoughts, for it was better to give people hope that something useful was being done, than to dash such hope away.

"All stray dogs are being killed," Whittington said. "Cats as well. Perhaps they contribute to the spread of the pestilence."

"Perhaps," Bolingbroke said. "Is there nothing else we can do?"

Whittington looked to one of the clerks. "Well . . . someone has suggested that we fill a barge with peeled onions and float it down the Thames when the winds are southerly. Then the tart scent of the onions will blow over London and—"

"Then set whoever thought that one up to the peeling of the several tons of onions needed to fill a barge," Bolingbroke said. "When he is done, and finished his weeping, I shall be willing to consider the proposition in more detail." He paused. "Dick, this is something I would rather not speak of, but I think we must . . . what of the dead?"

"They are being collected in grave carts," Whittington said, now looking out the window with unfocused eyes, "and being trundled to plague pits even now being dug in the fields beyond London."

"Sweet Jesu help us all," Bolingbroke whispered.

MARY READ the short, terse letter the courier had given her wordlessly, then handed it out with a shaking hand to Neville.

Neville exchanged a glance with Margaret, took the letter, read it, then cursed under his breath.

"Pestilence," he said, and handed the letter on to Margaret, who read it aloud for the benefit of the other of Mary's ladies who crowded about with huge, frightened eyes. Rumours from London had reached them early in the morning, but to now have confirmation of the worst . . .

"*Beloved Queen,*" Margaret read in a low voice, "*I greet you well. Know that pestilence has gripped London since yesterday afternoon. Many have died, more are infected, and the city tosses in the throes of torment. I beg you to remain in Windsor, where I might be more assured of your safety. Know that I am well, and in the Tower, whose walls have thus far kept the pestilence at bay. Pray to Lord Jesus for our deliverance. Your loving husband and king, Bolingbroke."*

Margaret lowered the letter, staring at Neville. "Sweet Jesu," she breathed as several of the ladies about her exchanged shocked looks.

Mary, lying as usual on her couch by the window, now struggled to sit up straight. "I must go to London," she said.

"Mary!" Neville and Margaret said together.

"No," Neville continued, risking a hand on Mary's shoulder. "You are too ill—"

"No, I am not," Mary said.

"—and you can do little to help," Neville finished. "Sweet Jesu, madam, what do you think you *can* do?"

Mary regarded Neville steadily. "I can give comfort, Tom. I can be with my people."

"Mary," Neville said, abandoning all attempts at formality, "You can barely walk *now*. You are in too much pain. You—"

"I *am* going, Tom. I cannot sit here and twiddle my thumbs while London dies."

"Then I'm going with you," Neville said.

Mary hesitated, then smiled. "Thank you, Tom. Your adeptness with the last rites will no doubt be more than useful."

"And I," Margaret said, as concerned as her husband that Mary should have as much support as possible, but unable to suppress a twinge of jealousy at Tom's care for Mary.

"No!" Thomas stared at her. "You cannot. The children need you. . . ." The thought that *both* women would be in danger was unexpectedly too much for him. He did not want to risk them both.

"The children shall stay here safe with Agnes. Mary will need me as much as you." Margaret looked Neville directly in the eye. "You know both of us will be safe."

The archangel needs both of us alive to play out the final drama, Neville thought, and he nodded. They would both live.

He did not see Mary's thoughtful gaze move between him and Margaret.

Chapter IV

Thursday 23rd May 1381

✝

EMMA HAWKINS HURRIED down Carter Lane by St Paul's, then ducked into a small alley. The streets were deserted save for a few scurrying people, and those wretched souls manning the plague carts on which were piled the dead. Fires coughed and spluttered on their diet of wood, brimstone and saltpetre at intersections and in marketplaces: their noxious fumes twisted and writhed into the air, tangling about eaves and overhangs before rising into a sky made scarlet with the sunset and the smoke of the fires.

There was the faint sound of wailing and sobbing in the air, anguish seeping out from behind closed doors and shuttered windows where men and women and children lay dying in unspeakable agony. Occasionally the muted, sombre tones of shroud-wrapped bells tolled indifferently from one of the city's parish churches.

Death lurked everywhere: in the stench of uncollected corpses upon the air, in the miasma of the fires, in the sewage choking the gutters, in the soft lament from tight-closed houses. Emma gathered her shawl more tightly about her face, gagging as she coughed, and regretted her decision to walk the streets in search of custom.

But she and her daughter needed to be fed, whatever

crisis gripped the city, and Emma knew she would get God-all custom huddling at home behind closed doors. She stopped briefly, leaning against a closed door, and tried to catch her breath. Well, it was time she admitted she was going to get God-all custom out here as well. No point in even hoping. She should get home. Her daughter Jocelyn would be worried about her—she'd spent an hour this morning begging her mother not to go out into the streets—and the longer Emma stayed outside, the more likely the pestilence would snatch at her.

Ah, that she *could* not think about! Pestilence crawled over the entire city, dealing death to scores every hour, and Emma simply refused to contemplate the idea that she—or Jocelyn—might be struck as well. Fate had already been unkind enough to her. It wouldn't deal her this death blow . . . would it?

If only Jocelyn was older. Emma couldn't afford to die yet. Jocelyn was only eight. Too young to work, too young to marry, and too young (by a year or two) to follow her mother out into the streets. Not that Emma would wish that on Jocelyn. It was too great a burden of sin for her frail shoulders.

"Only one of us need spend eternity in hell," Emma whispered. "And I will not have it be my daughter."

She struggled a little farther down the alley. The air was thick with the noxious stink of brimstone and ash—was she in hell already? Had she died without knowing?—and night was closing in about her fast. Too fast. Emma coughed again, and then almost panicked as she tasted blood in her mouth.

No! No! She'd bitten her tongue . . . that's all. Please sweet Jesu, let that be all!

Emma groped along one wall with one hand until she found a gate. She opened it, stumbling through into a courtyard, then hurried as best she could to the small door set to one side of the yard. Here she and Jocelyn lived in their two tiny rooms. Small, dismal, cold, but *home*.

She heard Jocelyn's small voice pipe a welcome,

then, horribly, the deeper voice of her landlord, Richard Harrison.

"Come to collect the rent, my dear," he said.

"Now?" Emma whispered, closing the door behind her and drawing the shawl back from her head. Her face was thin, her hair more grey than fair, her eyes enormous and black.

A faint flush glowed on her forehead and cheeks.

"Now?" she repeated, incredulous. The city was dying, gripped in pestilence sent from hell, and *Harrison had come to collect the rent?*

Then her mouth twisted bitterly. Why not? Why not, when he might be too dead to enjoy it tomorrow?

Emma folded her shawl and nodded towards the other room. "Quickly, then. I have Jocelyn's supper to prepare."

Harrison grinned. "You're in no position to tell me quick or no," he said. "Rent's rent, and it must be paid as owed."

Emma shot him a black look, then smiled at Jocelyn. "We won't be long," she said, then walked into the tiny, inner room.

All it held was a narrow bed and a stool.

Emma looked at the bed, unbuttoning her dress, and sighed as the door closed behind her and she felt the great bulk of Harrison fill the room.

HE WAS big and heavy and cumbersome and painful, but all of this Emma blocked out through years of experience. She arched her back as best she could with Harrison's weight atop her, and moaned with as much feigned pleasure as she could manage, and closed her eyes against Harrison's sweaty, straining face above hers, and her mind against the ponderous thrusting of his body.

Sweet Jesu, why was he taking so long? Reluctantly, Emma opened her eyes.

Harrison's round, pasty-skinned face wobbled above her. His eyes were closed, and his expression was one of the greatest concentration. His hips continued to thrust himself deep into her, his massive belly crushing her against the bed, the rest of his weight supported on arms locked rigid and splayed to either side of her body.

Thankful his eyes were closed, Emma allowed herself a grimace of distaste. *Everything* about him wobbled— his face, his fleshy shoulders, the rolls of fat down his back, his buttocks.

And it all sweated, great glistening globules of—

Emma went rigid, her eyes starting, then she screamed and tried to writhe away.

Under his left armpit was a massive, black swelling!

"Am I driving you wild?" he whispered, his eyes still closed. "Am I? Am I?"

Emma screamed again, trying with all her strength to topple the man off her. But he was too heavy, too strong, too determined in the sating of his lust.

His efforts increased, and as he did so the bubo in his armpit swelled until the skin enclosing it stretched thin and tight.

Sweet Jesu, this was Death riding her. God's judgement on her sinful life.

The door to the room flew open. Jocelyn, her face crinkled in worry at her mother's screaming.

Emma saw her over Harrison's heaving shoulders, and she screamed yet again, not only with fear this time, but with horror that Jocelyn should finally see what she had spent eight years keeping from her.

Harrison climaxed, and as he did so, the bubo in his armpit burst.

HE WAS long gone now, his face lax, his eyes glazed, and apparently still unaware of what his body harboured. He'd left the instant he'd pulled himself free from her body, and shucked on his clothes. Then he pushed past Jocelyn, still standing, staring at her mother on the bed. When the outer door had slammed behind him, Emma pulled the soiled sheets about her, trying to not only hide her nakedness, but also to clean off the filth from the burst bubo.

Jocelyn had stood, staring, frightened, until Emma quietly asked her to fetch a pail of water from the other room so that she might wash herself.

Now, sitting shivering before the small fire in the inadequate grate, Emma knew that she, and probably her beloved daughter, were doomed.

Death had been a-visiting.

Outside a dog howled once, then was silent.

Emma shivered some more.

Jocelyn sat down at Emma's feet, and silently held out to her mother a piece of bread. Emma took it, even though she felt ill, and forced down a few bites.

Satisfied, Jocelyn lowered her head to watch the flames, and once her gaze had turned away, Emma hid the bread in a pocket in her skirt. She reached out a trembling hand, and touched Jocelyn's shining fair hair.

What will happen to her when I am dead? Emma wondered, then began to weep, silently, despairingly.

Then, on cue, the fever struck, and Emma shuddered.

"Mama?" Jocelyn twisted about. "Mama?"

"Jocelyn . . ."

"I will fetch the physician."

Emma smiled tiredly. "I have no coin with which to pay the physician," she whispered.

"Then I will fetch the monks to take you to Saint Bartholomew's."

Emma began to laugh, a grating, grinding sound that was more sob than laugh. "I have no virtues with which to pay the monks," she said. "I am *un*virtuous, and they will not save me. Their hospital is as unobtainable to me as is heaven."

"Then *I* will save you," the young girl said with such a determined air that Emma almost believed her.

With the utmost effort, Emma raised a shaking hand and touched her child's cheek. "You are so beautiful," she said.

Chapter V

Friday 24th May 1381

— i —

✣

MARY LEANED FORWARD very slightly, just enough to touch Neville's arm to stop him, then stared about in horror.

They'd entered London across the bridge a few minutes ago after a careful two-day journey from Windsor. The journey had not tired Mary as she'd feared it would. Men rather than horses had carried her litter, and they were as gentle as might be. Her physician, Nicholas Culpeper, travelled with her entourage, and made sure that she took regular doses of monkshood and opium poppy. The strength of the mixture should have fogged her mind, but Mary was so overwrought with the horror she knew had descended on London that she managed to remain both relatively pain-free and clear-headed, something for which she thanked sweet Jesu many times daily.

They'd set out from Windsor at daybreak on Wednesday. Thomas Neville led the entourage, which consisted of Mary herself, Margaret Neville, one other noblewoman, Lady Alicia Lynley (Mary's other ladies were so terrified at the thought of returning to a pestilence-ridden London that Mary had bid them from her service),

Neville's squire Sir Robert Courtenay, Nicholas Culpeper, two of his apprentices, and an escort of fifty armed men-at-arms.

They had approached London from Southwark. Here Mary had excused from her company the greater number of her men-at-arms, Lady Alicia Lynley, and Culpeper's two apprentices. They would journey on to the Tower by boat to apprise the king of her arrival in London.

Here also Mary had alighted from her litter, saying only that she felt well enough to ride something small and manageable, and the litter would be too cumbersome to negotiate the twisted, narrow streets of London with ease.

At this Neville had argued vehemently with Mary, saying she could do little within the ravaged city, that it was suicide to even think of entering, and that she would be vastly better off going straight to the Tower and to Bolingbroke, both of which were, at the least, pestilence-free.

Mary had listened to him with the utmost courtesy, saying once he had paused to draw an indignant breath that if he and Margaret did not fear for their lives, then neither should she. Besides, she would do more good for the Londoners *in* London than walled within the safety of the Tower, would she not?

Neville, as Margaret, tried for another hour to persuade Mary not to enter London. In the end, Mary had been forced to command them to allow her. She was queen, and as queen she was going to enter London to do what she might.

And so they went, everyone walking save Mary, who sat atop a sweet-tempered pale cream donkey that Neville had found for her in the stables of one of the Southwark inns.

Its owner was long dead, and the donkey seemed pleased at being pressed once more into service. It appeared also instinctively to know Mary's frailty, for it stepped slow and sweetly, gently easing down each hoof so that Mary might not be jolted.

And thus, Neville leading Mary's donkey, Courtenay

and Margaret walking on the other side, and Culpeper bringing up the rear with the remaining ten men-at-arms, they crossed London Bridge.

ARMED MEN had stopped them halfway across at the drawbridge, but had let them through the instant they recognised Mary. When the party gained the intersection of New Fish Street and Thames Street on the city end of the bridge, they all stood still, slowly coming to terms with the horror that had enveloped London.

Evening had fallen, but it did little to hide the hellish streetscape. Red, noxious smoke billowed everywhere. Fires sparked and roared in the intersections ahead. People, little more than huddled humps, scuttled from doorway to doorway. A cart, overloaded with corpses and drawn by an emaciated limping horse, emerged momentarily from the roiling smoke, rattling slowly down the cobbled surface of New Fish Street. A grotesquely cloaked and masked shadowed figure tugged at the horse by its bridle, and, even after the cart had vanished back within the smoke, Mary and her escort could hear the man cursing at the poor beast, trying to make it hobble faster.

Through this nightmarish landscape filtered the noise of lament, and above all clung such a stench of rotting flesh that Mary had to hold her gloved hand to her mouth for a moment or two to stop herself from gagging.

A muffled bell tolled once, twice, and then jangled frantically as if whoever held its rope had succumbed to convulsions.

It suddenly fell silent.

"Is this Satan's work?" Mary whispered, finally lowering her hand.

There was a silence. "God's retribution, more like," Margaret said in a toneless voice.

Neville glanced at her. Her face was drawn and pale where it wasn't clouded by the flickering shadows of the flames and smoke. Her eyes stared, unblinking, straight ahead.

Mary turned her head so she could see Margaret herself. "God? Why would He visit us with such agony?"

"Because He hates Hal," Margaret said.

"But if He hates *Hal*, then why destroy London? Why destroy the innocent?"

Margaret looked away from the hellish landscape before her and towards Mary. "Because that is what He is best at," she said softly.

"Madam," Culpeper said, stepping forth. He was a thin, flame-haired man with a great beaked nose that currently sported a bunch of herbs tied under it. This bundle was attached to two strings that ran behind each ear. Every time Culpeper moved, the bundle of herbs jiggled slightly from side to side. Neville thought it made the physician look ridiculous. But, he supposed, if the herbs gave the man comfort in this most comfortless of times, then who was he to laugh?

Culpeper glanced at Margaret, who was now staring at him with a somewhat disdainful expression on her beautiful face, then addressed his queen again. "Madam, my Lady Neville is distressed, and perhaps she does not know the import of her words."

Margaret rolled her eyes slightly.

"This pestilence is a judgement, surely," Culpeper continued, "but we must not question God. We are only sinful mortals, and cannot understand God's handiwork."

"I'm sure that will give you enormous comfort when you lie shrieking in agony in your pestilence bed," Margaret murmured.

Culpeper flushed, then frowned. He looked about to remonstrate with Margaret when everyone's attention was caught by the sound of footsteps.

They were light and rapid, approaching down New Fish Street.

Neville moved a little closer to Mary's donkey, and he glanced behind at the men-at-arms.

They moved up, drawing swords, even though it was obvious that only one person approached, and that a child from the lightness of the steps.

The next moment a child did indeed emerge from out of the fire, smoke and gloom. She was young, only seven or eight, and slight even for her age. Her bare arms and face were grimy, perhaps from the smoke and soot that drifted about from the brimstone fires, while shoulder-length hair that was, under normal circumstances, probably very fair, clung to her cheeks and neck in oily tendrils.

Huge black eyes stared at the group of men-at-arms and nobles who blocked her path, and she sucked in a breath of anxiety.

She was trembling, but whether from effort or fright, none could tell.

She was dirty, but, all were relieved to note, did not display any signs of pestilence.

The child took a hesitant step forward, then, with an unerring instinct for who was the most likely to aid her, she ran to kneel before Mary's donkey.

"Blessed Lady!" the child stammered, holding out her hands in supplication. "I beg your aid."

Mary smiled, and beckoned the child to rise and come to stand by her donkey's shoulder.

Neville moved very slightly out of the way, but he made sure that he remained close enough to prevent any trouble should the little girl suddenly produce a dagger from her skirts.

Mary reached out a hand and touched the child's cheek. "You shall have my aid," she said in a gentle voice. "But first, tell me, how should I call you?"

"Jocelyn." The girl's eyes were fixed on Mary's face as if she thought her an angel.

"What a lovely name," Mary said. "I am Mary, and thus you shall call me."

Neville opened his mouth to object. Mary was the

child's queen, and the child ought to realise that she should address her queen with more respect than just—

With an amused glance Mary silenced whatever Neville might have been going to say, before addressing Jocelyn again.

"Jocelyn, child, why do you run with such haste? Should you not be home with your mother and father?"

"I have no father," Jocelyn said, "and my mother is sick, near to dying. Please, will you help her?"

"There *are* hospitals," Culpeper murmured, using a forefinger to press the herb bundle the closer to his nostrils.

Jocelyn began to cry, pitiful hiccupping sobs that shook her shoulders. "I asked the monks at Saint Bartholomew's," she said, her stammering even worse now, "but they refused. They said my mother had been struck down for her sins, and that she should learn to . . . to endure. I was running to Saint Katherine's across the bridge, hoping that I might find someone to aid my mother."

"And so you have!" Mary said. "See? I have with me a physician—" Culpeper started to say something, but Mary silenced him with a wave of her hand. "—and a lady to aid me, and," she turned her head very slightly to smile at Neville, "a man who can give your mother absolution if that will aid her more than medicines can. Come," she looked at Jocelyn again, "will you lead us to her?"

Jocelyn was still crying, but her sobs had quietened, and she managed a small smile. "Thank you, Mary."

"Would you like me to hold your hand as we walk?" Margaret said, stepping forward and squatting down before the child. She smoothed a lock of Jocelyn's grimy hair away from her forehead with tender fingers.

Jocelyn stared a moment at her, thinking she had never seen a lovelier lady, then nodded. Margaret rose, took the girl's hand, and they turned west into Thames Street.

* * *

THEY WALKED at a brisk pace, Margaret and Jocelyn leading, Neville staying close to Mary in case she needed support to keep upright, Courtenay on the other side of the donkey, Culpeper using his forefinger to keep the herbs pressed close to his nose and looking from right to left as if he expected further waifs to accost them, and the men-at-arms bringing up the rear.

After a few minutes Jocelyn twisted back to address Mary. "We live in an alley near Saint Paul's," she said.

"Then the bells must give you great joy," Mary said.

"They keep me awake," Jocelyn replied, turning back to the street before them, and Margaret suppressed a smile.

They'd walked only a few more minutes, but close enough now to see the spire of St Paul's emerging from the brimstone haze like a long-necked sea monster, when a vicious snarl stopped them in their tracks.

They stared, looking about them.

There was nothing but the twisting, drifting smoke.

The snarl sounded again, low and, if possible, even more malevolent than previously.

Neville and Courtenay both drew their swords, Neville nodding to the men-at-arms to position themselves about Mary.

"It is nothing to worry about," he said to Mary. "A stray, perhaps, terrified of the smoke and stench."

"Tom," Margaret said very quietly.

He looked to her. She was staring ahead as, very slowly, she backed herself and Jocelyn up to within the protective circle of armed men.

Neville followed her gaze.

There was something emerging from the red and black smoke in front of them. A shape, vaguely four-legged, and black, forming among the twisting tendrils and sparks within the fumes. But a *dog*. It seemed huge, as if—

The beast moved forward several steps, and the smoke swirled back to reveal it.

A massive, grotesque hound, almost as big as the donkey on which Mary sat. Its shoulders were so muscled they appeared out of proportion to the rest of its body. Its legs were slim, but stiff as if ready to spring, its coat and skin eaten away by scores of suppurating sores.

Malignant yellow eyes glared unblinkingly at them above a twisting, snarling muzzle.

"Tom," Mary whispered.

He hefted his sword, as if about to step forward and confront the hound, but Margaret caught at his arm.

"No!" she said. "You cannot touch it. It is . . . it is the black Dog of Pestilence. God's wrath incarnate."

Neville stared at the Dog, trying to gain its measure. That it was a supernatural beast he had no doubt. But God's beast?

"A retributive strike," Margaret whispered, now staring at him with strange-lit eyes, and Neville understood that only he would be able to hear her voice. "God's vengeance on the English for having supported Hal's rise to the throne. Sweet Jesu aid us, Tom."

Then she turned back to the Dog. "Go. Go! We will have none of you here."

The Dog stalked forward another two steps on stiff legs, his hackles raised, snarling and snapping at Margaret.

Jocelyn had shrunk back into Margaret's skirts, and Margaret pushed the girl behind her.

"Go," Margaret said, now whispering. "You cannot touch us. Not yet."

The Dog growled one more time, low and vicious, its disappointment wrinkling about its snout and eyes. Then it turned slowly, almost insolently, and stalked away into a side alley.

A few heartbeats after the Dog had disappeared into the dark, shrieks and wails issued forth from the alley's smoke-shrouded homes.

"And so the pestilence finds new victims," Margaret said. She locked eyes briefly with Neville—*God's vengeance*—then dropped her head and smiled at Jocelyn still clinging to the back of her skirts. "See, darling, the Dog has gone. Come, lead us to your mother."

Jocelyn looked to Mary for reassurance, received it in the form of a smile, then very slowly led them forward once more.

JOCELYN AND her mother lived off a tiny enclosed courtyard, which itself ran off a narrow, bleak alley. When they gained the courtyard Neville lifted Mary down from the donkey, holding her arm as she found her balance.

Mary gazed about her with wide, almost disbelieving eyes.

Never had she seen such squalor in her life.

The courtyard was perhaps twenty feet by twenty, its cobbles so old and worn that they had disintegrated almost into gravel. In one corner lay a muck heap, the only means the inhabitants of this court had to dispose of their waste. Two small, almost skeletal pigs nosed about in it, and Mary had to turn away, sickened by what she saw smeared across their muzzles.

The courtyard was surrounded on three sides by buildings that leaned so far into the yard that they stayed upright only by virtue of the heavy wooden supports that had been manoeuvred into position underneath them. Damp and mould ran up the stone walls in long green streaks. The few windows in the buildings were tiny, and filled with waxed cloth rather than glass. Smoke seeped out from rents in two of the cloth windows—there were no chimneys.

Doors hung askew, rags fluttered from nails, dirt and dung piled in doorways, water ran in thin trails down plasterwork.

This was not the work of the pestilence, but of the ordinary, everyday squalor of the poorest of London's citizens.

"Madam," Neville said, reading the horror in Mary's

eyes and watching as one gloved hand flew to cover her nose and mouth, "we do not have to stay. We can send aid without having to enter ourselves. Let me—"

"No." Mary shook her head. "I will go in. I promised. But, oh, Tom, such squalor! I never knew . . ."

He shrugged. "Welcome to London's bleak heart, madam." He turned to the men-at-arms, directing several of them to take watch about the courtyard, several others, including Courtenay, to guard the entrance to the alley, and two more to make their way back to the Tower to make sure Bolingbroke knew where they were.

"No," Mary murmured.

"He has a right to know, madam," Neville said, and Mary sighed, and acquiesced.

"Mary?" Jocelyn called softly from a doorway on the northern side of the courtyard. "Hurry, please!"

Then she disappeared inside.

Mary locked eyes first with Margaret, then with Neville, then walked towards the doorway.

"Culpeper," she said, "ensure that you come with me."

Culpeper sighed, but he followed Mary, Margaret and Neville inside.

As they entered the building, several round, pale faces appeared at some of the upper windows, their eyes and mouths opened wide and glistening in faint light.

Chapter VI

Friday 24th May 1381

— ii —

✛

EMMA LAY CURLED in a foetal position on her bed. Suffering coursed through her. She burned with fever, and wanted nothing more than to toss and turn to try to seek in such movement some relief from its raging, but buboes filled her armpits and groin, and any movement made them sear with such torment that Emma would shriek in agony.

She was dying, and she knew it.

In itself the pain did not cause Emma the greatest distress. Instead, the knowledge that she would die alone (Jocelyn had been gone twelve hours or more, and the fact that she *was* gone gave Emma some hope that her daughter had escaped this death pit of a city) and unshriven, condemned to the fiery, tormented pits of hell because no priest was present to hear her confession, was making Emma's final few hours of life pitiful in the extreme.

This was hell in waiting.

Jocelyn's fate also weighed heavily on her mind. Her daughter was too young to be able to care for herself. She would be cast into servitude, or perhaps snatched to be sold into slavery to the Moors. Worse, the criminal underworld of London would find her, and force her into prostitution. Jocelyn was young and fair, and some noble would pay many gold pieces to be able to rob her of her virginity.

Emma wept silent, wretched tears that coursed down her cheeks. Jocelyn would suffer no matter what happened: either the pestilence would seize her and condemn her to an agonising death in a gutter, or men would seize her, and condemn her to a life of whoring for every man that had coin enough to pay for her.

And, as Emma well knew, once Jocelyn grew older and lost her youthful bloom, that meant every man who came her way, fat, ugly, scabbed or otherwise. Anyone, if just to keep some food in her mouth. Anyone, if only to keep alive.

There was a sound, but in her state of fevered agony and despair, Emma paid it no attention. There were always sounds: men, bending over you; rats, scampering past your pillow; the even-more-wretched-than-she, scraping fingernails against closed doors; and always, always, the censuring bells of St Paul's, ringing out their judgement, *hell awaits, hell awaits, hell awaits* . . .

The sound came again, and Emma moaned, for surely it could mean only more misery. Who now? Harrison, come to claim next week's rent? Some backstreet boy, come to steal her pitiful belongings? Someone from the watch, perhaps, come to poke her to see if she were dead yet?

Soon her corpse would be tossed onto one of the creaking death carts. Soon she would be cast down into the blackness of a plague pit.

Is this all that life was?

"Jocelyn tells me that you are Mistress Emma Hawkins," said a soft voice, and Emma felt someone sit carefully on the edge of the bed, "and that you are her mother. She has asked me to aid you."

Emma tried to open her eyes, but they were gummed closed. "Who . . . ?" she croaked, blindly reaching out a hand.

"Shhh," the voice said, and then Emma heard it whispering to someone else in the room. *Who? Jocelyn? Was Jocelyn here?*

Emma sobbed, unable to bear the thought of her daughter witnessing her miserable, tormented death.

"Shhh," the soft, gentle voice said again. "Here." And a blessedly cool and moist cloth was wiped tenderly across her face, wiping clean her eyes, and trickling moisture into her dry mouth.

Emma caught at the cloth between her teeth, sucking as much moisture out of it as she could. She heard the voice again, speaking quietly to someone, asking for water.

There were footsteps, not hurried, but quick, and then the woman on Emma's bed had slid one hand beneath her neck, raising her head forward and pressing a goblet to her lips.

The water was cool, and like nectar from heaven.

Emma drank greedily, and the woman withdrew the goblet. "Not so fast, Emma. You will make yourself ill."

Emma made a small sound. "Ill? Madam, can you not see my condition? Am I not ill enough already? Give me more water, please, I beg you."

And Emma finally managed to open her eyes, and see her saviour.

A face swam before her, and Emma had to blink several times to bring it into focus. A woman with a gentle face—gentle because its bearer, too, suffered. Wan but clear skin. Huge, kind, hazel eyes. Soft honey hair coiled under the finest of lawn headdresses. And the sweetest of mouths, curled in a smile so loving that Emma thought her heart would break.

"Blessed Lady," she whispered. "Blessed Mary!"

A shadow passed over the woman's face, then it cleared, and she smiled all the sweeter. "Nay, Emma, just a poor woman such as yourself. And my name *is* Mary—you must have recognised me from the day of my marriage."

Emma frowned. Not the Blessed Mary? But her name was still Mary? Then she remembered. She remembered a bright and sunny day, and a crowd about St Paul's. She remembered fair Prince Hal, riding to his wedding. And she remembered the girl that he had wed, the modest Lady Mary Bohun.

And this woman wore her face.

The Queen of England sat on her bed, and wiped her brow?

"Madam," Emma whispered, "what do you *here?*"

Mary indicated the several people standing about her in the cramped room: a handsome nobleman, black-haired and bearded, frowning at her; a noblewoman, beautiful beyond belief, and standing at the queen's shoulder; a red-haired thin man with a ridiculous bundle tied under his nose . . . he looked vaguely familiar, and Emma fleetingly wondered if she had serviced him sometime.

And there, staring at her from behind the beautiful woman's skirts, was her daughter, Jocelyn. Emma tried to smile at her, but failed.

"I and my friends," said the queen, "are here to aid you, Emma. I had come with my retinue from Windsor to do what I could for my poor people of London, when your lovely daughter, Jocelyn," and she held out her hand, and drew Jocelyn forth to stand at Emma's bedside, "begged me to aid you. I would not refuse her, nor you."

"Madam," whispered Emma, "please leave me! You will die if you stay. I am so hideous. Oh, see, see how hideous I am! Go! Go! I do not want to be the one to kill you."

Mary leaned forward and placed her free hand on Emma's mouth. "I would be honoured to think that, in aiding you, I might myself die, Emma. You are not hideous, but beautiful."

"You do not know what I am!"

"A whore," Culpeper put in. "I can smell it about this hovel."

The expression of sweetness in Mary's face did not alter, or even flinch. "You are a beautiful woman, a mother, and you are in need," Mary said. "I care not what you are, or what you might have been, or what sins you think weigh down your soul. Emma, you are dying, but I can ease you into that dying, and it will be my great honour to do so."

Again the tears trickled down Emma's face. She could not believe that this woman—this wondrous, noble woman—could sit there and look upon her with no judgement or loathing in her face.

"If you have love within you, and mercy to give," Emma said, "then give it to my daughter, not me. Jocelyn needs a protectress—"

"Say no more, Emma. I shall take Jocelyn into my household, for I think she shall make the best of companions, and ensure her future, but that does not mean that I should therefore abandon you. I do not ask such prices. Now, Jocelyn, sit here by your mother, and wipe her face and brow thus. Yes, good girl. Emma, I will return in a moment. I need to talk to my physician."

And Mary rose, smiled, and turned away.

Both Neville and Margaret instantly put arms about her, for she swayed as she stood.

She thanked them with a nod and smile, and it was a measure of her own weariness and discomfort that she allowed their arms to stay about her.

"Culpeper," she said, "what can you do for this woman?"

Culpeper looked at the queen, then, with increasing incredulity, at Emma lying on her bed. "Do for her, madam? I can do nothing for her. See, she is close to death. Why her mind does not wander with such a fever, I do not know, but I can only think that—"

"Thank you," Mary said, "but I believe there *is* something you can do for Emma. What of the potion that you mix for me? Will it not ease this woman's agony?"

Again Culpeper's eyes slithered from the queen to the dying woman, then back to the queen. "But, madam, I have so very little, and you need—"

"My need is inconsequential compared to this poor

woman's," Mary said, and her tone was like steel. "And you can find new herbs enough at any one of the city's hospitals or apothecary shops to mix a new batch. Now, where is it?"

Sighing, and setting his face into the most injured of expressions, Culpeper withdrew a vial from a pocket inside his cloak.

"Good." Mary took the vial, then turned to Neville. "Tom, will you shrive this woman? Cleanse her soul so that she may attain salvation?"

Neville glanced at Emma. "I am no longer a priest, madam," he said, "but it is the comfort and the words that matter, not the vehicle that utters them. Yes, I can shrive and comfort her."

He was rewarded with beautiful, grateful smiles from both Margaret and Mary.

"It is only love that matters, Tom," Margaret said. "Only that, and I think love is something that Emma has in full."

Neville held her eyes for a long moment, then gave her a small smile in return.

"Madam," he said to Mary, "I will need to shrive her before she takes that potion. She must remain clearheaded. Margaret, will you fetch me a bowl of fresh water? Or," he glanced about their surroundings, "a bowl of as clean water as you can manage."

He turned to Jocelyn, squatting down beside her mother, so that he could look her in the eye. "My dear," he said, "I must speak with your mother now. Will you wait with your queen? And can you find her a stool so that she might rest?"

Jocelyn regarded Neville with huge solemn eyes, then she nodded, turned, and did as he asked, finding a stool in the outer room and dragging it back into her mother's death room for Mary to sit upon.

As Jocelyn moved away, Neville rose, then sank down again on Emma's bed. After the briefest of hesitations, he took both the woman's dry, chapped and feverish hands in his.

"Emma," he said in a gentle voice, "I spent many years as a Dominican friar before," he smiled, and glanced at Margaret, "I met a woman who led me astray from my vows." His smile and the light, teasing nature of his voice took all potential sting and retribution out of his words. "I no longer wear my robes, or adhere to my vows. Nevertheless, would you like me to hear your confession, and shrive you of your sins?"

"Can I be shriven?" Emma asked. "I have so many sins, and, as the physician said, I am nothing but a common whore. How can you forgive such as me?"

Thomas Neville said nothing for a long moment. Instead, his thoughts cast back to those days when he'd renounced all whores, when he'd hated them beyond all reason . . . when he'd hated all women beyond reason.

He remembered the whore in the streets of Rome who had cursed him, and told him that one day he would hand his soul on a platter to a whore. *You will offer her your eternal damnation in return for her love!*

And then he remembered what Jesus Christ had said to him on the hill of Calvary. *Love saves; it does not damn.*

Jesus Christ, God of the Demons.

And yet what would he rather do here? Damn this woman into God's hell for her sins *(for men's sin in lusting after her? For the angels' sins in lusting after women?)*, or save her into Christ's world of love?

What should he do?

He remembered Alice, his mistress, and her horrible death because he had refused to acknowledge their child. Then he had run from love, fearing it. He remembered what Margaret had done for Lancaster, and to where Lancaster had gone. A field of lilies, under a clear blue sky, and the empty cross sitting atop the flowered hill. He and Tyler had gone home, to love, Bolingbroke had said, and Neville knew his choice was the easiest of all to make.

"Have you loved?" he said.

Her brow creased, as much in pain, Neville thought, as in reflection. "Yes, of course," she said. "I loved my parents, and they me. My grandmother adored me, and I her. And," her eyes shifted to where Jocelyn sat on the floor by Mary's feet, "I love my daughter, and she loves me."

Neville smiled. Emma had loved, and was loved, and she would be saved because of it.

If I had not learned to love, dared to love, Neville thought, *then I would have damned myself for all time.*

Then a stranger, and far stronger thought occurred to him. *If the angels have never loved, and refuse to love, then do they exist in hell, and not heaven?*

Neville suddenly realised his thoughts were drifting off, and he collected himself, remembering what Margaret had said to Lancaster. Now, Neville repeated those words for Emma. "Then what a blessed life you have had, and what love you have given. Your grandmother, your parents, your child have all had of you what they should: your love and your care. You have had from them the same love and care. Embrace your passing with joy, Emma, not with thoughts of sin."

"But—"

"You have been loved," Neville said firmly, his hands tightening about hers, "and you have loved. Is there anything else?"

Emma stared at him, blinking her tears away. Very slowly she smiled.

So deeply was everyone concentrating on Emma and Thomas Neville that without exception they all jumped when the voice spoke from the doorway.

"Well said, Tom. There is nothing else, indeed."

And Hal Bolingbroke, King of England, walked into the already crowded and close chamber.

Chapter VII

Friday 24th May 1381

— iii —

✠

EMMA BLINKED, AND smiled, for she recognised him, but did not otherwise fuss. Too much had happened already this night, and she was too close to her own death to be bothered overmuch by the King of England's entrance into her mean chamber.

Bolingbroke paused by Mary long enough to lay a hand on her shoulder and nod a greeting, then walked to Emma's bedside to stand by Neville.

"This is Mistress Emma Hawkins," Neville said softly, his gaze remaining on Emma's face. Then he raised his eyes to Bolingbroke. "Your queen is come to aid the Londoners in their horror, Your Grace, and she is here to witness Emma's passing into—" He stopped, unsure of what she might be passing into. Heaven as guarded by the angels, certainly not, and ever more certainly not the angels' construction of hell.

"Her passing into love," said Bolingbroke, and, leaning down a little, touched Emma's swollen face. Boils and pustules now disfigured it, blowing up the flesh about her mouth and eyes.

"Thank you," whispered Emma, and Bolingbroke nodded, then moved away. He whispered something to Culpeper, who vanished, returning a few minutes later with several more stools he'd purloined from the dwelling next door.

Neville rose from the bed and helped Culpeper arrange them about the confined space. Mary moved to a stool at the head of Emma's bed, Margaret sat on the bed itself beside Emma, Jocelyn with her, while Bolingbroke and Neville sat on two stools set just back from the bed; Culpeper, murmuring excuses, removed himself completely from the death chamber.

Mary and Margaret took turns wiping Emma's face with damp cloths, while Jocelyn held her mother's hand and silently wept.

Time passed.

"You came quickly," Neville eventually murmured to Bolingbroke.

"I was on my way from the Tower when I met your men-at-arms approaching the bridge," Bolingbroke replied.

Neville raised his eyebrows in silent query.

"Whittington and I," said Bolingbroke, "thought to walk the streets of London. We could not bear to think that the Londoners suffered while we waited out the pestilence locked in the silence of the Tower."

"You are not afraid?"

"Of the pestilence? Nay. It cannot touch us." Bolingbroke's steady pale grey eyes caught Neville's brown ones. "Not my brothers and sisters of the angel-children. This is a pestilence designed to punish the ordinary men and women who supported me. The louder they cheered, the more violently they die." He looked back to Emma. She'd drunk the potion that Margaret had fed her drop by drop, but even so she still moaned. "The pestilence also serves as a means to turn the people against me. It is not a good omen with which to begin a reign, Tom."

Neville thought of the horrors God had visited on the Egyptian king and his people in order to force him to free

Moses and the Israelites. "Sweet Jesu," he whispered, "what else might we expect?"

Now Bolingbroke had turned his piercing eyes back to Neville. "I don't know, Tom. It was a question I was about to ask *you*."

Neville jerked his eyes away, studying Emma. *Jesu, these were ordinary men and women, doing the best they could in their daily travails. And for this God has lashed them with His disgusting pestilential vengeance?* Then Neville jerked slightly on his stool as a revelation—it was too powerful to be called a thought—surged through him. *God and his angels, and their Church on earth, were nothing but vehicles of hate and fear and vengeance. The demons, the angel-children, embraced Christ's message of love.*

Emma moaned, louder now, and Mary leaned forward to add her hand to that of Jocelyn's as it held Emma's. "Your agony will ease soon," she whispered.

Emma opened her eyes—mere slits now between her swollen lids. "Mary," she whispered, repeating what she'd said when she'd first realised Mary was in her chamber. "Blessed Mary!"

Mary shifted uncomfortably on her stool, a faint flush of embarrassment on her cheeks. "Her mind wanders," she said to Margaret, who was looking at her with an odd expression in her eyes. "The liquor is so strong."

"Maybe," murmured Margaret, remembering the strange things that Mary herself had said while under its influence.

Emma now freed her hand from her daughter's, and gripped Mary's hand tightly. She twisted her head on her pillow so she could stare Mary directly in the face.

"Mary, Mary," she said. "What you have lost you will find again."

"Emma, I have lost nothing, I want for nothing—"

"Save your husband's love," Emma croaked. "Never mind, sweet Mary, Blessed Mary, it shall be yours again soon."

Now Mary's flush deepened, and she studiously avoided looking at Bolingbroke. "Emma—"

"You have loved, you are loved, and you will be loved," said Emma, and then she died with nothing more dramatic than a long, comfortable sigh.

There was a lengthy silence, eventually broken by Jocelyn, who began to cry anew. Margaret gathered her into her arms, comforting her.

But she kept her eyes on Mary, sitting straight and still on her stool.

"We will wash her, and make her clean," Mary said. "And then we will have her conveyed to a churchyard where she shall be buried."

"Mary," Bolingbroke said, rising from his stool. "This is not a task you should be engaged in. I can find—"

"No, Hal. I would like to do this for Emma. It will not take long, and it will be no effort."

"Mary," Bolingbroke said in a stronger voice, "I cannot allow it. You have already exposed yourself far too much to the pestilence, and I will *not* have you handling this woman's noxious corpse!"

"I am dying anyway," Mary said in a matter-of-fact tone, "and whether it be from the black imp eating me within, or the black pestilence that will swell me without, is neither here nor there."

"Mary—"

"I can do good *here,* Hal, not cloistered up in some silken chamber. If nothing else I can bring comfort to the dying. I can let them know that their queen cares about them, and suffers alongside them in their extremity."

"It is the same reason you are here, Hal," Neville put in quietly. "London cannot be left to suffer alone. And Mary has Margaret and myself to care for her. When we see that she needs to rest, then she *will* rest. When we see that she needs to eat, then she *will* eat. And when we see that she needs to—"

"Then she *will* do it," Mary finished for him, with a smile. "Hal, please, do not worry about me. If you wish, I will go to one of the hospitals, and do what I can there, rather than wander the streets."

Bolingbroke looked at her, knowing that if the hospitals were filled with the victims of the pestilence then they might be more dangerous than the streets.

But then, did she not say she was dying anyway? Who was he to gainsay her?

He nodded tersely. "Very well. Tom, Margaret, I charge you with her care. Keep Culpeper close by you at all times, and if at any time it appears necessary, then you escort my queen to the Tower . . . no matter how she protests."

Everyone nodded agreeably.

"Come, Margaret, Jocelyn," Mary said. "Gather together some water and some towels, for we have Emma to see to."

Bolingbroke watched for a brief moment, then turned to Neville. "Keep her safe," he said, then left the room. Neville heard footsteps outside, then hooves as Bolingbroke and his escort rode away.

"I will wait in the outer chamber," he said to Margaret, "for this ritual is women's business."

MUCH LATER, when the women were done, and bearers arrived from St Mary-le-Bow church to escort Emma Hawkins' body to the churchyard, Mary finally consented to allow Margaret and Neville, Jocelyn close behind, to help her outside.

As they stepped into the tiny courtyard, they halted in amazement. Some forty or fifty people—ordinary Londoners—had crowded into the confined space.

"What is this?" said Neville.

The crowd parted a little, and Dick Whittington stepped forth. "One of Emma Hawkins' neighbours saw our queen enter her lodgings," he said, "and word spread. My queen, I speak for all these good people here, and for all Londoners, in thanking you for your mercy and goodness."

And he dropped to one knee, sweeping his cap off his head as he did so.

One by one the other people in the courtyard did likewise, and as Mary moved slowly towards her donkey, many reached out and touched the hem of her gown.

"Beloved lady," they whispered.

Chapter VIII

Sunday 26th May 1381

— i —

✠

FOR THREE DAYS the Dog of Pestilence stalked London, striking down innocent and sinner alike, leaving thousands to perish alone huddled in gutters or slumped in darkened alleyways. The stench of ripe decay hung like a pall over the city as muffled church bells pealed an incessant mournful toll and masked and cloaked men walked the streets, escorting creaking carts laden with the dead to the death pits dug in orchards and gardens within the city walls. In some churchyards the ground level rose two feet or more as the soil absorbed scores and scores of freshly swollen and ripening corpses; some crypts were filled to the ceiling with bodies; some wells had to be closed, as body fluids from over-packed graveyards seeped into them.

Scavenging dogs and pigs scrambled over the humped soil of the churchyards, digging with feet and snouts for the food so close beneath.

Church wardens could shoo them off, but they returned, along with the ravening crows, as soon as the wardens turned their backs.

The city gates were closed and locked. No one was allowed in or out.

The city's population gradually sank beneath the soil.

MARY BASED herself at a hastily established hospital within the guildhall.

The guildhall's internal spaces were given over to row after row of low, wide and commodious beds, each accommodating two or three victims of the pestilence. Nuns and monks moved among the rows, doing what they could for the desperate souls writhing and tossing in agony. Mary, with Jocelyn almost constantly at her side, and Margaret, Neville and Culpeper helped as best they could. Even Culpeper forgot his airs and distaste as he pierced buboes, lanced arms and legs, and trickled potions down throats swollen with pustules and fever.

Neville did his best when he saw the opportunity, offering comfort to the dying and aiding here and there by feeding fluids to those who could take them, but mostly he was concerned with Mary. He made sure she slept and rested regularly, encouraged her to eat broths and morsels to keep up her strength, and fed her small sips of Culpeper's liquor whenever he thought the shadows of pain behind her eyes grew too dense. Faced with so much suffering, Mary was disinclined to pamper her own pain, and so Neville often had to fight to make her sip some of the liquor. Those times when he managed to get her to take enough of it that she slipped into a sleep were occasions he counted as small victories.

Sunday evening was one such victory. Mary had been on her feet for hours, moving from bed to bed, and in the end Neville almost had to hold her down and force the liquor down her throat. But eventually she took it, and consented to lie down on the bed that Neville and Margaret had caused to be made up for her in a small alcove.

Margaret and Jocelyn, exhausted, lay down on pallets

beside her, and within minutes all three had slipped into a deep sleep.

Satisfied, Neville sank down to the floor himself. He leaned against the wall, relishing the coolness of the stone as it seeped through his clothes, and rested his head back. He did not mean to sleep, for the women needed to be watched, but within heartbeats his eyes slowly closed, and moments after that his chin sank down to his chest, and a low snore rumbled from his throat.

NEVILLE JERKED awake. What had happened? Something was different . . . something wrong . . . he turned his head. Mary, Margaret and Jocelyn still slept. He looked back to what he could see of the hall.

No one moved.

Neville blinked, coming to his senses.

No one moved? Someone was always moving . . . the nuns, a monk, a physician, or the porters come to drag away yet another victim.

But now no one moved.

Neville rose to his feet as silently as he could, again glancing at the sleeping women to satisfy himself that they were alive.

Then he looked back to the hall, taking the few steps to the edge of the alcove and looking up and down the hall's length.

Rows upon rows of beds, filled with the writhing, tossing ill.

But no one moved among the beds. No nuns, no monks, no porters, no weeping, wailing family members come to farewell their loved ones.

An eerie silence hung over the hall. The people on the beds moved, but they made no sound.

Strange, for normally their moaning and weeping filled every hour of the day.

And the light was different. The guildhall was lit from windows high in the walls, and this natural light was augmented with torches and lamps. Now the windows were dark, for evening had fallen, but the torches still guttered in their sconces, and the lamps still glowed.

Over and above this, though, shone a silvery light.

A most unearthly light.

Neville moved forward a few paces, coming to a stop in one of the aisles.

The sick twisted to either side of him, their eyes staring, their mouths gaping in agony, their hands clutching at bedcovers.

Neville paid them no heed. He looked over his shoulder, again satisfying himself that Mary, Margaret and Jocelyn remained safe.

When he turned his head back, there was a man standing in the now open doorway at the far end of the hall. A bright, silvery light shone from behind him, so Neville could make out no features, but he knew instantly who it was.

Archangel Michael.

The archangel slowly stepped forward. He was different from how Neville had ever seen him previously. Normally the archangel hid the majority of his features inside a great golden light. Now that light was gone, and the archangel strode forth in what Neville instinctively knew was his natural form.

He was incredibly beautiful. Heavenly, as only an angel could be.

His naked body was slim but well-muscled, and glimmered with a faint silvery air. The hair on his head, in his armpits and at his groin was glittering white and tightly curled. His skin glowed with the faintest undertone of pink. His face . . . his face was both majestic and sensual at the same moment. Beautifully proportioned angles and planes framed a well-shaped, full-lipped mouth, straight nose and deep, black eyes.

He was wingless.

The archangel strode close to Neville, then stopped. A smile played about his lips.

"I have come to take you into the Field of Angels," he said. "What mortals call the Kingdom of Heaven."

Chapter IX

Sunday 26th May 1381

— ii —

✠

"HOW LONG HAS it been, Archangel?" Neville said. "I thought you had forgot me."

The archangel smiled, but it was a cold, hard thing. "Forget you? Never, Thomas. You have always been at the forefront of my thoughts." His voice was strong, and strangely melodious, as if it were underscored with the music of bells.

"And yet—"

"And yet I have left you to the lies and manipulations of the demons? Yes, that I have. And you know *why*, Thomas . . . don't you?"

"So I could see the lies and manipulations for what they were."

"Yes. Margaret and her ever-damned brother have shown themselves for what they are. Cursed manipulators, destroyers, murderers."

"Your children."

The archangel smiled. "Yes. My children. But this place of stench and suffering is not the right place to discuss this, Thomas. Will you come with me now? Into the Field of Angels?"

Neville hesitated, not willing to leave what remained of the earthly realm, even if it *were* a place of stench and suffering. "Am I dead?"

"No. You cannot—" The archangel broke off, and a sly expression slithered over his features. "But I go too fast. Thomas, you are not dead, and you will not die this day. I invite you into the Field of Angels as a guest only. You may leave when you wish."

If you wish. The qualifier hung in the air between them.

Neville hesitated, then gave a curt nod.

"Then discard your clothing," Archangel Michael said, "for it will corrupt Heaven with its mortal stench."

Neville did as he was commanded, unbuckling his sword belt and letting it slide to the floor, drawing his tunic and undershirt over his head and dropping them at the foot of the nearest bed, then stepping out of his boots, hose and under-drawers. He turned away as he disrobed, strangely uncomfortable that the archangel demand he be naked.

When Neville turned back to face the angel, slowly letting the final article of clothing slip to the floor, Archangel Michael allowed his black eyes to travel infinitely slowly up and down Neville's naked body, as if assessing. "You have no scars," he remarked. "Your body is very beautiful, indeed. Strange, perhaps, for a man so committed to war."

"I have always healed well," Neville said.

And yet again the sly expression slithered over the archangel's face. "Of course you have," he said, turning to walk towards the doorway. "Follow me."

Neville followed the archangel, the silvery light beyond the door growing stronger with every step closer they took. As he walked he allowed himself to study the archangel's body as the archangel had so recently studied his. It was almost impossibly beautiful: muscles strong and rippling beneath unflawed skin, sinuous movement that combined both masculine and feminine qualities, limbs so well-shaped that they seemed as perfect as marble carvings.

I am very lovely, said the archangel in Neville's mind, and Neville found it impossible to disagree with him.

Then, abruptly, they were through the door, and Neville left the mortal world behind him.

Archangel Michael had led him into what appeared to be an infinite gently undulating field of multi-coloured flowers. The flowers were such as Neville had never seen before. They were massive, almost grossly so, reaching upwards on leafless thick stems to thigh height. Their colours were over-rich—tawdry—and their texture was heavy and fleshy. They gave off a scent which hung so intense and cloying in the humid air that Neville felt slightly nauseated by it.

The field was dotted with hundreds of stumps of long-dead trees, the wood grey and split.

Above all hung, not a sky, but a heaviness of silvery light.

Everything about the Field of the Angels seemed to Neville to be false and oppressive. He had an almost panicky urge to cover his genitals, only managing to keep his hands at his side with considerable effort.

This is heaven?

They walked forward, and as Neville stepped into the field of flowers, he brushed against some of the gaudy blooms.

They were cold, and brittle, as if made of ice, and they shattered as he touched them.

Neville jumped, then walked more carefully, trying his best not to touch these strange, counterfeit flowers.

Or were they perfection, and the soft, gentle blooms of earth the lie?

The archangel led Neville farther into the Field of Angels, and as they walked, angels in the hundreds rose from their hiding places among the brittle flowers. They were all made as Archangel Michael: the white-marbled bodies, impossibly beautiful, with chiselled features dominated by their black eyes and crisp white curls.

None of them was winged.

"Wings are but a figment of the mortal imagination," said the archangel, now walking at Neville's side. "We are not so flawed that we need wings to fly." The archangel's voice was thick with sarcasm.

Neville nodded, but did not respond, working to keep both his thoughts and his face bland although every nerve in his body was at screaming point, every muscle knotted and fearful, and every thought jumbled and confused.

This is heaven? This?

The other angels, their black eyes fixed on Neville's every movement, sat down on the tree stumps, one angel to each stump. There they crouched, legs drawn up, arms locked about their knees, only their eyes moving as Michael and Neville walked through the field.

Neville thought they looked a little like the gargoyles he'd seen so many times crouching at the top of cathedrals and churches.

As the gargoyles crouched on churches, so the angels crouched in heaven, looking down, watching, watching, watching . . .

Desperate to keep his mind away from the imagery that flooded it, Neville addressed the archangel some two paces ahead of him. "You told me the demons were from hell," he said. "Foul creatures that needed to be destroyed. But I find that instead they are the by-products of your lust, begotten on the bodies of unsuspecting women. They are heaven's children, not hell's! How can I condemn them for that?"

"I do not ask that you condemn them for that," the archangel said, "only for what they are."

He stopped, turning about to face Neville. "You *know* them for what they are. Troublemakers at best—need I mention Wat Tyler's name?—and cruel, manipulative murderers at worst. Hal. Margaret."

"They are not—"

"What? *Not* cruel, manipulative murderers? How did Margaret and Bolingbroke trap you into loving her? Not through reason, Thomas, but through the cruellest of manipulations. How did Bolingbroke gain the throne of England? Through a series of well-timed and oh-so-well-planned murders. There was *nothing* haphazard about the blood Bolingbroke spilt on the way to his crowning achievement."

The archangel's mouth curled a little at his pun, then he went on: "Thomas, nothing about your task is pretty or tasteful. If left to their own devices, Bolingbroke and his kind will destroy the peace of the current order. Mankind will be thrust into chaos. You can stop that. Choose between them or the angels. Choose one way, and the demons will overrun earth and turn it to their will. Choose another, and heaven will triumph."

Neville moved a little, then flinched as he felt the cold caress of the false flowers against his body.

If he moved too quickly, if he made the wrong move, would they slice into his flesh?

"The demons speak of love," he said. "The freedom for individual men and women to choose their own destiny, the freedom to love. They say that mankind's salvation is not your way, but theirs."

The archangel's fists clenched at his side, and about them several other angels moved from their crouches to stand watchful by their tree stumps. "Love? Love is weakness."

Love does not damn; it only saves. Neville clung to Christ's words, trying desperately to keep his face neutral. Everything about this horrible, cold, oppressive place made him think only of escape.

"For the mighty, perhaps," Neville said, and this seemed to appease the archangel, for he relaxed.

"For all," Michael said. Then he laughed, and its sound was as brittle and dangerous as the flowers that surrounded them. "And yet the demons have chosen the most easy of tests for you!"

Easy for you, perhaps, Neville thought, and then he jumped, for suddenly a patch of flowers to his right vanished, and in their place crouched the beautiful young whore of Rome, whom Thomas had thrown to the ground in a fit of temper.

She stared at him with hate-filled eyes. "I curse you, Friar Thomas!" she cried. "One day one of my sisters will seize your soul and condemn you to hell for eternity. A whore will steal your soul. Nay, I pray to the Virgin Mary, that you will *offer* her your soul on a platter. You will offer her your eternal damnation in return for her love."

The apparition vanished; in its place was Archangel Michael's ice-sharp voice. "And on your choice rests the fate of mankind. If you condemn yourself for love, then you condemn mankind."

And then the archangel's voice changed, becoming infused with triumph. "But how can you ever choose for Margaret? How? You might love her . . . but the test, the choice, demands unconditional love. There can be no place for hesitancy, even for an instant, for then all would be lost. Do you love Margaret unconditionally, Thomas? Do you? Do you? Do *you?*"

Neville was aware that all about the entire assembly of angels had risen from their stumps and were now crowding about him. He could hardly breathe, and he wondered where God was, in this thicket of angels.

"No," he whispered. "She tricked me into loving her. I do nonetheless love her, but she tricked me. I was the one raped, not her. There is and will always be that single hesitancy. It is not . . ." *Oh sweet Jesu, he did not want to say these words, but they were the truth, and the combined will of the angels was forcing the truth out from the very pit of his soul* ". . . it is not an unconditional love."

Archangel Michael screamed with laughter. "And when it comes to the test, will you hand her your soul on a platter, Beloved? Will you? Will you? Will you?"

And all about, Neville heard the whispers: *Will you? Will you? Will you?*

"No," he said, his words now barely audible. "I want to, but I cannot."

Archangel Michael's face contorted in a horrible grimace of ecstasy, and about them in the field the angels erupted in exultation.

Margaret loses! Margaret loses!

"You see," said Michael, now speaking in a warm and reasonable tone, "you are unable to do anything but the truth. That is your blood speaking. You have been well bred indeed."

Bred to our standards, came the whisper of the angelic assembly about Neville. *Bred to be one among us.*

Unmindful of the pain caused by the shattering of the cold, brittle flowers with his movement, Neville sank to his knees, covered his face with his hands, and wept.

"LET ME show you our prize," Archangel Michael said, "for I think you deserve some cheer." He and Neville, now back on his feet, were still within the field of false flowers. The other angels had retreated to crouch on their tree stumps, their backs now to Michael and Neville.

Neville felt very cold, as if his very soul had been reduced to a state near to that of the flowers. He knew now what he wanted to do—free mankind from the grip of the angels—but he also knew *(No. No! He only feared it. He still had a choice, he still had a choice. Please, sweet Jesu, please let me still have a choice!)* that he could not do it. He could not hand his soul to Margaret.

Not with that single dark irksome doubt contained within their love.

That single hesitancy.

Archangel Michael began to walk forward very slowly, and Neville followed, as if he had no control over his muscles.

"We had no thought for our issue," the archangel said, "until *he* was born."

Neville had to think a moment, trying to work out what the archangel referred to. "Jesus," he said finally, remembering what Hal and Margaret had told him.

"We had not realised how dangerous, how malicious, how destructive the imps could be until *he* began his depraved campaign to win mankind's soul over to his cause."

Neville did not respond, keeping his eyes ahead. There was a smudge on the horizon now, and he realised they walked towards a small hill. He concentrated on that hill, trying not to think about what the angels had forced him to confront.

He had no choice. None. His love for Margaret was not unconditional enough.

"He was frightful," said the archangel. His speed had picked up a little now. "We had to do something. We created hell—such a wonder! And we enlisted the talents of special men, true men, to aid us."

Neville nodded, not needing to answer. The Select with their book of incantations, thrusting down the angels' issue into hell each year on the Nameless Day.

"We keep *him* trapped up here, though."

"Why?"

"He is a Master Trickster. Too dangerous to allow contact with others of his kind."

"And then you constructed the Church," Neville said. "To further limit the damage." They were very close to the small hill now. It was barren of flowers, apparently nothing more than a heap of dirt and gravel, and Neville could see that there was a cross atop it.

He suddenly thought of when Lancaster and Tyler had died during the peasant rebellion. Their spirits had left their corpses and walked into a field of flowers with a small hill with the cross atop it rising in the distance. *That* was the true heaven, he realised, not this cold, barren landscape of hate. *That* was the heaven Christ promised his followers, not this angelic nightmare.

He concentrated on the cross, and on the figure of the man fixed to it, and it gave him back some of his strength.

He no longer felt naked, and he moved more confidently.

"Yes," said Archangel Michael. "*His* word had spread too far. It was too seductive, winning men and women away from their duty to us. Frightful. Dangerous. So we took his word and made it our own." The archangel laughed. "We took his offer of freedom and made of it a prison."

Michael stopped suddenly and swung about to face Neville. "You have learned a great deal in the past two years," he said. "You know *why* mankind cannot be allowed his freedom, don't you?"

"He would destroy himself." Neville was now concentrating so hard on the figure on the cross that he found conversation with the devil at his side much easier. He knew what to say, for he knew what Michael wanted to hear.

After all, had he not been a good and devoted student of the Church?

"Yes." The archangel's voice was relieved. "Mankind cannot handle its own destiny. Too dangerous a toy. We must do it for them. Guide them as children need to be guided. Now, you see what we approach?"

"Yes." Neville could see very well. They were climbing the hill now, approaching the cross at its summit. Neville slipped a little here and there on the loose gravel, but Michael moved effortlessly, as if he glided over cold marble.

They reached the top, halting.

"Behold the Master Trickster," Archangel Michael said.

Hesitantly, almost too scared to dare to look into Christ's face, Thomas Neville lifted his head.

The cross itself was of twisted, blackened wood, as though the tree it had been cut from had died in a forest fire. It was rough, splintery, desolate, and marked in places by dark stains: sweat, perhaps, or blood.

Finally, Neville allowed himself to look at Christ.

In this cold, barren, malicious landscape of heaven,

there was only one warm, living thing, and that was Christ on his cross.

Christ had been nailed to his torment through his wrists and his feet, and Neville could see that, in order to breathe, Christ had to constantly use the muscles of his shoulders and chest to lift himself up so his lungs could draw breath. His muscles were trembling with the exertion of continually supporting himself against suffocation, his chest shuddering with the effort of drawing breath into lungs torn and bleeding.

Yet even so, even despite the trails of blood and sweat that ran down flesh grimy and stained, Christ's body was as beautiful—*far more so*—than those of the angels. He was well but finely muscled, his shoulders broad, his hips lean, his arms and legs shapely. Where not covered with either grime or blood, his skin was pale, marked in places with traces of fine dark body hair.

It was a beautiful body, the body both of the warrior and of the lover.

But nothing caught at Neville's heart and mind and soul so much as Christ's face. His hair was black, like Neville's own, and his light beard was stiff with the sweat and blood that trickled down from where the crown of thorns pierced his forehead. His face was composed of hard angles and planes with a hooked nose over a well-shaped mouth, yet despite its angularity, his face radiated nothing but warmth and compassion. It was as knowing as that of the angels, yet its knowing consisted of generosity, not judgement.

His eyes were black, like the angels', but loving, so very much unlike the angels'.

He was in physical torment, but Neville could see that Christ cared for only one thing, and that thing was Neville.

"How does God allow His Son to suffer so?" whispered Neville.

"God?" said Archangel Michael, then laughed uproariously.

Christ turned his head, flinching with the pain of the effort, and looked at Michael. His expression was sad.

Then he looked back at Neville, intensely, curiously, as if wondering what the man would make of what Michael said next.

"There is no God," said Michael, and laughed even further at the shock on Neville's face. "God is nothing more than the collective will and endeavour of the angels."

"No God?" whispered Neville. He'd sunk to his knees, staring unbelievingly at Michael.

"No God," agreed Michael. "God as a single entity is a phantasm. It is easier for the simple souls of mankind to worship a single entity than a collective grouping."

"So Christ is the son of . . ." Neville now looked up at Christ, drawing all the comfort he could from the sympathy in the man's eyes.

"All of us," said Michael. "A collective effort. We thought he was to be one of us, the one to finally consolidate our grip on mankind. But," his voice hardened into absolute hatred, "he betrayed us, seeking instead to free mankind from our will."

I almost succeeded. Christ spoke into Neville's mind, and somehow Neville understood that Michael was not aware of Christ's words. *I almost succeeded . . . Now it is up to you. You are mankind's final chance. You alone.*

But how? Neville thought. *How? There is but the one test, and I cannot choose the way I want.*

Christ's face suffused with love and comfort. *You will choose the way your heart directs you, Thomas. Trust me. Trust me. Trust your own heart.*

"And now we have him trapped," Michael continued, his eyes on Christ. "Trapped, where he can no longer wreak his havoc."

Then the archangel lowered his head and looked Neville straight in the eye. "Not like our next effort. *He* works our will as if an extension of our own thoughts. There will be no mistake this time." His mouth twisted, frightful and unloving. "Beloved."

* * *

NEVILLE STUMBLED through the guildhall, its occupants still under the thrall of the archangel. He almost fell over in his dash to his clothes, feeling the cold of heaven penetrating to his bones. He grabbed at his clothes and boots, pulling them on as fast as his shaking muscles would allow, then rebuckled his sword belt about his hips.

His hands were trembling so badly, he cut two fingers on the buckle, and when he tried to put his boots on he dropped one of them three times before it finally consented to slide on his foot.

Clothed, he felt only very slightly more in control—how could clothes comfort the turmoil in his mind?

He turned, looking back to the door. Silvery light still shone through, and Neville could see the faint outline of Archangel Michael, standing watching him.

Then the archangel turned, and walked into the light, and the doors slammed behind him, and the hall woke.

Hands grabbed at Neville: the dying, seeking some last hope of succour. He pulled away, and walked as steadily as he could back to the alcove where Mary, Margaret and Jocelyn still slept. There he sank to the floor, his back against the wall, staring at the sleeping forms of the two women and the girl.

There was no God save the collective will of the angels? God was nothing but the ultimate sum of those cold, heartless creatures? And if Jesus was the product of their collective effort, what had Archangel Michael meant when he said that their latest effort acted only as an extension of their will?

Neville wrapped his arms about himself, shivering, driving away that last thought, concentrating instead on what he had seen in the Field of the Angels.

Desolate, malicious. *Heaven!*

If nothing else, Neville now knew exactly what choice he wanted to take when the time came for him to choose.

Freedom for mankind, freedom from the chains of the angels.

The mission that Christ had started but had failed to accomplish.

But to do that, Neville would have to hand his soul to Margaret, and that he knew he could not do, however much he *wanted* to do it.

Just that single niggle. That single doubt. That single piece of knowledge that she had abused his trust, and if she had done that once, then she might do it again—even if unwillingly or unknowingly.

Just one single hesitancy, but one that would damn mankind forever.

"Damn you, Margaret," he whispered, then winced, wishing he could take back the words.

Her actions had allowed him to love, to see that love saved, not damned.

Yet in the doing, Margaret had sabotaged her own cause.

"Please, sweet Jesu," Neville whispered. "Tell me what to do."

But there was no answer, and Neville felt very alone and very unsure.

For a long time he sat, staring at the wall, loathing the angels and what they were going to force him to do.

Chapter X

Sunday 26th May 1381

— iii —

✝

"DID I NOT say the Lord our God would send an omen?" said Thorseby. "What further sign do you need than this pestilence? If you do not move, and soon, then the pestilence shall envelop all England."

Sign of God or not, Hotspur well knew the advantages the sudden eruption of the pestilence had given him. First Exeter's revolt. Nasty, but not deadly enough to Bolingbroke's reputation for Hotspur to be sure of any chance of success if *he* then moved.

But now this. A clear sign of God's ill will. The rumours of what had happened in St Paul's with the supernatural appearance of the black Dog of Pestilence while Bolingbroke had been viewing Richard's murdered corpse would almost certainly ensure England would rise up against Bolingbroke should an alternative present itself.

And Hotspur meant that alternative to be himself. The golden hero from the north, untainted by any association with Bolingbroke—Hotspur had not kept himself apart from Bolingbroke since his landing at Ravenspur for nothing—who could restore England to godly rule and a golden age.

Lord God, what that would mean in terms of power for the Percy family! *Both the Lancasters and the Nevilles would lose all—there would be no one and no thing left to challenge Hotspur's claim to the throne.*

"*Good King Harry! Good King Harry!*"

Aye, Hotspur could hear it now.

"I am going to need your help," Hotspur said to Thorseby.

"You have it, my lord."

"Good." Hotspur paused, thinking. Thorseby was good for much of the Church . . . but he would need more than whispering friars and monks to aid his cause. Hotspur needed swords, and many of them.

And allies . . . men that Bolingbroke would never suspect to throw in their lot with Hotspur.

"Thorseby," Hotspur said, all doubt now gone from his mind. "I will need some of your friars, well horsed and able to move swiftly down the roads of England, to carry messages for me." *Great black crows, nurturing murderous intents.*

"You have them, my lord."

Hotspur nodded, then smiled. The crown would feel good on his brow. "Then you are my man, Thorseby."

Chapter XI

Monday 27th May 1381

— i —

✠

THE COLD EVENTUALLY grew unbearable, so bad that not only was Neville's shaking verging on the painful, but his hopeless thoughts had grown disordered and uncontrolled. He could see nuns, monks and physicians moving about the guildhall, could see the sick writhing about their beds, and yet none of them appeared beset by such cold. Mary, Margaret and Jocelyn slept close to him with nothing but thin blankets about them, and yet neither did they shiver.

Perhaps the cold was heaven sent to remind him of his purpose. To control him, perhaps.

Neville tried to concentrate his thoughts, but they were scattering all over the place. No God but the collective will of the angels . . . the cries and screams of the dying . . . Mary, trying not to cry in pain as she tended those only marginally sicker than she . . . the black Dog of Pestilence, stalking through London . . . the cold, cold hell of heaven . . . Margaret nursing their son . . . Jesus Christ in agony on his cross for fourteen hundred years . . . himself, forced into a decision that he loathed beyond anything he could imagine . . .

Neville lowered his head into his arms and concentrated on the memory of the suffering Christ, driving away all other thoughts. He remembered Jesus' dark eyes settling on him, their compassion, their love . . . and all the time he struggled to raise his shoulders and torso so that he could draw great, painful bubbling breaths into his tortured body.

Dangerous, malicious, destructive, Archangel Michael had said.

Christ, who died for love so that mankind could be saved, freed from the chains of the angels.

"Dangerous? Malicious? Destructive?" Neville whispered. "I cannot believe that to be so. No, no. *You* are the dangerous and malicious one, Michael!"

He raised his head, intending to meditate on the small crucifix that hung on the wall of the alcove. Hoping to drive away the more painful of his thoughts.

But instead of meditating or praying, Neville found himself staring at it with wide, disbelieving eyes.

The crucifix was small, no taller than the length of Neville's forearm, and carved from a block of solid wood. It was good English workmanship, for despite its smallness, the form of Christ was lifelike in the extreme.

Too lifelike perhaps, for, as Neville watched, the body of Jesus Christ contorted in agony on the cross. His head turned, and seemed to stare directly at Neville.

Do not despair, Thomas.

"Why not?" he whispered. "Sweet Lord Christ, I want to free mankind from the grip of the angels, but I cannot. I cannot! I cannot freely hand my soul to Margaret—"

Thomas, do you not remember what I said to you as you stood beneath my dying body?

Neville fought to remember. "You told me to trust you. But what can you do, what can anyone do? How will trust help me?"

Trust me, Thomas. That is all that I ask.

Neville laughed bitterly. Trust. It was a terrible thing to ask when he knew the angels had him trapped. He could never give Margaret his soul. Not freely. Not completely.

Free me. Trust me.

"Free you? How?"

Free me.

"How?"

The figure of Christ twisted and writhed in agony. *I am nailed to the cross—*

"How? How do I free you?"

I am nailed to the cross . . .

Neville sobbed, inching forward on his hands and knees towards the crucifix. Christ's body now twisted in such agony that rivulets of blood seeped down the wall. "How?" he whispered. "Sweet Jesu, tell me how to free you!"

I am nailed . . .

"Sweet Jesu!"

I am nailed . . .

I am nailed . . .

. . . nailed . . .

And then Neville blinked, and the blood had gone, and the body nailed to the crucifix was gone, and Neville was left crying softly, his hand still outstretched in silent supplication.

How? How could he free the Lord Jesus Christ?

He slowly lowered his hand, resting his head on the cold stone floor, and wept.

Chapter XII

Monday 27th May 1381

— ii —

✠

"TOM?"

Startled, Neville raised his head. Mary had risen and was sitting on the edge of her bed. She put a finger to her lips, indicating Margaret and Jocelyn, then gestured for Neville to aid her.

Nothing in her expression indicated she had seen or heard any of the exchange between Christ and Neville.

He rose, walked over to her—hobbling slightly with his cold, stiff muscles—and took her arm.

"The chapel," she whispered. "I would like to pray awhile, I think, and perhaps talk with you."

Neville felt her tremble slightly, and she leaned more heavily upon him.

"You need to eat something," he said, "before we can talk."

HE LED her first to the area where a nun was ladling broth into bowls, where he sat her down and forced her to drink a half-bowl of broth and several pieces of milk-soaked bread, then into the cool dimness of the guildhall's chapel. Flickering red light lit the chapel, a combination both of the continually burning fires and of the dawn.

"Madam, may we speak?" Neville said, sitting down beside Mary on a bench.

If she was irritated at his forgetfulness of her wish to pray first, she did not show it. "Only if you call me Mary, Tom. I am too tired and weary to cope with the continual 'madams.'"

He hesitated, and, seeing his uncertainty, Mary reached to him and took his hand between hers.

Neville looked down at her hands, and saw that they were so thin that the bones appeared ready to break through her fragile skin.

"Mary," he said, "you are so ill . . ."

"Aye," she said, "and you have known that for so long now there is no reason to remark further upon it."

He smiled a little at the tartness in her tone, and she coloured at the expression in his eyes. Her entire body stiffened, and Neville's smile grew wider.

"And you have known for so long now how greatly I adore you," he said with a light teasing tone, grateful that, unknowingly, she was giving him a reason to jest away some of his troubles, "that you should not now be acting the coy virgin with me."

Mary relaxed, and laughed softly. "Aye. We have both seen too much to hide behind coy exteriors. Tom, what is on your mind? Your eyes are clouded with such pain that I can hardly bear it."

Neville looked at the altar, his eyes fixed on the crucifix behind it.

How, Lord Christ? How do I free you?

He faced Mary again. "I have been given a problem, Mary," he said. "Actually, several problems, but there is one that perhaps I shall concentrate on first. First this solution presents itself, then that, and then I find I cannot choose between them for worry that I might pick the wrong one."

"And you would ask my advice?"

"Aye." He paused, thinking, then spoke again. "A man begs me to free him. To me he appears as if love incarnate, for he speaks of nothing but love, and thinks that love is the highest thing a man or a woman can aspire to."

"Yes . . . ?"

"Yet others, beings of power and majesty, tell me that this man is evil incarnate . . . that if he is freed to walk earth malevolence and disaster will follow in his footsteps."

"Beings of power and majesty?"

Neville hesitated, then decided to tell Mary the truth. "Angels, Mary. You have heard, surely, that the Archangel Michael has appeared to me?"

Mary nodded. She'd heard the gossip about why Thomas Neville had left the Dominican Order. "You claimed to be following the archangel's orders in discovering some evil." She frowned. "This man? This man you think is love, but the angels claim is evil?"

"Aye. He is the embodiment of the evil the angels have sent me to destroy."

"But now you want to free him? *Not* to destroy him?"

"Aye."

"Tom . . . to go against the wishes of God's messengers. Surely you must have misunderstood this man? Surely he only presents a chimera of love and goodness to hide the evil within?"

Again Neville glanced at the crucifix. "No. I believe that he does truly represent love, Mary. The angels . . . the angels are cruel creatures . . ."

"But they must be cruel, surely? Tom, I do not understand . . . why . . . *how* can you go against the wishes of the angels? I cannot think that you could possibly want to let this man free at all."

And yet again Neville glanced at the crucifix, and this time Mary did not miss his look.

"Have you prayed to Jesus Christ our Lord, Tom? Have you sought His guidance in this matter?"

"Mary." Neville took both her hands between his own, holding them with the utmost gentleness. "Mary, it is Jesus Christ who the angels say is the embodiment of all that is evil."

"What? Tom, I do not understand. How can sweet Jesu embody evil?" Unbidden, a memory surfaced in Mary's mind. A memory of . . . a dream, perhaps? A strange dream . . . a dream of great grief, of loss. She frowned.

"Mary?"

"Ah!" She jerked her head, as if waking herself out of some stupor. "It is nothing. Tom . . . I cannot believe that Jesus Christ our Lord embodies evil. I simply cannot. I *will* not. No, it *can't* be."

Again Neville looked at her strangely, and Mary knew it was because of the slight note of hysteria that had tinged her last words. Why so upset? It was not simply because the notion that Christ embodied evil upset her genuine piety . . . it was almost as if the charge struck to the heart of her being.

"Aye, how can he indeed . . ." Neville bowed his head, staring at Mary's hands between his, thinking deeply.

Whom could he trust, if not this woman?

"Mary," he said finally, raising his face to hers, "I have taken this single problem out of a much larger one, and, as much as I am loath to trouble you with my burden, I think I will go mad if I do not talk with someone about it. Mary, this will be difficult, unbelievable, and it will shatter much of what you believe. Mary, I do not . . . I cannot . . ."

She pulled one of her hands free, and lifted it to his face. "Tom, so often I am left untold, and left out of people's plans and schemes and secrets. I do not care if what you have to tell me shatters everything I hold dear, for to know that you hold me beloved enough to tell me . . . well, that is recompense enough." She smiled. "I am dying, Tom. Who better to confess to than a dying woman?"

"Mary, I shouldn't have spoken . . . this is too great a burden . . ."

"You are tormented, Tom." Her finger stroked gently up and down his cheek. "And I have already lived through such torment that to hear a little more will do me no injury at all."

She hesitated, and frowned slightly, as if wondering what she herself meant by that. Then her expression cleared, and she leaned forward and kissed Neville's cheek exceedingly gently.

"Confess all, Tom, and I shall take your secrets nowhere but to my grave."

ON *HIS cross in heaven, Christ writhed in torment.*

But, strangely, his face was suffused with joy. "Thank you, Mary," he whispered. "Thank you."

Chapter XIII

Monday 27th May 1381

— iii —

✝

MARGARET HOVERED IN a half-sleep, too exhausted to take the final step to wakefulness. The past few days had been appalling; a never-ending nightmare of tending the hopeless, of sponging down corpses befouled with pus and blood and black faeces, of wondering how much longer she could continue without retching out every morsel of food she had ever consumed, of praying endlessly, over and over in desperate rote, that Rosalind and Bohun would remain safe in Windsor. Every hour she would have to find a bucket of water and scrub her face and hands and arms, trying to get the odour of death out of her skin. But it was a hopeless task. Margaret thought that the stench of the dying and of their foul fluids had so impregnated her flesh that she would never, never be rid of their stink.

And her clothes. Her gown and under tunic were stiff with dried blood . . . and worse. Her hair was hopeless: so solid with sweat that Margaret thought it was permanently matted. Perhaps she would have to take shears to it and cut the tangled, dried mess off. It would be easier than trying to clean and comb it.

As she slept Margaret had dreamed of tearing herself free of her clothes, throwing them on a fire, and jumping into a delightfully cool pond of spring water. There she would scrub and scrub at flesh and hair until everything—the encrustations, the stains, the lice and fleas, the terrible, terrible stench—were gone and she was pale and clean once more.

To drift into wakefulness, realising that she still stank and that her soiled clothes still clung to her, was a wretched experience.

Margaret lay a few minutes, eyes shut, trying to control her despair. She could hear the moans and wails of the dying beyond the alcove, she could *smell* their stink, and she could hear the shuffling, exhausted feet of their carers.

Nothing had changed since she lay down to sleep, nothing had improved for the better, and there was no hope that this day would bring anything but a continuation, and perhaps even a worsening, of the horrible dying about her.

She moved very slightly, and winced. Every muscle ached—her neck, shoulders and hips were especially painful.

"Sweet Jesu," she murmured, then made a supreme effort and opened her eyes. If she were feeling so sore and exhausted, then how was Mary coping? The woman had not complained once during these past days, even though Margaret knew there were times when she had to bite her lip to stop herself crying out with the pain coursing through her body. Mary permitted herself to take enough of Culpeper's liquor to dull the pain, but never enough to completely dissipate it, for that would fog her mind and send her to sleep. "And how can I sleep," she would say to Margaret or Neville whenever they pleaded with her to rest, "when so many need me?"

Margaret could not deny that Mary's very presence did some good. Mary might not have had the power to heal, or to ease pain, but she eased spirits and minds with her very presence. That the Queen of England cared enough to spend her days and nights tending the ill gave more comfort than almost anything else could have done— save the sudden and miraculous discovery of a cure for the pestilence.

Finally, late last night, Mary had agreed to rest. Only for a few hours, but she would rest.

Once she'd settled Mary on her bed, Margaret had almost collapsed with her own exhaustion. Now she slowly blinked, accustoming her eyes to the light in the hall beyond the alcove.

Sweet Jesu! It was mid-morning. She'd slept for over ten hours.

And Mary hadn't woken? Margaret swung her legs over the side of her bed and sat up, twisting about to check Mary. *Please, sweet Jesu, that she hadn't died during the night . . .*

Margaret stared for a long moment at the tangled, empty blankets of Mary's bed before she actually realised that Mary wasn't there.

Sighing, Margaret struggled to her feet. Mary was undoubtedly already back at the bedsides of the ill while she, Margaret, had overslept by hours.

She glanced at Jocelyn, wrapped in her blanket and breathing deeply in sleep. She did not wake her: the girl had seen and done enough already.

Sighing yet again, and running her hands over her hair in a useless attempt to restore it to some order, Margaret walked into the hall and the stench of death.

MARY'S FACE was very still. She'd listened for over two hours as Neville had talked. What she'd heard left her cold and numb . . . but not disbelieving, for so much of it fitted with what she had seen of both Bolingbroke and Margaret, and with some of the strange dreams she'd had when she'd imbibed too much of Culpeper's liquor.

Strange dreams . . . sent to her by Jesus?

Neville held Mary's hand, watching her face carefully.

"It took me many months to come to terms with this knowledge," he said in a very gentle voice, "and I had not had to deal with it all in one indigestible lump as you must now do. But, Mary, I am glad I have told you. I need so much to have someone I could trust to talk to."

"I needed to know much earlier than this," Mary said, her eyes downcast, ignoring Neville's final remark. Of all the things that Neville had told her—demons, angels, and an eventual decision that would either damn mankind or free it—Mary caught onto the one that was closest to her own life. "My husband . . . the Demon-King? How could you not have told me?"

"Mary—"

She waved her free hand dismissively. "No, no, I know why you did not tell me. I thank you that you have now. . . ."

She lapsed into silence. "I cannot believe that our Lord Jesus Christ can be evil," she whispered finally. "But I do believe that what you have told me of the angels, and this strange-flowered place they inhabit, *is* evil. They are so cruel."

"In all of this," Neville said, "Christ's love and compassion has proved the rock that I can cling to. When Margaret betrayed me, when I think of what Hal has done to gain the throne, and of what he might do, when I discovered that demons are not the product of hell at all, but of the angels' lust, then thought of Christ has comforted me. Even though," his mouth quirked, "he is indeed 'demonry' personified . . . at least as the angels define it."

Mary drew in a deep breath. "There is a strange road before you, Tom. Before all of us. Before England."

"Aye, that there is."

A silence fell between them. It was a comforting, companionable silence, both adrift in their thoughts, yet glad of the other's presence.

"You wish to free Jesus?"

"Aye."

"Then you must do it," Mary said firmly, patting Neville's hand.

Neville looked at her carefully. "But perhaps I have been misled by Jesus. Perhaps I do not see the danger—"

"No. There is no danger. Tom, there is something I must tell you."

Neville smiled, and raised an eyebrow slightly. "Do not tell me that the angels have confided in you as well!"

Mary laughed softly. "Nay. But . . . Tom, I had a dream one night, just before we left Windsor to come to London. I had dismissed it as a phantasm of Culpeper's liquor, but now . . ."

She stopped, then shrugged. "I dreamed that I was loved, and that I loved, although everyone in the world seemed set against me." Mary hesitated, deciding not to tell Neville of the frightful end of her dream. "There was a lesson in that dream, I think," she continued. "Perhaps it was sent by Christ. Tom, I *cannot* believe Christ evil. I cannot. That dream was no lie. Neither was yours, when Christ told you to love Margaret."

She paused. "Love does not damn," she whispered. "It only saves. Oh, Tom, free him! Free him!"

"How?" he asked softly. "He is trapped in heaven, and I have not the power to free him from there."

She squeezed his hand, and sighed, and for a few minutes there was silence between them.

"What must I do?" Mary eventually said. "Now that I know, what must I do?"

"Be yourself," Neville said. "Do what you think is right. There is nothing else that you can do. But . . . do not tell Hal that you are aware of who he is, and of what battle is being fought about you. That would be—"

"Dangerous," Mary said with a small smile, and squeezed Neville's hand. "I know that. My life teeters on a dangerous thread anyway, Tom. Now that I know of the bond between Catherine and Hal, I can understand his longing, and his frustration in that longing. Now I understand the calculation in his eyes when he looks at me. At least," she touched her gown where it lay over her belly, "this canker in my womb means I need not share his bed any longer. I could not do that, not now that I know of the men he destroyed in order to reach the throne."

Knowing that I may well be next, she thought, and knew she did not have to voice that thought to Neville.

"Tom," she said. "How do you feel about Hal?"

"There has been such a bond of friendship between us," he said, "and for so many years that it will, I think, never break completely. Yet that friendship is now darkened. I watch Hal, and wonder if sometimes his ambition clouds his judgement. I wonder what that might mean for England, and for mankind. And I know that Hal watches me."

"And Margaret?" Mary said very softly. "How do you feel for her? Especially after . . . after . . ." What Neville had told her about Richard's and de Vere's rape of Margaret had left her numb with disbelief. That Margaret and Bolingbroke could have been so manipulative . . . that they had put both Neville and her through a horror so contrived . . .

Neville watched Mary's face carefully, knowing some of what she was thinking. Bolingbroke and Margaret's manipulations had hurt Mary as well.

"Especially after her 'rape'?" Neville sighed, rubbing his eyes as if so tired he could barely string two thoughts together. "She and Hal caused me to love, and I do not regret that love."

"But—"

"But I do regret the manner in which it was achieved. The lies, the treachery. Of you, sweet lady, as much as of me." His mouth quirked. "And of what could they have been thinking? Did they truly believe that I would wave away the cunning manner in which they manipulated my guilt as if it were of no consequence? That it would not affect the manner in which I love Margaret?"

"You *do* love her?"

"Oh, aye, I do love her. But, Mary, oh sweet Jesu, Mary, how can I give her my soul on a platter?"

"Surely you can forgive her?"

"I *have* forgiven her, Mary. I could not love her if I

hadn't forgiven her. But that doesn't mean I can willingly hand her my soul."

"Why not?"

"Because to hand her my soul, to hand *anyone* my soul, requires a trust and a love and a respect and an honour so complete that it consumes every fibre of my being. With Margaret—with my love for Margaret—there is now a tiny hesitancy. But that single slight hesitancy, that single scruple, will be enough to damn mankind. I cannot afford any hesitancy at all."

Mary briefly closed her eyes, pitying both Neville and Margaret. Her hand groped for his, and they sat a long while in silence, each lost in their own thoughts of Christ.

"TOM! MARY! Thank the Lord Christ."

Both Neville's and Mary's heads jerked up, and they pulled their hands apart. Margaret stood at the door of the chapel, breathing heavily, as if she had been running, or perhaps panicking.

She walked into the chapel, then stopped a few paces away from the bench where Mary and her husband sat. "What do you here?" she said. "Madam, are you well?"

"Well enough," Mary said, smiling gently at Margaret. "Tom and I came here to pray, and talk a little. We did not wish to wake you."

Mary glanced at Neville, who gave a little nod, then she addressed Margaret again. "Tom and I have been talking." She paused, holding Margaret's gaze. She was about to go on, but Neville interrupted her.

"Of inconsequential things, Margaret," he said. "We needed some lightness after our immersion in the death beyond this chapel."

He trusts Margaret so little, Mary thought, stunned, *that he will not tell her that now I know of the battle between the angels and demons? And of the nature of my husband?*

She looked at Margaret, and saw the unhappiness

there. *Lord Jesu, aid him to make the right decision! Aid him to give his soul to this woman so that mankind may at last be freed.*

Margaret looked between Neville and Mary, attempted a smile, failed, then spoke hastily to cover her confusion and distress. "Tom, perhaps you can join with me in persuading the queen, our beloved lady, that she should take better care of herself? She has spent far too much of her precious energy in aiding the sick, when she should be conserving her strength for her own battles ahead."

"Margaret speaks sense," Neville said. "Mary, what can you do here, as tired and ill as you are? Please, rest a day or so at the very least."

"What can I do here, tired and ill as I am? I can give hope, and perhaps some comfort," Mary said. "Tom, Margaret, I cannot walk away from these people. Now," she stood up, "I have been a-wasting my time here in this peaceful chapel for these past hours while men and women have been dying in despair in the hall beyond. My self-absorption is reprehensible."

"Mary, no!" Margaret said, and reached out a hand.

Mary looked at her kindly. "Will you help me, my Lady Neville?"

Margaret shot Neville a despairing look, then sighed. "Of course, madam."

Chapter XIV

Monday 27th May 1381

— iv —

✠

AND SO BEGAN the nightmare once more. Mary may have been told of matters so great they affected both heaven and hell, but that was as nothing to her when ordinary men and women and children lay dying in agony in the room beyond. She, accompanied by Margaret, Jocelyn (who refused to leave Mary's side), the Lady Alicia Lynley (who had returned from the Tower), and two nuns, moved from bed to bed, daubing, sponging, and murmuring what comfort they could.

To Mary, it seemed that the comfort must be of very little use. Nothing she could do could ease the pain and horror of the pestilence that gripped these people. Nothing she did could ease their worry about the spouses or children they left behind. Nothing she could do could ease the forthcoming loss of their lives.

What Mary did not realise was the level of comfort she *did* bring to every person she stopped by for a few minutes, and even to the mass crowded within the guildhall as a whole. Here she was, the Queen of England, demonstrating with her very presence the love and care she bore for the common folk of her realm. How many other queens would have done this much? Mary was so ill her-self, yet she still cared more about them than she did her own comfort and easement.

To the common folk of London, not only those in the guildhall, but to everyone within the city who had heard of her presence and work among those struck down with the pestilence, Mary embodied the ideal virtuous queen. She was nobility and care and love personified, and in many more than one instance, when a person prayed to the Blessed Virgin herself, they envisioned not a cold statue before them, but the lined and exhausted face of their queen.

King Hal might direct relief efforts from the Tower, and might even stride the streets offering words or hope, but his wife was among them, and bore the full weight of their grief about her own shoulders.

By noon the stench within the guildhall had become al-most unbearable. The day was unseasonably hot, and the brimstone fires and their thick, drifting smoke only made the heat worse. Jocelyn had finally succumbed to her weariness and the heat, and Mary had sent her to sleep an hour or so in the small antechamber. As the heat had thickened through the morning, all the ladies, Mary in-cluded, had stripped away their heavy-sleeved tunics and robes, and worked only in aprons over their linen under-tunics. Dank sweat stained the necklines and armpits of these undertunics, and their hair hung in greasy tendrils, clinging to sweaty, grimy necks. Mary and Margaret, one each side of the bed, attended three small children rang-ing in ages from four to eight. The pestilence had struck the children, all girls, in its most virulent form. Instead of the pustules and buboes erupting on the skin, they had formed inside the poor children's bodies. Now the girls lay screaming, in so much agony from their internal swellings that they could not move. Mary and Margaret could not even sponge them down, for every movement, every touch, only increased their agony.

Margaret wanted more than anything to be able to use

what little ability she had to ease their pain, but she was exhausted beyond measure, and knew that she had no power left within her to aid these three girls.

"How can God justify such horrific vengeance on these innocents," she whispered, tears streaming down her face. "How? How?"

Mary shifted slightly on the bed, then flinched as two of the girls screamed in agony at the movement. "There is no justification," she began, but stopped and raised her head at a commotion towards the doors at the rear of the guildhall.

People were shrieking, panicking, falling over themselves in an effort to clamber away from something that stood just inside the doors.

Wincing at the effort—and the girls' cries at her movement—Mary stood upright, peering with red-rimmed eyes, trying to see what had frightened people into such a panic.

For an instant a gap appeared in the press of people, and she saw what so terrified them.

Coldness overwhelmed her, then that was quickly consumed by such a rush of anger as Mary had never felt before.

"Let me through," she said as people rushed down the centre aisle of the hall. "Let me through."

Somehow, Margaret behind her, Mary managed to move towards the outer doors of the hall. People streamed towards her, but without fail all moved aside at the last moment, leaving her passage forward unimpeded. From his place at the other end of the hall where he'd been talking to Robert Courtenay, Neville pushed forward as well, moving quickly to reach Mary and Margaret.

Finally, she stood face-to-face with the creature that had caused the panic.

"Get you gone from this hall, this city, and this realm," Mary said in an even voice. "You are not wanted, nor welcomed."

The black Dog of Pestilence snarled at her, low and vicious. It had grown in the past days, as if it had fed off the death that had followed in its passing, and now stood the size of a small pony. Its hide was, if anything, covered with more, and larger, weeping sores than before.

Its small, piggy eyes were now bright red.

"Get you gone," Mary whispered. She heard Margaret and Neville move up behind her, and felt Margaret's hand on her shoulder. Neville stood slightly to one side, his hand on the haft of his sword.

The Dog took a stiff step forward, and snapped, scattering thick yellowed saliva to either side.

Behind her was only stillness, but Mary could feel the entire hall watching, holding its breath.

"I say to you once more," Mary said evenly, "get you gone from this place. I like you not."

A frightful shudder ran through the Dog's body. It snapped several more times, moving ever closer with every snap until it stood only a pace from Mary.

"Mary," Margaret whispered, "please, get away from it." Beside her came the rasp of steel as Neville drew his sword.

"I am not afraid," Mary said, addressing the Dog rather than Margaret or Neville, "of either death or of this foul beast that stands before me. I say to you, Dog, take me if you will . . . if you think that my flesh is so sinful that you think it deserves the touch of your vileness."

She paused, and her fists clenched at her sides. "Otherwise, I command you to begone from this place! Begone, Dog. *Go!*"

The Dog snarled and snapped and slavered and postured, but it did not advance. Rather, it took a half-step back.

Neville, meanwhile, was watching Mary rather than the Dog, his eyes narrowed in thought.

"I am Mary, Queen of England," she said. "I *am* England. If you want to punish England, then take me instead of the innocent. Otherwise, get you gone."

She stepped forward one step, and half raised a fist. *"Get out of here!"*

And the Dog, with one final snarling howl, turned and fled.

Mary staggered, and Margaret wrapped her arms about her, steadying her. "He could not bear to face goodness," she whispered, tears streaming down her face. "Well done, Mary."

Behind them, on the bed they had risen from, the three little girls gasped, then blinked.

All their pain had gone.

NEVILLE LAY in bed, weary, waiting for Margaret to join him. After the strange events of the day, they'd come back to the Tower apartments; slowly, for it seemed that all London had turned out to cheer Mary.

The news of her banishment of the Dog of Pestilence had spread out from the guildhall on a wave of relief and joy and, coupled with the instantaneous recovery of everyone suffering from the pestilence, people had poured out into the streets to honour her.

Neville smiled. Mary had been exhausted, and so obviously in pain, but at the same time she'd been delighted and uplifted by the gratefulness and love shown her.

"Beloved Lady," they'd called her, and Neville could not think of a better title to bestow on her. Beloved Lady, indeed.

Full of surprises.

"Tom?"

He blinked, and turned his head. Margaret had finished her bathing and now, naked, was crawling into their bed. He reached out for her, holding her close to his body, and burying his face in her hair.

"Tom," she whispered, rubbing close against his body, as clean and as sweet as hers after his earlier bath. "I am glad to have my husband back."

He kissed her, then began to slowly caress her breasts. "You have no need to be jealous of Mary. I love her only as everyone else does."

"And if she were fit and well and free of any spousal encumbrance? And you the same?"

Neville rolled Margaret onto her back. "It would still be you in my bed, Meg." He covered her body with his, teasing her with intent, but not action.

She moaned, trying with her hands to push him down into her. "But would you want her as a wife? Would you love her?"

"You are my wife, and I love you."

"But—" She gasped as Neville finally pushed himself inside her body, making love to her with long, slow, powerful strokes. He kissed her, deep and sweet, massaging her breasts and belly with firm, knowing hands.

"But," she finally managed, dragging her mouth away from his, and trying to keep her mind intact amid the sweet onslaught of his loving, "do you love me enough to hand me your—?"

"Jesus Christ, Margaret!" Annoyed that she persisted in trying to further her *(the demons')* cause at a moment when all he had wanted was to enjoy her company and her love, Neville pulled away, rolling over to his side of the bed. "Can you not leave that alone?"

There was a long, bitter silence.

"If I had been Mary," Margaret eventually said, "you would not have rolled away."

PART THREE

Shrewsbury

Also we do allege, saie & entend to prove that thou hast caused kynge Richarde our soueraigne lorde and thine, traiterously within the castell of Poumfret, without the consent or iudgement of the lordes of the realme, by the space of fiftene daies and so many nightes (which is horible emong christian people to be heard) with honger, thirste and colde to perishe, to be murdered [and then] thou by extorte power, diddest usurpe and take the kyngdom of Englande . . . uniustly and wrongly, contrary to thyne othe . . . for the whiche cause we defy thee, thy fautoures and complices as comen traytoures and destroyers of the realme.

—Excerpts from the statement made by
Northumberland and Hotspur prior to
the battle of Shrewsbury

Chapter I

Wednesday 29th May 1381

✠

THEY TROTTED IN long snaking lines down the mountains and valleys to vanish within the drifting mists. They reemerged just as the great wall rose before them, and shouted when they saw it, thrusting fists and pikes into the night air. This was a day they'd longed for through vast, hateful centuries. Many exposed themselves to the stonework, demonstrating their ancient malice for all who cared to see. By dawn they were through into Cumberland, passing underneath gated arches opened by silent, resentful Englishmen.

The horsemen, thousands of them, moved in clattering lines past Carlisle, whose terrified citizens shuttered themselves tight inside their homes. Rain fell, sheeting down in grey, cold rivers, but the horsemen ignored it, for this cold and wet was as a home to them. They pushed their small, tough horses into a canter, riding through the dark mid-morning of West Warde Forest and then further south towards the hills and Copeland Forest.

Finally, as the afternoon grew grim and chill, they approached the village of Black Hal just above the border of Lancashire.

There lay the English army, and in a tangle of wild beards and colourful tartans the Scots pushed their exhausted mounts into a gallop, and raised their pikes and swords, and rode to meet their hated enemy.

SIR HENRY Percy, Harry Hotspur, stood frowning in the doorway of the porch where he had made his headquarters.

"Douglas," he said to the man who'd come to stand at his shoulder, "I hope to God you can keep them under some semblance of order. I need an army, not a rabble."

Archibald, fourth Earl of Douglas, grinned amiably. He was a huge man, all muscle and darkness, and all grace of movement and manner. "They're hot-hearted lads," he said, in a voice that was thickened by only the barest of Scottish brogues, "but true-hearted. And they are mine. They will do whatever I tell them."

Hotspur chewed the inside of his cheek, wondering if Douglas would stay true to the bargain they'd hammered out between them. Allowing this Scottish army to mingle with his went against everything he'd fought for his entire life.

"I've too much to lose to move against you," Douglas said softly.

Still Hotspur did not answer, his dark eyes flickering over the English and Scottish camps before him. The tension was palpable, and Hotspur wondered if he shouldn't have kept the two encampments farther apart.

"They're going to have to fight together," Douglas said softly. "Best for them to learn to bed together now."

"Are you a magician to so read my thoughts?"

Douglas laughed. "'Tis the fey fairy blood of our people, laddie. Come, our captains can keep the peace between your men and mine, and there's food awaiting us in the church."

Hotspur lingered briefly, glancing once more over the English and Scots. *Sweet Jesu in Heaven, let this alliance hold together just long enough for it to do what I need.*

Then he turned his back on the gathering darkness, and walked into the brilliantly lit church.

There his commanders awaited him, as well as the grim Prior General Thoreseby. The man was always hovering about in shadows, too eager to lean into any conversation he encountered and whisper his hatred of Bolingbroke. Hotspur well knew that Thoreseby's obsession with Thomas Neville had spilled over into an equally vile hatred of Bolingbroke, and that perhaps all Thoreseby said should not be believed. But Thoreseby appealed to Hotspur's own long-nurtured resentment of Bolingbroke, and of Bolingbroke's too-loving alliance with the Percys' rival, Raby, the Earl of Westmorland.

Above all, England did not need another Lancaster . . . and most certainly not as king. That would spell disaster for the Percys and their ambitions.

Apart from Hotspur's and Douglas' commanders and Thoreseby, there were several other men present. The Earl of Fife, Douglas' son, also named Archibald. With him sat the earls of Orkney, Angus and Moray. All, as Douglas, had been taken prisoner by Hotspur at the battle of Hombildon Hill. And all, as Douglas, were now allies rather than prisoners.

Partners in a coalition so fantastic that had they been told of it several months ago, they would have laughed at, and then beheaded, the fool who thought to relate it to them.

Fantastic it might be, but if successful, it would bring everyone concerned such riches, and such power, that the fantastic needed to be taken very seriously indeed.

"And so the vengeance in the hand of God readies itself to strike," Thoreseby whispered as Hotspur sat down.

Hotspur shot him a dark look, and wondered if he could possibly leave the madman behind when they marched south. He'd put up with the man for over six months, and that was six months too long.

But he'd been useful, bringing with him powerful factions from within the Church. Dominican friars had spent the last few months spreading rumours amid the English, whispering that Bolingbroke was not God-blessed, and that he'd taken the throne illegally amid a welter of murder. Once Hotspur was successful, and had taken Bolingbroke's head, then Thorseby would swing the might of the Church behind his own claim to the throne, crowning Hotspur with an aura of legitimacy.

Hotspur sighed as he accepted a cup of warmed wine from a valet. He needed Thorseby a while longer. But one day . . . one day . . .

"Have ye heard from ye father?" said Moray. The support of Hotspur's father, the Earl of Northumberland, was critical to their eventual success.

Hotspur drained the wine and handed the cup back to his valet. "Aye. He gathers men in Yorkshire and Northumberland."

"They are of little use to us in the northwest," observed Douglas.

"He will meet us in Cheshire," Hotspur said, staring at Douglas until the man averted his eyes. "Believe it."

"There are some," said Fife, keeping his voice indifferent, "who say that it seems passing strange that not seven months since the Percys helped put Bolingbroke on the throne they now seek to dethrone him."

"What the Percys make, they can unmake," Hotspur said. "We are the kingmakers of England. No one else."

"But are you sure you want to do this, laddie?" Douglas said. "My son speaks only what many whisper."

"*I* never rode with my father against Richard," Hotspur said. "I kept apart from Bolingbroke's slaughtering and murdering. Now I move against it. What is so 'passing strange' about that? *What?*"

He glared at the other men. "My father made an error of judgement. Now he seeks to rectify it. And why do *you* sit here and murmur and mumble about our actions? Do *you* not stand to gain as much as I?"

"Aye, aye, that we do," Douglas said, holding out his

hands placatingly. "We merely needed to be reassured as to the strength of your resolve, laddie. Bolingbroke was once your dear friend—"

"Once!" Hotspur said.

"Enough!" said a new voice, and everyone's head whipped up to look at the man who had now entered the church.

Hotspur rose, and managed a smile. "Uncle. Greetings. I am glad you are here. What news?"

Thomas Percy, Earl of Worcester, brother to the Earl of Northumberland and uncle to Hotspur, looked about carefully at each man present, then withdrew a parchment from underneath his cloak. "Glyndwr is with us."

Without exception, the face of every nobleman and warrior present broke into a huge grin of combined relief and triumph.

Thorseby, on the other hand, mumbled something uncomplimentary about dark magicians into his beard.

"Owain Glyndwr," Hotspur said, "the most powerful prince among the Welsh."

Douglas sent him a sardonic glance, and refrained from reminding Hotspur that, until three years ago, Owain Glyndwr had been a failed law student at the Inns of Court who had wandered back to his native Wales, proclaimed himself a prince of the ancient Powys line, and proceeded to stir up nationalistic Welsh resentment against the English. *Well,* Douglas thought, *to give the boy his due, he'd done a good job. Now tens of thousands of Welshmen would lay their lives down for him.* For Hotspur, now, if Glyndwr had indeed agreed to the terms of the alliance.

"He will . . ." Hotspur could not complete the answer.

"Meet us in Cheshire, as will your father," Worcester said. "Harry," he addressed Hotspur familiarly, "we will have so many tens of thousands with us that Bolingbroke will have no choice but to lie down and cower."

"And this island will finally be divided into three clear, independent and strong kingdoms," Hotspur said. "England, Scotland and Wales, confirmed by treaty, and bound by brotherhood!"

Douglas winced, thinking Hotspur was getting a bit carried away. Confirmed by treaty, yes, but they'd be bound by treason and regicide, not brotherhood.

"And so to Cheshire," Hotspur said. "And from there . . . England."

Chapter II

Thursday 30th May 1381

✛

"PARIS," SAID CHARLES. "I have set my mind to it." *Thank the sweet Lord Christ*, thought Catherine. *Finally, we move from Rheims.*

"May I enquire," asked Philip the Bad of Navarre from his place at the table next to Catherine, "why this sudden change of heart? We have been here"—he gestured about the hall of the palace Charles had commandeered (or rather, that his mother, Isabeau de Bavière had commandeered)—"some ten months, with most of us lusting after a change of scenery. But to this point you have always pouted your lip—"

"Philip!" Catherine said sharply, not wanting his insolence to push her brother into retracting his order.

"—and declared that Rheims was more to your liking, and that Paris was full of nothing but stinking drains and rebellious peasants."

"Paris," Charles said stubbornly.

"Why?" Catherine asked with as much gentleness as she could muster.

"Because . . ."

"Because reports from England," Joan said, her eyes steady on Catherine, "suggest that there are major troop movements in the north. Perhaps good King Hal," her mouth twisted very slightly, "is planning an invasion shortly. And, my beloved king wishes to go to Paris, where—"

"The walls are mightier than those about Rheims," Charles finished in a rush.

"You are not afraid," Catherine said, "that Paris might once again rise in rebellion at your presence? Do you not remember what occurred the last time we were there?"

"Joan shall keep me safe from any harm," Charles said, looking down at the napkin he was fumbling between his hands. "She is the Maid of France, and none would dare hurt her, or those she protects."

Catherine glanced at Joan, and saw a glint of humour in her eyes, as if she knew very well that there were many people who might hurt her.

Catherine felt a twinge of disquiet. Over these past two months Joan's sense of peace and contentment had not wavered. She and Catherine had talked privately on three or four occasions, and not once did Joan veer from her commitment to establishing Charles firmly on the throne of France. When Catherine argued with Joan that Charles was an imbecile, the worst choice for the throne of France that anyone could possibly imagine, Joan only smiled gently, and said his time would come. Catherine felt in Joan something that greatly disquieted her—that Joan not only knew of her fate, and not only accepted it, but also embraced it.

Perhaps she would come to her senses if her parents could speak with her. Had not Joan said she would end her days as a shepherdess?

Catherine's mouth lifted very slightly at the thought that not even sheep could be as stupid to herd as Charles so consistently proved himself to be.

Yes, perhaps all Joan needed was the temptation of her parents. The faint whiff of sheep, perhaps.

"Joan," she said, "would you like it if I arranged for your parents to meet you in Paris?"

Joan's face creased in a huge smile, and Catherine

thought that if she'd been in any company other than that which currently sat about this chamber, she would have clapped her hands.

"Thank you," Joan said. "You are a very generous woman, and sensitive to my needs."

The faint whiff of sheep, Catherine?

Catherine had the grace to flush very slightly, and it deepened as she saw how merrily Joan smiled at her.

"LET ME look at you," Philip said, his brow furrowed in pretended confusion. "Perchance let me pinch you, to see if you are still the Catherine I fell in love with so long ago. Ah, yes! You do feel the same . . . but . . . something about you confuses me, muddles me . . ."

They were alone, finally, in their apartments. Catherine's maid had just departed, leaving her mistress sitting in a chair by a fire with her glossy black hair unbound and flowing down her back, and her body encased in nothing but flimsy silk. Philip, for his part, still had his undershirt and hose on, but was hopping from foot to foot as he struggled to slide off his boots while poking Catherine in the shoulder.

Catherine laughed, a little self-consciously, for everyone in the hall had regarded her in startlement when she had been so unusually kind to Joan.

"Sometimes the little saint makes me feel sorry for her," she said. "So attached to Charles. Such peasantish loyalty and naivety."

"Ah . . ." Philip had finally managed to rid himself of his boots. He threw them into a darkened corner of the chamber, then lifted Catherine in his arms, sitting down in her chair and settling her upon his lap.

She smiled, and snuggled in close to his body. Who would have thought that one day she would be so happy and comfortable with Philip the Bad, ambitious king of Navarre, who had spent so many years plotting, and waging war, to gain the throne of France?

"You have saved me from madness these past months," Philip said softly, one hand stroking Catherine's hair. "This sitting about doing nothing. This waiting. This *not knowing*."

"Shush." Catherine kissed his mouth softly, knowing his frustration. Philip was a fighting man, a man of action and impetuosity, a man who was all for the *getting* and not for the constant drivelling inaction he'd been forced to endure. "Paris is one step closer for us."

"Yes? And how might that be? Was Joan right when she said that Bolingbroke was preparing to invade?"

Catherine could feel Philip tense underneath her. "I do not know what she has heard, sweetheart, but I do know that, whatever happens, Bolingbroke must invade sometime this year."

"Oh? And how do you know that? Has Bolingbroke been writing to you of his plans? Of his hopes? Of his love?"

Philip's voice had raised, and he pushed Catherine back a little so he could stare into her eyes.

"Nay," she said softly. "I have no communication with Bolingbroke. But I know him, and I know his ambition, and I am certain that he will be here this year."

"He wants you," Philip said, and drew Catherine back to him, sliding the silken robe from her body as he did so. "We both do. You are France. Whoever you accept takes France. That was my deal with Bolingbroke . . . or have you forgot it?"

Catherine shook her head, her eyes filling with tears.

"Marry me," he said.

His hands were sliding over her breasts, almost rough in their hunger, and Catherine wondered if it were her body he caressed, or the hills and valleys of France.

"I wish I could," she whispered.

Again he pushed her back, studying her face. Then he ran his hand down to her belly, and pressed lightly. "How long have we shared a bed, Catherine? Almost two years, give or take a few months. And yet not once have you bred to me. Not once. You said that—"

"I would give you any child of my body, Philip. Yes. That was part of the bargain between us."

"We are both young and healthy, and surely lusty enough to have filled half a village with our get by this stage. Tell me, Catherine, have you—?"

"No! Philip, believe me, I have hungered for a child of ours more than you could possibly know. I have neither ended a pregnancy, nor acted to prevent one. To have seen other women swell and breed at the slightest glance from a man has been . . . has been . . ."

"Hush. Hush now." Philip drew Catherine against him once more, cuddling her close. "God surely has his reasons."

And then he almost jumped, stunned by the sudden intensity of her weeping.

"If I had the courage," she eventually whispered, "then I would wed you. If I had the courage."

And if I thought that Bolingbroke would honour my choice, and the bargain between you.

SHE SLEPT, and Philip continued to hold her, his dark handsome face hard in the lamplight.

Slowly, slowly, his hand stroked her back.

Despite his gentle words to Catherine earlier, Philip simply didn't know what to think. Why hadn't Catherine fallen pregnant to him by now? Jesu! Almost two years. Did she still hold true to this ancient bargain with Bolingbroke, even after Bolingbroke had married Mary Bohun?

Why wouldn't Catherine marry him?

And if all those questions weren't enough, then why Catherine's sudden about-face to Joan in these past weeks? Catherine had hated Joan from the instant she'd first seen her . . . so why now this strange empathy with her?

Was Catherine still the one to partner him in his ambitions? She'd told him to wait, that their time would come . . . but what if Catherine was wrong?

Slowly, slowly, his hand stroked.

And then stopped.

Perhaps it would be best to watch for his own chance.

Chapter III

Sunday 2nd June 1381

✠

"TOM?"

Neville turned from the stallion he'd been brushing.

He looked about, making sure no one else was present. "Good morning to you, Hal."

Bolingbroke walked into the dim horse stall. The entire stable complex was quiet; most grooms and horsemen were in the Tower's chapel hearing Sunday Mass. He ran a hand down the stallion's smooth coat, admiring the sheen that the grey hairs picked up, even in this dimness.

"Not at Mass, Tom?"

Neville resumed his long, slow strokes. Mary had asked him to accompany her to Mass, but he'd demurred, saying he needed time alone to rid his head of his buzzing thoughts. Besides, Mary had a bevy of women, including Margaret, to attend her in chapel.

And perhaps it was best not to feed Margaret's jealousy and unease any more than he had to.

Neville had come to the stables to find some peace, to lose himself in the rhythmical grooming of his favourite horse. It had worked, because during his grooming, Neville had come to a decision within himself.

Trust Christ. Trust his own heart. And all would be well.

Having made his decision, Neville had felt a peace envelop him. The way forward was as yet dark, and his eventual decision full of unknowables, but if he could free Christ, then all would be well.

As Bolingbroke walked over to him, Neville slowed his stroking, then stopped altogether, resting his arm across the back of the horse as he looked at Bolingbroke. "I did not wish to go to Mass," he said.

Bolingbroke took the horse's halter in one hand, and softly rubbed the stallion's nose.

The horse snorted, and snuffled its nose across Bolingbroke's chest.

Bolingbroke waited.

Neville sighed. He supposed he ought to tell Bolingbroke *something* of what was going on. "The Archangel Michael spoke to me."

Bolingbroke straightened, and pushed the horse's nose away. "When?"

"About ten days ago. That final day of the pestilence."

"And?"

"He took me to the Field of Angels, Hal. Heaven, he called it."

Again Bolingbroke waited.

"It was foul," Neville said. "Foul."

"In what way?"

"In every way, and yet in only one way. It was cold and barren and full of falseness, reflecting the coldness and barrenness and falseness of the angels' souls."

You could have told me earlier, Bolingbroke thought. *Once I would have been the first one you would have rushed to.*

Then he realised how unfair that was. It was gift enough that Tom should be telling him now.

"I have known since . . . well, since you gave me the casket, just how heartless the angels are. But to see them in their own world . . ."

Bolingbroke almost asked what the angels wanted, then bit his tongue. He knew what they wanted well enough.

Neville suddenly threw the brush into a corner of the stall, making the horse jump and snort. "He made me feel like a puppet."

Bolingbroke had caught the horse's head, and was now stroking its cheek, soothing away its fright. "The angels have ever been loathsome creatures."

As he said that, Bolingbroke thought again about the strange, horrifying confidence that the Archangel Michael had in Neville. *What was it? Why did the angels believe so implicitly in Thomas?*

He opened his mouth to ask the question that consumed his nights and days—*Which way will you choose, Tom?*—but before he could speak there was a sudden rattle of hooves in the courtyard beyond, and both men's heads jerked towards the door. Voices shouted, and Bolingbroke pushed past Neville and strode into the courtyard.

NEVILLE ENTERED the courtyard a moment or two after Bolingbroke. Some two score men had ridden in on horses close to dropping from exhaustion. Their captain was even now speaking urgently to Bolingbroke, so forgetting himself that he had rested his hand on the king's shoulder.

Bolingbroke took no notice. He heard the man out, then nodded, thanked him, and sent him scurrying on his way.

Then he looked to where Neville was standing.

His eyes were wide with something that Neville thought looked surprisingly like loss.

THE CHAMBER that Bolingbroke had taken as his working chamber was alive with activity: shouted words, hands flung about, papers shuffled, men pacing back and forth, messengers running in and out. Most of Bolingbroke's advisers were there, including Ralph Neville— Baron Raby and Earl of Westmorland; Thomas Beauchamp—Earl of Warwick; the youthful Thomas

Mowbray—Earl of Nottingham and Duke of Norfolk; Michael de la Pole—Earl of Suffolk; and Sir Richard Sturry. All of them had been supporters during Bolingbroke's rebellion against Richard, and all had been richly rewarded since.

Of course, the Earl of Northumberland had also been more than instrumental in supporting Bolingbroke, and had been richly rewarded as well.

But he was not here now, had not been at Bolingbroke's court in many weeks, and this morning had brought the news that all of them had been dreading.

Horribly, the news was far, far worse than anyone could possibly have supposed.

"Well, it is no surprise, perhaps, that the Percys have proved so disloyal," Suffolk was now saying. "Northumberland has ever been the turncoat, and Hotspur has ever been the ambitious one."

Neville was standing behind a table covered with hastily unrolled maps, as well as the written reports of everyone from sheriffs to millers who had seen armies move this way or that. As Suffolk spoke, he happened to catch a glimpse of Bolingbroke's face, and saw again that fleeting expression of sorrow in his eyes.

Hotspur, his childhood friend, and now his betrayer.

"We must move fast," Mowbray said. "These reports are some days old. Sire . . ."

Bolingbroke grimaced, and looked about. Whatever pain had been in his eyes was now gone. "Of course we must move fast . . . but in which direction? Northumberland is moving in Yorkshire and Northumberland. Hotspur and his damned Scots alliance are on the move in Cumberland—no doubt in Lancashire by now—and Owain Glyndwr, by sweet Jesu's sake, in the northern reaches of Wales."

"They are all heading in one direction," Raby said, moving to the table. He ruffled about a little, found the map he was after, and stabbed his finger down. "Shropshire. The city of Shrewsbury."

"If they meet up, sire," Neville said, feeling the weight of Bolingbroke's eyes fall upon him, "then your task will be more than difficult."

Everyone could see Bolingbroke struggle with himself, trying to deny it, but he couldn't. Again he grimaced, and this time his pain was clear for all to see. "Scotland, Wales and the damned north of England, all arrayed against me. You are right, Tom. Raby, Nottingham, Warwick, Suffolk, Sturry . . . what numbers would Hotspur command?"

"If they all meet up," Warwick said slowly, not wanting to say the words, "then he could well have over sixty thousand."

"And currently? What does he command currently with just his men and the Scots?"

Raby again fidgeted among the reports. "Twenty thousand," he said eventually.

"Then I prefer the twenty thousand to the sixty," Bolingbroke said. "Our reaction must be three-pronged if we are to keep that sixty thousand separated. Raby, to you I give the most difficult of tasks—stop Northumberland before he can join his son."

Raby nodded, his face grim, then looked at Neville. They shared a silent understanding born of long association and deep respect: Raby's task would be horrendous, not just difficult. Not only would Raby have to ride hard and fast for the north, but his confrontation with Northumberland would bring with it all the accumulated bitterness of their long rivalry.

"Sire," Raby said, and half bowed. "If I may have your permission to retire."

"Go, go!" Bolingbroke said. Then, when Raby was halfway to the door of the chamber, Bolingbroke spoke again. "Ralph. May Christ ride with you."

Raby nodded, once, tersely, then was gone.

"Warwick? Suffolk? I need you to deal with our Welsh upstart. Can you manage?"

Warwick and Suffolk exchanged glances, then Warwick looked back to Bolingbroke and smiled. He'd never liked the Welsh. "Oh, aye, I think we can manage." He bowed, and both men left.

"And I," Bolingbroke said, "shall to Shrewsbury."

ONCE SOME order was restored, and men sent on their appointed tasks, Bolingbroke drew Neville aside for a quiet word.

"Tom, will you ride with me?"

Neville did not hesitate. "Aye."

Bolingbroke sighed in relief, which surprised Neville, for he'd not realised how unsure of him Bolingbroke had been. "Thank you. Tom . . ."

He hesitated, and seemed to drift off into such a dream world that after a moment or two had passed, Neville felt obliged to say something. "Hal?"

"I was thinking of Harry Hotspur, Tom, and of you and me. Of our wild childhood, of our friendship, and of the times we pledged to defend each other to the death. Even though I'd always known of Hotspur's ambition, and even though I knew my father's and my alliance with your uncle would undermine what friendship I had with Hotspur . . . this is still hard news to bear."

"A crown always attracts ambition, Hal. You know that."

Bolingbroke half smiled. "How polite you are. You want to say that perchance Richard felt as betrayed by me as I now feel betrayed by Hotspur."

"It had never crossed my mind, sire." Neville grinned.

Now Bolingbroke's smile stretched into a genuine expression of merriment. "Will you ride as my friend, Tom?"

"Aye, Hal, I will ride as your friend. I think I will enjoy setting aside questions of love and angels and demons for a few hard days' riding."

"Would that we could set them aside for ever, Tom." And Bolingbroke turned away.

Chapter IV

Wednesday 5th June 1381

— i —

✝

AS QUICKLY AS the pall and horror of pestilence had lifted from London, the shadow of major rebellion enveloped it. The joy that people had felt at their miraculous escape from almost inevitable death vanished, replaced with yet more uncertainty.

When Hal Bolingbroke ascended the throne, most people assumed that England would settle into a period of stability. Instead, the opposite appeared to be happening. Uncertainty over the manner, even the actual fact of Richard's death, spread whispered doubt about the legitimacy of Bolingbroke's monarchy. These whispered doubts became the stronger with Exeter's attempted coup during the Windsor tournament. Then, within moments, so it seemed, pestilence exploded through London and the immediate surrounding areas.

The black Dog of Pestilence, which no one had seen for some twenty years, once more stalked the lives of the innocent.

Now, Hotspur, and a rebellion the like of which the good people of England had never seen. An unholy—an *abominable*—alliance of the northern English, the Scots and the Welsh against the central and southern peoples of England.

Surely God had spoken? Surely *this* was the final word and judgement on the legitimacy of Bolingbroke's tenure as king?

Bolingbroke did not waste a single moment of those days that followed news of Hotspur's rebellion. From within the precinct of the Tower complex came the distant shouts of men, and the noise of horses being readied. Across the green meadows of East Smithfield adjacent to the Tower, where Wat Tyler had once made his fateful demands of Richard, spread the horse lines and encampments of thousands upon thousands of men-at-arms. Every day their numbers swelled as Bolingbroke called on the loyalties and obligations of nobles across southern England. Rumour had it that similarly large encampments of men and horses were building in Oxfordshire, Worcestershire and Warwickshire, waiting to join up with Bolingbroke's main force as it passed through on its way northwest.

But as men and arms and horses gathered, so did the ordinary people of London. Unsure, troubled, questioning, people grouped in increasingly large crowds in the major streets and squares leading to the Tower, and stood in shifting, murmuring clusters outside the East Smithfield encampment. The markets were filled with housewives and tradesmen, talking not of the overpricing of salted cod, or debating the qualities of the fine flannels of Belgium, but of the ever-increasing troubles of Hal Bolingbroke.

Sin attracted sin, did it not?

Among them moved yet more friars—those Whittington's watchmen were not able to detect and eject from the city—muttering of the dark evils that had enveloped England since Bolingbroke seized the throne from poor, young Richard, whose only fault was the naivety and impetuosity of youth. They talked of the strange deaths of

Edward III and the Black Prince, of the highly convenient deaths of Gloucester and Lancaster, and of how they cleared the way for Bolingbroke to assume the throne.

Once Richard was removed and murdered, of course.

Evil now sat the throne of England, they whispered, nodding their heads sagely, and blessing all whom they encountered. *Evil sits the throne of England, and until it be removed, until all traces of it are burned and destroyed, evil and its brother, despair, will multiply until all the good, God-fearing people of England have been crushed and destroyed.*

The crowds grew, and their mood grew darker. Fair Prince Hal had long vanished from their memories.

EARLY WEDNESDAY morning, Neville stood with several men-at-arms on the stone causeway just inside the Lion Gate. Behind them, in the Lion Tower, one lion, two tigers and a crocodile roared and croaked, sensing the bleak mood of the crowds gathering in the courtyard beyond the Lion Gate.

No doubt the giraffe, a gift to Edward III from one of the Muslim sultanates seven years ago, would also have been whimpering and murmuring were it not for the fact it had died from the pestilence.

"They've increased three-fold since yesterday evening, my lord," said one of the men-at-arms. His deeply seamed and browned face seemed impassive, yet when his eyes swung Neville's way, he could see that the soldier was gravely concerned.

"How quickly they forget," Neville murmured, turning his gaze now on the people who crowded just beyond the gate.

"They have not forgot the pestilence, my lord," said another of the soldiers, an almost gnome-like veteran of many battles, if the twisting scars on his left cheek and neck were anything to go by. "Not forgot the husbands and infants they saw tossed into the death pits. They have not forgot the stink of the rotting, nor the—"

"I understand!" Neville snapped. "Have *you* forgot how Queen Mary, ailing herself, further risked her own life to care for the dying?"

The soldier dropped his eyes, and then half turned his face away. Neville had the feeling that, to this soldier at least, even the memory of Mary's selflessness and mercy could not totally counteract the brooding misgivings of the moment.

He sighed. "Has the crowd done anything bar murmur and shuffle and stare?"

"Nay, my lord," replied the first soldier.

"Not *yet*," mumbled the gnome-like veteran.

Neville glared at him, then turned on his heel, mounted his horse, and rode back around the outer ward to the Garden Gate and so into the main complex of the Tower.

HE ARRIVED in Bolingbroke's royal chambers to find that Bolingbroke was already well aware of the unrest. Bolingbroke had several captains with him, as well as the Bishop of London, the Lord Mayor Dick Whittington, one of Bolingbroke's household lords, Owen Tudor, and the usual accompanying bevy of clerks, recorders, messengers and valets. Mary was there also, accompanied by several of her ladies.

Bolingbroke, dressed in a leather jerkin over his white shirt and hose, heard what Neville had to say, then nodded. "We ride out at dawn on the morrow and I cannot afford to leave London seething behind me." He gave a short laugh. "Imagine being caught between Hotspur and the Butchers' Guild of London, Tom."

Neville barely managed a smile at Bolingbroke's poor joke. The Butchers' Guild was notorious for its feast day parade violence, and its efficiency in dismembering any who got in their way. At any given time it seemed that a quarter of the guild's members were in prison awaiting trial for murder, another quarter were in the streets committing murder, yet another quarter were patrolling the streets with their hatchets and knives looking for an opportunity to do murder, and the final quarter were, reluctantly, in their workshops dismembering the already dead.

"We could try to disperse them, sire," said Dick Whittington, who'd joined Bolingbroke in the Tower the day previously. "I have several hundred well-armed men on watch, and—"

Bolingbroke silenced him with a wave. "Nay, Dick, I could not countenance that. Not setting Londoner against Londoner. Instead, set your men to spreading word that I will address the good citizens of London this evening at dusk, outside the encampment in East Smithfield."

Neville raised an eyebrow, both aghast and impressed at Bolingbroke's course of action. To address the crowds was good, a courageous choice. But to pick East Smithfield? Where Richard had ordered mass murder? And where the crowds might think that Bolingbroke meant to use the soldiers in the encampment to do the same thing?

"My lord?" Mary was seated on a couch near the window, and now she rose with a helping hand from one of her ladies.

Bolingbroke turned, smiling politely but impatiently at her. Mary looked wan and far more wasted than she had in previous weeks. The neckline of her gown gaped at shoulders and breast, and it appeared that Mary's arms barely had the strength to carry the weight of the gown's heavy sleeves. Her breasts were so flat as to be nonexistent, while her belly was swollen and, obviously, painful.

"My lord," Mary said again, and Neville heard a worrying breathlessness in her voice. "Allow me to come with you. Please. I might do some good."

Bolingbroke's face flushed, and Neville realised that he was angry.

"Mary, my love," Bolingbroke said, "I cannot allow it. You are too frail. Besides, the mood of the crowd is dangerous—"

"And that mood is why I should come with you," Mary said. Her own face had some colour in it now, and she tilted her chin determinedly. "I have a gentle voice and presence, and perchance I can soothe when—"

"When my words might only inflame? Think you that I cannot manage this on my own, Mary? Think you that you can save the day as you did at the tournament? Do you think me such an *incapable* king?"

"That is not what I meant, my lord, and well you know it."

Owen Tudor, his compassionate face grave under its greying red hair, glanced about at the appalled and embarrassed faces of the others who were in the chamber, then spoke quickly before Bolingbroke could respond. "Your Grace, madam, may I suggest something?"

Bolingbroke shot him a simmering look of anger, but waved his hand for Tudor to continue.

"I agree with my queen that she accompany you, sire, for she speaks well when she says that her presence might allay some of the more outward manifestations of anger. But, sire, you alone should speak, for this is not only your duty, but your right."

Bolingbroke gave him another long, hard stare, then nodded. "You speak sense, my Lord Tudor, although I still fear for my queen's safety."

"Then I will ride at her side, sire," said Neville quickly, before Tudor could jump in.

Tudor sent him an ambiguous look.

"So that I might watch over her for you," Neville continued. "Will you trust me with her life?"

Bolingbroke stared at Neville, then again he nodded. "With you more than with anyone else, Tom."

Then he turned aside, and began to speak of the preparations he would need to make for his evening's activity.

Mary also nodded, first at Tudor, who smiled and bowed slightly, and then at Neville, clearly relieved at the adroit manner in which they'd managed to defuse the situation, and sank back down to her couch.

"Our queen shall surely be safe with you, my Lord Neville," whispered Whittington in Neville's ear.

"Then make sure that your men also spread word that the queen, as ill as she is, will also attend this evening's audience with the king. Make sure the people know that."

"Oh, aye," Whittington said, and then he was gone.

Chapter V

Wednesday 5th June 1381

— ii —

✠

EAST SMITHFIELD GLITTERED in the dusk as the lights from a thousand torches glinted off hard steel and the angry, sceptical eyes of the crowd. People had moved from the streets and markets through the Tower gate into the meadows of East Smithfield. Normally filled with the sweet scent of cornflowers, columbines and dandelions at this time of the year, the fields were instead dust bowls, scarred with the recent excavations for death pits, as well as the more latter-day hooves and boots of Bolingbroke's growing army.

Just as the sun finally set, the sound of horns burst from the battlements of the Tower, and then the faint shout of those people still about the Lion Gate as King Henry and his party issued forth to meet with his people.

The crowd in East Smithfield strained, then surged forward, each member desperate to catch a glimpse of their king. A shout spread through their ranks: "The king draws near! The king draws near!"

And then, as Bolingbroke did indeed draw near, the crowd murmured, swelled, then sank back.

Bolingbroke rode in all the majesty he could muster,

and that was great indeed. His party numbered perhaps some twenty, or twenty-five—small, considering what Bolingbroke could have chosen to accompany him. But what his party lacked in numbers, it more than made up for with display. All were arrayed in the most sumptuous of garments: flowing silken robes of the richest jewel-like hues, embroidered in costly gold and silver threads; many of the greater nobles among them wore the crowns of their titles, as well their heraldic devices embroidered on their horses' hangings; gems glittered at throat and wrist and chest; chains of gold ran across shoulders; banners fluttered; great destriers snorted and snapped at any who pressed too close; and faces, stamped with the nobility and importance of the owner's rank, nevertheless managed to avoid haughtiness to radiate instead assurance and care.

At the head of this cavalcade rode Queen Mary, dressed in a long, flowing robe of silvered satin over the finest lawn gown. Under her crown, her dark honey-blond hair was left free to flow down her back and flutter in the wind of her passing. About her throat sat a wide collar of emeralds set in gold, and similar bands of gold and emeralds bound her wrists. She nodded gravely to the crowds as she passed, not making the error of smiling amid their doubts.

A half-pace behind her rode Lord Thomas Neville, as resplendently gowned and bejewelled as any other in the king's escort. He wore a scarlet surcoat over white armour about his chest and arms, and a golden sword in a scabbard that matched his surcoat bobbed at his left thigh. A great chain of gold and diamonds enclosed his neck and draped over his surcoat. His head was bare, his black hair and beard carefully trimmed, and his dark eyes never strayed from the queen's form, as if he rode ready to spring forward the instant she showed any weakness.

Bolingbroke rode three paces ahead of everyone else, and at counterpoint to everyone else in his party. For, unlike their beautifully gowned and richly adorned figures,

Bolingbroke rode completely unjewelled save for a simple crown about his silver gilt hair, and he wore, not resplendent robes, but plain leather armour over which draped a sleeveless tunic of chainmail. A war sword in a leather scabbard hung at his hip. His black destrier, similarly, wore nothing but the accoutrements of war: chainmail about its chest and flanks, armour and thick leather covering the vulnerable points of its neck.

This was a king under siege, yet prepared to meet that siege head on, and Bolingbroke wanted all to know it.

He rode deep into the crowd, stopping only when the press grew too thick to ride further.

"Good people," he called, standing in his stirrups and looking about at the crowd. "I beg you stand back a little. My queen is ill, and needs air with which to breathe."

He swivelled in the saddle, and smiled lovingly at Mary. "My lady, are you well?"

Mary, remembering well her duty not to speak, merely inclined her head, arranging about her face a loving smile to match her husband's.

The crowd murmured, then cheered a little.

"Good people!" Bolingbroke cried again, turning back to face the crowd. "You have carried such burdens of late. The pestilence, rumours—and worse—of rebellion and uprising, false rumours and whispers. Your lives have been disrupted and made capricious by the whims of fate and traitor alike. You want certainty and sunlight back in your lives, and I, of all among you, can understand that need.

"Good people! I know that there is little I can say to allay your misgivings. I know that only my *actions* can ease your minds and hearts. And I know also that you remember the plagues and uncertainties of recent weeks, and wonder if somehow this is a reflection on my right to reign over you."

Bolingbroke dropped his voice, although it still carried easily across the assembled masses. "I also wonder. I also am consumed with doubt. And I also know that this doubt must be laid to rest soon, or all my legitimacy will vanish, both in your eyes, and in God's.

"My fellow Englishmen, hear now my vow to you. Tomorrow I ride to meet with Hotspur, who leads the rebellion in the north. Let *God* be the judge. Let the *battlefield* be the trial of my right to reign as your monarch. And let *you* be the guardians of the crown until either I, or Hotspur, return to claim it."

Bolingbroke stood tall in his stirrups, his balance easy on the shifting, nervous horse beneath him. He let go the reins, and, raising both his hands, grasped the crown about his head.

"My brothers and sisters," he shouted. "May you guard the crown and majesty of England until God has made His decision!"

He raised the crown with both hands, holding it above his head, then, in a sudden, stunning movement, he tossed the crown into the crowd.

"Take it, and guard it," he shouted, his voice ringing over all of East Smithfield and into the city beyond, "and may God prove the final arbiter on my right to rule!"

He sank down into his saddle, holding the crowd captive with the intensity of his eyes.

"And, whoever comes back to reclaim that crown, may you never again question his right to rule. For what God has joined, may no man put asunder."

Chapter VI

Thursday 6th June 1381

✝

PHILIP DRAPED A comradely arm around Charles' shoulders, and flashed his charming grin into the man's face. "Charles, may I speak plainly, king to king?"

About them servants were taking down hangings and tapestries and folding them into great wooden chests, then piling pewter plate on top before carefully lowering and locking the lids. Others were rolling the heavy rugs from the floor, and pushing them to one side for labourers to lug outside to the awaiting carts.

Philip and Charles had to move smartly to one side to avoid the particularly energetic rug rolling of two servants, and Philip's arm tightened a little around Charles' shoulders as he led him towards a window seat that, being built into the wall, couldn't be packed and moved.

"About what?" said Charles, his eyes sliding in what he hoped was a surreptitious manner as he scanned the chamber for possible assassins.

"About your situation, my friend. It seems to me to be most hideous."

Charles sat down on the seat with a thump, and tried to move away from Philip's arm. But the King of Navarre was apparently most desirous of Charles' close physical companionship, for as Charles shuffled a few inches down the seat, so did Philip shuffle against him, tightening his arm as he did so.

"In what manner?" Charles said, hating the slight shrillness in his voice. His eyes darted about once more, this time looking to see if perhaps his mother was going to emerge from one of the chests to accuse him of unseemly weakness.

"Well . . ." Philip finally lifted his arm from Charles' shoulders, and leaned back in the seat, puffing his cheeks out on a breath as if his thoughts disturbed him greatly. "Firstly, my friend, there are the English."

Charles wriggled uncomfortably, and began studying a ragged nail on his left hand.

"I cannot but think that the rumours are correct—dear Hal is surely thinking of invading this summer."

Philip paused, damping down the amusement in his eyes at Charles' obvious discomfiture, and leaned forward, assuming an earnest expression. "So, how *are* your war preparations coming along?"

The ragged nail suddenly became of such extreme interest, and Charles bent his head over it so acutely, he managed to hide his face from Philip.

He chewed the nail enthusiastically, and mumbled something around his mouthful.

Philip grinned, enjoying the man's discomfiture, not so much out of mean-spiritedness, but because it would play directly into his own hands.

"You *do* have your war preparations well in hand . . . do you not?"

Again Charles mumbled something unintelligible. He shifted slightly on the seat so that his shoulder and back were half-facing Philip.

"Hmmm," Philip said thoughtfully. He screwed his eyes up against the light streaming in the windows and pretended an interest in the servants still scurrying about the almost completely defurnished chamber. "May I make a suggestion?"

Charles made no sound, but his nail biting came to a sudden end.

"Paris would be the perfect place to set in motion your plans for Bolingbroke's, and England's, complete humiliation, my friend," Philip said. "The city is so easily secured, yet so strategically positioned as to make it the perfect location to sally forth against any invading English army. Don't you agree?"

"Perhaps," Charles managed. His shoulder shifted slightly, and Philip caught a glimpse of an eye slanting in his direction.

"But you are king, and of such a mighty kingdom," Philip continued. "You have many burdens to bear. I cannot think how you manage to find the time to direct army preparations against the English as well."

Charles shifted a little more towards Philip. "Perhaps."

"Of course! Now . . ." Philip leaned forward. "I might be able to lift some of the care and burden of kingship from your hands."

"In what manner?"

"You are as yet young, and I have spent many more years in the battlefield than yourself. Perhaps I might be able to assist you in overseeing your war preparations?"

Charles thought about it. He knew it was dangerous to give Philip control like this. Very dangerous. Philip had attempted to double-cross his grandfather on numerous occasions . . . the years of experience Philip had on the battlefield were on the battlefield *against* France.

And who wanted Philip of Navarre commanding one's own army? That army was sure to be turned against one's own person the instant it served Philip's ambition.

Charles frowned. "No. I think not. I have the Maid of France. She will command my forces against whatever enemy arrays itself against me. I trust her. She speaks for God."

"Hmmm," said Philip, then fell silent, keeping his eyes

on four beefy labourers who were pushing and shoving a massive chest towards the doorway.

"Well," said Charles, "she *does* speak for God."

Philip lifted one of his own hands and began to study his own nails with an expression of intense concentration.

"And she will command my army. Successfully! I am perfectly safe with Joan about."

Philip glanced over his hand towards Charles, arching one of his black eyebrows.

"Joan . . ." Charles' voice drifted off. "She can help. Remember Orleans!"

Philip sighed, and put his hand down. "My friend," he said in the most sorrowful of tones. "We both know that Joan is no longer the woman . . . well, the saint she used to be. For months she moped about, and now in the past weeks she has done nothing but smile and enjoy the comforts of your hospitality. What talk has she made of crusades, and winning back France from the English? Why—none." His eyes darted around, as if checking for eavesdroppers. "I have even heard, my friend, that she has spoken of her desire to go home and tend her father's sheep once more . . . although, personally, I think she's simply decided to enjoy the luxury you wrap her in. Has she shown any interest in cladding herself in armour and riding out to war these days? No! Of course not. All she wants to do is live off you, my friend. She has you wrapped about her little finger."

"She hasn't! She hasn't!"

"Shush," Philip said urgently, laying a cautionary hand on Charles' arm. "Never let the servants see your panic, man. All I mean to point out," he continued in a more moderate voice, "is that Joan simply can't be relied on anymore. I mean to say, how many miracles has she popped out for you since you've been in Rheims? And who was it dropped your crown at your coronation? My sweet Lord Christ, man! If I hadn't caught that crown and handed it back . . . you might *still* be grubbing for it under the pews of the cathedral.

"Charles—" Philip dropped all the banter and foppishness out of his voice, leaning forward to stare directly into Charles' nervously shifting eyes. "—Joan cannot save France. She doesn't have the will anymore. Neither, to be blunt, can you. Give me the command of the armed forces and I damn well *will!*"

"I don't trust you," Charles said.

"You don't have a choice," Philip said. He rose, dusting down his tunic over his hip, where some dirt had smudged. "We have a week or so before we arrive in Paris. By then we will know with more certainty what is happening in England. And then, my dear boy, you will have to make a decision about what to do. You can't delay any longer. Either pick someone to command your forces . . . or make it easy for Bolingbroke and simply flee south to whatever whorehouse in the sun you have picked out for yourself."

And then he was off, striding across the floor without a backward glance.

Charles watched him go, trembling slightly at the harshness of Philip's tone.

ANNOYED WITH Charles, but not overly angry, for he knew it would take several overtures to win the faint-hearted idiot over to his plan, Philip ran nimbly down the main staircase of the palace. All about him he heard the noise of the move: the shrill voices of the cooks, rising out of the kitchens as they tried to both cook and pack at the same moment; the shuffle and snorting of horses in the courtyard; the curses of men as packs slipped and dislodged in the chaos. Catherine was elsewhere in the palace, closeted with her mother, Isabeau, and Philip thought he might as well take the opportunity of a few free minutes to check that his war stallions were being loaded properly into their transport.

Just as he reached the foot of the staircase, however, he came to an abrupt halt.

Standing some ten paces in front of him in the great hall of the palace were Regnault de Chartres, the Archbishop of Rheims, and Joan herself. De Chartres had remained within Charles' household ever since he'd examined Joan at La Roche-Guyon. Although he'd not found sufficient reason then to discredit her, Philip knew he'd been looking for an opportunity to do so ever since. Particularly since Joan had usurped his rightful role in crowning Charles in the cathedral of Rheims.

Now de Chartres was leaning over Joan, who was returning his stare without apparent effort. The archbishop's face was red-veined and incredulous, his pale blue eyes almost starting out of his head.

"May I ask you the question again?" he said, just as Philip sauntered up. "I cannot believe I heard you aright the first time you answered."

"If you wish," Joan said, and sighed. She glanced at Philip.

"The clerical brotherhood of Christendom," de Chartres said, "are greatly divided over which pope should be obeyed: our revered papal father Clement in Avignon, or the rude pig of an impostor, Urban, in Rome? As you have the ear of God," his lips curled in a faint sneer, "and seem on such intimate terms with the Archangels themselves—"

Joan's cheeks flushed, as if the archbishop's words angered her, but she kept her eyes steady on his.

Intrigued, Philip moved closer.

"—I ask you again, Joan of France, which pope do you say should be obeyed? Which one speaks on behalf of God?"

"And I say once more to you," Joan snapped, "that I do not care overmuch. I concern myself only with France, not with the dubious arguments of men. *Or* of Archangels."

And with a defiant look, first at de Chartres, then at Philip, she turned on her heel and marched off.

"One can almost sense her confusion," Philip said

softly, edging closer to de Chartres. "Perhaps . . . perhaps she has lost the ear of God? Perhaps the Archangels no longer visit her as once they did?"

De Chartres turned and studied Philip. Like everyone else, he didn't trust the man . . . but that didn't mean he might not make a useful ally. "Continue," he said.

Philip gave a slight shrug. "She may prove more dangerous than beneficial to both you and to me, my lord. To both the Church and to France."

"Yet who can touch her? France adores their miraculous Maid!"

"Well . . ." Philip said. He almost put his arm around the archbishop's shoulders as he had with Charles, then thought better of it. "I have a plan, my lord archbishop. Perchance you might care to hear of it?"

Chapter VII

Sunday 16th June 1381

✝

"HOTSPUR IS STILL some twenty miles north of the town, sire. And neither Northumberland's nor Glyndwr's forces appear to have yet joined with him."

Bolingbroke's shoulders visibly slumped in relief. His face looked grey in this late afternoon light, deep lines of exhaustion and care creasing his forehead and running down from nose to mouth. His beautiful silver-gilt hair was plastered to his skull by days of sweat, and the neckline of the undershirt peeking from his leather armour was stained and rank.

It had been a hard ride from London, collecting over six thousand soldiers and knights in Oxfordshire, and another five thousand each in Worcestershire and Warwickshire to combine with the force Bolingbroke had assembled in East Smithfield. Now Bolingbroke commanded an army some twenty thousand strong—a good size, and made up of experienced knights, foot solders and archers, but next to useless if Hotspur had managed to assemble his entire alliance.

They'd ridden into Shrewsbury two hours ago. The town mayor, well aware of the two armies moving towards Shrewsbury, had hastened to greet Bolingbroke, assuring him of Shrewsbury's continued loyalty and pledging the town's every resource to aid his king in repelling the rebels. Exhausted, irritable and impatient, Bolingbroke had wondered if the mayor would have said the same thing to Hotspur if he'd arrived first. But he thanked the man as graciously as he could manage, then waved him off, saying that he needed to confer with his lieutenants.

While the bulk of Bolingbroke's army was encamped outside the town walls, just to the south of the River Severn, which all but enclosed Shrewsbury, within the town the mayor had made available several adjoining townhouses for Bolingbroke and his commanders. They were comfortable and well appointed, and offered the men the first decent accommodation they'd had for over a week.

But before anyone could eat, or wash, or sleep, they needed to know the latest intelligence regarding Hotspur, Northumberland and Glyndwr. Bolingbroke had heard very little since he'd left London. He knew that Raby had reached the north . . . but did not know if he'd been in time to cut off Northumberland's march towards Hotspur's forces in the west. He knew that Warwick and Suffolk had reached the northern marches of Wales, but had they managed to turn aside Glyndwr's push north? For all Bolingbroke knew, he could have just ridden his army into the nightmarish situation of being caught in the pincers of three hostile armies.

The initial news from a scout waiting for Bolingbroke within his assigned townhouse had therefore been greeted with relief. At least Northumberland and Glyndwr had not yet joined with Hotspur.

But if not with Hotspur, then where were they?

Bolingbroke was in the main chamber of his townhouse with Thomas Neville, the Earls of Nottingham and Clarence, several of his leading commanders, John Norbury and Lord Owen Tudor, and an ever-shifting, whispering collection of squires and valets hovering about doorways and windows.

He was pacing back and forth before the unlit hearth,

waving off any attempts by his valet to unstrap him from his armour and snapping at any remark or observation from any of his commanders, when footsteps sounded at the door, and a messenger entered. Bolingbroke halted, staring at the man, who was even sweatier and exhausted than he felt.

"Sire," said the man, ducking his head, "I bring news from Ralph Neville, Baron of Raby and Earl of Westmorland. He sends his greetings, and—"

"For Christ's sweet sake," Bolingbroke snapped, stepping forward until he was within a pace of the now pale man, "just tell me your intelligence!"

"My Lord of Westmorland begs me to inform you that Northumberland's push westward is stopped, and that Hotspur may expect no aid from that quarter."

If the earlier news that Northumberland and Glyndwr had not yet joined with Hotspur brought relief, then this brought the kind of emotional release normally only associated with the unexpected lifting of a death order.

"Thank the sweet Lord Jesu!" Bolingbroke said, literally sinking down to his knees before the startled messenger. Bolingbroke leaned forward, grasped the messenger's hand, and kissed it, before standing and grinning at the expression on the man's face. "Norbury," Bolingbroke said, "see to it that this man has suitable reward for the sweetness of his intelligence."

Norbury, as relieved as any other in the chamber, smiled and beckoned the messenger away.

"Tom," Bolingbroke said, turning to Neville, "your uncle has saved me once again. I do not think there are enough rewards in this kingdom to honour him. What can I do?"

"Good service to you is all the reward my uncle needs," Neville said, too physically and emotionally exhausted to return Bolingbroke's grin. "Sire, please. You must rest, eat, and perhaps wash away some of the sweat of your travel and worries."

"Glyndwr . . ." Bolingbroke said.

"The Welsh bastard prince is the least of our worries," Nottingham said. "Northumberland and the tens of thousands he could have called up behind him was the greater threat. Now that he is stopped . . ."

"Aye," Bolingbroke said, finally sinking down into a chair and consenting to take a cup of warmed wine from his valet. "If we have to, then we can deal with Glyndwr. But I have faith in Warwick and Suffolk. I have no doubt that Glyndwr is even now scurrying back into the mountains of Wales."

His squire now stepped forward, and tried once more to relieve his master of some of his armour. But yet again Bolingbroke waved him away, asking him only to see to it that he lit the fire and set before it a tub of hot water.

"My lords," Bolingbroke said, "I do find that indeed I need some hours of rest. I excuse you to your own ablutions and meals."

The various men in the room turned to leave, but just as Neville had taken a step towards the door, Bolingbroke spoke again. "Tom. Will you stay and serve me? I would speak with you."

Neville nodded, helping himself to some warmed wine before sitting down in a chair by the window and waiting silently as Bolingbroke's valet set up the tub of warm water. Then, as the door closed behind the valet, Neville spoke.

"My lord, how may I serve you?"

"Aid me to untie some of these buckles to begin with."

Bolingbroke was fumbling with the buckles holding his leather armour to his body, and Neville wearily rose, walked over, and started to tug at straps himself.

Bolingbroke managed a smile. "I am sorry to ask you to do this, Tom. I know you as much as anyone need your meal and rest. But I wanted to talk to you . . . Ah! There! That is done!"

Neville lifted the massive chest and shoulder armour away from Bolingbroke's body, draping it over a nearby chair, then helped with the buckles about his hips and thighs.

Bolingbroke muttered and cursed, stripping away the armour and tossing it into a corner, then almost tearing off his filthy, sweat-stained undergarments.

"Sweet Jesu," he muttered as he finally managed to free himself from his last bit of clothing. "I thought those linens had melded with my skin."

He stretched, bent and touched his toes several times, then gingerly got into the steaming bath that his valet had put before the now-roaring fire.

"Tom," he said finally, "bring your wine and that stool and come sit by me awhile as I soak."

"About what do you want to talk?" Neville asked, sitting down next to the tub and eyeing the hot water enviously. He hoped his valet or his squire, Courtenay, were preparing his own tub in his chamber.

"About friendship," Bolingbroke said. He had stretched out as best he could in the tub, and now lay with his head on the rim, and the waters lapping at his chest.

His eyes were closed.

"It seems to me," Bolingbroke said softly, "that in my lifetime I have had two close friends—not counting my father, Lancaster. You, and Hotspur."

Neville watched Bolingbroke reflectively, sipping at his wine. "Not Margaret? Or Wat?" Wat had been Hal's brother, but had died terribly leading the Peasant's Revolt against King Richard.

Bolingbroke smiled, his eyes still closed. "Oh, I loved Wat, despite his intemperance in leading the rebellion, and still love Margaret. But my love for them is only tangentially a friendship. There is something about those few, strong friendships that are made beyond the bounds of family, Tom, that mark the boundaries of a man's life." He opened his eyes, and looked about. "Where did that damn valet put the soap?"

"Here." Neville tossed it to him, and watched for a few

moments as Bolingbroke soaped his chest and under-arms. He thought he knew where Bolingbroke wanted this conversation to go . . . and while he understood, was not sure that he wanted to go there himself.

"Myself and Hotspur," Neville finally said. "The friendship between three lonely boys, the friendship soldered in the heat of our learning to be men and warriors."

"Aye. Two deep friendships I made in my life, Tom. Just two, and both lost to me. Hotspur's friendship I lost when the ambitions of both our fathers and ourselves collided. Yours when you joined the Church."

"But I came back."

"Oh, aye, you came back to me. And for a sweet short time I thought I had your friendship back, Tom." Bolingbroke had given up all pretence at washing himself, and now lay back in the tub again, his head resting on its rim, his watchful eyes resting on Neville. "But then I lost it again, and it was not your doing that drove us apart, but mine."

"Hal, I do not want to talk of this again." Neville's voice was very, very tired, and his empty wine cup sagged between his hands. "What's done is done. I love Margaret still, and . . ."

"And?"

"And, you too, Hal. I cannot deny that." Neville grimaced, and let the cup fall to the floor. It hit the timbers with a clatter, then rolled away a few paces. Neville watched it until it had come to a stop, then resumed. "Hal, I am so sick of both angels and demons. And I am sick to death of having you watch me day and night and wonder what my decision will be."

Abruptly his eyes swivelled back to Bolingbroke. "Listen to me now, accept what I say, and then perhaps we can find some measure of friendship within this forest of wariness that has enveloped it." He paused. "I will do what I think is best, Hal. Not what is best for you, nor what is best for the crippled angels in their cold, sterile heaven, but what is best for mankind. I will do what my heart and soul scream at me to do. Can you accept that? And, accepting that, not bother me with what I might or might not choose? You can do nothing more than what you have already, Hal. Nothing."

Bolingbroke sighed, closing his eyes and sliding back in the tub briefly so that the water covered his head. He shook his head as he brought it back up, then wiped his eyes with a hand. "Aye, Tom. I can accept that." He sighed again, and Neville realised that the moisture in his eyes was not all due to the bathwater. "Would that Hotspur's friendship prove so easy to regain."

Frowning, Neville leaned forward slightly. "You would accept Hotspur's friendship again?"

"If I could persuade him away from his treason, then, aye, I would. Tom, Hotspur's scouts have no doubt informed him that I am now at Shrewsbury. By tomorrow noon at the latest he will be in the fields just to the north of here. I want to meet with him, talk with him, see if we can't settle this in some other manner than bloody warfare."

Was this statecraft speaking, Neville thought, *or the voice of a man sorrowing at the loss of a friend?*

"It is the voice of a man who hopes to use statecraft to win a friend back," Bolingbroke said softly, not looking at Neville.

Neville stared at him for a long minute. Finally he rose, retrieved his wine cup, and placed it on a nearby table. Then he put his hand briefly, gently, on Bolingbroke's shoulder before turning and leaving the room.

Once the door closed behind Neville, Bolingbroke rubbed his eyes once more with a hand, and whispered: "Oh, sweet Jesu, has any of this been worth what has been lost, and is yet to be lost?"

No one answered him.

PERHAPS BECAUSE he *was* so exhausted, Neville found it difficult to sleep. He tossed and turned, thinking over what had passed between him and Bolingbroke. In the end, while he finally drifted off to sleep as faint dawn light stained the muddy grey clouds over Shrewsbury, he decided that he could find some peace from what they'd said. Bolingbroke had been Neville's only friend during his youth and early manhood—Hotspur had never been as close to him as Neville had to Bolingbroke—and Neville did not think he could afford to lose him completely.

He did not want to lose him. Bolingbroke had lied to him and manipulated him, and had abused their friendship in the doing, but that did not prevent Neville from understanding Bolingbroke's reasons.

He was virtually asleep now, and his thoughts became softer, less formed. They had been so close as boys . . . weathered so many storms side by side . . . shared so much laughter . . . perhaps . . . perhaps it would be good to have Hal back as a friend.

For however long it lasted.

Chapter VIII

Monday 17th June 1381

✠

BOLINGBROKE HELD THE single-page letter in his hand, and only Neville, who was close enough and astute enough, could see that the king's hand trembled very slightly.

"He will meet with me," he said. "In the ploughed field with three oak trees beyond the town. Alone, save," his eyes lifted, glancing briefly at Neville before settling on his assembled commanders, "for Neville. We must both be unarmed."

"Sire!" Cumberland said. "This is folly. You cannot ride alone—my apologies, save for Neville—to meet with such an arch traitor. He is as soon likely to have one of his archers put an arrow through your breast as engage in gentle courtly parley!"

"Hotspur will not do that," Bolingbroke said. "I know him well. He may rail at me, but he will not stoop to cold-blooded murder."

"Sire—" tried Norbury.

"I have made up my mind," Bolingbroke said, carefully folding the letter. "Now, see to the arrangements."

As the others set to their tasks, grudgingly, murmuring among themselves, Bolingbroke locked eyes briefly with Neville.

The three old friends would meet one last time, to see if the old ties of that friendship would be enough to save staining the fields north of Shrewsbury with English blood.

THE WIND was cold, the sky still layered with the dirty brown clouds of dawn, the air thick and irritable with the dust lifted by the hooves of the thirty thousand horses of the armies to the north and south of Shrewsbury. It was hot, and the noise of insects shrilled through the air.

Neville and Bolingbroke sweated underneath their armour, and within half an hour of riding out from Shrewsbury, an escort of some three hundred men at their backs, they stank as badly as they had before their baths the previous night.

The ploughed field with the three oaks lay some two miles north of Shrewsbury along a badly rutted track. On either side, the fields waved thigh-high with grain crops, and the meadows along the several small streams they passed were thick with over-ripe hay.

But there was no one in the fields weeding the crops, or in the meadows scything the hay. Neville was uncomfortably reminded of that hot day he rode through northern France, wondering at the oddness of deserted fields before smelling the foulness of the roasting flesh.

He shuddered, and hoped his memory was not to be an omen.

It was early afternoon, the time Hotspur had said he would meet with Bolingbroke, and in the near distance Neville could see the dusty black earth of the ploughed field, with the three oaks standing in a sorry cluster in its southwestern corner.

There were a thousand glints of steel on the far side of the field—*a river of steel*, thought Neville—marking the position of Hotspur's escort. Presumably his army would be another mile or so behind that.

Hotspur had encamped his force of Scotsmen and Englishmen behind a mid-sized ridge some three miles north of Shrewsbury late the previous night. As soon as Bolingbroke had risen at dawn, and been informed of Hotspur's arrival, he'd sent the request that they meet. Hotspur's response had been only an hour in its delivery.

As they arrived at the southern edge of the field, Bolingbroke held up his hand, halting the advance of his escort. Then he looked at Neville, raising his eyebrows.

Neville nodded, and they kicked their horses forward.

Both he and Bolingbroke rode in full ceremonial armour, although minus any helm or helmet, or any weaponry. Their plate was gleaming white steel, marked with Bolingbroke's personal standard, as well the three Plantagenet lions. Their horses were decked out in as fine a manner, although their carefully washed and groomed coats were now coated with the fine dust that hung in the air.

As bad as our heads of hair, thought Neville, and wished that, somehow, either Hotspur or Bolingbroke could have magically arranged a damp day so that the dust might have been settled. He fought the urge to wipe his dry lips, and, as he saw a mounted figure emerge from the glittering steel at the far side of the field, cleared his throat quietly in order to try to bring some moisture back into his mouth.

"I am glad you are with me," Bolingbroke said from his position slightly to the front of Neville's left.

"I would not have let you come on your own," Neville said, and Bolingbroke flashed him a boyish grin.

Then they both focused on the rider approaching them, and any merriment on their faces died.

Hotspur rode a dark bay destrier, festooned in scarlet draperies. Hotspur's armour was scarlet also, with silver decorations. To Neville's eyes, he looked like the scourge of death riding to meet them.

"Hail, Harry Hotspur," said Bolingbroke as he reined his destrier to a halt. "What have I done, Harry, that you should so maltreat me?"

Hotspur, also helmetless, glanced between the two men, nodding at Neville, then settled his gaze on Bolingbroke.

"I have come to revenge Richard," Hotspur said, "and to settle legitimacy back on the English throne."

"That being yourself, of course," Bolingbroke said.

"God has spoken," Hotspur said. "The black Dog of Pestilence stalks your reign—"

"You speak in the riddles of fairy tales," Bolingbroke said. "Come now, Harry, what need is there of this? Turn about, now, and ride back to the north. Wall those Scots back in their mountains where they belong. Sweet Mary Mother of Christ, Harry, all you need do is bow before me and pledge your allegiance and I will give you all the honours I may."

Neville glanced at Bolingbroke. Hal's voice had almost broken on that last phrase.

"The Percys can never hope for any justice under a Lancastrian sun," Hotspur said. "You would have had us killed as you had Richard. We needed to move to save ourselves."

"Harry . . ." Bolingbroke edged his horse closer to Hotspur, who just as quickly edged his horse away a few paces.

"Harry," Bolingbroke said again, "does the friendship between us mean nothing?"

"Our 'friendship' died many years ago, Hal," Hotspur said. "We have only tolerated each other since then."

"I remember a year or so past," Bolingbroke said, "when we laughed together in London at the feasts and tilting matches of Christmastide. We were friends then, surely."

"Ah, yes," Hotspur said. "Was that not the same Christmastide that our beloved King Edward died, and the Black Prince with him? The same Christmas when the first of several Plantagenet impediments to your eventual seizure of the throne dropped dead?"

Neville shifted uncomfortably on his horse, and dropped his eyes.

Hotspur did not fail to notice it. "Yes, I see that Tom remembers. How is it, Tom, that you sit on that side of this ploughed field, and not mine?"

Neville raised his eyes again. "My loyalty is to Bolingbroke," he said.

Hotspur sneered. "Your loyalty has ever been to the Lancastrian house, Tom. You even abandoned your clerical vows when Lancaster snapped his fingers in your face. I knew it even when we were boys. I could never trust you. Never."

"Christ, Harry," Bolingbroke said, holding out a mailed hand in entreaty. "Why must it come to this? Why blemish English soil with English blood? What do you want? What can I give you?"

Hotspur held Bolingbroke's gaze easily. "Your throne and your death," he said. "And not necessarily in that order."

"Harry, no! There must be some means, some way, some *thing* that we can do—"

"Listen to yourself, Bolingbroke. Begging me to go away. You are a fool!"

"Hal speaks to you as friend to friend," Neville said quietly. "He speaks to you as an Englishman begging you not to put that in motion which will see Englishmen killed. He asks you to remember who you are, and what once was between you and him."

"Who we are? What once lay between us?" Hotspur laughed incredulously. "He is Lancaster, and I am Percy, and our houses have ever been rivals. I will *not* sit by and watch a Lancaster take the throne of England."

"Your father supported him. Gave him the throne," Neville shouted, finally losing his temper.

"But *I* did not! *I* did not simper all about London singing, 'Fair Prince Hal! Sweet Prince Hal!' I have never given Bolingbroke my loyalty, and will surely not do so now. As to my father . . . he has finally seen sense—"

"And *you* will oversee the death of the great House of Percy if you persist in this foolishness," Bolingbroke said. All friendship, all humour, all entreaty had fallen from his voice. "Your father will not be joining you here, as you surely must have heard by now."

Hotspur's glowering face was all the confirmation that Bolingbroke needed.

"And Glyndwr has lost himself in the misty Welsh valleys—or so my intelligence reported to me not an hour ago. Have you heard different? No?"

Bolingbroke paused, calming his voice. "Harry, one last chance. Bow to me now, disband your force, and your house will not suffer. But carry this treason forward and I will destroy your house—your father, your uncles and cousins, your own infant son. All will perish."

Hotspur's face twisted with loathing. "And that's all you have ever wanted to do, isn't it, Bolingbroke? From the moment we were boys together you wanted to destroy me."

"No," Bolingbroke said. "I loved you then and I love you now. Pledge to me, Harry, and you and yours will prosper."

Neville, watching, couldn't believe the depth of Hotspur's hatred and overweening ambition. Bolingbroke was giving him every opportunity to back away, to plead some passing madness, and to retire home to his family.

And Hotspur was determined to refuse him.

"Don't do this, Harry," Neville whispered, appalled at what Hotspur was about to set in motion.

But Hotspur was intent on Bolingbroke, and did not hear Neville. "I will *not* wait for the knife in the back," he said. "This is Percy's time, Bolingbroke. Tomorrow will prove it. I have twenty-one thousand battle-hardened men behind me. What do you have?"

"Men who love me," Bolingbroke said softly, then he swung his horse about and kicked it into a canter.

He did not look back as he rode away.

"Tomorrow, mid-morning," Hotspur said to Neville. "Here. This field. Battlefield."

"Harry—"

"I will see you dead, too," Hotspur said. "You should

have pinned your hopes and ambition with the House of Percy, Tom, not Lancaster."

Then he swung his horse about and galloped off.

Neville was left sitting his horse in the dry, dusty hot field, wondering at what friendship had come to.

He raised his head, staring about, and fancied he could already hear the screams of the dead and dying, and see the pools of hot blood soaking into the earth.

Thus ends all friendship, he thought, remembering his indulgent thoughts of the night past, *in the bitterness of bloody ambition. What will happen to Hal and myself?*

Chapter IX

Tuesday 18th June 1381

✝

THE SEA SURGED and receded, swollen and heavy. It pounded against the twin rocks of ambition and resolve, dragging under men and horses, conscious but uncaring of their screaming and dying. Overhead circled crows and ravens, dipping and soaring, riding the sea of death below.

The battle raged.

The two forces met at nine of the clock in the morning. Hotspur had positioned his forces atop a ridge, forcing King Hal to cross the ploughed field to meet him. Bolingbroke's forces protected their advance with volley after volley of arrows, met with stoic shields and returning arrow fire by Hotspur's force. Then the two forces met in a rolling thunderous shriek of steel against steel and the scream of horses. The forces merged in a chaotic melee, swelling first this way, then that, then in a different direction altogether as if, locked together, the two armies formed one gigantic, convulsing animal.

For two hours they fought, roiling back and forth, the injured with nowhere to go but to be sucked under the ocean of battling men, to be lost forever in the trampled dust of the depths.

Then, just after eleven of the clock, Hotspur called in

the Scots he'd been holding in reserve. The Scots, several thousand strong, attacked from the western flank, slamming into the twisted, muddled melee. Their faces were striped with war paint, their mouths open and gaping and shouting battle cries the like of which had never been heard below the border regions before.

Their impact carried the full force of their hatred for the English. Bolingbroke's army faltered, stumbled, then rallied at Bolingbroke's scream of encouragement.

And then, disaster.

Neville was fighting close to Bolingbroke's side. Their section was doing well, advancing slowly but steadily forward towards Hotspur's standard. Bolingbroke himself fought in a tight, contained manner, wasting not a movement or a breath, and killing with quiet efficiency. When the Scots broke upon their left flank, Bolingbroke stood in his stirrups, rallying his army with his extraordinary, clear voice, calling for calm and effort in the face of the new threat.

"I am your king!" he called. "And with me at your head, *nothing* can deflect our purpose!"

At that exact moment, and just as Neville had twisted his head to stare towards Bolingbroke, an arrow dipped out of the sky. It caught the sunlight, shimmering as if on fire, and plummeted earthwards.

Bolingbroke himself seemed aware of it, for, as fate would have it, just before it struck he raised his helmeted head and stared upwards.

The arrow sliced neatly into the right eye slot of his visor, shuddering as it impacted.

"Hal!" Neville screamed, digging spurs into his stallion as he twisted its head towards Bolingbroke.

Bolingbroke wavered, once, twice, then toppled to one side.

Men screamed about him, several reaching to grab him before he fell to the ground.

Neville pushed through several ranks of fighting men, killing once or twice with thoughtless swings of his sword, reaching Bolingbroke's side just as helping hands pushed him back into his saddle.

"Hal," Neville said again. "Hal?"

Bolingbroke had dropped both his sword and the reins of his horse, but as Neville spoke he managed to wave one hand weakly, then pointed urgently to his helmet.

Neville looked about—ranks of Bolingbroke's personal guard had closed in around them. They had a few minutes, at least.

Neville scabbarded his own sword, drew off his mailed gloves, and grabbed at Bolingbroke's helmet.

The arrow still stuck obscenely out of the eye slot, and now blood bubbled forth, sliding down Bolingbroke's visor.

"The king is murdered!" someone several paces distant screamed. "The king is murdered!"

"The king is alive, damn you," Neville shouted back, but the refrain had been taken up, rolling through the ranks.

"The king is dead! The king is dead!"

Neville's fingers fumbled with the straps of the helmet, but he had no idea how he could get it off without perhaps fatally dislodging the arrow in Bolingbroke's face.

Please, sweet Jesu, not his eye. Not his eye.

But Bolingbroke took the decision, quite literally, out of Neville's hands.

As Neville fumbled with the helmet, Bolingbroke reached up with both his hands, grabbed the arrow, and jerked it out.

Blood flooded out of the eye slot, and down his neck underneath the helmet.

"Jesu, Hal," Neville hissed, then finally managed to lift the helmet away from Bolingbroke's head and hand it to a man-at-arms standing by.

Neville grabbed at a torn piece of banner another man handed him, wiping away the worst of the blood from Bolingbroke's face.

"Thank the Lord Christ," Neville murmured. The arrow had narrowly missed Bolingbroke's eye, embedding itself in the flesh above his right cheekbone.

"How deeply did it bite?" Neville said as Bolingbroke took the now blood-soaked rag from him and held it firmly against the wound.

"Deep enough," Bolingbroke said, wincing as he pressed hard against the wound. "My cheekbone is split asunder."

"Then your beauty is all but ruined," Neville said, trying to grin, "and the ladies shall be desolate. Hal—"

"I know, I know, I will speak in a moment. Here, find me something cleaner."

Neville tossed aside the bloodied rag, then handed Bolingbroke a larger and cleaner piece of the banner. Bolingbroke pressed it against his cheek.

"There, that will do. It must. The surgeons can stitch it up once I win this field. No, don't give me back the helmet. Men must see that it is I, alive. Where's my sword? Ah, thank you my good man. Tom, I thank you also. Now you must take up your own sword, for I think I can see a flock of black Scots fighting their way through to us."

Without further ado, Bolingbroke grabbed his sword, gave his cheek a final wipe, then gathered up the reins of his stallion.

"Men of England!" he shouted across the battlefield. "Think you that an arrow could harm me? That a mere arrow could strike me from my throne? Here I am! Bloodied, but only into a prettier picture of the warrior king. Men of England, the traitor's chance has come and gone. Take up your swords and bows once more, one final time, and seize the victory that fate has handed us!"

And so saying, he plunged back into the fray.

Bolingbroke's words, coming so instantly after his men had thought him dead, galvanised them as nothing else could have done. There rode their king, fighting like a berserker deep into the enemy lines as if uncaring of his own safety.

Nothing could harm him. Nothing could stop him.

The sight gave them added strength at the same time it sapped the resolve of their enemies, and within minutes Bolingbroke's force had turned the tide of the battle. The fighting continued in the tumbled, chaotic manner that it had been fought thus far, but now both the Scots and the northern Englishmen fighting for Hotspur fell back just that little more easily, and fell maimed or dead just that little more quickly than they had previously.

Neville stuck to Bolingbroke's back, defending him as best he could. They were fighting halfway up the slope of the ridge now, and Neville could see that Hotspur's standard fluttered but a few paces away.

"Hal!" he gasped.

"I know," he heard Bolingbroke reply.

"He will try to escape," Neville said.

"No," came the soft response. "I think that is the last thing that Hotspur will do."

Bolingbroke struck several more men, and spoke again. "I think that Hotspur would prefer to die defiant, than to escape and live with his shame."

Neville looked about. Hotspur's forces had thinned considerably now, and he and Bolingbroke were surrounded by their own men. Even as he watched, he saw a score or more of Hotspur's soldiers throw down their weapons and turn and flee.

Most didn't make it, struck in the back and neck as they fled.

"Hotspur," Bolingbroke called, "tell your men to lay down their weapons. It is over."

Seven or eight paces away, Hotspur turned his bay stallion towards Bolingbroke. He said not a word, but hacked his way viciously towards Bolingbroke.

Then his horse stumbled, a sword sticking out of its neck, and sank to its knees.

Nimbly, for all his heavy armour, Hotspur leapt to the ground, hefting his sword as if he thought to take on Bolingbroke's entire army by himself.

"Watch my back," Bolingbroke shouted to Neville, but

he was too late, for Neville had already pushed his horse forward, and struck the sword from Hotspur's hand.

Bolingbroke muttered a curse, then looked about. "Send the word," he shouted to a nearby man-at-arms. "King Hal has Hotspur! Hotspur is taken!"

As the shout rang out, Bolingbroke dismounted, stumbling a little as he did so. He touched his cheek gingerly with one mailed finger, then hefted his sword, and walked slowly forward.

"Harry Hotspur," he said. "What have you done?"

Hotspur stood, surrounded by men on horses, their swords pointed towards his head. Someone, Neville perhaps, for he now stood slightly to one side, had removed Hotspur's helmet.

Hotspur's face was sweaty, his cheeks and forehead splotched with the marks of his helmet and his effort on the field, his eyes brilliant with hatred and anger.

"I have done what I needed to," he said. "That I failed is my own shame."

Bolingbroke advanced another step. "Go down on your knees before me, pledge yourself to me, and you will yet live."

Hotspur's face contorted, then he spat at Bolingbroke's feet.

A man-at-arms standing directly behind Hotspur swore, and gave Hotspur such an almighty shove between his shoulder blades that he fell to his hands and knees.

"Pledge to me," Bolingbroke said again, more softly this time, "and you will yet live."

Hotspur struggled to his knees, raising his face to Bolingbroke. "Bastard," he said. "Kill me and you will die an ignominious death."

"I am not talking of killing!" Bolingbroke said. He was now very close to Hotspur. "I am talking only of pledging loyalty. Do you not remember those times when we were boys together? Friends united against whatever the world threw in our path."

"Those boys are dead and gone," Hotspur said. "You

lost my loyalty many years ago, Hal. Do not think that you can wring it from me with threats now."

"I do not threaten, Harry. For sweet Jesu's sake. For the sake of that long-lost friendship . . . *do not make me kill you.*"

"I would rather be dead by your sword, than living treacherously at your side," Hotspur snarled. "If you do not have the courage to do it, Bolingbroke, then ask Tom. I'm sure he'd manage."

"Harry!" Bolingbroke cried. He turned his head for a moment, struggling with himself, his sword resting on its tip on the blood-soaked earth.

"You did not hesitate to murder Richard," Hotspur said, his entire face twisted in a sneer. "Why hesitate to so murder me?"

"Because you were once my friend," Bolingbroke whispered, "and because once I loved you."

And with that, he hefted his sword in both hands and, to the accompaniment of Hotspur's wild laughter, smote the man's head from his shoulders.

Chapter X

Wednesday 19th June 1381

✝

SO CONFIDENT HAD Prior General Richard Thorseby been of Hotspur's victory against Bolingbroke—how could he fail with Scotland and Wales allied with him, and God so clearly on his side?—Thorseby had removed himself from Hotspur's encampment at Black Hal in southern Cumberland to arrive at Blackfriars in London within two days of Bolingbroke's move north.

This proved to be a rash decision.

In the early hours of the morning after the battle of Shrewsbury, well before news arrived in London of Bolingbroke's victory, Thorseby woke to see something dark and forbidding slipping in the door of the chamber to stand at the foot of his bed.

At first he thought it one of those strange cloaked figures who had periodically appeared to him while he was with Hotspur in the Scottish borderlands, whispering to him that Bolingbroke was unloved of God and must be overthrown.

But then the figure crouching at the foot of his bed moved, and Thorseby realised that it was not only not cloaked, but utterly unclothed and horribly, horribly solid.

"We've had enough of you," the creature whispered, and Thorseby scrabbled about in bed until he was sitting.

"Lord Jesu Christ," he began in a harsh whisper.

"Do not invoke *his* name with your filthy mouth," said the creature, and it moved slightly, revealing itself in a shaft of pale moonlight that filtered through a high window.

Thorseby's chest tightened in horror, and he found that he could not breathe.

A demon crouched at the foot of his bed. *Oh sweet Jesu, see his horns! His humped back! His claws!*

"Do you remember what you and Tresilian once discussed regarding Thomas Neville?" said the demon, rising to its full height of some seven feet.

Thorseby, incapable of movement save to clutch his bed linens the tighter to his chest, gibbered something meaningless.

"You thought to murder him by a means most foul," said the demon, and suddenly sat down on Thorseby's bed.

His weight rested fully on Thorseby's feet, and the Prior General could feel his bones crunching under the creature's body.

He whimpered in pain.

The creature took no notice. "I know," it said, "because Tresilian talked to me about it once. About how pleased you were that Neville was going to be . . . what was it . . . be drawn and quartered, and then have his cock sliced off and forced down his throat, followed after a lengthy interval by his balls and bowels."

The creature grinned, revealed small pointed teeth. "Of course, that didn't eventuate, did it, because honest men saw to it that Neville was released from your custody. Even Tresilian, after his initial enthusiasm, realised that Neville was a far better man alive than dead.

"But not you. Oh no, not you. You've spent these past months scheming and planning, and turning your ire against *everyone* Neville is connected to. We can't have that, Thorseby. Not at all. I'm terribly afraid that you shall have to die."

Thorseby screeched, his eyes bulging, his shoulders twisting in the effort to free his legs from under the demon's weight.

It grinned, enjoying the man's terror. "And what better fate for Prior General Richard Thorseby than a hanging and a quartering, followed by a good disembowelling and a stuffing of his mouth and throat with his privy parts."

Thorseby forgot his horror of the creature, and leaned forward to beat at it with his fists.

The demon swatted aside his fists with ease. "Of course, hanging and quartering will be too tedious in this small chamber, so I'll content myself with a mere disembowelling followed by a genital mutilation. You'll bleed to death, Thorseby, in agony, before anyone thinks to come wake you from your oversleep. Will that suffice, do you think?"

And then the demon leaned forward himself, and seized the Prior General in his clawed hands.

"MY LORD Mayor!" said the gateman at Ludgate, glancing at the dawn sky, "you are out and about early!"

"Ah, my good man," said Dick Whittington, passing the gateman a coin, "a Lord Mayor's work is never done."

And so saying, he walked down Watling Street towards St Paul's, whistling merrily despite the exhaustion that marked his face.

Chapter XI

Thursday 27th June 1381

— i —

✠

TOM, TOM, WHY *do you not free me?*

Neville twisted about, unable to tear his eyes away from the contorted, bleeding figure on the cross.

Tom? Have I not suffered enough? Free me!

"How, sweet lord?" Neville whispered. "How?"

I am nailed to this cross, Tom. Nailed . . .

"How? I cannot penetrate heaven!"

Nailed to this cross, Tom, as I am nailed to ten thousand score crosses about Christendom.

As he had many times previously, whenever Christ appeared before him, begging to be freed, Neville extended his hands. "How? How?"

Nailed . . . nailed . . . take out the nails, Tom.

"How?" Neville cried.

Christ's face twisted, and he gasped, as if the agony was finally about to consume him. Then he took a deep, ragged breath, and managed to speak again in a heavy rasp.

Mary. Go to Mary. She prays before the answer.

"Mary?"

Nails, Tom. I am bound only by nails.

And then the vision vanished, and Neville started, aware once more of his surroundings.

HE SAT under a bower in the gardens of the Tower complex. They had returned to London some three days previously, Bolingbroke riding triumphant, if a little battered, at the head of his army, Hotspur's staring, lifeless head on a pike in his hand.

The London crowds had seethed about them, screaming their adulation. They'd ridden into London via Ludgate and, in the square before St Paul's, Dick Whittington himself had met Bolingbroke. In his hands he'd held Bolingbroke's crown.

Bolingbroke's throne was finally safe, from English hands, at least.

Neville rose to his feet, his legs and hands trembling with the remaining emotions of his vision.

Go to Mary? She prays before the answer?

Neville took a deep breath, striding through the gardens to the gate in the wall surrounding the palace complex.

Go to Mary? She prays before the answer?

He went first to her chambers, thinking that Mary might be praying before the small altar she'd had erected in the corner of her bedroom. But she was not there, and, hearing that, Neville had no need to ask further of her ladies where she might be.

He made his way to the Tower's church, the Chapel of St John, situated against the eastern wall of the White Tower, where it sat sandwiched between it and the Wardrobe Tower.

Neville reached the outer door, then hesitated. Margaret sat in the gardens to one side of the chapel, together with her maid Agnes, and her and Neville's two children, Rosalind and Bohun. Jocelyn, daughter of the prostitute Emma, had also joined the group. It was almost midday, and the group sat in the shade of a small pear tree, tossing woollen balls for the younger children to play with, and scratching behind the ears and across the stomachs of two grey and white lapdogs, lolling on the lawns in delight at the caresses.

"Tom," Margaret said, half-rising, then sinking down again at Neville's gesture. "What do you here?"

"I look for Mary. Is she within?" He nodded at the closed door of the chapel.

Margaret and Agnes shared a glance. "Aye," Margaret replied. "She is praying. Tom, she asked not to be disturbed."

"I—"

"She most particularly asked me to—"

"Keep *me* away?" Neville said softly, incredulously, and Margaret lowered her eyes.

"Nay. She did not mention your name specifically."

"Then I shall go in," Neville said. "Margaret, do not fret. I will not disturb Mary overlong."

He laid a hand to the old iron door handle, turned it, then slipped quietly into the chapel, closing the door behind him soundlessly.

"Would that he sought *me* out so assiduously," Margaret murmured.

Why talk so much, and so often, with Mary, when he could so easily share with her?

Rosalind looked up from her play with her woollen ball, and frowned at her mother. She scrambled the foot or two distance between them, and clambered into Margaret's lap.

Mama, said Rosalind's childish voice in her mother's mind, *do not fret. I am sure that Papa loves you.*

Margaret stared incredulously at her child, and breathed in a draught of pure panic.

Ohsweetjesuohsweetjesuohsweetjesu!

ST JOHN'S Chapel had been built some three hundred years previously, during the reigns of the early Norman kings. Its builders had constructed it in the usual heavy Norman style—small windows, heavy arches, thick walls—but had somehow nonetheless managed to give the chapel both warmth and intimacy. It was constructed in the round: an outer thick wall with narrow but tall stained glass windows, and an inner wall, pierced with two tiers of similarly narrow but tall stone arches. Light flooded in through the outer windows, through the arches and into the small space of the circular chapel within.

Mary was on her knees on a cushion before a simple altar of stone. A linen had been thrown over the stone, and candles and incense placed upon it. Behind the altar, hanging from one of the stone columns supporting the arches, hung a life-sized statue of Jesus, attached, as always, to the cross.

Free me. I am nailed.

Neville trembled, and the slight noise his movement made aroused Mary from her devotions. She looked over her shoulder.

"Tom?" Her voice was cross. "What do you here?"

Free me! I am nailed here, as I am nailed to ten thousand score crucifixes about Christendom.

"Mary . . ." His voice had dried up, and he could go no further. All Neville could do was stare at the statue of Jesus on its cross.

It was different, vastly different, to most representations of Christ on the cross. Generally, crucifixes were carved out of a single block of wood or stone, but this one was not. The craftsman had taken two pieces of wood and carved them separately: one piece formed the cross, one the body of Christ.

Mary prays before the answer. Free me.

And the craftsman had affixed the body of Christ to the cross by nailing it at wrists and through the crossed feet.

Un-nail me, Tom.

"Tom?" Mary was struggling to rise, and Neville moved forward to aid her, although he did not take his eyes from the cross.

"Tom, *what are you doing here?*"

"I have come to free Christ, Mary," he whispered, and she gasped, and turned her head to follow his gaze.

The eyes of Christ were open, staring at them, great pools of black agony.

As they stared, a tear trickled down one cheek.

Free me, Tom. Now.

Chapter XII

Thursday 27th June 1381

— ii —

✝

THE CARVED CRUCIFIX had been fastened into the stone wall with bolts behind the two arms of the cross, but Neville was lucky—

Is this "luck," Tom?

—that the weight of the statuary rested almost entirely on a small stone shelf under the base of the cross, and not on the bolts. These were loose, and rusted, and when Neville climbed onto the base of the statue, grabbing onto Christ's shoulder for support with one hand, he found that he could use the dagger to prise the bolts loose with little effort.

One bolt fell free, and the entire crucifix shuddered, and shifted on the wall.

Neville almost lost his grip. He hesitated, regained his balance, then turned his attention to the bolt holding the other arm of the cross. As he did so, his gaze glanced across the face of the Christ figure, so close to his own.

The eyes were still wide open, black with pain, staring into Neville's.

Alive.

"Tom?"

Neville dragged his eyes away from Christ's, and looked behind him. "Mary! Stand back. This is going to fall at any moment."

"But, Tom—"

"Do as I say!"

Mary hesitated, then took several shuffling steps back, staring at Neville, who was now working on the remaining bolt. The statue shuddered, and shifted again, far more violently this time, and Neville leaped clear just as the massive wooden cross and statue fell off the wall.

It hit the altar, almost crushing it, then somersaulted forward, landing with a ringing crash . . . right at Mary's feet.

Christ's head lay only some six inches from the tip of her soft leather shoe, and Mary moaned softly, for Christ's eyes were open, full of life and agony, and staring right at her.

She drew in a slow deep breath, hearing it rattle in her throat.

Christ was alive, and looking at her as though . . . as though . . .

"Are you hurt?"

Mary looked up, blinking, feeling half-frozen with shock.

Christ's eyes were alive, and staring at her.

"No . . . no. I am unhurt. Tom . . ."

"Wait, Mary. Wait."

Neville knelt at the base of the statue, using the hilt of his dagger to lever out the iron nail that had been used to fasten Christ's feet to the lower portion of the cross.

With a scream of protest, the nail came free.

Mary wavered on her feet, then caught her balance, her mouth slightly open, her eyes wide above them.

Neville shuffled forward to the top of the cross, bending over the nail driven into Christ's right wrist.

He slid the hilt of the dagger under the head of the nail and grunted as he leaned his shoulders into the effort of tearing out the nail.

Mary heard a distant scream, of anger rather than of fright, and she looked about, but could see nothing.

She looked back down.

The nail was almost free, and with a final grunt of effort from Neville, it popped out.

Neville stood, and stepped over Christ's body to the left wrist and the last nail.

Now several screams sounded, and the fury and threat within them made Mary cry out in fear. She half turned, expecting armed knights, perhaps, to come charging into the chapel to do her to death with their swords.

But there was no one there. The chapel lay quiet and empty behind her.

"Lady, do not fear," said a soft voice, and Mary whipped about and looked down to where the voice had come from.

She gasped, and stepped back.

The wooden statue of Christ was now no longer quite wooden. Apart from the single limb still nailed to the left arm of the cross, the statue was living, breathing flesh. Pale flesh, wretched with pain and streaked with blood and sweat, but, nevertheless, flesh.

Christ's head and face twisted up and towards her, and he was smiling. Gently. Lovingly.

"Do not fear, Mary," he said again.

Mary vacillated between her continuing shock and an intense emotion she could not immediately identify. She thought she should be frightened, fearful, but she was not. She was beyond movement, beyond speech. All she could do was stare into the gently smiling face of Christ.

Then the face winced, and cried out in pain, and Mary heard the screech as the final nail popped free.

Christ pushed the crown of thorns from his brow, then rolled over, away from the cross, revealing deep lash welts on his back. He curled his arms about his body briefly, holding his wrists tight against his chest as if to ease the throbbing pain within them, then very slowly managed to get to his feet, stumbling a little as he did so.

Neither Mary nor Neville, now standing as well, moved to help him.

Christ took a deep breath, then straightened his body. The wounds in his flesh—in his wrists, his feet, his side and across his brow and back—abruptly vanished, and as they faded so did the lines of pain in his face fade with them.

He looked to Neville. "I do thank you, brother," he said, "for you have ended my agony, and gone some way to ending another's. Please, tell no one what you have done here today, for it would serve no purpose."

Then he looked to Mary and, if possible, his face softened even more. "Mary," he said in a voice that was so full of longing that Neville's eyes filled with unbidden tears. "Mary . . ."

Intense emotion flooded Mary. She had never felt this way before, and had never imagined she could feel this powerfully. She couldn't identify the emotion—she thought it may have been joy combined with overwhelming relief, but couldn't understand why she should feel this way—and knew only that before anything else she wanted to step over to Christ, to touch him, to *feel* his living warmth and let it reassure her. But before she could move to him, Christ vanished, and Neville and Mary were left staring at the space that he had inhabited.

Before either could move, or speak, there came a soft unidentifiable sound, and the empty cross at their feet vanished.

Neville turned to look at the altar: it was whole again, the cross and its carved figure once more attached to the stone pillar as if nothing had happened.

And yet, the carving of Christ seemed somehow empty, as if it no longer held what once it had.

MARGARET SOMEHOW managed to drag her eyes away from Rosalind still staring at her from her lap, to

Agnes who sat similarly shocked a pace away from her. Patently, Agnes had caught the mind thought as well.

But how could this be? Rosalind was more mortal than angel-child. She had none of the abilities of her mother. Only angel children had those . . . only angel children had those . . .

"Who fathered that child, Margaret?" Agnes said in a strange, rasping voice.

"Tom, Tom, Tom only."

"But—"

"Wait!" Margaret looked to where Bohun sat on the grass, tugging playfully at one of the lapdog's ears.

Bohun, she called.

The boy twisted about, looking at her inquiringly.

"Sweet Jesu," Agnes muttered. She stared at Margaret, eyes wide with fear.

"Who is Tom, Margaret? *What* is Tom?"

Margaret began slowly to shake her head back and forth. Not in answer, but in denial.

No wonder the angels were so confident of him! Sweet Jesu in heaven, Hal, what are we going to do?

STILL UTTERLY unable to speak, Mary very slowly turned her head to look at Neville. After a minute he met her eyes. He sheathed his dagger, needing three tries to do it, and made as if to speak, but whatever he wanted to say was stopped by a choral shriek of fury.

What have you done? What have you done?

Angels, a score of them, crowding the lower end of the chapel. They throbbed with light, a furious, vengeful light, and as Mary shrank in terror towards Neville, they advanced up the chapel towards the altar.

Neville put an arm about Mary, holding her trembling form close to his. "I set him free," he said in an even tone.

Why? Why? He is the Master Trickster. Have you been tricked, Thomas? Is that why you did this?

"You say you know beyond a shadow of a doubt," Neville said, "that I will not give Margaret my soul. That your children, the demons, will not win. That being so, why are you so afraid?" He paused, long and meaningfully. "Surely you can trap him again?"

Even as he said it, Neville wondered that the angels had not realised he'd been working to free Christ until after the event. Perhaps they were weaker than he thought.

The Archangel Michael stepped forward from the clutch of angels. *You tread a dangerous path, Thomas. Be sure you know what you do.*

Then he turned very slowly, and regarded Mary. *Bitch whore. I should have known that you would have been here. I suppose you imagine that the circle is complete now.* And then, horrifically, the archangel spat at Mary.

She flinched, and Neville's hold about her tightened.

"Michael—" he began, but the archangel turned on him in fury.

What do you with your arm about her? Has she not caused enough pain?

For a long moment Neville and the archangel stared at each other, then, suddenly, all the angels were gone, and Mary and Neville were left alone in the chapel.

Mary opened her mouth to speak, but her initial word came out a sob, and Neville turned to her, concerned. "Mary?"

"How could he have said that to me?" she eventually managed. "Bitch whore?" She half laughed, half sobbed. "What did he mean? What have I done to deserve that?"

"The angels thrive on vileness and distress, Mary," Neville said as gently as he could. "And 'bitch whore' is but their normal term of endearment as far as women are concerned."

She shuddered. "I feel unwell, Tom. Will you escort me back to my apartments?"

* * *

THAT NIGHT, when Neville turned to Margaret in their bed, she wriggled away, saying only that she felt nauseated—brought on by the heat perhaps—and that she preferred to sleep.

In truth she slept not a wink that night. She lay awake, staring at the night shadows that chased themselves across the walls of their chamber.

When would she be able to find time to see Hal? Alone?

Chapter XIII

Saturday 29th June 1381

✠

BOLINGBROKE STOOD AT the window of the White Tower, gazing out over London. "Ah, my friends," he said softly, "for the first time in months I feel safe!"

"Glyndwr? Northumberland?" Neville said, speaking for all of Bolingbroke's councillors in the chamber that morning.

Bolingbroke turned to face them. His right cheek was still swollen and mottled purple and brown about the angry red tissue, but it was healing well, and the physicians had told him he would likely have only a small scar to show for his battle injury.

"Glyndwr is vanished into the mountains of Wales," he said, "and without a strong English ally then that is where he will stay, spending his ambition warring with local Welsh lords and petty princes. Northumberland . . . well, Northumberland has gone into exile, taking what remains of his family with him."

"Is that wise?" Dick Whittington sat in a huge chair underneath another of the chamber's many windows. In his lap he held a remarkably plump cat, which he stroked absently.

"Wise? Do you mean 'Should I not have had him executed?' Well, maybe so, but in this instance I thought mercy best called for. Northumberland will not trouble me again. I have confiscated all his lands, and without that wealth to back him, his power is gone." Bolingbroke paused. "His ambition, of course, died with Hotspur."

He walked slowly into the centre of the chamber, briefly meeting every man's eyes as he did so. "Internal ferment is at an end. True, there may be still some minor lords muttering in their dark castles, but there will be no more serious threat of rebellion. Not now that Exeter, Northumberland and Hotspur have been negated."

"And so, sire?" Neville asked.

"And so?" Bolingbroke laughed. "How well you know me, Tom. And now . . . France!"

"France?" Sir Richard Sturry, one of Bolingbroke's closest and most respected advisers, shared a concerned glance with several of the other men present. "But surely . . ."

"Surely *what*, Sturry? When would be a better time? England is at peace, and rebels disposed of. Better, the rebels' wealth and lands have found their way into the royal purse." Bolingbroke smiled. "I shall not even have to ask Parliament for the funds for this campaign. I want France and *I* shall pay for it."

Neville thought those words had a particularly ominous ring, but he paid them little heed. For the past few days his mind had been consumed with curiosity and wonder in equal amounts. Wonder that he'd managed to free Christ, curiosity as to where he'd gone. Neville had somehow thought that there would be rumour of a new prophet gathering crowds in the marketplaces and fields of London, or strange word of miracles being wrought amid the poor and hopeless. But there'd been nothing. It was as if, once freed, Christ had vanished.

Perhaps he thought his work was done.

"And the bonus," Bolingbroke continued, "is that after the troubles of the past few weeks, I have a force almost completely assembled. Once Westmorland comes back from the north, with both his forces and those of

Northumberland's that he has been able to requisition, and Warwick and Suffolk from the west, I shall have an invading army such as England has not been able to raise in generations.

"And *now* is the time to strike," Bolingbroke continued, his face growing flushed with his enthusiasm and the force of his argument. "Pretty boy Charles is sitting playing his harp and refusing to be king, while this miraculous Maid Joan seems to have sunk into a mire of do-nothingness. Who has seen or heard anything of her in months? My friends, I can add the crown of France to that of England by late autumn. Are you with me? Are you with me?"

Neville finally surfaced from his reverie. "All England is with you, Hal. You know that."

BOLINGBROKE STRODE down the narrow corridors that joined the White Tower with the royal apartment buildings, his stride bouncy and jaunty. He greeted every guard he passed along the way by name, smiling and nodding at their returned greetings.

Everything was going far better than he'd expected. To be frank, he'd thought he might have to wait until the following year to launch his campaign into France, but Hotspur's rebellion had inadvertently played into his hands. Now England was secured, *and* he had the force at hand with which to deal with France.

And with Joan. And, finally, with Catherine.

His face lost some of its ebullience as he crossed under the archway that marked the outer wall of the royal apartments.

Catherine . . . how many years had he waited for her? Longed for her?

And to see her throw herself at Philip. Catherine well knew why he'd been forced to marry Mary—Christ alone knew how much he'd needed Mary's lands and wealth to launch his own bid for the English throne. And Catherine also knew that Mary was ill, destined not to live long.

Why could she not have waited?

Bolingbroke's face now shadowed with jealousy and anger, the emotions directed both at Catherine and at Mary. Damn Mary, how much longer was she going to take to die? Why cling so desperately to life when she knew her *duty* was to die?

What would happen if he won both France and Catherine and Mary was still clinging grimly to life?

What truly irked Bolingbroke was the place Mary had in the hearts of the English people. To the English, Mary was the Beloved Lady, almost a reincarnation of the Virgin Mary herself.

To Bolingbroke, she was becoming more of an irritation every day she continued to draw breath. He'd done his best for her, he'd been kind to her, he'd elevated her beyond anything she could have dreamed possible. And yet she refused to fulfil her part of the bargain.

Her place was to die, and yet she would not do so.

And so, angered and irritable, Bolingbroke banged through the door into Mary's chamber for his obligatory daily visit to her sickbed.

At least he'd be able to escape her in France.

AS USUAL, Mary was lying in her bed already, even though it was barely late afternoon. Outside, the sunlight still lay golden over the roofs and orchards of London. In this chamber, the curtains had been drawn and the lamps lit, as if Mary wanted to will forward the night.

Bolingbroke nodded to several of Mary's ladies, Margaret among them, who drew back from the bed as he approached, then sat himself down on the edge of his wife's bed.

"My dear," he said, then floundered into a silence as he fought for, yet could not find, words to continue.

She looked ill, grey and wasted, but then she always did. It was hardly anything new.

She smiled, but it did not reach her eyes. "You look excited about something, husband. Will you tell me?"

"I have decided to mount a campaign into France this summer, my dear. The time has never been better."

Her face lost any trace of humour. "Ah," she whispered. "Catherine. You must be happy that you will go to her finally."

Bolingbroke's expression darkened. He looked down, as if searching for something to distract him, and saw one of Mary's skeletal hands lying on the coverlet.

He reached out and picked it up, both marvelling at, and loathing, its thinness. "On the contrary, beloved," he said, his voice hard in its expressionlessness, "my thoughts shall be with you every moment that we are separated."

Mary started to say something, then stopped, her brow creasing. "My lord," she finally said, "I see no need for us to be separated at all. A queen's place is with her husband the king. I shall travel with you."

"What?" Bolingbroke dropped Mary's hand, ignoring her wince of pain. "You cannot come with me. An army encampment is no place for a woman, let alone one as ill as you."

"Philippa travelled with her husband Edward, your grandfather, on many of his campaigns," she said.

"Philippa was not sick unto death when she did so."

"I am well enough to travel," Mary said, her face now set into resolute stubbornness. "I *will* travel with you, and with England's hopes."

Bolingbroke stood up, his own face set and hard. "Then blame me not if your want finally kills you," he snapped, ignoring the gasps from the ladies standing a respectful distance from the bed. "War is no place for a woman sliding slowly into death. If you die in France, Mary, I will bear no responsibility, for it shall be as a result of your foolishness alone."

"It shall be my responsibility alone," Mary murmured

in agreement, and then smiled a little, as if at an inward thought.

WHEN NEVILLE left Bolingbroke's chamber, he'd wandered through the Tower complex, and out into London. He wasn't altogether sure why, only that a strange curiosity pulled him forward. It was Saturday, a major market day, and the crowds thronging Cheapside, the main thoroughfare through London, were dense and chaotic, and so Neville eventually ducked down a narrow side street where the close overhanging of the buildings rendered the air cool and dim. Here were the workshops and homes of craftsmen, mostly closed, but some open. Neville's pace slowed a little as he spied the glow of lamplight coming from a workshop several houses down on his left.

He stopped, staring at it.

There was no particular reason why he should be so curious about this single workshop. The lamplight in the dim alley certainly wasn't out of place, for Neville doubted full sunlight would ever penetrate the narrow street. Even the fact that the craftsman within was working—the noise of hammers emanated distinctly from the window—should not have been too much of a surprise. Craftsmen took much joy in their work, and this particular man might simply be celebrating London's release by returning to his craft . . . or trying to forget the loss of a loved one in the sweat of his labour.

The hammering stopped, and a shadow moved behind the window.

Neville walked slowly forward.

The shadow moved again, and Neville realised the man was standing, watching him.

Neville walked to the open door, then stopped on the doorstep, looking in.

The workshop was the domain of a carpenter. The lathe, worktable and tools of the carpenter filled the larger portion of the work space, while wood shavings littered the floor. A broom stood to one side, together with a pan—the carpenter was just about to clean up then.

Neville took a deep breath, and looked at the man standing in the half-shadows. "May I enter, good sir?"

"Certainly," said the carpenter, and stepped forward so that Neville could see him clearly.

He was a man in his mid-thirties, lean yet strong, with curly black hair tied back into the nape of his neck with a leather thong, and a well-clipped beard. His face was lined, as if he'd suffered loss, or pain, but his dark eyes were kindly, and full of humour.

"You are new hereabouts," said Neville.

The carpenter grinned. "And how would you know?" he said. "You are a fine lord, and your usual haunt the gaudy palaces of royalty. You cannot tell me you know the carpenter workshops of London so well that a gain or a loss among us comes immediately to your attention. So, if I may, what do you here, my fine lord?"

"May I enter a little further?" Neville said, and the carpenter nodded.

"So long as you don't get in the way of my broom," he said, picking the implement up and beginning to use it to sweep up the shavings.

"I was walking," said Neville, "and saw the light in your window, and thought to speak with you."

"Ah," said the carpenter, working furiously with the broom.

Neville opened his mouth, closed it, and wondered how he could say what he needed to ask. "Carpenter," he managed eventually, "what shall I call you?"

The carpenter looked up briefly from his broom. "James," he said, and Neville nodded.

"James, what will I do? How can I make the decision that I know is best?"

James the carpenter did not look up from his sweeping. "You know what to do."

"Trust you," Neville whispered.

James looked up briefly, smiled, then resumed his sweeping. All was well in his world, so it seemed.

Neville walked over to the worktable, wondering how best to move his thoughts into words. There was so much he wanted to say, and yet no way he knew to say it. Helpless, he studied the table. There were several pieces of beautifully turned and polished wood on its top, inlaid in a decorative pattern with a darker and redder wood, and Neville ran his hand slowly down one of the pieces.

"This work is wondrous," he said. "What are you making?"

James stopped his sweeping, leaned on the broom, and looked at the pieces of wood on the table.

"That is a casket," he said. "My marriage bed."

Startled, Neville looked at the carpenter. *His marriage bed was to be a casket?* "I think your betrothed must be an extraordinary lady. Is she here with you now? Cooking a meal in the kitchen, perhaps?"

James grinned. "No, good sir. My lady has yet to die."

Then he picked up the broom, and waved it at Neville, and as he wielded it, the workshop and carpenter vanished, and Neville was left standing once more on Cheapside, jostled by the crowds.

"SIRE? MAY I have a brief word?"

Bolingbroke stopped in his stride, midway to the door of Mary's chamber. "My Lady Neville, what can I do for you?"

Margaret glanced around.

We need only a moment, Hal. But I must talk with you. Please, bear with my subterfuge.

"I was hoping, sire, that you will permit Doctor Culpeper to travel with the lady your wife to France?"

"Who my lady wife includes in her entourage is of no matter to me, so long as they do not harry or inconvenience my army." *What is it? Be brief, Meg. We cannot*

stand here gabbling on about nonsense for much longer.
"I suppose Culpeper's skills will no doubt be needed."

"Then I thank you, sire, for your reassurance. Doctor Culpeper's liquor brings your lady wife much relief." *Hal, I know why the angels are so confident of Tom.*

Bolingbroke glanced around, wondering what further he could say to keep their inane conversation going. Several other women were passing close by them on their way to prepare Mary for the night and were glancing curiously at Lady Neville and the king.

"Perhaps Culpeper has an apprentice or two who might also prove useful." *Why?*

"I am certain of it, sire." *Hal . . . this afternoon I realised that Rosalind, and Bohun, can speak as you and I do now. They are full-blooded angel children.*

But how is that possible? Tom is not— Bolingbroke suddenly stopped, staring horrified at Margaret.

Tom is not quite what we thought he was, Hal, she whispered into his mind. *No wonder the angels are so confident. Tom—*

No!

Tom is an angel himself.

PART FOUR

The Crippled Angel

An army great our King prepared,
that was both good & strong;
& from Sowhampton is our King
with all his Nauy gone.
he landed in France both safe and sound
with all his warlike traine;
vnto a towne called Harffleete first
he marched vp amaine.
and when he had beseeged the same,
against these fensed walls
to batter down their statlye towers
he sent his English balls.
and he bad them yeeld up to him
themselves & eke their towne,
or else he sware vnto the earth
with cannon to beate them downe.

—Excerpts from Agincourte Battell,
late medieval ballad

Chapter I

Sunday 30th June 1381

✣

PARIS ROARED: "JOAN! Joan! Joan!"

Charles and his entourage entered Paris from the northern gate, but people had been lining the approach road for several miles before the walls of Paris had even been visible. The roar of the crowd, the throwing of flowers, and the sudden leaning forward and touching of the saintly Maid's armour was all very well, but Charles had not forgotten that in the past the Parisians had risen in revolt, determined to do away with their king and to effect some kind of *democracy,* by all the saints in heaven. He hoped that their devotion to Joan would keep him safe this time.

He glanced nervously at the crowds—those he could see through the ranks of mounted men-at-arms he had stationed about his person—wondering if he might see a surly glance thrown his way, a hint of subterfuge, perhaps, even the glint of steel as a dagger was surreptitiously drawn. But all Charles saw was joy and relief and pride, mostly directed towards Joan, true, but that was all to the good, for Joan would keep the masses away from him. Keep them loyal, and remind them of their place in the greater scheme of things.

Charles was not happy at the reports that continued to

come out of England. There had been a revolt, a serious one, but Bolingbroke had managed to put it down in a battle that, rumour had it, claimed over fifteen thousand lives. After his success, however, Bolingbroke had not disbanded the army he had needed to quell the rebels. Instead, intelligence had it that men, horses, equipment and supplies were moving inexorably towards the Cinque Ports from where a French invasion would surely be launched.

Potential site of rebellion or not, Paris was looking ever better to Charles. Its walls were difficult to breach, and the city was well prepared for a siege. Bolingbroke might hope to starve Charles into submission, but if he managed to ignore what was going on outside the walls, and perhaps ask the troubadours to lift the volume of their entertainment, then he would surely survive any attack. Bolingbroke would get bored and go home eventually.

All would be well if he just ignored everything that was worrisome and irritating.

All would be well . . . so long as he could trust those who promised to protect him.

Suddenly nervous, Charles slid his eyes before him to where Joan rode her roan stallion. She was some four or five paces ahead, her horse's pace slowed now to a walk as the citizens of Paris surged about her.

Contrariwise, Charles and his immediate escort rode without any serious impediment at all, save the road blockage about Joan ahead of them.

Joan was leaning down and touching as many hands and faces as she could. Her face seemed both grave and happy all at the same moment. Her mouth smiled, and spoke cheerful words, but her eyes were sorrowful, as if heavy thoughts consumed her.

Why so grave? thought Charles, screwing his face as he tried to think it through. *Should she not be joyous at this reception, at this public adoration? If not, then why not? What did she know? What secret did she not tell him? Did she know of a traitor? A treachery? Was* she *the treachery?*

Charles swallowed, and wondered if trapping himself within Paris was such a good idea, after all.

He glanced behind him to where Philip of Navarre rode.

Philip was staring straight at him with his intense black eyes.

Charles almost slipped out of his saddle in his haste to turn back to the front again.

Philip?

No, no. Not Philip. He had to trust Philip. Who else could save him? Philip was right, Joan and Bolingbroke were the true thorns in his side. Joan had grown useless and unsure (the gravity in her eyes when they should have been joyous was truth enough of that), and Bolingbroke was a repellent Plantagenet born and bred . . . all of them were determined to have France at any cost.

And the nastily efficient manner in which Bolingbroke had put down Hotspur's rebellion was indication enough of his martial ability.

Charles had not yet given Philip total control of his army—for which the man was constantly pressing him—although in the previous week he'd allowed him to begin preparations for war. But Charles was now thinking it might be the time to delegate military control to Philip. It would be best that way. He could keep both the Parisians and the English at a safe distance.

Cheered by his decision, Charles smiled and began waving at the crowds. Most ignored him, preferring to mob Joan, but the Maid herself saw Charles' attempts to be gracious.

She turned in the saddle, throwing back one arm to indicate Charles.

"There rides your king!" she shouted. "Charles, saviour of the French!"

Charles' heart lurched nastily within his chest, and his face paled.

"Charles is France! Charles is France!" she shouted.

Eyes swivelled in Charles' direction, stayed long enough to see the king's nervous attempts to moisten his lips, and the manner in which his hands trembled as they fumbled about his reins, then turned once more to Joan.

"He will lead you to victory," Joan shouted, now standing in her saddle, her eyes shining with the fervour she'd once reserved for the archangel. "Charles will save France! Charles will save France. Hail France! Hail Charles!"

Charles almost panicked. And any respect he'd ever had for Joan fled at that precise moment.

Damn, she was dangerous.

He turned about to look at Philip once more.

Philip stared at him, a sardonic smile playing about his lips. *I told you she was dangerous.*

Charles returned his gaze to Joan. Damn her! Damn her!

Charles was now *completely* determined to hand military control to Philip. At least Philip wouldn't ask, or expect, him to ride with the army. Philip would allow him to remain safely tucked away in whatever palace seemed safest at the time. Philip would always take care of him.

Philip was best, and Joan was looking more and more treacherous every minute.

The crowd still roared and surged about Joan, ignoring her continued impassioned pleas to consider Charles as their saviour.

They might be ill-bred, but they didn't consider themselves stupid.

THE SLOW ride through the crowds meant that they didn't reach the royal palace before late afternoon. By then, everyone from Maid of France to king to lowliest foot soldier assigned as escort was tired, irritable, and wanted nothing more than to eat, then fall down somewhere vaguely comfortable and sleep.

But for Joan, both eating and sleeping were denied her for an hour or so. And yet, she minded not in the least.

As they rode into the courtyard of the palace, a man and a woman emerged from a doorway, standing shyly to one side as valets and servants fussed about the royalty and nobility.

Joan saw them only after she'd dismounted, and handed the more easily removed bits of her armour to a valet.

"Mama?" she whispered. "Papa?"

Catherine had said that she would arrange for Zabillet and Jacques d'Arc to meet Joan in Paris, but Joan had hardly dared to believe it.

Now she rushed over to her parents as far as her exhausted body and heavy armour would allow. She hesitated just as she reached them, clearly wanting to hug them, and yet not wishing to crush them against her armour, and so she dropped to one knee before them, and bowed her head, asking humbly for her parents' blessing.

Jacques' hair and beard were grey now, and his face more lined with care since Joan had last seen him. But his eyes were still warm, and full of love and compassion for his daughter. He stepped forward, and placed his hand on her bowed head.

"Jeanette . . ." he said, and her heart almost broke as he spoke the diminutive of her name. "Jeanette, you always have had, and will always have our love. Do not kneel before us."

Joan lifted her face, and took one of her parents' hands in each of her own. "I want so much to come home with you," she said, "but I cannot. Not yet." Tears formed in her eyes, and slid down her cheeks.

Zabillet's heart almost broke. "You must do as the angels tell you," she said. "We know that."

A peculiar expression came over Joan's face. "I do as my Lord Jesus Christ tells me, and no other."

There was a step behind her, and Jacques and Zabillet looked up, their faces blushing and unsure. "Madam," Jacques said, and bowed deeply as his wife curtsied.

Joan looked around.

Catherine had walked over from her horse, hobbling a little with the stiffness in her body caused by their long ride. She held out a hand to Joan, aiding her to rise.

As soon as she'd regained her feet, Joan also bowed as deeply as her armour would allow her before Catherine. "I do thank you," she said, "for this act was nothing but kindness on your part."

Catherine smiled, nodding a greeting at Jacques and Zabillet, but speaking to Joan. "I would speak with you later," she said. "Perhaps before you retire?"

"Gladly," said Joan.

"JOAN," CATHERINE said to her many hours later as both met in a small chapel in the vaults under the royal palace. "Why not go home with your parents?"

Joan shot her an amused glance, then picked up a small wooden statue of the Virgin from the altar. She stroked it gently with her fingers, as if drawing comfort from it.

"You think to be rid of me so easily?"

"We are no longer the enemies we once were," Catherine said, cross that Joan had chosen that manner in which to respond.

Joan sighed, and put the statue of the Virgin back in its place. "No, not enemies, but I do not think 'friends' yet, either, Catherine. I do not loathe you, I do not fear you, and I understand you, but I do not think myself your friend. You want either Bolingbroke or Philip for France; I want Charles."

Catherine studied the girl's face for a moment, then sank down on the cushions scattered over the steps before the altar. She was very tired, and would be glad to go to bed.

She thought she would have it to herself this night. Philip would be closeted with his commanders and his newfound authority in the war rooms of the palace.

"Oh, Joan," she said, concern making her voice husky. "If you stay, you will die. Both Philip and Charles plan your downfall, and the good Archbishop Regnault de Chartres as well, if the whispers I hear are correct. I beg you to go home with your parents. Mind your father's sheep. Joan, *Charles* plans your downfall as much as anyone. Why this loyalty to him? If you want to save France, why think him the man to do it?"

Joan sat down beside her, staring towards the back wall of the chapel. This late at night there were only two or three oil lamps lit about the altar, and the back wall was covered in flickering shadows.

"Is Philip the man to save France?" she asked softly, her eyes still on the shadowy wall. "Or Bolingbroke?"

Her eyes suddenly shifted back to Catherine. "Both men want France for themselves, and for their own ambitions. Both men will *rape* France."

"And what will Charles do?" Catherine cried. "Suddenly find his spirit and courage and lead France into a glorious and secure future? *Charles?*"

Joan's mouth quirked in genuine amusement. "Charles. Yes, he will. Charles does not yet know himself."

Catherine laughed shortly, disbelievingly. "Charles will do nothing but lead France into muddlement and disarray. He is a fool. Joan . . . if you stay here, you will die. And what will that accomplish? Go home. I say that, not because my scheming wants you out of the way, but because I do not want you to die for nothing."

"I will not die for nothing," Joan said very softly, reaching out to take Catherine's hand. "My death will accomplish France's freedom. It is a simple thing to do, a simple act for a simple girl, and I will not shirk it."

"And is this what the archangel told you?" Catherine said, her voice full of bitterness.

"No," said Joan, smiling secretively, and not explaining her answer. "Catherine, what I do is for joy. Joy for my parents and my village and my homeland. And I do it because I know that my death will give Charles what he needs to be a true king to France."

"You are a fool, Joan," said Catherine, but her voice held no hostility, only despair.

Aye, thought Joan, *once I* was *a fool, but no more.*

"Why care so much for me, Catherine?" she asked. "Why care so much for my fate?"

Catherine took a long while answering. "Because you have been so grievously handled by the angels. As grievously handled as their children."

"Where have you been hiding this heart all these years?" said Joan. She leaned forward and kissed Catherine's cheek gently. "Now go to your bed. You and I are both tired, and if we stay here any longer, we shall weep."

Catherine smiled. "And that would not do, would it? Not for the Maid of France, nor for the Princess Catherine."

Joan grinned, and helped Catherine to rise.

"Charles is an idiot," she said, "but he will not be so forever."

Chapter II

Friday 26th July 1381

☩

HAVING ORDERED ENGLAND'S affairs as best he could, and leaving behind Ralph Raby, Earl of Westmorland, as Justiciar to govern England, Bolingbroke embarked for France a little shy of a month after his announcement to invade. Three score ships set sail from the Cinque Ports, fat with archers, men-at-arms, knights, valets, horses and all the weapons, armour, gear, and as much of their sustenance as they could manage. Ships glistening not only with the spray of the Narrow Seas and the hot sun above, but also with the jewel-like banners, pennants and sails that strained at every masthead and pole and rope, and with the shimmer of light from the helmets and weapons of those men-at-arms on top of the decks.

Three score ships, carrying an army of thirty-five thousand: England's chance at France.

The preparations for this invasion force had not gone unnoticed by France. Philip of Navarre, now in control of Charles' military force, was almost certain of Bolingbroke's destination: Harfleur, the garrison that guarded the mouth of the Seine. Bolingbroke would come straight for Paris—no use dawdling sightseeing about the provinces when the crown both literally and metaphorically rested in Paris—and if he wanted to secure his approach to Paris, he would need to subdue Harfleur.

Philip had every intention of ensuring that Bolingbroke got bogged down in the salt marshes surrounding Harfleur.

He and Bolingbroke may have made a bargain regarding France—once both Joan and Charles were disposed of, whoever Catherine gave her hand to in marriage received the throne—but Philip trusted Bolingbroke not an inch.

He trusted Catherine even less. She refused to marry him, and thus her heart must be set on Bolingbroke. Philip knew he was going to have to fight to finally wrest the crown away from Joan, Charles *and* Bolingbroke and his Englishmen.

Harfleur had for generations been a well-defended town and garrison. By the time the English fleet hove into view at the head of the wide bay leading to the mouth of the Seine on the dawn of the twenty-sixth of July, it was virtually unassailable.

BOLINGBROKE STOOD on the deck of his flagship, the *Grace Dieu,* staring at the coastline fifty yards away. The ship swayed vigorously beneath his feet, tugging impatiently at its anchor, but he did not notice his movement. The coastline, and the geography of the landscape surrounding Harfleur, occupied his entire attention.

"There," he said, pointing. "Land there and climb to the top of the hill. It will be the best spot from which to observe, and too far from Harfleur's walls for arrow flight. Get back as soon as you can . . . I want to begin disembarkation today."

The two men who stood beside him, Lord Hungerford and Sir Gilbert Umfraville, nodded, then turned and led a party of some thirty-six men down rope ladders to two small boats bobbing at the *Grace Dieu*'s side.

Bolingbroke waited until he saw them land, scurrying for cover and the path to the top of the rolling hills to the northwest of Harfleur, then he went below to oversee the final preparations for landing.

As he was about to duck down into the hatchway he saw Neville standing at the stern of the ship.

They stared at each other, locking eyes, then Bolingbroke disappeared below.

NEVILLE CONTINUED watching the now empty hatchway for some time before returning his gaze to the choppy seas and the row after row of ships at anchor behind the *Grace Dieu*.

For the past few weeks, ever since that day he had talked with James the carpenter in his workshop in London, both Bolingbroke and Margaret had been assiduously avoiding him. This was an easy matter on Bolingbroke's part, for he was a king, not only governing one realm, but preparing an invasion of another, and he had many things to occupy him. On those few occasions Bolingbroke could not manage to avoid Neville, he spoke with Neville stiffly and coolly, as if he were the most treasonous piece of filth in the realm.

What friendship they had reforged before Shrewsbury was patently torn asunder.

Margaret had a more difficult time of avoidance, for Neville was her husband, and she must share his bed at night. Nevertheless, Neville felt such a vast distance between them within that bed that she might as well have been inhabiting the mythical Cathay. She would hardly speak to him, replying only in monosyllables whenever he tried to engage her in conversation, and refusing to meet his eyes. He saw more of her back than any other side of her.

It was, in many respects, a return to the Margaret who had so rejected him after her rape at Richard's and de Vere's hands.

So, Margaret and Bolingbroke avoided him, and turned their backs to him. What had he done? Did they somehow know of what he did in St John's Chapel within the Tower complex? Were they somehow angry that Christ was freed from his torment?

Or had he committed some other sin?

Whatever it was, Neville found he did not care overmuch. Bolingbroke and he had been drifting apart for a very long time. A brief reunion of their friendship during the campaign against Hotspur was apparently not enough to bridge permanently the divide between them. Margaret and he ... well ... he loved her, and wanted whatever had come between them to be resolved, but he was not going to moon after her, or chase after her, or beg her forgiveness as he had after her rape. If she did not want to come to him and broach whatever troubled her, then it must needs continue to trouble her.

Neville had other things on his mind.

The decision. It would be made here, in France. Bolingbroke had long ago told him this, and now Neville could *feel* it, tugging at his blood. Here, in France, and within weeks at the most. Everyone who needed to be a part of that decision was present: Margaret, as part of Mary's entourage; Bolingbroke; Joan—presumably still with Charles, but Neville had no doubt that sooner or later fate would see her in Bolingbroke's camp; and Neville himself. At least his children were well out of it, sent back home to Halstow Hall in the company of Agnes and a grumbling Robert Courtenay, who would have vastly preferred to be participating in the glory of a final French defeat than minding two small children.

Of all the thoughts that eased Neville's mind, the knowledge that if all went well, he could return to the love of his children comforted him the most.

If all went well.

Neville assumed that Bolingbroke and Margaret were as much aware of the closeness of the decision as he was himself, and he wondered that they so damaged their cause in turning their backs and hearts against him. What ploy was this on their part? Did they not need him to so love Margaret that he would hand her his soul? Neville wondered if their coldness was a conscious ploy. After all, these tactics had worked perfectly once before, bringing him to love's heel, and it was not beyond the realms of possibility that they would try it again.

After all, they surely sensed his hesitancy towards Margaret. Perhaps they knew they now needed to pull out all stops in their effort to win him utterly to their cause.

Neville slowly shook his head, his eyes unfocused, the ships in the distance only shimmering shapes in the rapidly strengthening sun. *Did they not yet realise how he hated to be manipulated? And did they not realise how much he wanted to be able to hand Margaret his soul? To deny the angels?*

"Ah!" Neville said softly, blinking as he suddenly became aware of the time. Mary would be awake by now, and hopefully washed and tended and gowned by Margaret and her other ladies. Neville moved towards the hatchway, thinking to spend breakfast with Mary. He had found himself spending almost all day with her recently, more time than usual. Partly this was because of Bolingbroke's and Margaret's coolness towards him, but it was also because of their shared experience in the Chapel of St John's. Neville had told Mary of the carpenter he'd met in the workshop off Cheapside (although he had not told her of what James the carpenter was making), and every day they spoke of it, marvelling. Neville still had no idea how he would manage to navigate the angels' test, but he trusted in Christ that he would find a way to free mankind through giving his soul unhesitatingly to Margaret.

If only she wasn't treating him so badly . . .

HUNGERFORD AND Umfraville were back by midday, having concluded safely their scouting and observation of Harfleur. After listening to their reports, Bolingbroke gave the order to disembark. Three by three the ships took their turn in approaching a sandy spit a few miles to the west of Harfleur, somewhat protected from the rolling waves and winds of the Narrow Seas. There the ships disgorged their cargo of war.

The process was agonisingly slow. Only a few ships could approach the spit at any given time, and then it took them a good few hours each to unload. Three days passed, three days of Bolingbroke and his commanders anxiously pressing for everyone to hurry, before the process was complete.

Neville happened to be on the spit as the last ship disembarked its cargo. These were mostly workmen—blacksmiths, carpenters, armourers, grooms and cooks—and just as Neville was about to turn away, a familiar figure caught his eye.

James the carpenter, bowed and stooped under what was unmistakably an intricately carved casket, slowly made his way down the gangplank.

He saw Neville staring at him, nodded and smiled, then continued towards the English camp with the rest of the tradesmen.

Chapter III

Tuesday 30th July 1381

✚

BOLINGBROKE ESTABLISHED HIS camp only a mile distant from Harfleur in the gently rolling hills to its northwest. On the Saturday, while still waiting for the majority of his force to disembark, Bolingbroke had sent north the Earl of Suffolk and a force of some two thousand men to circle Harfleur in an effort to secure the three roadways that led into the town.

They were only partially successful, as Bolingbroke now heard.

The Earl of Warwick was leaning over a map on a trestle table that had been set up in front of Bolingbroke's pavilion. A shade had been erected over the table and the men grouped about under it to protect themselves from the hot sun. Before them the ground slowly sank towards Harfleur, its walls and twenty-six towers aflutter with pennants.

"The French knew we were coming," Warwick said, and Bolingbroke hitched a shoulder up.

"Of course. Our preparations could not have gone unnoticed."

"Yes . . . well," Warwick replied. "They knew enough in advance, and had enough forethought in advance, to protect Harfleur with everything they could. See." His finger jabbed down at the river valley to the north of the town. "They've dammed the River Lézande, and now the valley is nothing but a lake a hundred yards wide. Suffolk had to detour above it, and it took him a day longer than expected."

Now Warwick's finger fell on the salt marshes to the east of the town. They were bisected by a single road. "Harfleur managed to get in a convoy of food and other supplies on Sunday afternoon and evening, before Suffolk could complete his encirclement. Three hundred carts and some five score pack mules crossed the road."

Bolingbroke muttered a curse. "But Suffolk has now managed to encircle the town?"

"Aye, as best he can." Warwick's finger drew a wide arc on the map from their position in the west, across the northern flooded river valley and then down to the east of Harfleur to the coastline. "We have them surrounded on land on three sides, and, of course—"

"Our ships cover the south in the bay," Bolingbroke completed for him. He raised his head from the map once more and stared at the vista before him. Harfleur was encircled by the English, true, but it was also very, very well defended. Assaulting this town would be difficult in the extreme. Harfleur sat on the bay formed by the expansive mouth of the River Seine. To the north was the river valley of the Lézande, now dammed, although water from the river still flowed through the town. To the east were salt marshes. To the south the bay, entrance into the port of Harfleur being via a small harbour. This was now crisscrossed with heavy chains below the surface of the water, and Bolingbroke knew there was no way he could sail his ships into the harbour itself.

Harfleur was surrounded by a perimeter wall of some two miles. It was well constructed, protected by its twenty-six towers—some with cannon—and a moat. Only three gates broached the wall. One to the northeast (leading to the now flooded river valley), one to the southeast (leading to the salt marsh road) and one to the southwest (leading to the hills upon which the English were now encamped). All three gates were heavily protected by wooden barbicans, earthworks and an extra moat dug about all three.

And each would be a bastard to approach, let alone broach. Bolingbroke's preferred method, to bombard the wall and towers about all three gates and then ram them once the defences were in disarray, was not going to work here. Both the placement of the wood and earthworks and the wide moats made that impossible.

That left an all-out attack on the walls—an option not to be considered until the town had been starved and bombarded through a lengthy siege—or . . .

"Tunnelling," Bolingbroke said. "It is our only option. I can't afford to waste months here starving Harfleur into submission while Philip and Charles manage to deploy their army to their best advantage."

Warwick and the other commanders present all nodded. They'd reached the same conclusion themselves. Tunnelling under a town's walls until they collapsed was a tried and proven tactic, and Bolingbroke had among his engineers some of the most experienced tunnellers in Christendom. With luck and effort, Harfleur's defeat could be accomplished within two weeks.

With luck, and the grace of God.

"Meanwhile," said Bolingbroke, "we can set the artillery on these hills, spanning the entire west and northwest section of the walls." He pointed to three spots, one to the south of him, and two to the north. "There, there and there. Bombard the walls by day and night. The French will be so consumed with trying to negate the effects of the bombardment they will hopefully neglect to set aside men to observe for tunnelling."

He paused, returning his gaze to study the town itself. "Target the walls, but also the steeple of the church of Saint Martin. It will no doubt cause much distress if we manage to demolish their beloved church."

And with that he turned away.

* * *

BY THAT evening the artillery had moved their three massive cannon into position. The cannon were new, commissioned by Bolingbroke at the start of his reign, and the biggest Christendom had yet seen. Cumbersome, bulky, difficult and always with the potential to blow up in everyone's faces, the cannon could nevertheless hurl two hundred pound missiles well over a mile in distance. The entire army seemed to have adopted them as mascots, and had given all three names.

London sat atop a hill nearest to the coast, from where it could bombard the harbour and southwestern portions of Harfleur's walls. The grimly but aptly named *England's Messenger* sat in the central portion of the western hills, from where it could send its message of hate and ill will deep into the town. And, finally, the *Beloved Mary* was positioned farther to the north, from where she could spit her missiles into the northern defences of Harfleur. (Mary, when she'd heard the men had named one of the cannon for her, was said to have shuddered and to have turned aside her head.)

That night began the bombardment of Harfleur.

Chapter IV

Monday 5th August 1381

✛

"WHERE IS HE do you think, Tom?"

Neville did not have to ask of whom Mary spoke. "Somewhere close, I am sure."

"I dreamed of him last night."

Neville's first reaction to this statement was one of utter gratefulness—at least Mary had managed some sleep. Her condition was now pitiful, and Neville did not think she was long for this world.

Was she the reason the carpenter carried the casket?

The voyage itself had almost killed her. Neville remembered how ill Mary had been after their voyage into exile in Flanders; now she looked tenfold worse than she had then. She had lost so much weight she was skeletal. Her bones showed through her flesh, and her skin had collapsed so greatly about her face she looked more like breathing skull than living woman. Her skin was papery and grey, her eyes dull, her lips cracked.

Two of her bones in her left arm had broken in the effort to lift her out of the *Grace Dieu,* and the arm rested encased in a sling and cushioned splints. Mary was now so fragile that every movement threatened to break her apart.

Normally Neville would have held her hand, now all he

did was stroke the back of her right hand very gently with his forefinger, careful not to break the papery skin.

"Did Culpeper give you a dose of his liquor?" he asked, wondering if this is what had aided her to sleep.

"Nay." Her tongue, grey and swollen, licked at her lips. "I refused his liquor last night."

Neville wondered at her strength, not only in enduring the agony that must now be coursing through her, but also at resisting the entreaties of her ladies, no doubt distraught that she would refuse the numbing liquor.

"I wanted to see," Mary continued, "if my dreams were caused by the liquor . . . or by something else."

Neville smiled very softly, glad for her, knowing that Christ in truth must have come to her.

"I dreamed of a carpenter's shop," she said. "It was full of the sweet scent of shavings, and soft, gentle light. I saw our Lord there, working. He turned, as if knowing my presence, and smiled at me, loving, comforting, and said my name. I woke then, and for several hours I had no pain."

"It is a shame we cannot bottle dreams," Neville said, "for methinks they do you much more good than Culpeper's liquor."

Mary laughed, a little breathlessly, and when she spoke again it was to talk of other things.

LATER THAT evening a delegation of Englishmen rode deep into the orchards four miles to the northwest of their encampment, gathering fruit for the army. They'd grown tired of the dull fare of army provisions, and the apples on these trees looked as tempting as any they'd ever seen.

Chapter V

Wednesday 7th August 1381

✠

MASTER GILES, BOLINGBROKE'S chief engineer, flinched as yet another dull thunder rolled over his head. He was crouched deep in a tunnel, somewhere in the no-man's-land between the hills of the English encampment and the western walls of Harfleur.

The thunder of *London* was followed a half-second later by an enormous rumble, and Giles crouched even further, his arms laced protectively over his head. Clods of dirt crumbled over him, but nothing worse, and after a moment he dared peek out from under his arms.

The tunnel was low enough that everyone within it had to crouch, but reasonably wide, so that they could pass each other with ease. Wood, carried all the way from England, for Bolingbroke had long anticipated his need of tunnelling, shored up the hanging wall, or roof, of the tunnel. Dull light glowed from oil lamps placed regularly the length of the tunnel, enough light to show that Giles was as filthy as every other man sorry enough to have to work down here.

"How close are we?" muttered Jack Williamson, apprentice to Giles.

"Too close for comfort," Giles replied. "I don't want

any of us in this tunnel once it gets too much further. Hear that rumble after *London* fired?"

Williamson nodded.

"That was masonry falling from Harfleur's wall," Giles said. "If we're close enough to hear that . . ."

Williamson took a deep breath, unconsciously looking over his shoulder towards their escape route. "How much longer then?"

"A day. Then we set the explosives."

A day, thought Williamson. *A day . . . why didn't I take up potting, like my father wished?*

Giles moved cautiously forward, murmuring to the miners before him, then shouldering past them to inspect the face of the tunnel. "Dig down now," he said. "About three yards. The foundations of the wall will not be far ahead of us. Then dig the pit north. Within twenty yards you should connect up with your neighbouring tunnel."

The idea was to dig great trenches, perhaps some thirty yards in length, under the foundations of the wall. These would then be packed with explosives and, when set off, the section of wall should, in theory, come tumbling down.

Giles murmured encouragement to the miners, clapped one of them on the shoulder, then rejoined Williamson. "Let's get out of here," he said.

Williamson nodded eagerly.

Chapter VI

Thursday 8th August 1381

✠

"IS ALL IN readiness?" Bolingbroke asked Master Giles. The engineer glanced at the king. The man's face was tense, and the skin about his eyes and mouth so tight that the engineer thought the king was likely suffering a pounding headache.

"Yes, sire," he said, returning his gaze to Harfleur a mile distant. Both he and the king, plus a score of commanders, messengers and assorted valets stood before Bolingbroke's pavilion on the hill overlooking the town and harbour. "I need only to give the signal."

And that everything *was* in readiness was, to Master Giles' mind, a profound miracle. He'd spent the entire night in the tunnel, a quavering Williamson at his side, setting most of the explosives himself. Yesterday afternoon many of the miners had begun to complain of griping in the guts. Within an hour or so, their griping had turned to such massive diarrhoea that they'd had to return to their spots within the encampment to rest. Giles was forced to find replacements for them—and that was not the easiest of tasks. Few ordinary soldiers wanted to go down, or had the ability or skills to work within, the tunnels, and so those left had to perform herculean tasks in order to get both pits and explosives ready.

This morning Williamson reported to Giles that five of the miners struck with the griping had died during the night.

Rumour had it that several score men had died among the entire encampment, and that the French had resorted to poisoning in order to thwart the English attempts to broach the walls.

"The bombardment went well last night," Bolingbroke said reflectively. His right hand rubbed at a spot on his temple, and Master Giles' sympathy went out to him. He would not like to be responsible for twenty thousand men and a nation's hopes in this dog of a country whose natives resorted to unchivalric poisoning to repel their enemies. No wonder he had a headache.

"Aye, Your Grace," Giles said, then continued to answer the question he knew was lurking behind Bolingbroke's statement. "*London, England's Messenger* and the *Beloved Mary,* as well as fifteen of the smaller cannon, are primed, ready to fire. If it please God that these explosives work, then their bombardment will complete Harfleur's doom."

"You are a good man," Bolingbroke said, his fingers still working at his temple. "I am well served in you."

Giles ducked his head, both pleased and embarrassed at the same time. He had only done his job, and he would lay down his life for this king if it were required.

Bolingbroke's eyes slid Giles' way, and he smiled. "Perhaps a bombardment might shake this headache loose, Giles?"

"I pray it be so, Your Grace."

Bolingbroke smiled. "I think only an English victory shall cure this throbbing, Giles. I shall not rest until the mayor and council of Harfleur are bent on their knees before me."

He gestured at Hungerford and Suffolk, both standing close. "All is in readiness?"

"Aye, Your Grace," both replied simultaneously.

Bolingbroke took a deep breath. "Good, then let us begin. Giles, the signal, if you please."

Giles inclined his head. "Your Grace." He stepped over to a man-at-arms and took from him his pike. About its sharpened end Giles fastened a length of crimson cloth, then he hefted the pike, and waved it slowly from side to side above his head.

Behind them, in the dip of the hills hidden from French eyes, miners scurried into the openings of mines, eager to light the fuses and then retreat back into daylight.

"Pray to sweet Jesu," Bolingbroke muttered, "that we blow up the French and not us!"

There ensued long, tense moments of waiting. Deep beneath his feet Bolingbroke knew that sparks were blazing along almost a mile of fuse lines, running towards six pits with their bellyfuls of explosives.

If this did not work, he did not know what else he could do. A lengthy siege was, well, too lengthy, and he could not afford to leave Harfleur intact at his back. Sweet Jesu, hear me now, let this succeed . . . let this succeed . . .

The earth lurched under Bolingbroke's feet, and he grabbed at Giles for support. There came a low rumble, more felt than heard, and then, for just a moment, there was both silence and stillness.

"Giles?" Bolingbroke said finally. "What—?"

He stopped, mouth agape. The entire western section of Harfleur's walls suddenly sagged. Then, slowly, slowly, slowly, seven of the towers along the length of that section began to topple backwards, into the town itself. Most of the wall itself toppled into the moat, completely filling it.

"Now!" Bolingbroke shouted. "Now!"

Giles turned about and began to wave his hands frantically. Moments later the bellies and mouths of *London, England's Messenger* and the *Beloved Mary* boomed and belched, sending incendiary shells hurtling towards the town. Another pause, another few heartbeats, then the shells hit, all on the now-tumbled-down southwest gate.

Bolingbroke stared, taking one tense step forward, waiting for the smoke to clear.

Then he breathed out in relief: the incendiary shells had set both gate and the wooden barbicans about it on fire. The entire western section, walls, towers, moat barbicans and gate, were now destroyed.

Harfleur's defences were broached.

WITHIN THE hour Bolingbroke sent a message with Lord Hungerford to the mayor and aldermen of Harfleur. It was a simple message, and honest, for Bolingbroke was well aware that if he won this country, he would also need to win its citizens' love. *Fear not, for I am not come to waste either your land or your lives. Surrender now, peacefully, and all will be well.*

By that evening, Hungerford returned with the news Bolingbroke wanted. An hour behind Hungerford would follow the mayor and twelve aldermen of Harfleur, delivering to the English king the first conquest of his French campaign.

Chapter VII

Monday 12th August 1381

— i —

✢

PHILIP FOLDED THE letter, then tapped it reflectively against his teeth once or twice as he regarded the Earl of Suffolk and his five-man escort.

Then he glanced at Charles, sitting nervous and fidgety in the chair at his side. Charles looked at him, perhaps hoping for a glance at the letter, but Philip had absolutely no intention of allowing the man to see it at all. No, this was between himself and Bolingbroke only.

"You may rest here this night," Philip finally said to Suffolk, "and enjoy His Grace's hospitality."

At that Charles' eyes widened, as if he thought Philip meant that he should himself keep the English delegation amused through the night.

Philip sighed. "And in the morning you shall have safe escort back to the English lines."

"And the answer, Your Grace?" Suffolk said with a slight bow of acknowledgement of Philip's assurance of safety.

"You may tell Bolingbroke that I am not one to forget my obligations," Philip said. "He will know to what I refer."

Again Suffolk bowed and, taking his leave, turned to

withdraw himself and his delegation from the presence of the two kings.

"Wait," Philip called, standing from his chair. He walked over to Suffolk. "Also tell your King Bolingbroke," he said to the earl in a low voice, "that his gift shall not come without a price. Twenty thousand gold pieces, I think."

"Your Grace, I do not think that—"

"Bolingbroke asks for too much for free," Philip hissed, "including my goodwill. Tell him that his gift comes for a price, and that price is twenty thousand gold pieces."

Suffolk's face froze. He glanced behind Philip to Charles, slouched in his chair and chewing on a fingernail as he watched what was going on in the centre of the hall. "Perhaps His Grace the King Charles ought to be—"

"This is a contract between *me* and *Bolingbroke,* you rat-eyed wart. Just do as you are told."

For a long moment Suffolk held Philip's furious stare, then he capitulated. He took a long step backwards, bowed yet once more, then turned and exited the hall, his delegation at his back.

"Philip?" Charles called. "What was all that about? Let me see Bolingbroke's letter."

"Do you want to lead France's army yourself?" Philip said, pivoting on a heel to face Charles. "Would *you* like to be the one facing England's cannon on the dawn that is surely coming?"

Charles flushed, as much at Philip's anger as at the idea that he should personally lead France's army. "No, no, of course not, Philip. But I was just curious. What can Bolingbroke have wanted?"

You simpleton, Philip thought, but he moderated his voice as he replied. "He wants victory, as always," he said. "This," he waved the letter about, "was merely an opening ploy in the great game which is about to commence."

"But you have agreed to do what he asked?"

"I do not dance to his tune. I only intend to manipulate

Bolingbroke's ambition to France's advantage. Now, if you will excuse me, I have a war to win . . . as you are so patently loath to do yourself."

Then Philip turned smartly on his heel and left the hall.

HE WALKED into the palace gardens, wincing a little at the smell of the raw sewage and rotting animal corpses that clogged the Seine. *Sweet Lord. The stench of this city!* Then he put the odour from his mind as he once more read the contents of Bolingbroke's letter.

> *Philip,*
> *I come to conclude the bargain we made in Gravensteen one year past precisely. Hand to me Joan, the Maid of France, that I may dispose of her as I will. Then we will bow both our wills before Catherine, so that she may decide which of us she takes as husband . . . and thus which of us takes France to wife.*
> *Philip. You will by now have heard that Harfleur is fallen. No town, no city, no man can withstand me. You do not wish to take this to the battlefield. Hand me Joan, then we allow Catherine to make the choice.*
> *Send me your agreeance by Suffolk, and I shall expect the Maid within the week.*

Philip snorted in derision then slowly tore the letter into tiny pieces before dunking them into a fishpond, where trout eagerly ate them. *Allow Catherine to make the choice, indeed.* Once he'd been sure of her—certainly he'd been sure of her when he'd made that stupid pact with Bolingbroke!—but now? No, not now. She refused to wed him; she refused to give him a child.

All this she must be reserving for Bolingbroke.

Philip no longer believed either her loving caresses or her protestations of love.

So . . . what to do?

Philip considered his options.

Giving Joan to Bolingbroke could only work to Philip's advantage. One, it would mean that Bolingbroke would believe that Philip was still going to adhere to the bargain they'd made in Gravensteen. Two, it would get Joan out of Philip's way once and for all. (Philip had no doubts that Bolingbroke meant to put her to death . . . he certainly couldn't afford to keep her alive.) Joan was too damned determined to ensure Charles' place on France's throne. She definitely needed to go . . . and giving her, anonymously as it were, to the English would be the best way to do it. The French would blame the English, and Philip could wail with the best of them. That led to the third and best reason to hand Joan over to Bolingbroke. The girl was France's mascot, its saint, its star of fortune. The French people would go berserk with rage the instant the English got their horrid hands on their Maid. It would rouse them as nothing else would.

Frankly, Philip no longer liked Bolingbroke's chances once he faced an infuriated and obsessively vengeful French army and nation. Making sure that Joan found her way into the hands of the English only ever worked in his favour.

In this instance, Philip fully intended keeping his part of the bargain between himself and Bolingbroke. Of course, to do it successfully, he'd need to involve Regnault de Chartres, for if Philip handed the girl in body to Bolingbroke, then de Chartres would need to hand him the ammunition to try her. There would be no need to share the twenty thousand gold pieces with the archbishop, for Philip did not expect Bolingbroke to pay it; if Philip had acquiesced to Bolingbroke's demand without demurring in some manner then Bolingbroke would have been instantly suspicious.

But to keep the second part of the bargain? Allow Catherine to make the choice? No. That Philip could never allow to happen.

Philip meant to hand Joan over to the English and then, while they were consumed with rigging a trial and then a death, he would swing his army north, preparing to attack the English from behind. Even now, he'd heard, Bolingbroke was leading his army into Rouen (which had capitulated without a struggle). The city was a third of the way along the Seine towards Paris, and it would give Philip ample room to swing north and then behind the English lines.

Philip sat down on a bench, stretching his legs out in the hot sun, and grinned.

He'd heard that Bolingbroke was having some troubles. In the days after his capture of Harfleur, almost half of his army had fallen ill with such desperate griping in the guts that many of them were unable to move. Ten thousand, Philip had heard from his spies, had either succumbed to the griping, or were so ill they'd been shipped back to England.

Worse, at least for Bolingbroke, was that the disease showed no sign of abating. No one knew precisely what had caused it—many cited the unripened apples that the English had eaten in the cartload from orchards to the northwest of Harfleur—but it was decimating England's finest.

Philip closed his eyes and tilted his face back in order to enjoy the full caress of the sun, sending a quick prayer of gratefulness to God and his angels for their timely aid.

Soon Bolingbroke would have twin evils to counter: the spreading sickness within his army, and the wrath of the French people for murdering their beloved Maid.

Chapter VIII

Monday 12th August 1381

— ii —

✠

JOAN PACED BACK and forth, back and forth, her mouth dry with nerves and her stomach roiling with fear. She'd known there would be a betrayal, and had known from which direction it was likely to come, but now that it was nigh . . . well, premonition was never the most easy of companions.

The news regarding Harfleur's fall had come two days ago, and the arrival of Bolingbroke's envoy this morning. Joan had no doubts whatsoever that the betrayal would come soon.

She wondered vaguely what price Philip had demanded for her capture.

Thirty pieces of silver, or had the price gone up since Christ's time?

Ah! Joan shook herself out of her thoughts. She drew in a deep breath, closing her eyes, and prayed for courage to the Lord Jesus Christ and the woman who comforted him.

For a long moment she stood still, her eyes closed, her head thrown back, and then she smiled very slightly, her peace of mind restored.

She opened her eyes, then walked to the door of her chamber.

CHARLES WAS in a slumber so light, it could hardly be called a sleep. Far from a haven, Paris now seemed a trap—the cursed Bolingbroke was within a few days' march. Why on earth had he come *here* of all places? Why hadn't he fled south? Sweet Lord Christ. Who was it persuaded him to Paris in the first instance?

It must have been Philip, dark-browed, dark-hearted Philip. He couldn't have possibly thought of this all by himself.

Had he done the right thing in giving Philip control of the military? Could he be trusted?

No.

Could he wrest control away from Philip and give it to someone else?

No. Philip would never stand for it. Even now the snake was likely sending assassination squads to his chamber.

Charles whimpered, then jerked into full wakefulness. He pulled the sheet to his chin, his eyes moving fearfully about the dark room.

Was that chest there when he'd gone to bed?

Yes, he supposed so.

Was that table slightly out of place, as if someone had pushed against it while moving softly about in the dark?

Yes, almost certainly so.

Charles whimpered again, squirming further down beneath his covers.

A draught of air slid softly, almost apologetically, over his face.

For an instant Charles did not react. Everyone expected draughts in something as leaky and cold as the Louvre.

Save that his chamber was closed tight against the night *(and assassins)* and there should be no draught.

Charles drew in a terrified breath, breaking out into a sweat.

"Who's there?" he said. "Who? I command you, stand forth!"

What was he saying? What was he saying? Perhaps he should pretend to go back to asleep, and then whoever was in the room might leave. Might . . .

"It is only me, Your Grace," said a soft voice, and Charles managed a sigh of relief.

Which instantly turned into imperious anger. "What are you doing here, Joan? What, I say? My private chamber is no place for you."

"There was a time you would not have said so," Joan said, emerging from the shadows clinging to the tightly shuttered windows. "There was a time when you would have drawn comfort from my presence."

"You dare not speak to me like that," Charles said, emerging from under his covers to stare at the girl. She'd stopped a foot or so from his bed, and now had the extraordinarily bad manners to sink down onto her knees, leaning her elbows on the bed and clasping her hands in an attitude of prayer.

"What are you doing? Go away."

"Charles," she said, giving him the benefit of no title or flatteries, "my time is almost nigh. Soon I will be betrayed—"

"Go *away!*"

"—and you will be left by yourself. Charles, you must not despair—"

"Have you led assassins here?" he asked as her opening statements finally sank through into his consciousness. "Have you?"

Joan finally rose. "They will come for me tonight, I expect, but—"

Charles gave a wail of fear. *"Get out of this chamber. Guard! Guard!"*

Joan's right hand snaked out and delivered a hearty slap to Charles' cheek. "Be quiet and listen to me."

Charles was shocked into silence. She had hit him. Her! The Maid! Was *she* an assassin? *Lord Jesus Christ, save me now! Lord Jesus Christ, save me now!*

"*Listen* to me, Charles! By the morning you will be on your own. Paris is dangerous, too dangerous for you."

She finally had his complete attention.

"Flee south, somewhere safe, somewhere surrounded by loyal French counts and vassals. Wait for word."

"Wait for word? What do you mean?"

She smiled very sadly, even though she knew he could not see it. "Wait for word, Charles. You will know it when it comes for you."

Charles did not like the sound of that at all. "Joan," he began, then wailed in terror as the door to his chamber burst open.

Five men, all darkly cloaked and masked, leaped into the room.

Steel glinted in the faint light.

Charles gave another shriek, trying to clamber over to the other side of the bed, but hampered by the suddenly wet, urine-soaked sheets that clung about his lap and upper legs.

"Be still," Joan whispered. "They have not come for you."

She faced her abductors calmly. "With whose authority do you come for me?" she asked as the first of the men reached her.

"With this authority, lady," said the first of the men, and he clubbed her over her head with the hilt of his sword.

Joan slumped to the floor, clinging to the last vestiges of a consciousness riven by Charles' shrieks: *Take her! Take her! Leave me alone!*

You poor fool, she thought, sliding deeper into unconsciousness. *One day you will look back to this moment and think it the most cowardly of your life.*

And with that thought she blacked out completely.

Chapter IX

Thursday 15th August 1381

— i —

✠

NICHOLAS CULPEPER WIPED his forehead with his forearm; its sleeve was stained a light brown with two days' worth of his sweat. He slowly sat on the bed of the soldier, cursing his stiff back, and hoping that it was stiff only because of his two days of work without rest, and not as a harbinger of disease.

This bloody flux that now consumed the English army was almost as bad as the pestilence that had gripped London.

It was not killing so fast, nor so horribly, but kill it did, and increasing numbers of men died each day. They'd moved from Harfleur, where the flux had first struck, to Rouen two days ago, the passage of the English army marked by a trail of bloodstained shit.

Thank sweet Jesu that the French had not the forethought—or the ability—to attack while they were on the march. Christ, the archers were too doubled over to be able to draw their bows, and few knights dared put on a single piece of armour, let alone mount a horse, for fear they'd have to squat in the roadside dust the instant they did so.

"Fetch me a bowl and water, and a cup of the opium and primrose infusion," Culpeper said to the nearest of his assistants, Will Cooper. As Cooper went to do his master's bidding, Culpeper sighed, sponging the face of the man on the bed. He wished he had a better stock of herbs, and more variety, than those he'd brought with him. Apart from his duties to the queen (*who, praise Jesu, had not been struck with the flux . . . yet*), Culpeper had expected his duties, as those of every other physician travelling with the English army, to encompass battlefield wounds . . . not the squirting misery that now confronted him.

Cooper returned with a cup of the infusion, and Culpeper gently raised the man's head and dribbled the liquid between his lips. The opium would relieve the agony in the man's gut, while both it and the primrose would go some way towards calming the almost continual spasms that gripped his bowel.

The man gulped, his face sheened with grey sweat, then collapsed back onto his pillow.

He moaned and rolled over, curving himself about his belly, his eyes staring, his hands clawing at the mattress.

Culpeper rose hurriedly, taking a step back as the man's bowels voided themselves in a violent spasm, his face screwing up in distaste at the foul stench that rose from the bed.

"Find someone to clean him up," he said to Cooper.

Will Cooper, a young man of twenty-two or -three years and with a remarkable stoicism of expression given the circumstances of the moment, silently said a quick prayer of gratefulness that at least Culpeper hadn't asked him to clean the soldier up. But finding someone *else* to do it wasn't going to be easy. The sick numbered three hundred in this market hall alone, stretched out in rows on thin pallets, and there were only some ten or twelve assorted servants and as yet unaffected soldiers available to aid them.

And every one of the sick squirted at least five or six

times an hour. The problem was not only in the lack of helpers, but also in the ever-increasing number of rags, linens and herbal preparations needed to clean and treat the sick.

"First the pestilence, and now this," Cooper said.

Culpeper looked at him sharply. "And what do you mean by that?"

Cooper gave a small shrug. "Many mutter between their spasms that King Hal is a singularly unlucky man," he said. "Rebellion, pestilence, and now this bloody flux. It is like the seven plagues that God rained down on the Pharaoh for daring to keep Moses and the Israelites enslaved. What else shall we endure?"

Culpeper blew his breath out in exasperation, fighting the urge to slap Cooper's face. "This bloody flux was caused by the men gorging themselves on unripe apples," he said.

"But so *many* men, and not all of them apple eaters," Cooper murmured.

"*And* caused by the unhealthy air of the salt marshes about Harfleur," Culpeper said. "And who knows how it continues to spread among the soldiers. All these men, living in such close, unsanitary quarters . . . Now, get moving, Cooper, or I'll set you to washing the rags the servants use to wipe the men's arses. Move!"

Cooper scurried off.

BOLINGBROKE STOOD at the window of his main day chamber of Rouen's castle, staring at the city spread out before him. Rouen was a particularly beautiful city, with majestic spires and towers, gilded roofs, marbled balconies and intricately carved wooden fretwork on most buildings. Beautiful it remained after the English had occupied it two days ago, but only superficially, for now those gilded roofs and intricate fretwork hid requisitioned halls and the larger houses, all filled with the cries and the stench of the sick and dying.

Bolingbroke's army was already decimated by thirty percent, and only the Lord Christ knew how many more would die before this sickness had passed.

To lose his chance at the French crown because his men were squirting their lives down the sewers. He hit the window frame in sheer frustration, turning back into the room.

As usual, most of his commanders were present (although three, including Hungerford, were themselves so ill with the flux, they looked like being able to leave their beds only in caskets), as also was Neville, standing in a corner, his arms folded, watching Bolingbroke intently.

Bolingbroke sent him a hard, suspicious look, then addressed the Earl of Suffolk, newly returned from his mission to Paris.

"Twenty thousand gold pieces! Where shall I get that from? I should send him twenty thousand carts laden with the effluent my men have voided. That should be his due."

"Your Grace—" Suffolk began.

"There was never mention of monetary payment in the bargain he and I made," Bolingbroke continued, picking up an empty goblet from a table, then throwing it across the room in frustration and anger. *Damn the angels for the affliction they'd sent!*

Bolingbroke shot Neville another foul look.

Suffolk shifted uncomfortably on his feet, trading looks with several of the other commanders. He wished Raby was here, rather than in England keeping watch over the realm, for Ralph Neville always had a calming effect on Bolingbroke.

And more than a damn shame that Lancaster himself was dead, for more than anyone he could have prevailed upon Bolingbroke to keep a cool head.

"Philip is playing games," Warwick said. No one present made the mistake of believing they were dealing with Charles in this matter. "This morning's intelligence reports that he's jumping up and down, crying foul; that the English have stolen away his beloved Maid of France, and that all good Frenchmen must come to their nation's aid."

Bolingbroke, now fiddling with a tassel on a wall hanging, snorted in disgust. "At least we know he's taken her," he said. "And has her hidden away somewhere." He turned away from the tassel and regarded the roomful of men once more. "He will give her to us, never fear."

"That may work against us, much as we might want to get our hands on the heretic whore," Suffolk said, again trading looks with Warwick and the other commander in the room, the Earl of Nottingham.

"And in what manner might that be?" Bolingbroke snapped.

"It is sometimes better *not* to give one's enemy a martyr to inspire them," Nottingham said softly, moving forward. For a young man, he was unusually perceptive. "Better, perhaps, that we allow this Joan to lead France to defeat in battle. Her power over her people will then be lost."

"Better," Bolingbroke all but shouted, "to burn her and show them she is normal flesh and blood than to risk her *winning* the damn battle."

There was an utter silence in the room as eyes dropped away from Bolingbroke. Never before had he spoken of defeat.

"Our men are dying," Bolingbroke continued in a far more reasonable tone. "We had a moderately sized but fine army when we left England. Now we have a tiny army racked with disease. If you don't think that leaves us vulnerable to defeat on the battlefield . . . then think again.

"Joan is our bitter enemy," he continued, now even more softly. "Perhaps even the witch who has sent this plague upon us. She needs to die."

"Your Grace," said Neville, unfolding his arms and standing off the wall on which he'd been leaning. "My Lord of Nottingham has spoken sense. The Maid's power is fading anyway. . . . How many battles has she won recently? Better, perhaps, to—"

"Better that I should burn you instead, traitor," Bolingbroke yelled, striding forward and poking Neville in the chest with a stabbing forefinger. "Better that *you* die before the last of my men empties his bowels out in the gutters of France."

Bolingbroke's outburst caused a commotion within the chamber.

"Your Grace!" Suffolk said, coming to stand beside an obviously shocked Neville. "My Lord Neville is hardly a traitor. What has he done that you so accuse him?"

Bolingbroke's eyes shifted about the murmuring group, and he abruptly backed down. "You must excuse me," he said. "I've had so little sleep, and am riven with concern for my wife." He waved his hand, hinting at other vague problems.

"Perhaps you need to rest, Your Grace," said Sir John Norbury, who'd been standing silent with Owen Tudor to this point.

"Yes, you're right, I do need to rest," Bolingbroke said, stretching his face in an unconvincing attempt at a smile. "If perhaps you could excuse me for the moment."

The group bowed, murmuring their farewells, but just as they started to move away, Bolingbroke spoke again. "Tom, stay, if you will. I should apologise for my unfortunate words."

"I AM a traitor?" Neville said quietly when the last man to leave the room had closed the door behind him. "In what manner am I 'traitor'?" Neville knew that Bolingbroke had no intention at all of apologising for his attack . . . he'd just wanted to be able to continue it in private.

"In what manner 'traitor,' Tom? Oh, what pretty words!" Bolingbroke's voice was heavy with sarcasm.

"What *is* this?" Neville said, walking to within a pace of Bolingbroke and staring belligerently into his face. "You and Margaret have these past weeks treated me as if I were a pariah. For what reason? Do you think to manipulate my guilt again as once you did? Think you to *force* me into tossing my soul into Margaret's manipulative care? Christ, Hal, how better to turn me *against* you?"

"You have never had *any* intention of choosing in my, Margaret's, or mankind's favour."

"I have every intention of doing so, but *you* make it too difficult for me. Damn you, Hal! *Damn you!*"

"Damning me has always been your intention, hasn't it, Tom?" Bolingbroke said very quietly, his eyes unflinching as they stared into Neville's furious brown ones. "You have ever pretended to be my friend while always remaining my secret enemy."

"Ah!" Frustrated, Neville turned away. "For the sweet Lord's sake, Hal, what do you mean?"

"Rosalind," Bolingbroke said, watching Neville's back carefully. "Bohun."

Neville turned around again, his face creased in puzzlement. *"What?"*

"Your children have betrayed you, Tom."

"Of what do you speak, Hal?"

"Seven weeks ago, Tom, seven weeks ago, Rosalind spoke into Margaret's mind. When Margaret tested Bohun, she found that he, too, had the same ability. No mortal has that power. None."

"But Rosalind and Bohun have as their mother an angel-child, Hal. Surely . . ." Neville's voice drifted off as he remembered what Margaret had once told him . . . that the children of the angel-children, if one parent was a mere mortal, were as all mortal children. They had no powers at all: no shape-shifting, no mind-reading, no witchery of any sort.

Neville suddenly realised his mouth was hanging open, and he snapped it shut.

"Yes." Bolingbroke was walking *(stalking)* very slowly closer to him. "Rosalind and Bohun *should* be as mortals, shouldn't they? But they have the full range of abilities as do all angel-children, Tom. *As do all angel-children!*"

"You cannot mean . . ." Again Neville drifted into a silence as he remembered what the Archangel Michael had said to him when they were standing before Christ's cross in the Field of Angels. There was no God save the combined will of the angels . . . Jesus was the child of the combined will of the angels . . . Jesus had proved himself a frightful burden to the angels, trying to free mankind from their grip, therefore the angels had imprisoned him on the cross . . . but he was *"Not like our next effort. He works our will as if an extension of our own thoughts. There will be no mistake this time . . . Beloved."*

"Beloved?" Neville whispered, staring at the whorls in the grain of the floor planking. *Rosalind and Bohun were full-bred angel-children?*

He looked up at Bolingbroke, now so very close, his eyes the piercing murder of the plunging hawk.

"I am an angel?" Neville whispered. *Jesus was an angel, too?*

Brother, he had called me.

Bolingbroke's mouth opened, twisting with the full measure of his rage and hate, and he reached for Neville with hands hooked into claws.

Chapter X

Thursday 15th August 1381

— ii —

✝

NEVILLE SIDESTEPPED, AND began to laugh. It was weak at first, but then it turned into the full-blown hilarity of true humour.

"An angel!" he said, now laughing so hard he had to rest his hands on his thighs. "An angel! An *angel!*"

Bolingbroke had stopped, his hands slowly lowering to his sides, his face wreathed in confusion at Neville's reaction. "You did not know?"

Neville sobered. "No, I did not know, although I think the signs had been there for me to see for months, if not years. An angel! Oh, Lord Jesus Christ . . . an *angel!*"

He abruptly sank down into a chair that, fortuitously, sat right behind him. "An angel, an angel . . ." he muttered. "I should have known. All the signs were there." The angels calling him "Beloved," his quick healing, his luck in war . . . so many things.

Why he was picked for the angels' crusade against the demons.

He finally looked up at Bolingbroke, still standing, and regarding Neville with absolute bewilderment.

"It changes nothing," Neville said. "Nothing."

"But . . ."

"I am not your enemy, Hal. I have never been. And if I am an angel . . . well, then I am a most crippled one."

"Crippled?"

"Crippled by love, Hal, as Jesus is."

Bolingbroke's face creased even more. "Jesus is . . ."

"Sweet Jesu is an angel as well. Engendered by the combined will of the angels." Neville paused. "Sweet Lord," he murmured, "what my poor mother must have gone through, to have been visited by the combined will of the angels."

Then he stood up. "You must excuse me, Hal. I have some words to pass with my wife, I think."

And then he was gone, leaving Bolingbroke still standing, still bewildered, staring after him.

MARGARET STOOD in a trancelike fugue, staring at her hands as they dipped in and out of the soapy water in the large basin on the table before her . . . in and out . . . in and out. All she had been doing this morning was wash out linens dirtied during the care of Mary. Bedgowns, flannels, small linen squares to drape dampened over Mary's brow, pillow covers, sheets, undergarments, towels . . .

In and out . . . in and out . . . wring and drape over the drying rack. Pick up next piece to wash. In and out . . . in and out . . .

Mary, she hoped, was asleep in her bed. Margaret had given her an extra dose of Culpeper's liquor an hour ago when she'd heard Mary wake moaning from a nap. Margaret had followed up Culpeper's herbal with a little of her own power, rubbed gently into Margaret's hands.

She hoped it helped . . . but little seemed to help Mary now. The growth in her womb had clearly spread so deep into the woman's bones that every movement threatened to break her apart. Already her left arm was broken, the bones refusing to heal, and every time Margaret aided Mary's other ladies to turn her over, or to wash her, or to lift her, she feared they might snap Mary's spine, or neck.

Mary weighed less than the eight-year-old Jocelyn now. Her body was virtually fleshless, her skin alternately yellow or grey, depending on whether it was morning light or evening light that bathed her. Her hair was dank and lifeless, falling out in great chunks.

The sweat that poured out of her during her night fevers stank of death.

Yet through all this, through all her pain and suffering, Mary's temper was invariably sweet, her thankfulness for what Margaret and her other ladies did for her genuine.

Margaret picked up another piece of soiled linen, glancing at Mary as she did so. The queen's bed was set against the window on the far wall of the chamber from where Mary could see into the gardens whenever she felt well enough to do so.

Right now, however, she appeared deeply asleep. Her head lolled to one side on the pillow, her hands rested open and relaxed on the light coverlet.

A small speck of dribble had dried and crusted in one corner of her mouth, and Margaret supposed she ought to wipe it away, but to do so would be to waken Mary, and that Margaret did not want.

She dipped the linen into the soapy water and began washing it. Mary's other ladies were in the chamber next door, sleeping away some of their exhaustion, garnered while tending Mary through a sleepless night. Jocelyn lay with them. She'd sat by Mary's bedside during the long night, singing sweet ballads in her youthful voice, keeping Mary's mind blessedly detached from the agony of her flesh.

Jocelyn was a gift from whatever benign benevolency thought occasionally to watch over Mary, for her sunny temperament and honeyed voice kept Mary at peace through many a long hour.

Margaret sighed, slipping deeper into her fugue. She was tired, but these linens needed to be done, and their doing kept her from tossing restlessly on her pallet in the chamber with the other ladies.

Thoughts of Tom, and of what he was, had kept her awake for many a long night.

Those nights when Mary dismissed her from her service to lie beside Tom were agony, for she wondered at what point Tom would turn on her, and strike her down with angelic fury.

Christ Lord, they had thought they could turn Tom to their way of seeing and understanding. How foolish of them. How blind.

"Sweet Jesu," she whispered, "I had loved him so much."

"Then why cease?" whispered Neville's voice, and strong arms wrapped themselves about her waist, pulling her back against his body.

Margaret stifled a shriek, but could not stop herself going rigid with fright.

"I have just come from Hal," Neville continued in a low voice, his lips against her right ear. "Hal made me see myself for what I am."

He stopped, and Margaret knew he expected her to say something. She tried to glance towards Mary to see if Tom's entrance had wakened her, but Neville swung her to the right a fraction, towards the drying rack festooned with damp laundry, just enough that Margaret could not see Mary at all.

"An angel," she said, her voice laced with venom.

"An angel," he repeated. "Ah, Margaret, my love. I did not suddenly 'become' an angel, but have been one all my life. Unknowing—I only understood it just now when Hal, brimming with fury, told me—but an angel nevertheless. I am so sorry I did not know. I should have. How I must have scared you when you discovered it."

His arms tightened about her, pulling her very tight against his body. She could feel him, feel his warmth and strength through his clothes, feel him move against her.

"No wonder I was such a bigoted crusader as a Dominican friar." His mouth brushed against her ear, then her cheek. "No wonder Archangel Michael kept calling me 'Beloved.' No wonder he believed in me so much, even when it seemed as though I strayed into the path of the demons. But he should have been more concerned, because I strayed too far. You crippled me, Margaret. You corrupted me beyond knowing when you made me love you."

He began to move from leg to leg, slowly, gently, as if rocking to some silent tune. As he moved, he forced her to move with him until they both rocked from side to side, slowly, gently.

"I still don't think that the angels have any idea. They think I remain pure. Untouched. Unloved."

"But—" Margaret managed.

"But *what?* Margaret, do you remember what I said to you that night in Kenilworth? That night when I confessed my love to you."

"You said many things to me that night."

"Aye, that I did. Well, do you remember what I said when you taxed me with the contention that I could not afford to love you, because when the time came for the choice, I would choose mankind's salvation before you."

"I remember," she said in a low voice.

"And what did I reply to that?"

"That when the time came, you would allow love to make the choice for you."

"Aye," he whispered, so softly that she had to strain to hear him, even though he was close. "Love killed the cold pious man I had been . . . that had been the angel within me."

His arms about her waist relaxed, and he turned her about to face him. "Jesus is an angel, too, Margaret. But do you fear him? Nay, of course not. He has loved also, and that broke apart the angel within him." Neville grinned, the expression on his face reminding Margaret very much of that sweet long-ago night at Kenilworth. "We were both most vilely crippled. Perhaps because we were tainted from birth."

"What do you mean?"

"He means," came Mary's weak voice from her bed, "that both Jesus and he were born of human mothers."

MARGARET SWUNG towards Mary, pulling herself half-free from Neville's hold. *"You knew?"*

"Not of this last, no. But of many things."

Margaret looked between Mary and Neville. "She *knew?*" she said to her husband.

"I told Mary during the time of the pestilence in London of the nature of the battle that consumes the angels and their children," Neville said. "Mary has been my confidante in many things."

"And I not?" Margaret said softly.

Neville led her stiff and unyielding towards Mary, where he sat down carefully on Mary's bed, pulling Margaret against him.

"Mary has no stake in this matter," he said. "She has not tried to pull me one way or the other. And," he looked to Mary as if silently seeking her permission for what he was about to say next. He seemed to receive it, for he went on, "Mary's mind and soul have the clarity of near death. I can say to her what I can say to no other. *But,*" his hands about Margaret's waist pulled her tense body down to his lap, "I cannot say to her what I now say to you. That you are my love, and my wife, and the mother of my children, and that you come before all others in my life. I love Mary, but not as a man loves a woman. Although," now he turned and winked mischievously at Mary, "had I not been so tied by love to my wife I might have been tempted to battle Hal to death in the tourneying field for her hand in marriage."

To his relief both women laughed. Margaret, particularly, relaxed, finally allowing some of her jealousy for Mary to slip away. *He had told her he loved her in front of Mary, confirmed their bonds before Mary . . . But he confided in Mary when he has not confided in me.*

"Margaret," Neville said softly, "when it comes to the

choice, and Christ knows it will be soon, I swear before you and on the lives of our children that I *will* allow love to make the decision for me, angel blood or no angel blood. My loyalty and desires are with mankind, not the deformed, loveless beasts that inhabit heaven. I can give you no more assurance than that."

"So you will choose in my favour?" Margaret asked.

Neville suppressed an irritated sigh. "I will allow love to make the decision for me, Meg. Love alone."

And may Jesus aid me to rid myself of that dark irk which still clutters my conscience. Because if it does not go, Margaret, then I know not what I will do. . . .

Margaret nodded, smiled a little, and rose. "I will fetch a damp cloth to wash your face, madam," she said to Mary, and walked over to the drying rack.

Mary watched her go, then, once she was far enough away, whispered to Neville: "You have not told her Christ walks again on earth. That you freed him from the cross in the Chapel of St John."

Neville shook his head. "He does not want her to know, Mary. You know that."

She nodded, but said nothing, for then Margaret returned.

Chapter XI

Thursday 15th August 1381

— iii —

✝

NEVILLE LAY CURLED about Margaret, more asleep than awake. They'd made love this night, and it had gone well, if Neville had sensed (and sensed that Margaret did, also) a distance between them. They'd embraced, and done what was needed to achieve their sexual union, and had then talked softly and tenderly, speaking words of love.

But still that distance.

Neville remembered the last time he and Margaret had attempted to make love, when Margaret had said bitterly that he would not have pulled away from her had she been Mary. He wondered if what she had said had any truth in it, and then dismissed the thought. He'd never thought of, nor regarded, Mary in sexual terms. He could not imagine making love to her, even if she had been healthy. Margaret was wrong to be so jealous of her. Mary had done no harm, and could not possibly do any.

Neville drifted further into sleep, only barely conscious of the darkened chamber about them. Then, just as he was about to tip over into the dark cup of unconsciousness, his nose twitched, as if irritated by some cloying scent.

He murmured, and shifted, rubbing at his nose briefly with the back of his hand.

He drifted back into sleep.

Again, the heavy, syrupy scent, and this time Neville had to stifle a sneeze.

He blinked, rubbing his nose again, and finally opened his eyes.

As he did so, the room exploded in golden light.

HE STOOD, shuddering, naked, amid the brittle, false flowers of the Field of the Angels. About him circled the entire fraternity of the angels. Their bodies glowed a marbled silver, their eyes a hard obsidian black. They moved slowly, their circle some four or five angels deep, their eyes still on him, never leaving him, trapping him.

About their feet they had shattered the fragile multicoloured flowers into a hard-trodden track of crystallised fragments.

"Hail, brother," said one, stepping forward out of his circling comrades. It was Michael, the angels' emissary to Neville.

Neville did not reply. He watched Michael carefully, his eyes occasionally flickering to the thick circle of angels moving about them.

"You have discovered the truth about your heritage," Michael said. He shrugged slightly. "We thought you'd realise it sooner."

Still Neville did not answer. He was freezing, his flesh dimpling, and he had to fight to keep his arms relaxed at his side rather than wrapping them about himself in an attempt to get warm.

Michael smiled, and as he did so the entire assembly of angels smiled: cold, malicious, and very, very certain.

"We have always been sure of you," Michael said. "We

did not make the same mistake with you as we did with Christ."

"And what was that?" Neville said softly. He was shivering now, and feeling nauseated.

"We have always wanted to ensure the complete enslavement of mankind to our will," said another archangel who stepped out of the ring of circling angels to stand at Michael's shoulder, and Neville knew that it was Gabriel.

"We have been working towards this since the dawn of time itself," Gabriel continued. He saw the question forming on Neville's face, and answered it before he had a chance to voice it. "We have always been," Gabriel said. "Always a part of creation, always gaining our sustenance from the adoration of lesser beings. But relying on adoration from such capricious creatures as mortal men has ever been a chancy thing. We need to enslave them completely. But completing the process of enslavement necessitated one of our kind physically being present on earth. It meant one of our number physically becoming a man."

As one, the circling angels screwed their faces into expressions of utter disgust.

"Even had one of us wanted to do that," and the expression on Gabriel's face left no doubt that none of the angels had stepped forward to volunteer, "it would have been impossible. We cannot appear in physical form within the mortal sphere."

"So we took the next best step of creating another of our kind within the womb of a woman," said Michael. "Not an angel-*child,* of which horrors there were plenty enough, but a fully formed angel. He would then work his will—*our* will—and lead mankind into a complete enslavement to our wishes."

"But it all went wrong," Gabriel said, and as one, all the angels snarled, then hissed, and Neville had to use every measure of self-control he possessed to stop himself from trying to break through the circle and escape. He found it difficult to believe that the angels, while professing repugnance for mankind, nonetheless could not resist the lust they felt for women. It was a matter, Neville thought, of loathing the thing they could not resist, and then seeking to enslave it in order to save themselves. Their hatred of mankind was merely a reflection of their hatred for themselves.

How could he be one such as these? One such as these *horrors?*

"Christ went berserk." Yet another archangel stepped forth from the circle. Uriel, this time. "He tried to *free* mankind instead of enslaving them."

"He was corrupted," Gabriel said.

"Precisely," said Uriel.

"Because he had a human mother," Neville said softly, remembering what Mary had said.

For a moment the angels did not reply. The only sound was that of the circling horde's shuffling feet through the shards of the flowers, the only existence the corral of their flat, black eyes.

"Because he had a human mother," Michael repeated.

"A bitch mother!" the assembly of angels cried as one.

"I have had a human mother," Neville said softly. "I must be corrupted, too. Why so confident that I will choose in your favour?"

Michael smiled, and all the angels smiled with him.

The depth of cold suddenly increased twofold, and now Neville could not stop himself from shivering.

"We know what you think and what you want," Michael said. "You want to hand your soul to the bitch-whore Margaret, to free mankind from our chains forever."

Total silence, save for the shuffling of feet.

"How sweet," whispered Uriel.

"How foolish," said another Archangel, Sariel, stepping forth into the circle. With him walked the Archangels Raguel and Raphael. Neville was now hemmed in by two circles: the outer one of angels, and the smaller inner core of Archangels.

"You see, dear corrupted brother of ours," Michael said, "where you think is choice, is none at all. You *have* no choice."

"I will *always* have choice," hissed Neville, now truly frightened. He'd finally given up trying to keep his arms at his sides, and now he wrapped them about himself, trying to keep some of the cold of heaven at bay.

"No, no, no," said Michael. "In your darkest moments you admit to yourself that you cannot hand your soul to Margaret. There is that slight hesitancy, that slight doubt. She used you, tricked you once—"

"Like all women," cried Gabriel and Uriel as one.

"And that single instance," said Michael, "that single trickery—"

"That single, dark irk!" said Raguel.

"—means you cannot choose for her," finished Michael.

"Then there are good women, true women, who I can—"

"Whom you love without reservation, Thomas?" Sariel said. "And who are *whores?*"

"Remember the prophecy as spoken by that whore in the street of Rome, Thomas?" said Michael. "Remember? One day one of my sisters will seize your soul and condemn you to hell for eternity! A whore will steal your soul! *Nay, I pray to the Virgin Mary, that you will offer her your soul on a platter! You will offer her your eternal damnation in return for her love!*"

"A whore, Thomas," said Uriel. "Not a good woman, nor a true woman. Not even a slightly wanton woman. A *whore*. A harlot who prostitutes her flesh for coin to any man who can pay. A whore whom you love so unreservedly that you would beg her to take your soul."

"And that whore," whispered the congregation of angels, "is not Margaret. Not Margaret twice over—you do not love her unreservedly, and she is no whore. She may not be truly virtuous, but she is no whore. Not Margaret . . . *not* Margaret."

Not Margaret . . . not Margaret . . . *never* Margaret . . .

"Then who, Thomas?" said Michael. "How many filthy purveyors of carnality, whom you love unreservedly and unhesitatingly, *do* you have in reserve?"

"Christ tells me to trust him," Neville said, his voice panicked. "*Christ tells me to trust him.* He is my brother, and—"

Michael laughed. "How many whores does *he* have in reserve, Thomas? Freeing him from our prison has, in the end, done you no good at all. This choice will not be set before you in six years, or ten, but in a matter of weeks. Love, the kind of love that you need to be able to hand a woman your soul, takes months if not years to develop. Thomas," and suddenly his voice became a roar, and the entire assembly of angels stopped, and turned into the circle, their mouths opened in silent screams. "Thomas! You have no choice at all. You will choose in our favour, *because you have no choice in it.*"

The angels shrieked in hideous mirth, and Neville, terrified and hopeless, cowered on the ground of the field, his arms wrapped about his head.

You will *choose in our favour because there is no choice at all.*

"There is no choice," Michael whispered through the screaming laughter. "*There has never been one.* This time we have made sure. If you cannot hand your soul to your bitch-whore, do you know what happens then, Thomas? Do you? Your soul reverts to our care, back to the angels, where it originated and where it belongs. Mankind is ensnared forever, and you get to spend eternity with *us.*"

A scream sounded, and Neville only dimly realised that it was his voice.

"Welcome back to the brotherhood, Thomas."

PART FIVE

Agincourt

Now shrinketh rose & lilye-flowre
That whilen ber that swete savoure,
In somer, that swete tide.
Ne is no quene so stark ne stour,
Ne no levedy so bright in bour,
That ded ne shall byglid.

————

Now shrinketh rose and lily flower,
That once bore such sweet fragrance,
In summer, that sweet time.
There is no queen so mighty or strong,
Nor lady so bright in her bower,
That death shall not pass by.

—Late thirteenth-century English lyric

Chapter I

Friday 16th August 1381

— i —

✝

A STRONG PREMONITION of danger wakened Joan from her sleep. Why the arrival of such a premonition at this particular point she did not know, because it had been four days since she'd been abducted, bundled into a chest, and moved two days north of Paris on the tray of a jolting cart. Not even in those two days, when she'd been trapped in the dark chest, did Joan sense so much danger lurking about her.

But today, on this fine morning, and with no apparent reason, Joan woke with the sense that today would be one of extreme danger.

Her captors—Philip's men, naturally—had brought her to the small and somewhat tumbledown castle of Beaurevoir some eighty miles north of Paris. Here they placed her into the care of several well-dressed and mannered ladies of the minor nobility, a goodly contingent of stern-faced men-at-arms, and several priests, who examined her twice daily for an hour to see if they could detect any heretical leanings.

Joan stirred on her comfortable bed, hearing the noise

of her ladies rising when they realised she was awake. One of the women drew back the shutters, illuminating the chamber with the early morning sun. The chamber that formed her prison was very comfortably appointed, almost luxurious: the furniture was well made, tapestries hung from the walls, and Joan ate her meals from fine silver plates and drank well-seasoned wine from solid gold cups.

"Mademoiselle?" said one of the ladies, bending over Joan.

"I am awake," said Joan, and sat up.

The woman offered Joan a bowl and flannel with which to wash the sleep from her eyes, which Joan accepted gratefully. But Joan's face darkened as another lady approached carrying a richly wrought and embroidered crimson gown.

"I will not wear that abomination," Joan said.

"But you will look so beautiful in it," said the woman.

Joan sent her a scathing look, then reached for her usual garb, a man's tunic and leggings, even though they were soiled and stained from their continual wear for some five days.

The women, all three of them, tried again to persuade Joan to accept the gown, but Joan steadfastly refused. Every morning that she had been at Beaurevoir the four of them had engaged in the same ritual: the women begged Joan to wear the rich gown, and Joan refused.

Having finally managed to garb herself in her tunic and leggings, Joan then sat at the table and allowed the women to serve her some bread and fruit, accompanied by watered wine. She waved her companions away as she ate, preferring to breakfast in some measure of loneliness.

As she ate (or, rather, pushed the bread about the plate and chewed with effort upon a single apple), Joan sank into thought, trying to discover the reason for her sudden sense of danger.

That she was going to die, she knew, but she felt very much as if today she would be forced into a premature death that would not in any measure serve to aid France or Charles.

Joan momentarily closed her eyes and shuddered. Dying she had accepted, but only because she knew it would serve France so well. To die purposeless? Nay, that she could *not* accept.

"Mademoiselle?" came the concerned voice of one of the women, who had left her stool in the corner of the chamber and now approached Joan.

"Nothing," said Joan, waving the woman back. "Leave me."

As the woman retreated, Joan took another mouthful of apple. Where could the danger come from? Was one of her female companions hiding a dagger with which she thought to assassinate Joan? Was one of the priests even now building a premature pile of faggots in the courtyard outside? Was *Bolingbroke* riding here as she sat eating her futile breakfast, thinking to run her through with his sword?

"Mademoiselle? *Mademoiselle?*"

Joan looked up, knowing that there was no use trying to decipher her premonition. Whatever happened, the Lord Jesus Christ would protect her. "I think I would like to take my morning walk now, my lady. If it pleases you."

EACH OF the two mornings past, Joan's minders had escorted her up the narrow stone staircase to the flat roof of the southeastern tower of Beaurevoir castle. Here they had allowed her an hour of gentle pacing about the perimeter of the roof in the fresh air.

Today Joan walked up as usual, encased by her women, and murmured her thanks as they led her into the sunshine. Not only was the sun and fresh air welcome, but the view was spectacular. Rolling fields, not yet browned by months of summer heat, spread in every direction, interrupted only here and there by a stand of trees, or a tiny village. Birds fluttered overhead, sometimes landing on the roof not far from Joan's feet as if to beg from her a morsel of the breakfast she had left uneaten.

Joan spent several minutes standing motionless in the centre of the roof, her hands folded before her, her eyes resting on the peaceful view. The sense of danger had now grown so intense it dominated her consciousness.

She looked over her shoulder. Her two female companions were standing by the door to the stairwell, gossiping quietly. Farther away stood the three men-at-arms who had accompanied them, watching Joan, but not with any serious attention.

Not one of those five looked to have a single murderous intent lurking within their minds.

Joan looked back to the view before her . . . and gasped in horror.

Before her stood the very faintly illuminated figure of Archangel Michael.

You stupid peasant, thinking you could switch your allegiance from us to that Demon Trickster Jesus. Thinking you still have a role to play in the drama ahead. Fool! Have you not yet realised how utterly redundant you are? How useless?

And without waiting for any kind of answer, he lunged forward, enveloping Joan in his golden luminosity.

A second later, she felt herself being lifted up and hurled over the side of the tower.

Joan tried to scream, but the earth below rushed to meet her so fast that there was no time.

"MADEMOISELLE? MADEMOISELLE?"

Encased in such agony that she knew she must be dead, Joan managed to open one eye a fraction.

A man leaned over her. A craftsman by the leather tunic he wore, and the belt of tools at his waist.

"Help me," she whispered.

"How may I do that, mademoiselle," the man replied,

"when you are not even badly hurt. A little bump to your head, and a twisted ankle."

Suddenly Joan's pain vanished, and she felt her broken body miraculously knit itself whole again.

"Lord Jesu," she whispered.

He smiled at her, his eyes crinkling against the strong morning sun. "I have not forgotten you, Joan," he said, "nor forgotten how important you are to me. Do not doubt my love and need of you."

And then, suddenly, he was gone, and she was surrounded by the terrified faces of the men-at-arms who had rushed down from the tower roof.

"She lives!" cried one.

"And with barely a scratch!" said another.

"A miracle," Joan murmured, and closed her eyes and smiled, knowing how the angels must be screaming in frustration.

THIRTY-SIX HOURS later Philip's men came to take her away.

Chapter II

Friday 16th August 1381

— ii —

✝

CATHERINE PAUSED INSIDE the doorway, waiting for Philip to notice her. He was standing in a group by the window of the large chamber, gesticulating angrily with several of the French commanders, the Archbishop of Rheims, Regnault de Chartres, and the Provost General of Paris.

She wondered if this was the best possible time to try to speak with him. But when else? Philip had not come to her bed at all in the past two nights, and had made no attempt to see her during the days. He had been lured away, not by the charms of another woman, but by that heady mistress, War. France had roused as never before against the English threat—the English dogs had stolen their Maid—and this time the French were determined to push the invaders back beyond the Narrow Seas once and for all. Now men and horses and equipment gathered in increasing numbers in the fields and meadows above Paris. There was a sense of resolve, a sense of purpose, and a sense of unity that gripped all Catherine met (save, naturally, her brother, Charles) and that was to her so strange as to be quite remarkable. Joan's stealing had accomplished what very little else was able to: a forgetfulness of personal feuds and ambitions in preference for a united stand against the English.

If only Joan knew, thought Catherine, *she would be so happy.*

Then her mood darkened. France was going to war against England, but, more important and tragic for Catherine, Philip was going to war against Hal.

She suddenly realised Philip had seen her. A stillness had come over the group by the window, and all eyes had turned to her.

Catherine smiled—an expression meant to display confidence rather than amusement—and moved deeper into the chamber. She'd dressed carefully for this occasion: the deep crimson gown that Philip liked so much, jewels at her neck, upper arms and waist, and a delicate golden tracery of lace that trailed about her coiled dark hair and down her back.

"My lords," she said, inclining her head. "Surely this talk of war must not consume *all* your time? Are there no minutes left in your day for your women?"

The men glanced at each other, embarrassed and out of sorts with Catherine's entrance and words. There were great matters to be decided, a war to be won, invaders to be trod into the dust of the earth . . . this was no time for wives and lovers.

"Ah," Catherine said softly, "I have disturbed your talk."

She glanced at Philip. His dark gaze was riveted on her, his expression that of utter neutrality. Catherine knew him well enough, however, to know he was angry at her interruption.

"I irritate you," she continued, "I can see that. You think what I am and what I have to say is of little consequence. My lords . . ." Catherine sat on a thronelike chair that had been placed ready for Philip, her head and shoulders held elegantly, her hands carefully, deliberately, rearranging her full silken skirts into precisely the correct folds. She raised her head, regarding each man frankly, and continued. "And yet this woman *can* perhaps aid you." She tilted her head and regarded Philip. "If I said the right words, Philip, could I not win for you—?"

"Perhaps it would be better if Catherine and I spoke privately," Philip said. He waved away the group about him. "Meet with me again this evening, and bring with you the latest reports on both the English and our preparations."

The men filed out, slowly, reluctantly, their every movement stiff with affront that Catherine should have so interrupted them.

Finally, when all were gone, Philip closed the distance between himself and Catherine in three heavy strides, and leaned down, placing his hands on the arms of the chair so that his stiff arms trapped Catherine.

"What do you here?" he said, finally allowing his anger some freedom.

"What do *you* do here?" she countered. "Philip, what is going on? Joan is gone, taken by Hal, they say . . . although I have my doubts. And here you are, preparing to lead an army against Hal. Philip, you cannot win."

He stepped back from her. "I thank you for your confidence in me."

Catherine's shoulders slumped, and she looked down at her hands as they lay in her lap. "May I rephrase that last?" she said softly.

She received only silence for an answer.

Catherine looked up. "I do not want you to lose, Philip. I do not want to lose *you*."

Again, silence, although now his regard was more calculating than angry.

"You said that Hal and you had made a bargain. Together you would dispose of Joan, then you would let me decide France. Whoever I took as my husband would take France."

"Aye," he said.

"Then stop this foolish war," she said, "and marry me."

Nothing she could have said would have stunned Philip

more. For months, years, she had consistently refused to marry him.

"*What?*" he said.

"I do not want Hal," she said, her voice even softer now. "I want you. You will do better for France than either Hal or Charles. Marry me."

His eyes narrowed. "This is some trap."

She smiled, but sadly, knowing that she deserved his suspicion. "No. No more a trap than any marriage. Marry me."

"Catherine . . ." Philip came close, squatting down before her. He took both her hands in his. "Catherine. There will be war anyway. If Hal discovers that you have wed me . . ." He gave a short laugh. "My love . . . neither of us meant that bargain. The rejected suitor was *always* going to take out his frustration on the battlefield."

"I know. Marry me anyway."

"Catherine . . . why *now?*"

"Because I think the world is about to fall apart," Catherine said, and began to weep soundlessly, "and I would prefer it to fall apart while I am in your arms than distanced from them."

He lifted a hand and wiped away some of her tears. "Regnault de Chartres is undoubtedly close. His ear is pressed permanently to doors. Should I call him now?"

She nodded.

Chapter III

Monday 19th August 1381

(NIGHT)

✝

THE STUBBLE OF the grain field crackled underneath the boots of the men and the hard-iron hooves of the horses they led on loose reins.

The men walked slowly, loose-hipped, their eyes straight ahead, their heads and shoulders still, their arms wary by their sides.

Two groups of men approaching each other across the newly harvested barley field, each equally watchful. Every man among them wore smiles of disdainful confidence on their faces.

It was all show, all gamesmanship. Every man expected treachery to leap out at him from the night.

Above them hung a heavy moon. A thin haze of clouds gave it a sickly yellow sheen, as if it had somehow caught the miasma that had so recently enveloped the English army. It drooped dully in the sky, as if tired of hanging on amid the exuberance of the stars.

The air was hot and dusty, and most of the men glistened with sweat. But better this dark activity than tossing and turning sleepless on a pallet in camp.

Hal Bolingbroke, King of England, led the group of

twenty-five Englishmen. He was finely dressed in a crimson and forest-green tunic above ivory leggings and dark red Italian leather boots, wearing no armour and only a slim sword at his hip. His silver-gilt hair was left to lift in the breeze of his passing; his light grey eyes did not falter in their regard of the group that he approached.

A small purse hung at his waist.

Behind him walked seven nobles and eighteen sturdy and trustworthy men-at-arms who led the party's horses.

They had one spare.

The group who walked towards them were of a similar composition to the English party, save that they were led by a man in the rustling silken robes of an archbishop. The cleric walked as confidently as did the English king, his head held as high, his face as arrogant.

His eyes slipped to the small purse at Bolingbroke's waist, and he permitted himself a small smile of satisfaction.

"Greetings, King of England and Pretender to the French crown," said the cleric as, finally, the two groups came to a halt some two paces apart. "I am pleased that you appear so hearty, given the disease that has decimated your army."

Bolingbroke's face tightened. "Greetings, Archbishop. I regret to say that your concern has no grounding. My army is well, and fit. What little illness there was has passed."

Archbishop Regnault de Chartres smiled cynically. The reports that he and Philip had received put the English army at a fraction of its previous size. Eight thousand, perhaps. No more. Bolingbroke was finished.

But he was still useful.

"I have what you want," de Chartres said, seeing no point in wasting anyone's time. He gestured slightly with his left hand, and two of his men-at-arms brought forward a hooded and hunched figure.

The figure stumbled a little as it hit a raised sod of earth, but made no sound.

Bolingbroke stared at it, his eyes raised. "*This* is the mighty Maid of France? Where her powers? Her miracles?"

De Chartres shrugged dismissively. "I have not brought you miracles, Bolingbroke. Only the maid, Joan. Do what you will with her."

The men shoved the hooded girl forward, and she tripped, falling to her knees before Bolingbroke.

Bolingbroke smiled.

"And I have these for you," de Chartres continued. He snapped his fingers at one of the noblemen behind him, and the man handed him a packet of documents, tightly bound and sealed. De Chartres took them and stepped forward, handing them to Bolingbroke over Joan's bowed figure.

"You will find these useful, I think," the archbishop said. "They relate the girl's various heresies, and her sorceries."

Bolingbroke took the documents readily enough, but raised an eyebrow. "You are being generous, de Chartres."

"I am a man of God," de Chartres replied, and now it was Bolingbroke's turn to smile cynically.

"You have been careful, I hope," he said to the Frenchman. "It would not go well for you were your countrymen and women to discover your treachery to their Maid."

"I have been careful," de Chartres snapped. "Have you brought the money?"

"The twenty thousand gold pieces?" Bolingbroke laughed, and took the purse from the belt at his waist. He opened it, tipping a pile of silver coins into his hand. "I have brought only what you deserve, de Chartres. Thirty silver pieces, the regulation payment for any Judas."

He flipped the coins towards the archbishop, and they caught the moonlight as they arced into the night, glittering like magical dots of light as they fell in a tinkling heap, one by one, at de Chartres' feet.

He stared at them, but did not condescend to bend and pick them up.

"Do not think that she will do you any good," de Chartres finally said softly, lifting his head. Then he

swivelled about on his heel, and gestured to his party to
return the way they had come.

Bolingbroke stared after him for a moment, then
waved several of his men to come forward, grab Joan, and
hoist her onto the spare horse.

Then, just as Bolingbroke was mounting himself, de
Chartres stopped in his tracks, and spun about to shout a
final message.

"Good King Hal," he cried, "I almost forgot. Philip of
Navarre says that the final part of the bargain between
you is now also concluded."

Bolingbroke froze in the act of mounting, one leg
hanging awkwardly over his horse's back.

"He says that he hopes for your very best wishes," de
Chartres continued, and all could hear the laughter in his
voice, "on the occasion of his marriage to Catherine of
France. A happy ceremony which I was glad to perform
two nights ago."

Very, very slowly, Bolingbroke managed to lower his
leg across his horse and settle in his saddle. His face was
completely expressionless.

"But at least you now have Joan," de Chartres concluded. "And with her, Philip says, you must be content.
Perhaps you shall not wish to burn her after all."

He laughed, mocking and triumphant, and Bolingbroke
swung his horse about, and spurred him into a gallop.

THEY ARRIVED back in Rouen at dawn, Bolingbroke
still stony-faced at the head of his party. He led them to
the entrance below the castle that he had made his headquarters, to the dungeons, then commanded them in curt
words to lift Joan from where she'd been roped across her
horse and to follow him.

He led them deep into the underground vaulted chambers. The stone walls were damp with constantly dripping
water, and splotchy-dark with mould. Torches sputtered
in infrequent sconces, and everyone, save Bolingbroke,

stumbled, cursing, from time to time. Joan was in a pitiful state, for the hood still covered her features, and her hands were bound behind her back. Had not two men kept their fingers buried in the shoulder material of her tunic, she would have hardly been able to walk at all. As it was, she had twisted her left leg at some point, and now it dragged behind her.

Eventually Bolingbroke came to a halt before a door. Several men stood at guard outside, and to these men Bolingbroke nodded curtly. "Is it done?"

"Aye, Your Grace," replied a sergeant. "Exactly as you ordered."

"Good." Bolingbroke nodded to the sergeant, who produced a key from a bunch at his belt, unlocking and swinging the door inwards.

Bolingbroke took a torch from one of the sconces, and stepped into the chamber.

After a moment he emerged, his face satisfied, and nodded to the two men who held a half-fainting Joan between them.

They hustled her inside, Bolingbroke a half-step behind them.

He closed the door as he entered.

JOAN WHIMPERED, hating her weakness that she did so. Her entire body ached from the bruising ride tied across the horse's withers, and her head and ankle still pained her from her fall three days previous, but worst of all was the pain in her heart and soul.

Betrayed in such brutal fashion. But then she had expected that.

What had distressed her more than she had known was to be treated in a more worthless manner than was a common pig.

Brought here, to the heart of the hated English enemy camp, where, no doubt, they had tortures aplenty devised for her, to be applied with brutal glee that they'd finally got their hands on the Maid of France.

Christ be with me, she prayed. But here, in this dankness, and surrounded with Bolingbroke's enmity, she wondered if even Christ would be able to aid her.

Rough English hands grabbed at her simple clothing, and Joan cried out involuntarily. They tore from her body her tunic, and her breeches, and the plain undergarments she wore beneath.

Their hands rubbed against her breasts and belly, pinching, hurting, and she heard a snort of derisive laughter.

"No," she whispered, her face twisting in humiliation beneath the still-covering hood. "No!"

"You're too ugly for us, girl," said one coarse voice, and then the hood was lifted from her head.

Joan blinked, her eyes unaccustomed for many hours to any light at all. She crouched, trying with a touching inefficiency to hide her breasts and pubis, then looked up, squinting a little as a man held a torch above her head.

It was Hal Bolingbroke. Joan recognised him instantly from the vision Christ had vouchsafed her.

"Well met, Joan of Arc, Maid of France," Bolingbroke said. "You seem strange to me, for I had imagined a maiden of great strength and bravery. Instead, I find this crouching, trembling peasant."

He stepped back, turning the torch towards a wall. The chamber was quite roomy, and the torch barely lit what covered the wall.

But Joan saw clearly enough.

"I found this," Bolingbroke said conversationally, "in the great guildhall of this fair city. Apparently the guild's seamstresses and embroiderers had worked at it ceaselessly for a year. It has only just been completed. I brought it here." His voice hardened. "I thought it might cheer you."

Joan could hardly bear to look upon the huge tapestry.

It was most beautifully wrought, and most perfectly designed (although unintentionally on the part of its makers) to serve Bolingbroke's need to humiliate Joan.

It took as its subject Joan of Arc herself, depicting her at the height of her fame as she led the French forces against the English at the siege of Orleans. She was clad in gleaming white armour, riding her roan stallion. One arm was held on high, carrying a great banner depicting the heraldic devices of the Archangels Michael and Gabriel. Her visor was open, and her face shone with heaven's glory, her eyes fervent, trusting, believing.

"Where your armour now, Joan?" Bolingbroke asked as Joan finally tore her eyes away from the tapestry. "Where your glory? Where," his voice hardened into vindictiveness, "your angelic companions?"

His arm lowered, thrusting the torch almost into Joan's face. "Look at you, dirty, ugly, teary girl. How could I have thought that you were ever a worthy opponent of *mine?* Ah! Put her away, for I cannot bear to think that I wasted a night of my life, let alone thirty pieces of silver, on this sorry wench."

The two men-at-arms grabbed Joan by her upper arms, dragging her towards the centre of the chamber. She cried out, lifting her legs against her abdomen and attempting to hide her breasts with her hands.

They gave her no chance. Even as she dragged her legs upwards, the men lifted her high, throwing her through the opening of an iron cage suspended from the ceiling of the chamber.

Joan landed with a jolt and cried out in distress, for the floor of the cage was made of nothing more than crisscrossed roughened iron bars, and her skin scraped and tore as she slid across to the far wall of the cage, slamming her right shoulder and arm against it.

The cage door slammed, and she heard the sound of a lock being turned.

The two men-at-arms left and, after a very long pause, so did Bolingbroke.

The door banged shut behind him, leaving Joan suspended in her iron cage in the dark of her gaol.

After a few minutes of staring blankly into the silent darkness, her arms wrapped about her breasts in a vain attempt to negate the horror of her earlier humiliation, Joan began to cry, crushed by the hatred of Bolingbroke.

Chapter IV

Tuesday 20th August 1381

— i —

✝

THE DOOR SWUNG open suddenly, violently, crashing into the wall and springing halfway back into the room.

Joan jerked out of a half-slumber, crying out. She began to shake, as much from fear as from the cold that had almost frozen her.

A guard stepped in, holding out a torch. He grunted at the sight of Joan, huddled in the farthest corner of her cage, dirty and shivering.

Then he stepped back, and bowed.

Two men came in, awkwardly, carrying something between them.

Something that cried out as they stepped down into the chamber. Something they carried with the most infinite of gentleness.

A third man followed these two. He carried, not some as-yet-undetermined bundle, but a simple wooden chair with several blankets and a pillow on its seat.

Behind him came yet one more person. A woman, but she was hidden by the shadows and the shapes of the men moving in front of her, and Joan did not see her clearly.

Joan returned her attention to the two men who carried

the bundle. The third man had placed the chair directly before Joan's cage, arranging upon it the pillow and blankets, and now the two men lowered their charge toward the chair.

As they had carried it, so now they lowered it with such infinite gentleness, respect and love that Joan lost some of her terror. If this bundle was so loved and respected, then how could it mean harm?

The bundle—a woman, Joan could see that now—moaned as the men deposited her into the chair. She clutched at the right-hand arm of the chair with her hand; her left arm was bound up tightly in a sling. The two men hurried away, searching for more torches to place into wall sconces, while the other woman now came forward, and murmured soothing words to the woman in the chair, and wrapped her about in the blankets.

When the torches—five in all, their light now exposing Joan's shame for all to see—had been set into their sconces, the woman in the chair spoke.

"Leave us alone now with the Maid," she said, her voice firm and clear. "She can do us no harm."

The guard who had been standing all this time by the open door looked uncertain.

The woman in the chair, even though she did not turn her head to see him, sensed this uncertainty. "Go now," she said. "I will come to no harm."

The guard grunted yet again, shuffled about for a moment, then turned and left the chamber, closing the door behind him.

Joan, still huddled in the far corner of the cage, her arms wrapped about her nakedness, stared at her two visitors.

The woman in the chair was many things.

She was a queen, for although she wore no crown or jewels proclaiming her status, the essential majesty of her soul shone through her beautiful hazel eyes.

She was a woman dying, for Joan could clearly see her skeletal frame underneath her simple robe of white wool, overlaid at the shoulders by a sky-blue shawl. Her forthcoming death was also apparent in the colour and texture of her skin, for it was grey and papery, and in the thinness and dryness of her hair, which had fallen from her scalp in great patches.

And she was a woman somehow indefinably *magical.* This "magical" Joan could not clearly determine; it was merely something about, or, rather, *within* the woman. An unknown secret, perhaps. Something *unknown,* but . . . but something very, very blessed indeed.

She strongly reminded Joan of someone, but Joan could not quite place who. That she had seen this woman before Joan had no doubt . . . it was just that she could not place the *when* or the *where.*

But that did not matter. All that mattered was that this magical, otherworldly woman was here *now.*

Joan's eyes filled with tears of joy that she should be so graced with the presence of this woman.

The other woman, standing beside the chair of the dying queen, was incomparably beautiful. Joan did not think she had ever seen any woman so beauteous. She had dark, bronzed hair, shot through with ripples of gold. Her face was wonderfully moulded, her eyes the deepest black, her figure that of the most intimately desirable woman.

But this woman's beauty was tempered with sadness. This woman grieved. For what, Joan was not sure. Certainly for this dying queen, but her grief went deeper and further than that.

"Margaret," said the queen in a soft, gentle voice, "take my shawl and give it to this poor girl. I cannot believe that Hal would treat her so."

"No," said Joan, her voice cracking after almost twenty-four hours locked in this cold, damp prison. "No, madam, I beg you. Keep it about yourself, for it is so cold in here."

"I soon shall not feel the cold," said the queen. "Margaret, do as I ask."

The woman, Margaret, lifted the shawl away from the queen and carried it the two paces to the cage.

"Joan," she said, "wrap yourself in this. Please. It will give Mary pleasure that you do so."

Now that she was close, Joan realised that Margaret was a demon. Joan reached out a hand, took the shawl, and hastily wrapped it about her shoulders and over her breasts.

"I thank you," she said to Margaret, but including Mary in her words. Then, exclusively to Margaret, she said, "Who is your father?"

"My father is the Archangel Michael," she said.

Joan nodded. "Then I pity you." No wonder this woman was so sad, for she had been conceived in grief and born in yet more.

"I escort," Margaret said, turning back to the queen in her chair, "the Queen Mary, wife to Hal Bolingbroke."

"I am sorry," Mary said softly, "that for the moment I can do little else for you than to give you the shawl, and one of these blankets." She handed the item to Margaret, who passed it through to Joan. "When my husband departs this city, as I expect him to do within the next day or so, then I will be able to do more for you."

"What you have done is grace enough," Joan said quietly.

"My husband," Mary's voice hardened a little with that statement, "has feared you for a very long time. Joan of Arc, Maid of France, forgive him his fear."

"How can he not love and honour you?" said Joan, for she could see that Mary was, as a wife, a neglected and unloved companion.

"He thinks to love Catherine of France," said Margaret. "Do you know her?"

"Aye, of course I do," said Joan. "And *Bolingbroke* loves her? Then he will indeed have been distressed to have heard Regnault de Chartres' news . . . that she and Philip of Navarre have been wed these past four or five days."

Mary smiled, very slightly, very sadly. "Then no wonder it is that he has been thumping about this castle so thunderously. He will indeed have been grieved at the news."

"What did she hope to accomplish with that?" Margaret said, more to herself than anyone else.

"An end to the fighting, perhaps," Mary said. "Or maybe she hoped that Hal might return home if he thought she were now unattainable."

Her mouth twisted. "But there's nothing standing between Hal and Catherine—so far as Hal is concerned—that two quick deaths could not accomplish. As far as Philip is concerned, Hal prepares for it even now. He has gathered about him his army, and will soon march out to meet with Philip. I have heard rumours—and no doubt Hal has heard the certainty—that Philip is preparing to lead an army forth from Paris to repel the English once and for all."

"And this sickness that I have heard so much about?" said Joan. "Does Bolingbroke *have* an army to lead out?"

"Aye," replied Margaret, this time. "But much reduced. The sickness passed within days of our transferral here to Rouen. He leads no more than six and a half thousand men."

"But they have *Hal* at their head," said Mary softly, her eyes unfocused and far away, "and Hal is worth ten thousand men at the least."

"Madam," said Joan, "what do you here? Here in France, and here in this dungeon with me. You are ill, and should be at home, surrounded with those who love you."

"My home is wherever I am surrounded with those who love me." Mary held up her right hand for Margaret to hold. "And I am here in this dungeon with you, Joan, to let you know that you are also loved. Do not despair."

Joan lowered her head, blinking away her tears. This Mary was truly good in a way that Joan had never seen before.

Eventually, she raised her eyes again and spoke in a

quiet voice. "Is Thomas Neville with you? May I speak with him?"

Both Mary's and Margaret's faces fell. "We have not seen Tom in many days," said Margaret, her voice breaking. "We do not know where he is."

"We fear," said Mary. "Greatly."

Chapter V

Tuesday 20th August 1381

— ii —

✠

CATHERINE KNEW SHE was making a spectacle of
herself, knew that men were looking away in embarrassment, knew that her mother, Isabeau de Bavière, was
standing, arms folded, looking on in amusement, but
Catherine did not care.

All she knew was that Philip was going to his probable
death.

"Don't go!" Catherine cried once more, one hand
clinging to the stirrup leather of Philip's saddle, the other
grasping the strap holding his knee plate in place.

"Catherine—" he said.

"He will kill you!" Catherine said. "Hal is . . . is . . ."

Philip risked a glance about the courtyard. Several
score knights and men-at-arms, fully weaponed and
armed, sat their horses, waiting Philip's word and movement. In the streets outside another thousand waited.

And another twenty thousand awaited in the fields
north of Paris.

Philip was going to war.

"Bolingbroke's army is decimated," Philip said, his
voice low and caring. He reached down and took Cather-

ine's chin in his hand, tilting her face towards his. Her almost-hysteria did not embarrass him; rather, knowing Catherine's normal steely reserve and control, it touched him deeply. She cared enough to weep over his going, and Philip could not have asked for a better farewell gift.

"He is deep into what, for him, is enemy territory," Philip continued, his fingers caressing her chin. "France is rousing against him—soon Bolingbroke will commit the gross error of murdering Joan . . . if he hasn't already. That will be enough. That will lose him France, if not also his life. Catrine, darling, if I strike now I will win. Believe it."

But Catherine didn't believe it. For her the past few days had been a mixture of profound joy—she knew taking that final step into wedlock with Philip had been the right thing to do—and profound despair. From somewhere or someone, she knew not where or whom (*Joan? Margaret? Neville?*), black anguish had been washing over her in great breaking waves of misery.

Something, somewhere, was very, very wrong.

And Philip was riding into this maelstrom of uncertainty and despair.

And against *Hal*. Who had ever withstood *Hal?*

"He has much more than the six thousand men at his back," she whispered.

"What?" Philip frowned. "What do you know? Has he found more men?"

"No, no . . . oh, Philip, do not trust Hal—"

"Trust Bolingbroke? Never!" Philip laughed, then bent even further down and planted a kiss on her mouth. "Do not worry over me, Catrine. I have weathered greater storms than Bolingbroke."

"There *is* no greater storm than Bolingbroke," Catherine said. She reached up with both her hands and briefly, tenderly, held his face between them. "I love you, Philip. I have given you everything that I am."

"I will be back, Catrine. I *will.*"

Her hands dropped, and her mouth twisted. She could hear heaven itself laughing at that remark.

Then, impulsively, knowing she shouldn't do this, knowing that she tempted fate beyond all hope of redemption, she pulled Philip's face close to her own again.

"Philip, beloved," she whispered hastily into his ear, "know that on our wedding night I conceived your son."

Stunned, Philip jerked his head out of her hands, staring at her.

"You can't know——"

"I know," she said, staring at him, her clear blue eyes now calm and sure. "Believe me."

"Catrine . . ."

"Go now," she said, her voice breaking. "Go to your war." Philip stared at her a moment longer, his face full both of love and of question, then, abruptly, he raised his hand, and gave the signal.

Commands rang out through the courtyard and down the street outside. Philip held Catherine's eyes a moment longer, then he wheeled his horse's head about and kicked it into a canter.

Catherine watched until he'd disappeared beyond the courtyard gates and then she turned to go back inside.

"Very touching," said her mother, Isabeau, who'd come up behind her.

Catherine stared at her with eyes hard with grief. "Isn't it time you retired to one of your many castles full of willing stable lads, Mother?"

"Not when there's still power about for the grabbing."

"Very soon, Mother, there will be nothing about at all. It is all soon to come tumbling down. Everything. Everything. Soon there will be nothing left at all."

CATHERINE WALKED towards the apartments she shared with Philip (*had* shared, never would again . . .), but stopped, confused by the unusual scurrying of servants and valets about the wing of the palace containing the royal apartments.

"What is happening?" she asked a valet, whose arm she'd had to grab to make him stop and talk to her.

"The king is leaving," the man said, his thin, pale face gleaming with the sweat of either fear or effort.

Sweet Jesu! What was Charles up to now? "Leaving? Where?"

The valet's eyes blinked in confusion. "Where to, madam? Or where is the king?"

"Both, you idiot. Answer me!"

"The king is in his apartments," the valet stuttered, trying, but failing, to tug his arm out of Catherine's grip. "And he is fleeing . . . um . . . travelling south. I know not his destination."

Catherine muttered something very unflattering, then let the valet go. She turned on her heel, and walked quickly down the corridor that led to Charles' apartments.

The fool was in a flutter of fear. He'd managed to dress himself in at least three outfits, all crammed one on top of the other, and was now so confined by the stiff robes and tight seams that his arms stuck out stiffly at his sides and his face had gone a dusky pink in his efforts to breath through a throat enclosed by several layers of tightly laced high collars.

"What are you *doing?*" Catherine snapped at him.

"Getting myself to safety," Charles said, his voice squeaking in a most unmanly manner. Catherine could not be sure if this was due to fear, or the constriction of so many collars.

"By trying to disguise yourself as . . . as . . . as . . ." Words failed her, and Catherine contented herself with throwing her hands up in a gesture of utter disgust.

"The English dog bastards want to kill me," Charles said, and Catherine found herself unable to contradict that statement, at least.

"They'll torture me! Tear me limb from limb! Disembowel me!"

"And let's not forget slice off your balls and feed them

to the gutter dogs," said Isabeau de Bavière, who had just entered the room.

Catherine shot their mother a contemptuous look. Isabeau was not going to help anyone at the moment if she descended into her habitual sarcasm.

Charles whimpered, then turned around (almost overbalancing in his tight attire) and wobbled towards a chamberlain who was supervising the packing of several trunks. "Hurry! Hurry!" Charles cried. "The English are almost here."

"Well," said Isabeau, now speaking to her daughter, "I cannot but admit that Charles has good reason to fear for his safety. Paris shall become, I fear, a most unhealthy place for him once Bolingbroke sets Philip to one side."

"*If* Bolingbroke sets Philip to one side, madam," Catherine murmured.

Isabeau gave her a short, cynical smile. "*When*, my dear. As you know in your heart."

Catherine drew in a deep breath. "Are you sure you won't flee with my brother, madam? Paris is likely to become as unhealthy for you as it is for him."

"Oh, nay to both, I think. I am sure I can come to some accommodation with whoever wins in this battle for the French crown." Isabeau studied her daughter's face carefully. "I will wait for the outcome with you, Catherine. Here. In Paris."

"You think you can seduce the victor into granting your wishes?"

"No, Catherine. That I leave to you."

IT WAS only when she returned to her apartments that Catherine allowed herself the weakness and vulnerability of tears. Philip was never coming back. She knew that. Hal would win . . . by whatever means, he would emerge the victor against Philip. Philip was lost, France was lost . . . and Catherine was lost.

"Oh, sweet Jesu, help me," she sobbed, collapsing on

the floor by hers and Philip's bed and leaning her head into her arms where they rested on the coverlet. She wondered how it would be . . . would Hal stride into this very bedchamber, and force her to the bed and to his will? Or would he send for her . . . force her to come to him, enduring the cold stares of the English ranks through which she rode?

And what would he do when he discovered she was carrying Philip's child?

The thought that Hal might—*would*—force that child from her body caused Catherine to wail out loud. *Should she flee as well? To save Philip's child?*

"Oh, sweet Jesu, aid me now, aid me now," she sobbed.

"Madam?" came a hesitant voice behind her.

Startled, and angered that someone should have seen her in this state, Catherine sprang to her feet, whipping around to the door from where the voice had come.

A workman stood there, a length of wood over his shoulder, his face red with embarrassment that he should have disturbed such a fine lady.

"Who are you?" Catherine said, trying desperately to bring her tears under control.

"I was sent with this wood," said the man, a carpenter from the tools that hung at his belt, "to build a crib."

"What?" Catherine whispered.

The carpenter smiled at Catherine, adjusting the length of wood on his shoulder to a more comfortable position. "Madam, do not fret for your child."

"How . . . ?"

"I need you to do something, something for both yourself and for France. Will you do this?"

"What are you talking about? Who *are* you? What are you doing here?" Catherine stared at the man, wondering why she was standing here having this bizarre conversation with a craftsman. *How had he managed entrance into the palace in the first instance?* Should she shout for aid?

"Make sure your brother takes his crown with him when he leaves," the carpenter said.

"What?"

"Charles must have the crown, for he will be bereft without it."

And with that the carpenter ducked his head, as if apologising for his rude presence, and walked past the door out of sight.

Catherine stared for an instant, then ran to the door. She peered up and down the corridor beyond, but there was no one there.

"Charles must take the crown . . . ?" she whispered. "Why? Why?"

But then she thought that if Charles had the crown, then Hal would have the harder time of it trying to establish himself as the King of France (as she had no doubt he would soon do).

Without another thought, Catherine dashed the tears from her eyes and walked purposefully down the corridor, taking the turn that would eventually lead her to the jewel tower.

Chapter VI

Tuesday 20th August 1381

— iii —

✝

FOR DAYS, NEVILLE had existed in a state so melancholic, so despondent, so appalled, that he found it a wonder he could still draw breath.

He started fully awake from his vision of the Field of Angels, almost falling out of the bed he shared with Margaret.

He'd stared at her, wondering why she did not wake when it was so obvious that mankind only had a few more days, perhaps a few more weeks, of any measure of free will left.

Nearer and nearer draws the time, the time that shall surely be . . .

How foolish he had been, how proudful, to ever think that there *would* be a choice. The angels had come close to stumbling once before with Christ; they were not going to make the same mistake with him. They had allowed both the demons and Thomas himself to think that Margaret was the woman to whom he could gift his soul.

They had allowed both the demons and Thomas to trap themselves into a hopelessness.

That was all the events of the past few years had been—an opportunity to fall into a trap.

And Thomas had fallen . . .

FROM MARGARET'S bed, and then from their quarters in the castle, Neville had run into the night. His fear and his horror darkened his vision, and even where the way was well lit he crashed into pillars and corners and door frames until bruises matted the surface of his body and blood ran from a dozen cuts on his face and hands. The dawn still found him stumbling through narrow, dim alleys in the back quarters of Rouen, where small boys out collecting donkey dung at dawn laughed at him, and pinched at his flesh, and wondered whether this strange, naked man was crazed by drink, or women, or perhaps the moon, hanging so low and heavy in the sky.

Neville eventually found shelter of a kind in the low overhang of a stable roof. Damp, mouldy hay had been piled up under the eaves and, as morning finally dawned, he crawled deep inside the stinking mass, burying himself as deep as he could, wondering if the angels would ever find him here.

But he could not escape the words of the archangel: *There is no choice. There has never been one. This time we have made sure. Welcome to the brotherhood, Thomas.*

Those words never left Thomas' thoughts. The knowledge that he would be the one to damn mankind into eternal enslavement and that, having performed such an appalling task, he would then spend eternity locked in brotherhood with the foul creatures that inhabited heaven drove him so deep into despair that for hours that turned into days he was unable to leave his nasty burrow within the rotting hay. He sucked moisture from the loathsome mess whenever thirst drove him to the very edge of insanity (not that he was far from it in any case), scrabbled about hunting and squashing between his fingers the biting fleas and other insects that attacked his vulnerable flesh, and relieved himself into his bedding as needed, but *nothing* intruded on his sensibilities so much as to even come close to suggesting that it might be a good thing to escape this composting hideaway and find himself something a little more comfortable.

During the day the sounds of the city moving about him washed over him without making any impression on his misery. At night roaming dogs and pigs nuzzled and scraped at his covering layers of muck, trying to dig him out, but their efforts went ignored.

Thomas Neville just wanted to hide—hide from what the angels were going to force him to do.

There was no choice. There never had been. Everything that had gone before had been a jest, a jest on him and a jest on mankind.

There was no choice. The angels screamed in joy, capering about heaven. This time was their time.

There was no choice.

There never had been.

ON THE fifth night, trapped in his misery, a sound very gradually trespassed upon Neville's despair. It sounded for hours before Neville became aware of it, and then he listened to it for another hour or two more before he managed to emerge from his despair long enough to become even mildly curious about it.

It was the sound of a plane being drawn back and forth over a piece of wood. Back and forth, back and forth: an ever-patient carpenter in his workshop somewhere close to Neville's hideaway.

Neville grew to hate the sound. It angered him. It intruded upon his grief, his solitary despair, his selfish sorrow. Who was this Christ to so disturb him? Who was this Christ to set up shop so close to Neville's misery? *Didn't he know that all was lost? Would the man never give up? Damn him! Damn him! Damn him!*

Neville howled, so furious that he flung hay in every direction as he struggled out of his self-imposed imprisonment. *Didn't Christ know that all was lost?*

"I'll tell him," Neville mumbled, spitting out a bit of mouldy horse shit that had wedged itself between his front teeth. "I'll tell him, damn him. Why so cheerful? Why so cursed *hopeful? Doesn't he realise that when I am force to condemn mankind that he and his fellow demons will be curse as well?"*

He fell out of the muck heap onto the damp cobbles of the street, rolling some seven or eight paces down the slight slope until he managed to stop himself and rise to legs shaking from days of no food or use.

Neville stumbled a few paces down the alley. It was deep night, perhaps two or three in the morning, and the city was quiet.

Save for that cursed carpenter, still planing his wood somewhere close by.

Neville managed to walk further, ignoring the cramps that beset his calves and thighs. His face and body ran with sweat, his hands clenched at his sides.

The carpenter planed on, slowly, methodically, every stroke an obvious joy.

Why work wood, when there was no hope left? Didn't he know that within days, weeks at the most, he'd be back on his cross, hanging in agony?

Neville came to the end of the alley, leaning on the stone wall of a house for support as he heaved air in and out of his lungs.

There! There he was, the fool!

A faint light filtered from behind the shutters of a ground floor workshop three houses down the street. Neville, furious without being able to put a meaning to his fury, staggered towards the door of the workshop.

It was ajar, just very slightly, but enough for the hateful noise of the carpenter's efforts to seep out into the night air and wake Neville.

He reached the door and, without any of the hesitation

that had characterised his visit to Christ's London workshop, burst in.

And tumbled down the three steep steps to the floor. Neville hit the stone flagging heavily, his breath grunting out in a curse. He rolled over several times, his arms flailing, before he managed to stop himself.

He scrambled to his knees, then, awkwardly, to his feet, his hands held out to steady himself.

James the carpenter continued to steadily plane the large piece of wood on his worktable.

"What is it this time?" snarled Neville. "A casket? A breakfast table? Perhaps the axle of a cart?"

"A stake," said James, then nodded towards the far corner of the workshop. "I've set out a tub for you. Its water is warm, and comforting. There are some clothes on the stool to the side. I think you will find they will fit you well."

Then James' hands abruptly fell still, and he turned his face so he could stare at Neville, standing hostile and rigid in the centre of the workshop space. "We are brothers, you and I. What fits me, fits you."

Neville raised a hand, his face twisting with the strength of the emotion inside of him.

"I do not want to hear it," James said, turning back to his woodwork. "Not until you have washed, and clothed yourself."

"I do not—"

"What think you?" James yelled, now stepping away from his worktable altogether. "What think you, Thomas Neville, to so wallow in such self-absorbed misery?"

Neville blinked, unable to speak, completely stunned by James' sudden anger.

"I—"

"Are there no others in pain?" James continued, now standing directly before Neville. "Did you not think that your selfish despair might deepen their pain? Do you think yourself *alone* in this matter, isolated in your grandeur?"

James folded his arms, looking up and down Neville's naked body. "You are filthy," he said, both his eyes and tone flat. "The filthiness of your flesh reflects the state of your mind. You disgust me, Thomas. Wash yourself, for until then I cannot speak with you."

And with that he turned his back, and returned to his work table where he ran one hand softly up and down the length of wood he'd been smoothing. "Wash yourself," he whispered.

Neville stared at James' back, then his head dropped, and his shoulders slumped. He looked to the side, and saw the tub.

Steam rose from the water within.

Silently, abjectly, hating what his pride had brought him to, Neville walked over to the tub and lowered himself in.

"THEY BROUGHT me again to the Field of Angels," Neville said. He had washed, and dressed in the clothes James had set out for him, and now sat with James at a small table under the still-shuttered window.

He smelled sweet, and for no other reason that lifted his spirits.

"And?" James said, biting into a hunk of bread and cheese he had taken from the platter he had laid on the table between them. Ale stood in a jug to one side, and Neville sighed, and poured himself a beaker-full of the rich, foaming liquid.

"The decision is soon," he said, sipping the ale.

"Of course," said James. "Else I would not be here. And? What did they say or do to drive you into such self-absorbed—"

"Yes, yes, I know ... such self-absorbed misery. James," Neville put the beaker down with a thump, spilling a little of the ale, "you told me to trust you, and I have tried to do that. But what the angels showed me . . ."

"What?" James snapped, then smiled at the look in

Neville's eyes. "I am allowed to have a temper," he said. He reached out a hand and poked Neville in the centre of his chest. "It is one of the many things we share."

Neville half smiled, but his dejection would not allow it to flower fully. "The Archangels, all of them, ringed about me, trapped me, showed me that I have no choice but to choose in their favour when it comes to the decision."

"Ah," said James, "And what exactly did they say?"

Neville told James that the only way he could save mankind from an eternal enslavement to the angels was to hand his soul on a platter to a whore, to beg her to love him, to accept his soul.

"I had thought Margaret, but even if I could overcome my hesitancy in loving her I *still* could not hand her my soul because she is no whore. She may not be the epitome of saintly virtue, but Margaret is no whore, no street harlot. James, I thought I *had* a choice, but there is none. None. We have all been trapped, and we are all struggling useless in that trap."

James lowered his head, staring at his tanned forearms where they crossed on the table before him. Finally, he looked up with eyes gone very strange.

"In any apparent two-way fork in the path ahead," he said very quietly, his eyes locking into Neville's, "there is *always* a third way, a third path, a third potential choice that those who seek to control you do *not* want you to see, or to understand. Do not allow the angels to blind you, Thomas. Do not let your own anger and despair blind you. There *is* a third path, beyond Margaret, beyond the angels. Make sure that when the time comes, you are able to see it."

"But the angels said . . . the whore on the street of Rome said, that I must give my soul to a whore. A prostitute who I love and trust before all others. Who else but—?"

"You are blind, Thomas. I pray that the shutters shall be lifted from your eyes before it is too late. Now . . ."

James' voice stopped abruptly. He sat, his head cocked

as if listening, then suddenly his entire body jerked and went rigid. His brown eyes widened, appalled.

"Mary. Oh, in the name of all love . . . *Mary!*" James leapt to his feet, leaned across the table and dragged Neville up as well. "I have said too much. Thomas, you must get to Mary now. She needs you. *She needs you!* Go. *Go!*"

Neville took one more look at James' face, then ran for the door.

Chapter VII

Tuesday 20th August 1381

— iv —

✝

MARY AND MARGARET stayed many hours with Joan, sometimes talking, sometimes just sharing a companionable silence. By dawn, Mary was exhausted, and her pain too difficult to control, even for Margaret's use of her powers, and so she and Margaret called for the guards and said their farewells to Joan, promising more aid once Hal had gone to his war.

The two men with their thick blanket sling returned, gently positioning Mary between them, and returning her once more into the grim narrow windings of the passageways leading from the dungeons into the higher levels of the castle. Margaret walked a step or two behind, one hand constantly raised and hovering behind Mary's back, as if she might be able with that one hand to prevent a disaster if the two men should slip and lose their grip on their precious bundle.

She felt exhausted, drained, her muscles aching and her head throbbing. But if she felt this weary and aching, then how much pain must Mary be enduring? Margaret prayed they reached the upper levels in good time, and that when they entered Mary's chamber it would be to find that Culpeper had managed to discover an even stronger mixture of his dark, dangerous herbs that might serve to ease Mary's agony.

They ascended the narrow, winding stairs—the men stepping carefully, and with the utmost slowness, lest they slip on the damp stones and dislodge Mary from their care. The journey seemed to be taking hours, although Margaret knew they'd really only taken a few minutes to reach this point. Mary tried to keep quiet, but Margaret heard her sharp intakes of breath every time the men inadvertently jostled her, and could only imagine the pain she endured.

"Mary . . ." she said as they reached the top of the stairwell.

"I am well enough, Margaret," came the reply, but Mary's voice was tight and strained.

We should not have come, thought Margaret. *This was too much.*

But now that they'd reached the main levels of the castle the men made good and smooth time. They hastened through the main hall, populated at the moment by only a few sleeping men-at-arms and hunting hounds, then up yet another winding, but mercifully not so steep, stairwell. Mary's chamber was at the top of this stairwell.

Another few minutes only, thought Margaret, *and then we shall be well.*

Yet her hand hovered closer than ever to Mary's back.

Just as they reached the final few steps before the top of the stairwell, both of the men exclaimed softly, slowing to a complete halt.

"What is it?" said Margaret, her voice harsh with concern.

"My lady . . ." said one of the men . . . and then he screamed, flattening himself against the wall of the stairwell.

As he did so an explosion of golden light filled the

space before the group. Margaret had time for only one, brief, appalled look at what stood there—*an archangel, his arms raised above his head, his hands clawed, his face misshapen with hate, his entire being hurtling down the stairs towards the group*—before the man who had screamed fell against her, knocking her against the wall and momentarily stunning her as her head hit stone.

Bitch-whore! the archangel screamed. *Do not think that* this *time you will thwart our will!*

And then the archangel's scream was subsumed by something far more horrifying—Mary's shriek of terror as the archangel enveloped her and her two bearers in his heavenly anger.

Both the men dropped the blanket in an instinctive action to shield their faces with their arms.

The archangel pushed them to one side, reaching for Mary.

Whore-bitch! he screamed again.

"Mary," Margaret cried, reaching out through the confusion of falling bodies, trying to move herself so that as Mary fell Margaret might serve as some protection against the sharp edges of the stairs.

Mary shrieked, a formless plea for mercy.

The archangel roared, grabbed Mary by the hair and by the shoulder of her gown . . . and hurled her down the stairwell.

Now too horrified to even cry out, Margaret grabbed for Mary, but the archangel had tossed her high above her head, and all Margaret could do was turn and watch . . .

. . . as Mary's body bounced down the stone stairwell, disappearing around the gentle curve of the interior supporting wall.

Each time Mary bounced, Margaret could hear bones snap and break.

There was a sudden, stunning stillness. Margaret glanced above her—the two men were moaning, half-unconscious, slouched on the steps, and the archangel had vanished—then whipped her head downwards again as a thin wail of the most horrifying suffering came from the base of the stairwell.

"Mary," Margaret whispered, sliding and stumbling down the stairs. Her vision kept blinking in and out—her head throbbed abominably from the blow it had taken—and on at least two occasions Margaret blacked out momentarily as she slid downwards, but eventually she did make it to the foot of the stairs . . . and when she did, when she reached the final steps above the bottom of the stairwell, she came to a complete halt, blinking her eyes, trying desperately to believe that what she saw lying before her did not exist.

It could not exist, because for this degree of suffering to exist must surely mean the world was at an end.

Mary lay in a twisted nightmare on the flagging about two paces distant from the final step. Her head was contorted to one side, almost as if her neck had been wrung; her arms and legs lay at unnatural angles; her body was twisted back upon itself in a manner that suggested her back was snapped in two in more than one place.

Her body, as the floor beneath her, was wet with blood, and her robe, once such a pristine smooth silkiness, had peculiar little bumps in it.

Horrified, Margaret realised jagged bits of bone poking through Mary's flesh had raised those otherwise innocuous bumps.

One gleaming, white piece had actually punctured both Mary's flesh and her robe, jutting out a half-finger's length from her left shoulder.

But the most appalling thing of all was that Mary was completely conscious, completely aware of what had happened, and of the lingering torment in which she had been doomed to die.

Her eyes, wide and tortured, stared directly into Margaret's.

"Margaret," she whispered, and in that one word managed to convey both her suffering and her plea for Margaret to somehow, impossibly, make it all better.

Her mouth agape, her face white with horror, Margaret crawled forward on her hands and knees until she reached Mary's side.

She kneeled in a pool of Mary's blood, and held out shaking hands before her.

She did not know what to do with them. She wanted to touch Mary, but could not, for any touch would double her suffering.

Lord Christ, how were they going to move her?

Margaret's mouth worked uselessly, and her eyes filled with tears. The tremor in her hands increased so dramatically she had to hold them against her chest in an effort to keep them still.

"Mary . . ." she managed, then lifted her head and stared uselessly about the hall as people in their ones and twos began to walk towards Mary and Margaret. They approached slowly, hesitatingly, their steps leaden with horror.

"Help us," Margaret whispered, her tears overflowing her eyes and streaming down her cheeks. "Help us!"

Mary, still conscious, whimpering in both shock and the horrifying knowledge of her condition, had not once taken her eyes from Margaret's face.

"Help us," whispered Margaret one last, hopeless, time.

Chapter VIII

Tuesday 20th August 1381

— v —

✠

"PHILIP IS GATHERING an army together above Paris," said Thomas Beauchamp, the Earl of Warwick. "There can be no doubt that he will move soon."

"Philip is not a man to be underestimated," the Earl of Nottingham said, watching Bolingbroke's face carefully.

Bolingbroke heard the note of caution in Nottingham's voice, and raised his head from the map he was studying. He nodded an agreeance at Nottingham, observing the young man's slight shoulder-slump of relief.

"He has much experience," Bolingbroke said, once again studying the map, and tapping it with his fingers. He had gathered his commanders together at dawn in order to discuss their next move . . . which Philip looked like forcing on them.

He stood up and moved away from the map table. "Culpeper," he said, summoning the physician forward from where he stood by the door. "How goes this flux? The latest reports I had were that the flux had virtually run its course. Is this true?"

"The scourge is indeed almost gone, Your Grace," Culpeper said. "There are a few men suffering still, but not badly. Only two score men were newly infected once we left Harfleur. In a few days those that are still abed will have recovered enough to fight."

"We may not have a few days," Bolingbroke muttered, then waved a dismissal at Culpeper. "Thank you, Master Culpeper. Without you and your brigade of physicians I would not have an army left."

He waited until the physician had gone, then looked about at his three senior war commanders. "And exactly how many men *do* we have left?"

Warwick, Suffolk and Nottingham shared a quick glance, trying to decide who should speak the poor news. Finally, Warwick, the eldest, spoke.

"Less than eight thousand, Your Grace. But if you take into account the nine hundred you left at Harfleur to garrison the town and secure our retreat, and the similar number you'll need to leave here at Rouen . . ."

"I have an army of six thousand men only," Bolingbroke said. His face was bland, showing none of the emotion he must have been feeling. He waited a silent moment, then said, "And Philip?"

"The best intelligence we have," said Nottingham, "puts the total number at some twenty-five thousand. Almost all mounted men-at-arms and knights, and only perhaps some thousand archers."

"And our force?" Bolingbroke said.

"Of the six thousand you'll take to meet Philip, nine hundred are mounted men-at-arms and knights, and just over five thousand are archers."

Bolingbroke managed a smile. Stunningly, it looked genuine. "Then if we find a mud hole for Philip's heavy armoured cavalry to sink into, our archers will win the day, my friends. What say you?"

Suffolk laughed. "Shall I have a scout find us a suitable mud hole, Your Grace, then send them on to Philip requesting that he meet us there?"

Now all the men in the room laughed, glad to find a jest with which to relieve the tension.

Bolingbroke moved back to the map table, beckoning his war commanders over. "So, where will Philip go? Will he attack us direct . . . or . . . ?"

"He'll try to cut off our retreat and attack us from behind," said Warwick. "Lay siege to Rouen, if he has to. But he *will* make every effort to cut our retreat line back to Harfleur."

Bolingbroke nodded. "I agree. And his best route?"

Warwick hesitated, then let his finger trace a shallow arc through the country north of Paris. "He'll head far enough north in the hope that we might not realise his movements. Then, once he has moved west far enough, he'll swing south."

Suffolk had been watching Bolingbroke's face carefully. "Are you thinking of attacking him on his march, your grace?"

"Aye." Bolingbroke looked up from the map, and caught the uneasiness in Suffolk's eyes. "And you are thinking, my lord, that six thousand against twenty-five thousand are not good odds?"

"Your Grace, I did not mean to imply that—"

"You only spoke the truth, Suffolk. Six thousand against twenty-five is *not* good odds. But," Bolingbroke flashed his boyish grin, "of those six thousand, we have five thousand of England's best longbowmen, hand-picked, battle-hardened. What does Philip have? A motley collection of shiny-armoured knights whose only battle experience in recent years has been of monumental failure. Suffolk . . . my friends . . . when those men ride into battle all they will be thinking of is Poitiers. They will be remembering their rout there. They will quaver and shake, and they shall be ours."

"Are you sure they won't be remembering Orleans?" Nottingham said softly.

Now Bolingbroke did look annoyed. "They no longer have their precious Maid, Nottingham. They have lost her. She will not be able to aid them this time."

None of the three other men present thought it prudent

to remind Bolingbroke that Philip was using Joan's kidnap as a means by which to drive French nationalistic feeling to fever point. Whether with the French or not, the Maid was going to be a factor.

"We will march within forty-eight hours, or sooner if we have word of Philip's movements. We travel light, we take no cannon. The men carry eight days worth of provisions only. We march—" Bolingbroke studied the map, his finger tracing a route north from Rouen. "—here, to this village. I travelled through there some years ago. There is an open space just to the west of the village where, if I get there in time and position my six thousand, we will stand a good chance against Philip's twenty-five thousand."

Bolingbroke paused, his eyes on the map. Again, his finger tapped. "Here. Agincourt."

Then, before anyone could comment, the door burst open and a valet, wide-eyed with horror, ran in.

Chapter IX

Tuesday 20th August 1381

— vi —

✝

PANTING HEAVILY, FILLED with dread, Neville crashed through the twin doors of the hall. There was a group of people huddled at the far end of the hall, gathered at the foot of the stairwell, and he sped towards them.

As he did so a scream of pure agony tore through the hall.

"Mary!" Neville shouted, doubling his efforts to reach the group. Some ten paces away both his exhaustion and his apprehension caused one of his feet to slip out from under him, and he slid the last few paces on his hip, only managing to stop himself before he crashed into the group with the mightiest of efforts.

"Mary," he cried again, and the outer ring of people parted, and let him see what lay on the floor.

"Mary," he whispered, and rose to his knees, shuffling foward until he was at her side.

On Mary's other side, a pale and distraught Margaret stared at him. "What can we do?" she said. "What can we do?"

Neville leaned down one of his hands to take Mary's . . . then saw how her hand was disfigured. It seemed as though her skin contained, not a hand, but a shapeless mess of broken bone and tissue. *Lord Christ, every one of her bones must be shattered.*

"What . . . how . . . ?" he murmured, unable to tear his eyes away from Mary, who had now swivelled her eyes to stare at him.

"The archangel," Margaret whispered, and those two words contained all the knowledge Neville needed to know.

For a moment he remained silent, then he tipped back his head and roared, the sound filled both with anger and with an agony of sorrow.

He took a deep breath, and it appeared as though he would roar again, but Neville contained himself with a mighty effort, the muscles in his neck visibly tightening. Then, after another breath, he looked down at Mary, and smiled.

"May I help you?" he said. "Will you accept my aid?"

Mary was now clearly incapable of speech, but her lips moved, and she lowered her eyelids slowly at him.

Neville reached out a hand and gently stroked her forehead—the only part of her that he could see was not broken.

I am an angel, he thought, *and if I am ever going to use my heritage then it must be now.*

But when he tried to summon his heritage, nothing came. He strained, seeking within himself for the power that *must* be there . . .

He was an angel, for Christ's sake! An angel!

. . . but the only thing he managed was to continue to stroke Mary's forehead, hopelessly, trying to keep that hopelessness out of his face.

"Mary," he said again, his voice infused with the utmost gentleness, "I am going to lift you, and carry you to your chamber."

Her eyes widened in horror. *Let me die here. Don't touch me. Let me die here.*

Neville flinched. "Mary, I must. You cannot lie here."

A small mewling sound escaped her lips, and her eyes rounded in sheer terror.

Neville looked about. "Does anyone have a cloak, or a blanket, we could lie Mary on?"

WHAT HAPPENED next was a nightmare that Neville knew he would remember all the days he would be permitted to live. Someone fetched a thin blanket, and as gently as possible they edged Mary on to it.

Nothing could have prepared them for the agony she endured, nor for the shrieks of sheer torment that escaped her mouth. Her bones crackled, shifting every which way within her body, spearing into flesh that had thus far escaped major hurt, poking even further from the rents they'd already made in other parts of her body. She convulsed, just as they had managed to slide her to the blanket, her body arching off the floor. Then, to the thankfulness of everyone about her, she lost consciousness, her body sagging in a dead weight.

By that time, though, all about her were sobbing.

"I CAN do nothing more for her beyond what I have done already," said Culpeper, his ashen face staring down at the form lying on the bed. He had reached Mary's chamber at the same time that Neville, a mercifully unconscious Mary in his arms, had been carefully laying her down atop her bed.

"There must be *more* you can do," Neville said, sitting to one side of the bed. His face was haggard, his eyes almost terrifying in their intensity. He'd thought he would be able to do more himself—*had not Christ routinely managed miracles of regeneration?*—but he'd been able to do nothing more for Mary than torture her into a coma, and then physically lift her broken form in its blanket and carry her up those same stairs she'd been pushed down.

He would let no one else help him; he would carry Mary, alone.

Culpeper gave a disheartened shrug of his shoulders. "I have set those bones of hers that I could, and wrapped others. I have given her an infusion which will ease *some* of her pain when she reawakens. I have applied herbal poultices to her abrasions and open wounds. But, my lord . . . she has been so cruelly damaged . . . she cannot live through this. No one could. The best we can do for her now is to prepare her as gently for death as we can."

"*There must be more*," Neville said, rising to his feet. About them Mary's ladies murmured and shifted. Margaret stood still, one of her arms about Jocelyn's shoulders, hugging the girl tight into her own body.

"Tom," said a very gentle voice, and Bolingbroke stepped up behind Neville's shoulder. Everyone had been too distracted by Mary to notice his entrance.

Bolingbroke put a hand on Neville's shoulder, but stared down at his wife.

His face was expressionless, as that of a man who fights to control his emotions.

"What do *you* here?" Neville said, and several of the ladies gasped at his audacity and the venom in his tone.

"I cannot attend my own wife's deathbed?" Bolingbroke said, now lifting his eyes to stare at Neville.

"Mary should have about her only those who love her," Neville said.

"You forget yourself," Bolingbroke snapped.

"Do you think to play the part of the grieving husband?" Neville said, jerking his shoulder out from under Bolingbroke's hands. "Mary's 'accident' could not have come at a better time for you, could it?"

"Tom!" Margaret said. "Not here. Not now."

Neville stared at her, then forced himself to relax. "I beg forgiveness," he said to no one in particular, although his eyes shifted to Mary as he spoke. "This is not the time for ill-spoken words or angry thoughts. Not when we have the death watch of such a wondrous woman."

And, so saying, he sank back to his stool, his eyes still on Mary.

After a moment, Bolingbroke pulled up a stool and sat down beside him.

"I have time to watch," he said, "before I must to war."

Chapter X

Wednesday 21st August 1381

(NIGHT)

CATHERINE WONDERED IF she should have gone with her brother south to whatever safety he could find for himself, then, her every thought cynical, decided safety wouldn't be worth the constant company of Charles. So, desolate, she wandered the palace, her feet scuffing the bare stone flagging, her eyes downcast, the fingers of her hands tracing along walls as if she thought to find a way out of a maze. There were few people within the palace left to keep her company. Most servants had left at the same time as Charles, and the majority of the men-at-arms had taken themselves to the walls, ready to repel any attempt by Bolingbroke to lay siege to the city. Isabeau was one of Catherine's few remaining companions, but her mother's company made Catherine nervous. Whenever they were together, Catherine could feel Isabeau's calculating eyes upon her, and she knew Isabeau expected *(planned)* that Bolingbroke would emerge victorious against Philip. Catherine had no illusions left; Isabeau would use Catherine however she needed to, so she might assure her own place in the new order.

And so Catherine avoided Isabeau, preferring to leave her mother in solitary contemplation of her ambitions.

The strange carpenter who had appeared in her doorway telling her to pack Charles' crown had not returned, and the few people she'd asked about him had blinked at her in confusion.

There was no carpenter in the palace, she was told. Perhaps he had been a vagrant? An impostor? An English spy?

Well, vagrant or not, he had spoken of her child, and so Catherine had done as he had asked. She had derived a strange satisfaction from slipping the cloth-wrapped bundle of be-gemmed monarchy into the cart containing Charles' personal belongings. Hal would find the crown just that little harder to achieve now that he would have to chase around France for it. No doubt he had thought that Charles would have left it awaiting him in Paris.

Catherine sighed, and settled into a chair by a window overlooking the palace courtyard. She had little enough to do with her time. An hour ago a servant had brought her some food, which Catherine had dutifully eaten. Now there were several hours before she could disrobe and slip under the covers of her bed for the night.

An empty bed. A lonely night.

Catherine almost wept again, but she sniffed, held her breath, and managed to control her tears. She had cried too much this past day, and she would not cry again.

"Not for any man," she whispered. She would become hard and bitter like her mother. Manipulate men and thrones before her supper, and entire nations after. She would not love again. That was too hard, and too dangerous.

Catherine sat before the window, her eyes unfocused as dusk threw long shadows across the cobbled court below, and did not care at all that soon Thomas Neville would make his choice between her kind and their angelic fathers.

In fact, she vaguely hoped that Neville would choose whichever path led to assured destruction, because then it meant that she would not have to think, or to grieve, at all.

Then she would not have to exist in a world where Philip had died, and she was a prisoner of Hal's ambition.

"How could I ever have loved him?" she whispered,

her eyes still fixed unseeing on the dim courtyard, her mind now on Hal exclusively. She was quiet a very long time, thinking over her few meetings with Hal. Mostly they had been when she was very young, ten or eleven, when Hal had been eighteen or nineteen and as cocksure as any young prince of the blood was (and even more cocksure than most, knowing he was also the Demon-Prince with a potential world throne within his grasp). She had gloried in his attention to her, gloried in the secrets that they shared, believed him when he said that if she waited for him, wed him, then together they would unite the nations of England and France.

And after that . . . the world.

Catherine smiled dully. People thought Hal was only after the French throne. They did not know that his ambitions encompassed even greater glories than England and France combined.

Well, as a young girl, feeling the first flush of womanhood coursing through her veins, Catherine had been enthralled with both man and ambition. She would be Hal's mate, the keeper of his dreams, his one love before all others, his partner in the great battle against the angels, his *soul*.

But then Hal had sidestepped and married Mary Bohun—a small matter of money only, she'd been assured—but that had hurt and disillusioned.

And then, in her disillusionment, Catherine had taken Philip as a lover, and discovered . . . love.

But to what purpose? Philip would die at the point of Hal's ambition. Had she, Catherine, as good as killed him? Should she not have become his lover only? Not have married him?

Not have conceived his child?

Her hand slid to her belly. A week or so only. No mortal woman would know, but she did. A son. Philip's son. Poor boy, to have lost a father before either had ever held each other . . .

Catherine's entire being suddenly stilled. For a long

moment she held her stillness, then she blinked, refocusing her eyes on the world about her, her lips parting in a gasp of wonderment.

And then she smiled. Then laughed. And found joy in her heart again. Philip might be riding to his death, and she would always mourn him, but there was a revenge to be had here, and Catherine would take it.

Her entire body relaxed, and Catherine realised how tensely she had been holding herself. For no reason at all she thought of the carpenter again, his deep brown eyes, the quietude he had projected, and she smiled anew. He had been right, there was no need for her to fret about the child at all.

And every reason to rejoice.

Her eyes clouded again. Save for the loss of his father, of course.

But then she squared her shoulders, and shook away her doubts. No one had forced Philip to war; this was as much his decision as Hal's. She should not hold herself responsible for Philip's own ambition.

Catherine began to rise from her chair, then froze in the act. There was movement below in the courtyard. She finished rising then moved closer to the glass, resting her hands and forehead against its coolness.

A cart, and some three or four men, dressed as pedlars.

She almost smiled. They had come to collect their wares to peddle. Then Catherine *did* smile, for if these men snatched her away successfully, then Isabeau would be left alone in this empty palace, furious and frustrated that Catherine was with Bolingbroke and she, Isabeau, was left far distant from the machinations of power.

Her smile fading, Catherine turned aside. She walked over to the larger of the two bedside coffers, raising its lid and lifting out her cloak.

LORD OWEN Tudor pulled the hood of the cloak more tightly about his face. He couldn't believe they had come

this far this easily. The guards at the city gates had acted
as if enchanted, merely nodding to the group of disguised
men who had asked entry, and signalling for the gate to
be opened.

No one had questioned them in the streets as they'd
would their silent way towards the palace.

And now, here they were in the palace courtyard
itself—and it was deserted.

He looked over at Norbury, and found that Norbury
was looking at him with the same kind of expression that
Tudor expected was on his face.

This was too easy.

"It will get easier yet, my lords," said a soft feminine
voice, and Tudor's eyes jerked forward.

A woman had walked out from a doorway and now approached them. She wore a russet cloak about her slim
figure. The hood lay across her shoulders, revealing a
dark-haired woman of some particular beauty.

"You are English?" she said as she halted a few paces
away.

"My companions are English," said Tudor, half bowing. "But I am Welsh. Lord Owen Tudor, my lady."

She raised an eyebrow. From what she could see of him
under his hood, the man was of considerable comeliness.
Perhaps in his late thirties, tall, greying reddish-blond
hair and clipped beard, a weary, kind face with grey eyes.
"A Welshman? But I thought all Welshmen were un-
civilised dogs. And you, sir, do not look like a dog."

"And I," said Tudor without an instant's hesitation, his
eyes steady on Catherine's face, "thought all French
women gutter-bred harpies." He pointedly did not continue.

She gave a startled half-smile. "Forgive me, my Lord
Tudor. I spoke poorly."

"You did that. You are Catherine, Lady of France?"

"Aye."

"My lady . . ." Tudor hesitated, not sure how to continue. They'd thought they'd have to sling the woman
screaming over their shoulders, but he, at least, had not

thought out how to announce politely to her the fact of her abduction.

Now Catherine smiled fully, taken with the Welshman. "I am at your disposal, my Lord Tudor." She paused. "And I do not hold you responsible for what your lord has asked you to do in his behalf."

Tudor nodded, then stepped forward and held out his hand. "The cart is clean, my lady, and piled with pillows and comforts."

She held his eyes a long moment, then raised her arm and took his hand. "Then I entrust myself into your keeping, Lord Owen Tudor."

Chapter XI

Thursday 22nd August 1381

(EVENING)

"MY LADY," SAID Tudor, "I am sorry, but I have orders to take you directly to the king."

"Of course," Catherine said, trying to pull her gown and cloak straight as Tudor helped her out of the cart. They'd travelled nonstop through the night and most of this day, and now Catherine was tired, grimy and grumpy and her attire creased, stained and ill-fitting.

But of course Bolingbroke would brook no delay in inspecting his prize.

Catherine looked up at Tudor. The weariness on his face had increased dramatically. His skin was now almost as grey as his irises, and there were deep pouches under his eyes, and lines in his forehead and about his mouth.

"Will you escort me?" she asked softly.

"Gladly," he said, holding out his arm for her to take.

Catherine paused briefly to talk with Norbury and the men-at-arms who'd attended her on the cart, thanking them for their care and courtesy, then she nodded to Tudor and took his arm.

He led her into Bolingbroke's castle.

"I am surprised Bolingbroke has not yet ridden out to meet my husband," she said, slightly stressing the word "husband."

She had her reward as Tudor's arm jerked slightly. "The news of your marriage has only just reached us, my lady."

"I look forward to receiving the congratulations of Bolingbroke."

Tudor paused a moment, obviously considering whether or not to reply to her remark, then moved back to the safer territory of Catherine's original comment. "The king will move out tonight, madam. He has waited only to see you."

They were climbing the staircase now towards the royal apartments, and suddenly Catherine halted, her face white.

"Tudor," she said, "something has happened here. Something . . ."

"Something terrible, madam. Our beloved queen, Mary, fell down these steps almost two days ago. She was . . ." His voice caught, and Catherine studied his face carefully. This man loved Mary, *adored* her as a woman and a queen. There was no lust in his face—he had not thought of her as he might a paramour—but only grief, respect and devotion.

"She was hurt most grievously," Tudor finally continued in a low voice. "She is near death. She . . . she cannot last for much longer."

Catherine's hand tightened very slightly about Tudor's arm, and he gave her a small nod, acknowledging the comfort.

"Once I have seen Bolingbroke," Catherine said, "I would be most grateful if you could take me to see Mary. I have met her once before, and I honour her."

Tudor nodded again, not speaking, then continued to lead Catherine up the stairs.

BOLINGBROKE WAITED for Catherine in an antechamber, knowing the fact of her arrival a few minutes earlier. He was dressed in a leather jerkin over a warm shirt and above well-fitted leather breeches. A cloak, gloves and a sword lay to one side, ready to be donned.

There was a step outside, a low voice, and then the door opened.

Bolingbroke straightened, staring at the door.

Tudor entered, bowed slightly, then gestured to Catherine to enter.

Bolingbroke took a deep breath. It seemed decades since he had last seen Catherine, although in reality it had only been some twelve months since Philip brought her to Gravensteen.

She'd changed since then—grown a little thinner, her face a little wearier, her blue eyes a little harder.

She also looked exhausted and crumpled, but she still entered the room like a queen, her chin tilted up, her eyes flashing, her shoulders square.

Lord Christ, she would make him such a wondrous mate.

"Tudor," Bolingbroke said softly, his eyes not leaving Catherine who had halted a few paces inside the door, "leave us."

Tudor bowed again, and turned for the door.

"My Lord Tudor," said Catherine, her eyes as steady on Bolingbroke as his were on her. "I would have you stay. I am a married woman, and I would not like evil rumours of solitary meetings with another man to reach my husband."

Tudor halted, hesitant. He looked at Bolingbroke, who shot him a cold look. *Go.*

Tudor hesitated a heartbeat longer, then quietly closed the door, standing to one side of it. "I must respect the lady's wishes, Your Grace," he said.

Catherine's lips threatened to curve into a smile, but she managed to keep them under control. "I have heard of your wife Mary's tragedy, Your Grace," she said. "You must be heartbroken."

Bolingbroke was still staring furiously at Tudor, but at mention of Mary he looked back to Catherine. "Do not pretend grief," he said.

"I pretend nothing, Your Grace. I am sure that you are as grief-stricken at Mary's fate, as," her voice hardened, and she stressed the next phrase very particularly, "I would be should my husband meet an ill end."

"What did you think to do," Bolingbroke shouted suddenly, taking an aggressive step forward, "in marrying Philip?"

"I loved him," she spat back. "And still do."

Tudor had also taken a half-step forward, watching both Bolingbroke and Catherine carefully, but stopped as Bolingbroke shot him yet another furious glance.

"You have a better future before you," he said, "than Philip."

"And I think," she said, her voice suddenly soft, her eyes glittering with tears, "that I could have no better future than Philip."

There was a long silence, both staring at each other.

Finally, Tudor cleared his throat. "My lady has asked if she could see the queen," he said, expecting Bolingbroke to lash out at him, "in order to pay her respects."

"*Someone* should pay Mary respect," said Catherine, holding Bolingbroke's stare.

"The entire *world* pays Mary its respects," Bolingbroke said in a hard, ugly voice. "And I, for one, am right sick of it."

He turned abruptly away, striding to the table where rested his cloak, gloves and sword. "Tudor," he said, putting on his sword belt, "I hold you responsible for the Princess Catherine's safety while—"

"I am a queen," Catherine said. "Queen of Navarre." *Sweet Jesu,* she thought. *He has never loved me. He has only wanted me as a desire, as a triumph. He has never even* understood *the meaning of love.*

"Then I hold you damn well responsible for the *Queen of Navarre's* safety while I am gone."

Tudor bowed, wishing only that he could walk out of this room. "My lady queen," he said, opening the door. "May I escort you to Queen Mary?"

"Gladly, my lord," she said, then, as she was in the act of turning, paused and looked back at Bolingbroke, now fully cloaked and gloved. "Will you with us, Your Grace? To bid your wife farewell?"

"I have spent months bidding my wife farewell," Bolingbroke said. "I doubt she cares overmuch to hear another one from me."

"Your Grace—" said Tudor, shocked.

"There is a *war* to be won," Bolingbroke said, "and I do not have time to waste on the trivialities of women."

And with that he pushed past both Catherine and Tudor, and vanished through the door.

Catherine looked to Tudor, his face visibly showing his distress at Bolingbroke's last remark. She tried to find something to say, to comfort him, then realised there was nothing.

So she merely walked over, took his arm in a gentle hand, and together they went to see Mary.

THE CHAMBER was still, stuffy, warm. Candles burned in sconces and on many-branched stands.

Catherine, her hand still on Tudor's arm, stopped just inside the door and stared.

"Sweet Jesu," she said, her face appalled.

Several ladies on a bench against a distant wall started and rose up, as did Margaret and Neville, who had taken stools close to Mary's bed. Culpeper, too, hovering about the foot of the bed, Jocelyn hiding behind him, made a movement, and a noise of protest.

"Catherine," said Margaret. Her face, like all those about her, was lined and haggard, grey with anxiety and grief.

"I have been stolen," Catherine said by way of brief explanation. It was enough, for both Neville and Margaret nodded dully, as though they had expected this.

Catherine moved slowly across the room, coming to stand by Mary's bed.

What she saw shocked and horrified her. Mary, lying so broken it seemed a miracle that she could still draw breath.

Mary, her visible flesh chalky white save for four or five unnatural red streaks.

Mary, her eyes closed, sunken, not moving.

"Is she—?" Catherine could not finish.

"She is as close to dead as it is possible to be while still drawing breath," Neville said, and the grief and anger in his voice made Catherine raise her eyes to him.

He was sitting on a stool by Margaret, leaning forward, arms on knees, his hands dangling between his legs, uselessly wringing.

Everything about him—his slumping posture, his shadowed eyes, his wringing hands, his clammy skin—suggested a deep, agonising impotence, almost as if he thought he should be able to rectify the situation with a mere movement, or word.

Catherine's eyes returned to Mary. "Does she wake?"

"No," came Neville's harsh voice. "When . . . when we moved her from the foot of the stairs she lost her senses, and they have not returned. I pray they do not, for her agony would be too great to bear."

Catherine sighed, blinking back tears, then turned very slightly to where Tudor still stood by the doorway. "Will you bring me a stool, my lord? I would sit and keep watch as well."

Chapter XII

Saturday 31st August 1381

✝

BOLINGBROKE'S FACE, LIKE everyone else's within the English army, showed his exhaustion. They'd marched north for eight days, always adjusting both their pace and, to a mild degree, their direction as news came through of Philip's force. The men were tired, desperate for rest, but at least they'd reached Agincourt before Philip.

Just.

Bolingbroke sat his horse, his commanders and a score of mounted men-at-arms about him, on a small hill that overlooked the eastern approaches to the village and its surrounding fields. Some miles distant a dusty haze rose, obscuring whatever had caused it. But Bolingbroke did not need intelligence to tell him what rode beneath it.

Philip, and his twenty-five thousand.

"He knows we're here," Warwick said softly, his eyes fixed on the distant dust. "We saw several of his scouts not an hour ago."

"Good," said Bolingbroke. He studied the distance a while longer. "He will be here by this evening. We will battle tomorrow. I will not give him time to rest."

"And our men?"

"They have the rest of the day," Bolingbroke said,

checking the sun—it was a little before noon. "And tonight. Rest this afternoon, eat well at dusk, prepare this evening. Pray tonight."

"What do you intend to do?" asked Suffolk. "How are we to position?"

Bolingbroke pointed to the meadows directly before them. There was a stretch of land running roughly north-south for about twelve hundred yards. Some nine hundred yards wide at the northern perimeter, the stretch of land narrowed slightly to seven hundred yards at its centre, then ran an equal width of seven hundred yards to its southern border.

Dense woodland dropped away sharply to either side of the land's western and eastern borders. There was no escape in either of those two directions.

Essentially, the strip of land formed a funnel, widest at its northern end.

"We form our positions at the south," said Bolingbroke. He stood in his saddle, shielding his eyes against the sun, then pointed to a small meadowland a few hundred yards farther to the south of his chosen battle position. "We'll establish our camp there, forcing Philip to the north."

Warwick, the old and experienced campaigner, grinned as he realised what Bolingbroke was going to do. "And tonight, Your Grace, would you like us to pray for rain?"

"That would be very helpful," Bolingbroke said, returning Warwick's smile. Then he looked at his other commanders. "Keep your scouts in the field, report to me as soon as you know where Philip has encamped. Then, this evening, we'll hold a final war council in my tent." He looked at each man, his eyes steady, his voice confident. "The day *will* be ours tomorrow, my lords. This land belongs to England, not Philip."

And with that he wheeled his horse's head about and rode back to his army.

* * *

MARY LAY abed, her flesh suppurating from the wounds sustained eleven days ago.

The stink was dreadful.

About her sat, as they had for those eleven dreadful days, Catherine, Neville and Margaret. At one time or another, one of them would stumble to one of the makeshift cots that sat in a far corner of the room and snatch three or four hours' sleep, but most of each day and night, they sat, staring, weeping silently, keeping watch.

Apart from keeping Mary as clean as they could, and dripping fluids through her cracked and gaping lips, it was all they could do.

From time to time other members of the household joined in the watch. Sir Richard Sturry, who had not ridden with Bolingbroke. Lord Owen Tudor, who spent much of the day fetching and carrying food for the watchers, or quietly begging one or another of them to try to rest for an hour or so. Sir John Norbury came for a few minutes each day, as did the mayor of Rouen, Alain Montgies. Physicians shook their heads over Mary, while apothecaries left bundles of herbs and powders at the gates of the castle. Priests and friars, representatives of both papal camps amassing for the expected trial of the Maid of France, also tried to gain entrance to Mary's agonisingly slow death watch, but Neville asked that only one or two be admitted so that they might bless Mary's still, stinking form.

He wasn't sure if Mary wanted them or not, but he thought that she'd be hurt if he turned them all down.

The carpenter did not appear, and in his bleakest moments Neville thought he might hate him for that. *Surely he could have done something?*

But perhaps there *was* nothing to be done save watch and wait for Mary to let go her life. Perhaps the carpenter was sitting, waiting by the casket he had crafted, himself waiting for Mary to die.

Neville wondered why she hung on so tenaciously when it would be so easy to slip away.

He did not know that Mary dreamed.

* * *

PHILIP WAS tired, sweaty and not in a mood to jest. His scouts had heard rumours of the English army moving north, but hadn't been able to confirm it until today . . . and that confirmation came the worst possible way, with an actual sighting of the English army, moving slowly into an encampment to the east of the village of Agincourt.

"How many?" he snapped to the scout standing before him in his war tent.

"Not many," said the scout. "About a thousand horsemen, knights and men-at-arms, and some five or six thousand archers."

Philip's face twisted in disbelief. "He has archers only? What is he thinking of doing? Shooting rabbits for his supper?"

Philip's war commanders dutifully laughed, although the senior of them, Constable d'Albret, barely managed a smile.

"The English longbowmen are famed throughout Christendom," he said.

"But to have only a thousand horsemen," Philip said. "Is he mad? You can't win battles with archers!"

"My lord," said d'Albret very cautiously, "a single arrow from one of those longbows can penetrate the strongest armour."

"Yes, yes," Philip said, as he sat down in a campaign chair, gesturing to his commanders to also take seats. The scout he waved away. "So our first line will be vulnerable. But we have men and horses enough for *three* lines. We will override and overwhelm those archers within minutes of a cavalry charge. Archers are useless when trod into the dust by the heavy hooves of destriers."

A BREATH of foetid air filtered through the dim, silent chamber.

Neville jerked his head up from his half doze.

Mary's eyes were open, and her mouth worked, as if she tried to utter something.

"Mary," he croaked, his mouth and throat dry from hour upon hour of breathing in the decaying air of this chamber. "Mary?"

Beside him Margaret jerked into full awareness, as did Catherine on her stool on the other side of the bed. Owen Tudor, who'd been slumped on a bench a little farther away, awoke so suddenly he rolled off the bench and hit the floor with a thump and a muffled curse.

Neville, Margaret and Catherine leaned as close as they dared over Mary, wanting to touch her, knowing they couldn't.

"Mary," Neville said again, his voice full of grief and gentleness.

Mary's eyes slowly moved to each of the faces hanging above her. She blinked, her brow creasing in the slightest of frowns as if the faces confused her.

Margaret had dampened a towel, and now she wiped Mary's brow and lips with it. Mary sucked eagerly at its dampness, and so Margaret put the towel aside and picked up a beaker of lemon water, and spooned a few drops into Mary's mouth.

Mary's tongue, swollen and blackened, licked at her lips, and she sighed in pleasure, as if those lemon water drops had been a draught of the sweetest nectar on earth.

"Where is Joan?" she said in a voice so hoarse that the others barely understood her.

"Where is Joan?"

Owen Tudor, standing very slightly behind Catherine, looked to Neville, his eyebrows raised.

Neville nodded, and Tudor turned silently and left the room.

Margaret continued to spoon lemon water into Mary's mouth until Mary moaned slightly, and Margaret pulled back. She put the beaker of water down, jumping when it slipped and rattled against a bowl.

"I have been dreaming," Mary said, almost inaudibly,

"and yet I do not know if this is the dream, or if I am awake. My husband was here. Talking. Laughing softly. Where is my husband? Why has he gone away from me?"

"He has gone to war, many days ago," Margaret said, touching Mary's brow gently, stroking, giving what comfort she could. "There is a great war to be fought, and he must lead our army."

Mary moaned, stronger now, as if in the grip of agony. "No, no, he was *here,* with me, and he would never go to war. Never! Why are you lying to me—?"

"Mary," Neville said, "Bolingbroke went to war eight days ago. We know not what has happened to him." He hoped that would be enough for her.

Mary relaxed. "Oh, so *this* is the dream. Thank you, Tom. Thank you."

And then she drifted back into unconsciousness.

Back to where her husband waited to talk to her, and to ease her pain.

She laughed, but only in dream.

Chapter XIII

Saturday 31st August 1381

(NIGHT)

JOAN'S CONDITIONS HAD improved immeasurably in the past week. She'd been released from her cage, given clean and well-made (but not ostentatious or rich) clothing to don, and allowed the pleasant company of the wife of the castle dungeon keeper. She remained confined to her underground chamber, but her keepers had provided her with a good pallet, warm blankets, and light during the day.

All this had been accomplished because, Joan assumed, Bolingbroke had ridden off to war and Mary had subsequently ensured some alleviation of her distress. Joan was extremely thankful—simply to have her dignity restored was a gift of priceless value.

Yet the strange, wondrous Mary had not reappeared. Joan was sorrowful at that, but not surprised. The queen had been so patently ill, that time she had visited, that Joan supposed her condition had worsened in some manner in the past week.

And so Joan continued. She prayed to Jesus Christ and his exalted mother, the Blessed Virgin Mary, and that comforted her, and passed the hours.

* * *

ON THE final day in August, guards unlocked and opened her door late in the night. Joan was asleep, and woke suddenly, fearful, thinking that somehow Bolingbroke had returned and that her terror had begun.

She sat up from her pallet, pushing the blankets aside, blinking groggily.

A man she had not seen before came into the chamber. Tall, well proportioned, a tired, kindly face framed by greying reddish hair. He gave a small bow of acknowledgement, and spoke quietly.

"Mademoiselle, forgive me for disturbing you so impolitely. My name is Owen Tudor, and I am attached to Queen Mary and King Henry's household here in Rouen. May I ask you to accompany me? Queen Mary has asked for you."

"Is she not well?"

At that Owen Tudor paused. *Is she not well? How could he answer that?* "She is dying," he said. "She suffered terribly in a fall after she left here, and has been lying broken and insensible since. Just now she woke, and asked for you."

Joan nodded, slipping on her clothing as Tudor politely turned his back. She was ready in moments, and Tudor led her out of the cell and upwards towards Mary's death chamber.

NEVILLE LOOKED up as the door opened and Tudor ushered Joan inside.

He rose, then walked over to greet Joan.

Feeling a deep guilt at the way he had once spoken to her, and thought of her, he took her hand, and kissed it as if she were the noblest of ladies.

"Thomas Neville," Joan said, not so much surprised to see him (she had known he was close), but affected deeply by the sight of him after so long. When had they last spoken?

"In your father's hay store," Neville said, managing a

small smile even though Joan could see he was beset by grief. "Where Archangel Michael came to us, and set us forward on our—*his*—mission. Joan, we should talk, but first pay your respects to our beloved Lady Mary, who lies a-dying."

Joan nodded, returning Neville's smile, then allowed him to escort her across the chamber towards Mary's bed.

Behind them Tudor closed the door, then sat on a stool by the wall. Keeping watch, as he so often had through these long days and nights.

As Neville and Joan crossed the chamber, two women rose from stools either side of Mary's bed. Joan was not particularly surprised to see either of them: the beautiful demon Margaret, who had attended Mary on her visit to Joan's dungeon, and Catherine, no doubt here at Bolingbroke's will. Joan did not think she would have come of her own accord.

"She woke, and asked for you," said Neville softly as they drew to a halt by Mary's bed, "then slipped back into insensibility. We hope that she will wake again."

Joan stared at Mary, almost unable to comprehend the destruction that had been visited on this wondrous woman.

"Every bone in her body has been shattered," Catherine said, lifting her eyes from Mary to Joan.

"How?" Joan whispered, almost overcome by her pity and sorrow.

There was a silence. Then Margaret spoke.

"Archangel Michael pushed her," she said, and Joan's eyes flew up from their contemplation of Mary to stare at Margaret.

"*Why?*" she said. But somehow Joan knew why. Michael would have pushed Mary for the same reason he'd thrown her from the tower at Beaurevoir: somehow Mary threatened the angels' will. *Mary?*

Margaret's eyes filled with tears, and she spread her hands helplessly. "Why? Who can know the twisted reasoning within the archangel's mind. He said, 'Whorebitch! Do not think that *this* time you will thwart our will!' And then he pushed her, and destroyed her in the most cruel way imaginable."

Neville watched Joan carefully, not knowing how she regarded the archangels. "Joan," he said, "in the past months I have come to realise that—"

"The angels are cruel and capricious creatures," Joan finished for him. "I know that, Thomas. I am no longer their creature. I am for France, and for Christ."

"For *Christ?*" he said, staring at her.

"Aye," she said, and something in her eyes made Neville realise that James had, at some point, graced Joan with his presence.

He nodded, acknowledging her understanding. "But even Christ may not be able to help," he said, hating himself for the sudden flare of pain and fear he saw in Joan's eyes. He knew what she faced at Bolingbroke's hands, and knew also that the only hope she had was that Christ would, somehow, aid her.

"What do you know?" said Joan, her voice flat.

Neville looked from her to Catherine, then Margaret. "We shall need to sit," he said, "for I have a long tale to tell."

He fetched a short bench from a shadowy corner of the room, and indicated that he and Joan should sit upon it. Then, as Margaret and Catherine sat, glancing apprehensively at each other, Neville began to talk.

He told them of everything that had happened to him over the past few weeks, of the discovery of his true self, of his experiences in the Field of Angels, and of what he had learned there. He told them of the choice, the decision *(Hand his soul to Margaret, and save mankind? Or find himself unable to do that, and allow his soul to revert into the care of the angels, ensuring mankind's eternal enslavement to the will of the angels?)* that the angels would shortly force upon him, and of the manner in which they had ensured his eventual decision *must* be in their favour.

He did not tell them of how he'd freed Christ from the

cross, or of the strange presence of James the carpenter within his life. That knowledge was for only James to impart.

"Margaret," Neville finished, looking at her across Mary's broken body, "believe me that I would give anything to choose you, that I love you with all my heart, but that . . ."

Margaret's shoulders shuddered, and she raised a shaking hand to her mouth. Her face was horrified, her eyes shimmering with tears.

She stood, stumbling a little, and walked about the bed to fall to her knees before her husband. "Tom," she whispered, "you cannot choose me, because of something that *I* did. I know that. Oh, sweet Jesu, forgive me . . . forgive me . . ."

"Sweet Meg, you are not to blame." Neville stroked her face tenderly. "Even without that hesitancy I cannot choose you. Remember the curse? I must hand my soul to a whore, a *prostitute,* who I love unreservedly. You may be many things, my dear, but you are no whore."

He dropped his hand from Margaret's hand, and sighed. "Dear Christ, what am I to do? *What?*"

There was a very long silence as the three women contemplated the unthinkable. Thomas' soul would revert to the angels, and mankind would be doomed.

Joan lowered her head, fighting off bleak despair. All she'd gone through would be for nothing. France would be lost along with mankind's freedom.

Neville looked at their faces, then took a deep breath, hating that he was now about to give them unsubstantiated hope. "But . . . there may be a third way. A wise man once told me that in every seemingly two-way-only decision, there is always a shadowy third path. A third choice. If I can find that third choice, then perhaps I can keep mankind from an eternal enslavement to the angels."

"And that third path . . . ?" Catherine said.

"I do not know," Neville said softly. "I cannot see it, nor even comprehend it."

Everyone fell quiet again, lost in their own thoughts. Mary's breath continued to draw in and out, rasping in her dry throat. Eventually Catherine looked at her.

"Why did Archangel Michael hate Mary so much he had to try to kill her?" she said. "How could *she* thwart his will?"

Now everyone looked at Mary.

"Is she . . ." Margaret said, almost afraid to say the words. "Is *she* the third path? The third choice?"

Neville blinked, frowning. "Mary? Nay, for I cannot see how. I must give my soul, with unhesitating love, to a prostitute. Mary? Nay, never Mary."

Margaret's head sank back to its resting place on Neville's lap. "Not Mary," she whispered, and could not find the jealousy within her to be secretly glad.

EVERYONE HAD forgotten Owen Tudor's presence. He sat on his stool by the door, staring incredulously at the group of people across the chamber from him.

Chapter XIV

Sunday 1st September 1381

✝

THE MEN OF both armies rested, but they hardly slept. Partly this was due to the need to prepare armour, horses and weapons for the morrow, partly it was due to pre-battle tension, and partly it was due to the heavy rain which fell during the middle part of the night.

Bolingbroke, awake and standing under the overhang of his tent when the downpour began, smiled with deep satisfaction. Prayers were well and good, but they'd had nothing to do with this unseasonal deluge. Then he sighed, his shoulders sagging, exhaustion hitting home. The fatigue caused through the use of his powers, combined with the efforts of the eight-day march, was too great to allow him to stay awake any longer to savour his pre-battle triumph.

For the moment, Bolingbroke must to bed.

BOTH ARMIES had risen, eaten, and armoured and weaponed themselves by dawn. A half hour after dawn, they had moved into their respective positions at each end of the strip of land. To the north, the wider end, Philip had ordered his twenty-five thousand in three lines. In a last-minute addition to his original plan for a mounted charge, Philip had ordered most of his armoured knights and men-at-arms to dismount. The field was mud—the weight of horse and rider would bog everyone down. So need necessitated that the proud French walk rather than ride into battle.

But Philip was not unduly worried. The same conditions existed for the English as well—their mounted men would be worse than useless. So all the French had to contend with were the English longbowmen . . . and once Philip's twenty-five thousand reached them they could be easily dispatched.

To the south Bolingbroke had arranged his six thousand in a single line—he had no men for any succeeding lines, nor for a rear-guard to prevent any attack from the south.

It was a risk-all situation, but he'd no choice. With only six thousand, Bolingbroke couldn't afford a single luxury.

In this single line Bolingbroke had alternated units of men-at-arms and archers, the units of archers each being formed into wedges, their narrow ends at the front of the line. In that manner, Bolingbroke hoped to negate the worst of the onslaught of the French army's superior numbers.

If ever they reached the English . . .

By six the two armies were in position.

By seven no one had moved.

By eight no one had moved.

Nine and ten of the clock passed without any movement save for the fluttering of banners and the occasional catcalls across the twelve hundred yards that separated the two armies.

By eleven Bolingbroke had endured enough. He gave the signal for the English army to advance.

THEY HAD slept a little, one by one, and at dawn ate the breakfast sent in by the cooks. Then Margaret, Catherine and Joan, gently refusing the offers of aid from some of Mary's other ladies who had come with the dawn, washed Mary's unconscious form as best they could without doing her more damage, and gently changed the linens beneath her.

Then they sat, unspeaking, their eyes on Mary. Waiting.

Just before noon both Margaret and Catherine gasped, staring at each other.

"It has begun," Catherine said.

From his place by the door, Owen Tudor rose and walked quietly up behind Catherine. Hesitant, he lifted his hands, then placed them on her shoulders, offering what support he could.

He'd had time to do a great deal of thinking through the night.

SLOWLY, FOR they had to lift their feet high through the thick, clinging mud, the English line advanced. Every fifty yards or so Bolingbroke ordered a rest, so that his heavily armoured men-at-arms could catch their breath. Finally, after what seemed like an interminable march through the mud towards the jeering French, Bolingbroke called a final halt some six hundred yards shy of the French lines . . . just short of the French army's arrow range.

But just within the range needed for the English longbowmen.

The archers positioned stakes in the ground before them and then put arrow to bow, waiting.

Bolingbroke waited, his eyes searching out Philip's personal standard, then he gave the signal to shoot.

Instantly some five thousand arrows were in the air. Ten seconds later, while the first volley was still in the air, the archers loosed a second volley.

And so on, every ten seconds, for these men had been trained for years, and they could loose six arrows a minute.

Philip had no choice but to order his men forward. Needing to stop the archers as quickly as he could, he risked sending some four hundred horsemen forward with the front ranks of his dismounted men.

And so the French army attacked, straight into the narrowing funnel of the field.

MARY WOKE, gasping as if in pain. Her eyes stared wide and terrified. "What am I doing here?" she gasped in her frightful hoarse voice. "Who has condemned me to this hell?"

"You are with those who love you," Neville said. "And see? Here is Joan, who you asked for."

Mary turned her head, staring wildly at Joan. "This is not *your* place either, Joan. Are you trapped with me in this terrible dream?"

Joan leaned forward and rested her hand as gently as she could on a piece of Mary's arm that appeared least shattered. "We are all trapped," she said, a smile in her voice for Mary, "but I hope that we shall soon all be free."

TOO LATE did Philip, striding forward in the second of his three lines, realise the enormity of his mistake, but by then it was too late to stop, and impossible to turn back. His lines were nine hundred yards wide, the length of the northern end of the strip of land, but as they marched towards the English they found themselves being forced into a narrower and narrower section of land.

By the time the first ranks of the French were within twenty yards of the English, they had been crammed so tightly together that not a man of them could raise his arm to swing his weapon.

Neither, with all the thousands of men marching inexorably at their backs, could they turn back.

Instead, tens of thousands of arrows rained down on them every minute, plunging through armour with loud cracks. Those unlucky Frenchmen in the first ranks had two choices: attack, or panic.

Most panicked.

Men tried to turn and push their way back through the ranks of their comrades, or to push their way through to the sides of the field and a possible escape down the treacherous slopes of the wooded embankments. Their panic, as well as the constant rain of arrows from the sky, communicated itself to the entire French army, and soon the entire northern half of the land was covered both with panicking men seeking an escape, and with men trying to fight through the panic, mud and arrows to reach the English.

Men died in their thousands.

The arrows felled many of them, but just as deadly was the cramped conditions and the panic. As men fell wounded and dying, or had slipped in the mud because they'd been pushed or had slipped in their panic, the weight of their armour invariably brought down at least two other men.

Once in the mud, and under the weight of both armour and panic, few could rise again.

The arrows continued to rain down.

MARY BLINKED, and some reason returned to her eyes. She turned her head towards Margaret as much as she could, her lips flickering in a smile. "Do you have any more of that lemon water, Margaret? I would have some."

Distressed that she hadn't immediately thought of it herself, Margaret stood and reached for the beaker of lemon water (thankful that someone had previously had the forethought to refresh it this morning) and spooned a little of the liquid into Mary's mouth.

"If you wish," Margaret said softly, "I can send Jocelyn to fetch some of Culpeper's liquor."

"Ah, no need," Mary said. "I have no pain. I am feeling quite well." She tried to smile again, although her lips were so parched and cracked, and her tongue so swollen, that she only managed the barest of upward tilts to her lips. "It has been so long since I have been free from pain. . . ."

She accepted some more lemon water, then turned her head slightly in order to see Joan. "Do not fear, Maid. France will yet be saved." She paused, drank a little more, then continued: "France's mud is good for other things than growing plump onions."

Mary laughed a little, harsh and grating, then she quietened, looking to where Catherine sat. Owen Tudor still stood behind her, his hands on her shoulders.

"Never fear, Catherine," Mary whispered. "Love never dies; it simply moves elsewhere."

Then she closed her eyes again, and appeared to slip into a light doze rather than her previous insensible nothingness.

THE TINY English army took under thirty minutes to bring twenty-five thousand Frenchmen quite literally to their knees.

At about eleven thirty, Bolingbroke gave the signal for his own men-at-arms to advance.

They already had their orders: no quarter. So few themselves, the English could not afford to take prisoners for ransom. Instead, they drew knife and sword, and literally waded into the field of downed men struggling in the mud before them.

No quarter given.

It was slow work, hot and tiring, but the English men-at-arms and several thousand of the archers slowly worked their way through the field, carefully walking over the dead and injured. They prised open helmets, tore off plate armour, slit throats, and removed any small articles of jewellery that they might easily carry.

Over the field rose the frightful sound of thousands of

Frenchmen crying for mercy. They begged and screamed, but to no avail.

No quarter.

Very gradually the noise lessened as knives rose and fell.

For some time Bolingbroke sat his horse, his eyes moving carefully over the field before him.

Finally they came to rest on one particular area, and he dismounted, signalling some five or six men-at-arms to follow him.

Resplendent in his brilliant bejewelled white armour, a gold circlet enclosing a magnificent ruby about his helmet, Bolingbroke waded into the death with long, sure strides.

He drew his sword.

"PHILIP!" CRIED Catherine, starting from her stool.

Tudor's hands pushed her firmly, but gently, back down again. "You can do nothing, Catherine," he said. He hesitated before continuing. "Nothing but keep a death watch. You can do him that honour."

Catherine turned her head away, staring at a distant wall. "I find myself heartily sick of death watches," she said.

"This is all but a dream," Mary murmured. "Philip will be the better for his wakening. Do not despair, Catherine."

PHILIP HAD been caught like so many of his men. Several arrows had struck his armour, but none hard enough to penetrate. Instead, it was one of his own men who had felled him. Terrified, blind to reason, the knight had tried to push past Philip and escape through the back line. Instead, he'd brought both of them crashing to the mud.

Now Philip lay, trapped both by the weight of his armour and the weight of the man atop him.

The knight was dead now, for if Philip hadn't slid his knife into the eye slot of the man's helmet then his thrashing would surely have killed Philip.

But Philip still couldn't move. The dead man was atop him, too heavy to shift off (and both were surrounded by similar downed men in armour), and Philip was slowly being pushed deeper and deeper into the mud. Its cold fingers worked their way though the cracks in his armour, slowly filling the spaces with its weight. It was a slow death; eventually the liquefying mud would completely fill his helmet, and Philip would drown in its black embrace.

The back of his neck was frozen where the mud clung.

"This is the most foolish of deaths," Philip whispered. "Catrine, forgive me . . . forgive me."

Then there came a screech of metal, and the weight of the dead knight atop him rolled away.

CATHERINE LURCHED to her feet, screaming Philip's name.

Both Neville and Margaret also rose, distraught, and Tudor, whose hands Catherine had thrown off, now grabbed her to him, holding her tightly.

"Catherine," he whispered into her hair, "forgive me for not being able to help."

She began to sob, almost hysterical, choking on Philip's name.

BOLINGBROKE THREW his sword aside and leaned down, his breath harsh inside his helmet, and wrapped his hands about the fastenings holding Philip's helmet to his chest and back plates. He ripped the straps loose, then tore Philip's helmet off and hurled it several yards away.

Philip cried out, his arms moving weakly, not able to rise.

Bolingbroke retrieved his sword.

"You foolish bastard," Bolingbroke said, his voice issuing harsh and heavy from under his helmet. "You thought to have bested *me!*"

He raised his sword in both hands, bringing it high above his head.

Philip stared at him, his eyes curiously calm in his muddied face. At his sides, his arms spasmed once and then were still.

"France shall have you," he whispered, "and everything you hold dear."

Bolingbroke brought the sword arcing down in a flash of steel and screaming air.

"NO," CATHERINE cried, struggling in Tudor's arms. "No!"

"France shall have him," said Mary, "and everything he holds dear."

Catherine's body went stiff, then she whimpered, and slumped against Tudor's body.

"He should have loved," whispered Mary so quietly that none heard her, "for then he would not have lost."

RICH, HOT blood splattered across Bolingbroke's helmet. He drew in a deep breath, and tried to pull his sword from Philip's spine where it had wedged after it had completed its journey through the man's neck.

It was stuck fast.

Bolingbroke cursed, unsettled by Philip's last words, and wrenched at the sword.

It came free suddenly and, encased as he was in his own heavy armour, Bolingbroke toppled over backwards, landing in the liquefied muddied field with a tremendous splash.

There was instant pandemonium as those men-at-arms close by rushed to his aid. Four of them managed to grab at his arms and shoulders and raise Bolingbroke to his knees, then two of them worked at the straps holding his helmet in place.

There was a curious bubbling coming from within.

*   *   *

"FRANCE HAS him," Mary said, her expression one of all-consuming sadness.

DESPERATE, THE men cut through the straps with their knives, lifting the helmet off and tossing it aside.

Underneath the helmet Bolingbroke's head was entirely covered in thick, liquid mud which had seeped in with the force of his fall.

He was choking on it.

Hastily one of the men used the corner of a banner to wipe the mud free of Bolingbroke's face and to clean out his mouth and nostrils.

Bolingbroke tried to draw a deep breath, choked, made a wretched gargling cry, choked even more desperately, then leaned over, retching.

Great gouts of viscous black mud vomited forth from his mouth.

He took another breath, with much less difficulty this time, then leaned forward again and spewed forth more of the rotting, sodden earth that he'd swallowed.

Rivers of mud ran from his nose.

He choked, retched, vomited one final time, then managed to find breath enough to talk, and smile reassurance at the men-at-arms and knights who now surrounded him.

"France cannot kill me that easily," he rasped, and the circle of men laughed too loud in relief.

"TOM," MARY said, and, stunningly, managed to lift one of her shattered hands to take hold of his fingers.

She smiled, full of love and tenderness and peace.

"Tom," she said again, "I do love you so very much. Remember that."

And then she died.

*   *   *

MUCH LATER, after Mary's corpse had been washed and laid out as best it could be, a valet came through the door of the chamber, hesitated, then spoke quietly.

"The carpenter is here to measure our beloved queen for her casket," he said.

"Tell him," said Neville, "that he is far too late."

And with that he pushed past the servant and left the chamber.

He did not want to see the carpenter.

PART SIX

Mary

10000 frenchmen there were slaine
of enemies in the feeld,
& neere as many prisoners tane
that day were forced to yeeld.
thus had our King a happy day
& victorye ouer france;
he bought his foes vnder his feete
that late in pride did prance . . .
but then Katherine, the Kings fayre
daughter there,
being proued apparent his heyre,
with her maidens in most sweet attire
to King Harry did repayre;
and when she came before our King,
shee kneeled vpon her knee
desiring that his warres wold cease,
& that her loue wold bee.

—Excerpts from Agincourte Battell,
late medieval ballad

Chapter I

Friday 6th September 1381

✝

FIVE DAYS AFTER he had decimated the French at Agincourt, Bolingbroke strode into Catherine's chamber in Rouen.

She was waiting for him, serene, well groomed and robed in a brilliant sky-blue and ivory silken gown, sitting on a carved chest by the lead-paned window.

Her eyes were as glassy and as hard and as cold as the glass through which the sun streamed.

"My lady," Bolingbroke said, striding across the chamber before halting before her, bowing, and kissing the hand she raised. "I have tragic tidings—"

"I have already heard of your return," said Catherine, and almost smiled at the sudden flush of anger in Bolingbroke's eyes.

"Your husband is dead," he said softly, allowing her hand to drop back into her lap. "You are in need of a new one."

"And you are here to offer your hand?"

"Damn it, Catherine. We had an agreement."

"By law," she said, her voice both soft and hard, "I am allowed to say either yea or nay."

"There is no law between you and me."

"Apparently not."

They stared at each other, the silence growing colder with every passing heartbeat.

"I will burn Paris to the ground if you refuse me," Bolingbroke said suddenly.

"You terrify me," Catherine said, and turned her face towards the window.

Bolingbroke leaned forward, seized her left upper arm, and hauled her to her feet.

"We will marry this afternoon, after Mary's funeral Mass. No need to change your dress, you are well enough accoutred for what I need. But I would have you put a smile on your face, for I do not intend to wed with a wasp."

In response, Catherine smiled brittlely, falsely, "Will this do, my lord?"

Bolingbroke cursed, and let go her arm, swivelling about and walking for the door. "I will send your escort in two hours."

Then, just before he reached the door, Bolingbroke turned, stared at Catherine, then walked back to her. He grabbed her face in both his hands and kissed her deep and hard. She tried to tear herself away, but he was too strong, and when he'd finished, Catherine was red-faced and gasping.

"I will wive you on *my* terms," Bolingbroke said. "Not yours."

And then he was gone.

Catherine sat back in her chair, stared at the door, then lowered her face into a hand, weeping softly.

PEOPLE, NOBLES and commoners alike, French and English both, packed the great cathedral of Rouen for Mary's funeral Mass. It was a solemn affair, attended by genuine grief and loss. Mary's casket lay on a bier before the altar, covered in a crimson cloth, embroidered over with thousands of lilies and crowns.

She had been a woman, she had been a queen, and she

had been deeply loved, and the mourning for her was accomplished with all due respect and dignity.

A respect and dignity marred only by Bolingbroke's several bouts of coughing. He sat with Catherine and several earls and dukes in ornately carved chairs just to the right of the altar. Several times through the Mass he began to cough, almost choking on his phlegm on one occasion. Catherine ignored him, and it was left to the Earl of Suffolk to aid Bolingbroke as best he could.

But, by the time the monks had carried Mary's casket, still draped in its wondrous cloth, towards the side chapel where it was to be laid under the floor, Bolingbroke had managed to overcome whatever had tickled his throat.

No sooner had Mary's casket disappeared than Bolingbroke stood, taking Catherine's hand and forcing her to her feet beside him, and led her towards the waiting Bishop of Rouen.

"No point in waiting," he said to the bishop.

The bishop glanced nervously towards the nave. Most of the people who had come to pay their respects to Mary were now departing, and the cathedral was filled with the noise of their shuffling feet and murmured conversations.

Only a few people apparently intended to remain for Bolingbroke and Catherine's nuptials, Neville and Margaret among them.

"Bishop," said Bolingbroke, and the bishop licked his lips nervously, raising an unsteady hand for a blessing.

And so were wed Catherine of France and Bolingbroke, King of England, their nuptials accomplished to the shuffling of feet and the irreverent whisperings of departing mourners and the silent stares of those who remained to witness.

Once the abbreviated ceremony was done (Bolingbroke had informed the bishop that the marriage need only take the minimum of words), Bolingbroke lowered his head to kiss his bride.

Just as his mouth touched hers, Catherine's lips moved. "France shall have you," she whispered, her eyes staring into Bolingbroke's, her lips moving against his, "and everything you hold dear."

HE TOOK her directly back to his bedchamber to consummate the marriage—no need for the inconvenience of a wedding feast. He dismissed the ladies who had come to serve Catherine, and the valets who had come to attend him. He tore her lovely gown from her body, determined to wipe the look of disdain from her face, and bore her to his bed. He did not kiss her, he did not caress her, he merely jerked her limbs into the position he needed and plunged immediately into her body, taking satisfaction from her involuntary cry of pain and the defensive arching of her back.

"I want blood on the sheets," he whispered, thrusting into her again and again with all the force he could muster, "as any proud husband expects from the conquering of his new wife."

She bit and scratched, but she could do nothing to stop him. He was resolved to make her hurt and bleed and weep, and in all three objectives he succeeded.

It was his revenge for her love for Philip.

When he'd finally done, he pulled himself out of her and rolled onto his back, breathing heavily. "I'm sure we shall have a long and productive marriage," he said.

Catherine rolled away from him, curling up into a ball, hugging her belly, praying that his damage of her had not gone too deep.

Bolingbroke laughed softly, but then his laugh was cut off as another bout of coughing claimed him.

SHE CURLED into a protective ball about her belly, still asleep, still caught in her dream. She jerked, and cried out softly, then whimpered.

Her cry woke her husband. He rolled close to her, cuddling her, stroking her shoulder, gently waking her.

"*Do not be afraid,*" he whispered. "*You are here with me.*"

She blinked, finally rousing into full wakefulness.

One of her hands slid about her belly, checking. She sighed, relieved, and he felt her shoulders and back relax against him.

"*Our child is safe,*" he whispered against the roundness of her shoulder, and she felt his mouth smile.

"*I have been caught in the most vile dream,*" she said, very low.

"*I know.*"

She turned slightly, enough so she could look into his face. "*I dreamed I lived in a broken world of darkness with a man who hated me. I dreamed our child was nothing but a black malignant mass in my womb. I dreamed I was broken . . .*" She lifted one of her arms, frowning a little at its smooth round paleness, as if such wholeness was strange to her.

"*You are whole now,*" he said. "*And our child is living and warm cradled within you, not a dark malicious imp waiting to murder you.*"

"*Do people still hate us?*" she said, unable to believe they could possibly be safe.

"*No one hates us now. We are but simple folk. No one takes any note of us, no one sees us.*"

She relaxed even further, giving him a loving smile. She touched his face, marvelling at every angle, every line, every hollow.

"*In my dream,*" she said, knowing she could say this to him, "*there was one brightness.*"

"*And that was . . . ?*"

"*A man who loved me. Respected me. Trusted me. He was my friend.*"

"*And did you love him?*"

"*Aye, I did. I could weep before him, confide in him, trust him, and not doubt him. I had no shame before him.*"

"*Then he is a man to be treasured.*"

"*Aye,*" she said slowly. "*A man to be treasured.*"

Then she grinned, impishly, her hand slowly traversing his chest. "As are you."

He laughed, filled with wonder that she had finally returned to him. "As are you." He bent and kissed her.

Chapter II

Monday 9th September 1381

✝

PARIS STILL HELD out against Bolingbroke, but there was little he could do about it until reinforcements arrived from England. While he waited, Bolingbroke meant to dispose of Joan once and for all.

In this ambition, Bolingbroke had an unexpected ally. Isabeau de Bavière—now his mother-in-law—had somehow managed to extricate herself from Paris to arrive at Rouen in time for Joan's trial.

It was the least she could do for her daughter's new husband, she'd announced, and not even Catherine's studied indifference could wipe the triumphant smile from Isabeau's face.

Isabeau de Bavière had not only managed to reposition herself at the centre of power, but she had also arrived in time to slide the dagger deep into Joan's hated back.

Life for Isabeau was very good indeed.

THE TRIAL of Joan of Arc, Maid of France, for heresy and witchcraft began at eight of the clock of the morning of Monday the ninth of September and continued for a full twelve hours. It was conducted by Abbé de Fécamp, aided by French, Roman and English clerics, and all armed with the information that Regnault de Chartres had given them. Two years of jealousy, hatred, rumours, innuendo and bigotry fed their ardour to achieve a successful verdict ... and for them a successful verdict meant nothing less than a guilty verdict on as many charges as possible.

There had been many people, both within the Church and without it, who had lusted for this opportunity for a long time. Most of them had made their way to Rouen, determined that the court should hear their version of how the Maid had conducted sorcerous rituals, magicked several women into giving birth to deformed infants (and one five-legged rabbit), and uttered hundreds of heretical and hurtful criticisms of the true Church, exclusive mouthpiece of God and His angels. Her so-called miracles had been nothing but Satanic magical spells, her military skills an obscene parody of her womanhood, her alleged conversations with archangels delusional hysteria, or, worse, diabolical plottings with Satanic imps.

Joan might have a devoted following among the common people of France, but among both churchmen and nobles she had won many enemies. As much as they might detest the English, on this matter the French bishops were prepared to work with Bolingbroke. Joan must be stopped, and this court was just the vehicle to do it.

As quickly as possible so that the damage she'd wrought might be contained in timely fashion.

THE CASTLE in Rouen hosted the trial. Joan's guards woke her at dawn, offered her breakfast, which she had refused, then gave her the opportunity to pray and clothe herself. When the guards finally brought her into the chapel, Joan wore the same tunic and breeches that she had worn for so many months.

Her judges and their clerics were arrayed in a semicircle of benches and desks, their backs to the altar.

Their faces were grave, their eyes gleeful. They had her, and they knew it.

The trial began with a request by the Abbé de Fécamp for Joan to summarise as briefly as she could the history of her visions, and her campaign on behalf of the French king (who, the Abbé noted, was remarkable for his absence).

Joan, standing before them with her hands folded neatly across her abdomen, declined. "My visions have ever been personal," she said, "and my efforts on behalf of our gracious King Charles a matter of public record. I do not see why I must repeat them here."

"Mademoiselle," said the Abbé politely, even though his grey eyes were flinty with hatred, "there are many among us," several of the bishops to either side of the Abbé nodded, "who are concerned that these visions may not have been the work of the great Archangel Michael, but of Satan, disguised, whispering dark words into your ears. You must reveal what you know, or we shall be forced to think the worst."

Joan regarded the Abbé steadily. She did not answer.

"How," said the Bishop of Beauvais, who sat three places to the Abbé's left, "can we believe that the great archangel thought to confide himself in *you*, a common peasant girl?"

Joan almost did not respond, but just as the bishop was about to speak again, she said, "I suited his needs."

"His 'needs'?" said the bishop.

Joan remained silent.

"What do you mean by his 'needs'?" said the Abbé. "You surely do not suggest that the archangel had 'needs' as mortal sinful men have 'needs'?"

Now Joan hung her head, her cheeks mottling dark pink.

All the churchmen drew sharp breaths of horror.

"Are you implying," said Jean Lemaistre, the Dominican Vicar of the Holy Office of the Inquisition in Rouen, "that the archangel sought sexual comfort from *women?* Mademoiselle, I remind you that in this holy chamber you must speak the truth."

Now Joan raised her head, the colour in her cheeks coalescing into a bright red spot in each cheek. Her eyes were brilliant. "The Archangel Michael," she said, "is a sexually lascivious rapist. No more, no less."

Horrified before, the churchmen were now speechless. They stared at Joan, then they finally managed to turn their heads and stare at each other.

"As are all the angels," Joan said. *If they do not burn me for that, then they will not burn me for anything.*

The Abbé de Fécamp stared at Joan a moment longer, then turned in his chair and whispered to the friar who served as his aide. "Once we are done, we burn the transcript of this trial. I do not care *what* you put in its place, but this transcript must be buried for all time."

The friar nodded, understanding, and the Abbé turned back to Joan.

"You can have no evidence of this," he said. "Unless you claim that the archangel lay with *you.*"

There were impolite sniggers about the chapel. The Maid was too ugly for any man, let alone a mighty archangel, to contemplate lying with her.

"The archangel lay with my companion Marie," Joan said, "getting her with child—"

"She lies," said the Archbishop of Rheims, Regnault de Chartres. He had been listening to proceedings from a spot hidden behind a rood screen to one side of the altar. Now he stepped forth.

"The midwife Marie has admitted that she lay, shamelessly and adulterously, with a guard of the watch at La Roche-Guyon—"

"*You* lie," Joan began, but was halted from further speech by the appearance of a woman from the shadowy aisles of the chapel.

She was dressed splendidly in robes of bloodred silk and velvet, with ropes of pearls festooned about her jewelled girdle and collars of emeralds and garnets about her neck and wrists.

On her face she wore an expression, strangely combined, of loathing and triumph.

Isabeau de Bavière. "The good archbishop speaks nothing but truth," Isabeau said, her voice flat, then she turned to face the panel of clerics. "The midwife has admitted to me that she spent many nights in lustful copulation with the guard in question, my lords. When she found herself with child, the woman panicked, and thought to deflect blame from her sins by naming the archangel as the father.

"If that were not enough," Isabeau continued, "I myself once came upon them in the stables of the castle, naked and sweating as they sated their lust." She cast down her eyes. "I was appalled, not only at the midwife's lechery, but at her later claims."

"How can you," said Joan, her voice soft and compassionate, "a victim of the archangel's lust yourself, so seek to demean Marie? Can you not remember how terrified you were when you discovered yourself with child during a time when you knew you had slept with no man?"

Isabeau went pale, the only sign of her profound shock. *How did this peasant know about Catherine?* "Are you so great a witch," Isabeau finally managed, "that you would claim *I* copulated with the archangel?"

"If not," whispered one of the lesser clerics to the man seated beside him, "it would be the only male in Creation that de Bavière *hasn't* copulated with."

Isabeau heard the remark, as she was meant to, and she flushed with humiliation.

"Do you deny it, madam?" Joan said, and the pity in her face and voice pushed Isabeau into so deep a rage, and so great a hatred, that she did not even stop to consider how grievously she imperilled her soul with her next words.

"My lords," she said, her voice a hiss, "Marie was not the only wanton I came upon engaged in promiscuity within the spaces of La Roche-Guyon. I did spy Joan herself one afternoon, her mouth attached to the guard's privy member, pleasuring him in the only manner she could."

There was a collective gasp of horror among the gathered clerics.

"When the guard threatened to tell my son," Isabeau continued, "revealing to him that he trusted naught but a common harlot, Joan murdered him through her sorcerous arts, as she also similarly crippled two of his companions, true men both."

Joan shook her head very slightly, and looked away.

"Sorcerous arts, madam?" asked the Bishop of Beauvais.

Isabeau glanced at Joan, then looked back at the clerics. "She conjured up a golden hand, with which she murdered and maimed. I did not see this, but many did, and I doubt not their words.

"On a later occasion I spied her sorcery with my own eyes," Isabeau continued. She had regained control of her voice and features, and her face was composed, her shoulders straight, and her gaze level as she regarded Joan with a carefully constructed contempt.

"Yes, madam?" said the Abbé de Fécamp encouragingly, leaning forward.

"When my beloved son Charles was leading his army towards his magnificent victory at Orleans," Isabeau said, "we passed by the town of Montlhéry. Joan directed us to a small shrine dedicated to Saint Catherine, and there she performed sorcery before both myself, my son and my daughter. Using witchcraft, Joan transformed a rusting sword into a shining weapon of steel. Joan lifted this rusting piece from the ground, where it had lain for generations, and murmured over it, whereupon it transformed itself into new, polished steel."

"She performed sorcery before Saint Catherine's shrine?" the Abbé said.

Isabeau nodded, her face sad. "Aye, my lord, she did."

The clerics muttered among themselves for a few minutes, then the Abbé addressed Joan. "What have you to say for yourself, given the Lady de Bavière's evidence against you?"

"Naught but this, Abbé," Joan said, and turned so she faced Isabeau directly. "Do you remember, my lady, what happened to the guard at la Roche-Guyon who spoke lies against me? He died, although at the archangel's hand rather than mine. What fate awaits you, do you think, for your fabrications here this day?"

Isabeau's eyes widened, although whether in pretended or real shock was difficult to determine. "She threatens me," she cried, stepping back, one hand theatrically to her throat.

"I will never harm you," Joan said quietly.

"My lords," Isabeau said.

"We have heard enough, I think," said the Abbé. He looked to Isabeau. "Madam, we do thank you for your aid here this day. I can understand that your testimony must necessarily have been difficult."

"I swear that even *standing* in the presence of such foulness soils my soul," Isabeau murmured.

"If your soul has been soiled," Joan said, "then it has been through no work of mine. You have dragged yourself into the mud of meanness, madam. I have had no hand in it."

Isabeau reddened, angry that she had not managed to dent Joan's composure. She went to speak further, but Lemaistre waved her into silence.

"There is yet one more case of sorcery to be answered, Joan," he said. "Your tumble from the tower of Beaurevoir. How can any mortal man or woman fall that far and walk away unhurt? Did you fly your way down, like a witch?"

"Christ saved me," said Joan. "I did not save myself."

Lemaistre gave her a long look, then leaned over to confer with the Bishop of Beauvais. The bishop nodded, and Lemaistre turned his eyes back to Joan.

"We would like to hear why you chose to discard your womanly apparel and ride garbed in armour," he said. "Can you explain to us these ungodly actions?"

And so the questions and the accusations continued through the day and into the evening, Isabeau interjecting at every opportunity with her own pretended witnessing of Joan's witchcraft, until Joan was drooping with weariness and her accusators' voices harsh with judgement.

In the end, furious that they had not broken her, Jean Lemaistre pronounced their panel's judgement.

"This woman commonly known as Joan of Arc, Maid of France, is denounced and declared a sorceress, diviner, pseudo-prophetess, invoker of evil spirits, conspiratrix, superstitious. Implicated in and given to the practice of magic, wrongheaded as to our Catholic faith, and in several other articles of our faith sceptical and astray, sacrilegious, idolatrous, apostate, accursed and mischievous, blasphemous towards God and His Archangels, scandalous, seditious, disturber of peace, inciter of war, cruelly avid of human blood, inciting to bloodshed, having completely and shamelessly abandoned the decencies proper to her sex, and having immodestly adopted the dress and status of a man-at-arms . . ." His voice droned on, accusing her of so many heretical and sorcerous activities that few miscreants could have fitted them into six full lifetimes. "It is our unanimous opinion," Lemaistre eventually finished, "that you are a relapsed heretic, a witch and a sorceress, and that you are to be abandoned to the justice of the English king, Henry Bolingbroke, with the request," his lips curled maliciously, "that you shall be treated as mercifully as possible."

To one side Isabeau de Bavière's face relaxed into triumph. *Finally!* Merciful be damned. Joan was going to burn.

Joan gave a single nod, as if Lemaistre's verdict was nothing but what she had expected, but, as she turned to go, she gave a soft cry and collapsed to the floor.

For several minutes they stared at her, thinking this only a subterfuge on her part. But when she did not rise, the churchmen instructed a guard to walk over and inspect her.

He did so, first poking at her with his boot, then leaning down to roll her over a little distance.

"She is consumed with fever," he said.

THEY PUT Joan on a pallet in a small, windowless chamber off the main hall of the castle. Margaret, having heard of Joan's collapse, came hurrying and was allowed to tend her. Bolingbroke, having also been informed of Joan's collapse, sent for the physician Culpeper, then visited Joan himself.

The chamber was crowded, the lack of window, the closed door and the sputtering torches contributing to its airlessness.

"Well?" said Bolingbroke, as Culpeper finally stood back from the pallet.

Joan lay with her eyes closed, her face flushed and sweaty, her hands neatly folded across her breasts.

"She's exhausted and malnourished," Culpeper said. "She has been kept on her feet for twelve hours after spending many weeks imprisoned in poor conditions. Anyone might faint under such circumstances."

"So she will live?"

"Why do you *want* me to live?" Joan rasped from the bed. Her eyes had opened, and now stared directly at Bolingbroke.

By her side, Margaret laid a soft hand on Joan's arm.

Bolingbroke ignored Joan. "Take good care of her," he said to Culpeper. "She must not die a natural death. The Church court has handed her to *my* care and for *my* judgement." He choked a little on his last words, then coughed, short and harsh.

"Sire?" said Culpeper. "What ails you?"

"Nothing ails me," Bolingbroke snapped. "I —" He stopped suddenly, his eyes staring, then he gagged, then retched.

Black mud, perhaps several handfuls' worth, spewed

forth from his mouth. He coughed, coughed again, then managed to control his retching.

Bolingbroke slowly straightened, wiping his mouth with the back of one trembling hand. "Witch," he whispered, staring at Joan.

"This is not of my doing," she said. "I am finished. Weak. Powerless. France eats you of its own accord."

Margaret, for her part, stared at Bolingbroke with horrified eyes. "Hal? What is happening?"

"I have been ensorcelled," he yelled, then cleared his throat and spat a globule of mud into a corner of the chamber.

Margaret blinked at him, remembering the words that Mary had spoken in her final hours: *France shall have you, and everything you hold dear.*

"Get her well," Bolingbroke said to Margaret. "For once she is in the pink of health, I would have her burned."

Then he turned on his heel and left the chamber.

"I am well enough now to burn mightily well," Joan said to the closed door. "Burn me soon, I beg you."

"WHY DO you yearn for death so much?" Margaret whispered when Culpeper had left.

"Because I will succeed in death where I have failed in life." Joan closed her eyes briefly. "I pray it will be soon. France will eat Bolingbroke, and it needs my death to do so."

Then she rolled her head towards Margaret. "I have no one on this earth to live for. You have a husband and children. Do not mourn me, for so long as Thomas chooses a-right, then I shall be happy in death."

Margaret's eyes filled with tears, and she took Joan's hand. "In the end," she eventually said, "all of our fates rest with Tom, and his choice."

Joan tried to smile. "He *will* choose rightly, for he is a man who loves."

"But *who* is he to choose?" Her head bent, and a tear

rolled down her cheek. "We were so foolish to think we could best the angels. We have all been but puppets in their hands. Fate had us in its grasp from the moment we drew breath."

"Margaret has entirely missed her calling as a prophetess of doom," said a voice from the doorway.

Both Joan and Margaret turned their heads, surprised, for they had not heard the door open.

Neville stood just inside the door, and now he closed it, nodding thanks for his entry to the guard stationed outside.

Joan sat up, swinging her legs over the side of the bench on which lay her pallet.

Neville walked over and sat beside Joan. He smiled at both the women, but his eyes were too strained and tired to carry it off well. He let it fade, and reached out and took Margaret's hand.

"There is *always* choice left," he said, "even if it seems that all alternatives have been destroyed. I have to believe that."

Joan nodded, happy that Neville still believed.

"But you cannot choose me," Margaret said softly.

He looked her straight in the eye. "No, Margaret, I cannot choose you."

She turned away from him, her hands brushing the tears from her cheeks. "I wish my children were here with me," she said. "I wish I could hold them one last time. I wish—"

"Margaret . . ." Neville raised his hand to Margaret, then dropped it. He did not know what to say or do. James had told him there was a third option, a third choice, *but what was it?* Neville had spent every waking moment and much of his nightmarish sleeping time seeking the answer.

And yet there *was* no answer. There *was* no conveniently handy prostitute to whom Neville could unhesitatingly hand his soul . . . *beg* the woman to take his soul.

He was trapped by that damned curse, trapped by the Roman prostitute's prophecy. Trapped by her hatred of him.

Trapped by his own hatred of all women that he nurtured for so long. Trapped by his uncaring soul.

"I have spent my life as a foolish man," he whispered.

"You have spent your life as any angel would," said Margaret, still not looking at him, and to that Neville could only laugh briefly, humourlessly.

"Then I swear before both of you," he said, "that I will not choose as an angel would."

Joan opened her mouth to speak, but just then the door opened, and there stood William Hawkins, captain of Bolingbroke's castle guard.

"Mademoiselle," he said, his face flushing with the horror of the news he bore, "I am here to inform you that His Grace the King has just signed your execution order."

"When?" Joan said.

"Tomorrow noon," replied Hawkins. He hesitated, then left the chamber.

"Tomorrow," whispered Margaret. "We have less than a day."

"Trust in Christ," Joan said, staring at Neville. "If he said there was a third path, then he will make it plain to you."

"Would that I had your faith, Joan," Neville said. Then he stood, and kissed Margaret's forehead. "I will see you in the morning," he said. "There is something I must do tonight."

HE WENT straight to Bolingbroke, and was granted direct admittance.

"Why do you push this?" said Neville, striding up to Bolingbroke. "Do you not realise that the stake you build for Joan could just as easily hold all of mankind? You have forced the decision, damn you. All will be lost or won tomorrow . . . *how can you stand there so confident?*"

And even as he spoke the words, Neville remembered. He had not talked with Bolingbroke in weeks . . . and he had never told him what the angels had shown him.

The decision was already made. He would not give his soul to Margaret. He could not possibly give it to some unknown whore.

He must hand it to the angels.

But would telling Bolingbroke make any difference?

A slight movement out of the corner of his eye caught Neville's attention.

Catherine. Sitting in a shadowy corner. She shook her head very slightly, her face a mask of sadness. *It is of no use.*

"I have waited enough time," Bolingbroke said. If Neville was agitated, and Catherine dispirited, then Bolingbroke was a study in calm confidence. He turned away from Neville, and walked about his chamber a little, as if inspecting its rich appointments.

He stopped, and looked back to Neville. "It *is* time the decision was made, Tom. Time for the angels to be rejected, time for us to take command."

"Time for *you* to take command," Neville whispered, appalled. "Time for hatred to reign supreme. Look at Catherine, Hal. Does she look the loving and loved wife? Think of Mary, dying broken and unloved, eaten by your contempt of her. You have ever lectured me about the power of love, the damn *need* for love . . . but you are a man so consumed by hatred and ambition that you have become *every inch your father's son!*"

Bolingbroke's face darkened in fury. "How dare you—"

"How, *why,* should I choose in your favour, Hal? *Why?* Would I not condemn mankind to an even greater hell than that of the angels'?"

And suddenly, catastrophically, Neville slid into an even incomparably more vile damnation than that he'd been experiencing. He had thought he wanted to choose in the demons' favour, choose for mankind, choose *Margaret,* but now he realised that choosing Margaret would condemn mankind to an even greater disaster at Hal's hands than the one they would experience enslaved to the angels.

Choosing for the demons would not be choosing for mankind at all. They'd merely be passed from one enslavement to another.

Neville's face was a mask of horror, his eyes wide and, staring, he took a step backwards. Then another. Then one more.

He dimly realised that Bolingbroke was raging at him, that Catherine had stood up from her chair, a hand held to her horrified face, but none of this mattered.

None of this mattered, because he now realised he was triply trapped into choosing for the angels. He could never choose Margaret: firstly, because of that single hesitancy in his love for her, and, secondly, because she was no whore. And finally he could never choose Margaret because she represented the demons' path, and that path would condemn mankind to Hal's ambition.

There was laughter ringing about them, ringing through the chamber, and it was the laughter of the angels.

Neville turned and fled.

Chapter III

Tuesday 10th September 1381

✝

THE CROWD STARTED to gather in the square just outside the castle from dawn. News of the Maid's trail by the Church and the subsequent death sentence by the English king sat uneasily with them. Joan was the Maid of France—*surely not a witch, surely not a sorceress*—but their obedience to the Church, and their fear of what the Church might do to them should they make a fuss, kept their uneasiness to a sullen low murmur and the passing of uneasy looks between neighbours and friends.

Saints had been martyred before, it was almost the expected outcome for any saintly enterprise, and perhaps they should count themselves fortunate to be here to witness the passage of the Maid into the arms of God and His angels, where she surely belonged.

Carpenters and labourers had worked through the night to erect the scaffolding about the stake and to collect enough wood to ensure the Maid burned properly. The stake itself stood on a platform that had wood heaped beneath it and about it: a small space had been left clear so that Joan's gaolers could tie her securely to the stake.

A wooden board had been fastened to the top of the stake. On it were written words in red paint: *Jeanne who calls herself Maid of France, liar, pernicious deceiver of the people, sorceress, superstitious, blasphemer of God, presumptuous, boastful, idolatrous, cruel, dissolute, invoker of devils, apostate, schismatic, and heretic.*

The labourers had erected two stands a close but safe distance from the stake. In one would the English king, his entourage and the civilian notables of Rouen watch the proceedings, in the other the members of the Church who had gathered for the spectacle. Many of the clerics were already arriving, resplendent in newly laundered and brushed clerical robes of purple, crimson and black wool and silk, some of them wearing furs against the cool morning.

They fully expected to be able to discard them in the later warmth of the day.

The crowds were permitted to gather in the other two sides of the square, and in the spaces between the stands.

By nine of the clock there were some ten thousand gathered in the square. Among them was a scruffy, weary-faced English nobleman. He leaned against the supports of the stand where the king would shortly sit, his arms folded, his face staring at the stake. The skin beneath his black hair and above his unkempt beard was ashen, his eyes ringed with red, his mouth a thin-pressed white line.

Neville had spent the entire night roaming the streets of Rouen trying to find James. He'd shouted his name, he'd pounded on the doors of those carpenters' workshops he could find. He'd wept and screamed and sobbed.

But he had not found James.

Christ had deserted him today, it seemed.

Neville's eyes swung towards a movement in the crowd in front of the stake.

A man stood there, ethereal, exuding a faint unearthly aura. His features were all but hidden beneath a long, hooded, black cloak. All that Neville could see of him was a pale flash of a face deep under the hood, and the gleam of flat, black eyes.

The blackness of the cloak gave forth a faint, sickening light. A darkness that hung over the man, cloaking him from most eyes.

All eyes save those of another angel, or of one of their children.

Another movement, slightly to the left of the first cloaked man, and Neville's eyes flew that way.

There stood another black-cloaked and hooded man, exuding the same unearthly glimmer of darkness. On his hooded head sat a black obsidian crown, its points flickering in the light as if on dark fire.

An archangel.

Michael.

Neville stood up straight, letting his arms drop to his sides. His eyes moved about the crowd. There, there . . . there! The crowd was intermixed with a throng of angels, all blackly cloaked and hooded, some wearing the archangelic obsidian crowns.

All with pale faces under their hoods, all turned towards Neville, all with black eyes unblinking.

None among the human crowd realised their presence, or realised that every time they moved they bumped elbows or shoulders or hips with an angel come to gloat amid Neville's misery.

Hundreds of angels, the entire throng of heaven, moving very slowly to the front of the crowd so that they lined the semicircle of open space in the square.

Decision time, brother. Are you ready?

Neville briefly considered flight, *hungered* for the cowardice that would allow him to turn and flee.

But he could not.

"James," he whispered. "Where are you? Help me, please. Oh, sweet Jesu, help me . . . *help* me . . ."

A clarion of horns sounded, and Neville jumped.

The castle gates opened, and through them rode Bolingbroke atop a black destrier—*as black as the angels' cloaks*—Catherine riding a smaller palfrey at his side.

She was dressed in crimson, and it did nothing to soften the lines about her eyes, or the strain about her mouth.

Behind them rode Isabeau de Bavière, clad in demure grey, but with such a gleam of triumph in her eyes and her bearing that her entire face had lost its fragile air of beauty to a hard mask of malice. Isabeau was certain that, if nothing else, the horror of being burned alive would surely dent Joan's irritating composure.

Isabeau meant to enjoy Joan's death.

Following Isabeau rode a score of nobles, all splendidly accoutred, and perhaps a hundred heavily weaponed men-at-arms.

And behind them came a cart drawn by four great horses. On this cart sat a cage, and in this cage, clinging to its bars, stood Joan. She wore nothing but a simple unflattering sleeveless shift of undyed linen that came down to her calves; in places it clung in great patches to her skin where she had sweated. Joan's hair had been rough-cut very short to an uncombed dark cap about her head. Her eyes were wide, staring, but strangely calm. She almost seemed to be in another place. Neville wondered what she saw with those eyes . . . the market square, or something far more strange?

About her neck someone had hung a sign which read, simply, *Sorceress*.

Behind the cart walked Margaret, looking terrified rather than calm. Her clothing, while not quite so basic as Joan's, was almost as simple: a pale grey woollen robe, a simple corded belt tied low about her hips, a white lawn veil holding back her hair.

Neville's heart lurched within his chest, and his eyes filled with tears. *Poor Margaret. Did she think he had deserted her?*

But perhaps he had, for the angels had left him no room to manoeuvre, no room to gift Margaret his soul.

"Jesu! Jesu!" Neville whispered, not caring that his staring eyes and ashen face drew concerned looks from those in the crowd close to him. *Where is this third path, James? Where my third option?*

At that moment he saw Bolingbroke's face harden, and the man's hands jerk against his horse's reins as they tightened.

He'd just seen the angels ringed about the square.

Bolingbroke stared, then his eyes darted about until they found Neville, still close to the stand where Bolingbroke would eventually sit. His lips moved soundlessly, but Neville could hear Bolingbroke's voice in his head.

Do not fail me now, Neville. Do not fail Margaret.

Neville broke out into a sweat. *I will fail if I choose the path you point me at, Hal.*

Bolingbroke's face contorted, and Neville knew he struggled to contain his rage. If they'd been alone, if tens of thousands had not been watching, if the damned *angels* had not stood there gloating in their imminent victory, then Neville knew Bolingbroke would have been hard-pressed not to reach out and destroy him for that thought.

Far behind Bolingbroke, Margaret let out a soft cry of terror as she, too, caught a glimpse of the ranks of the angels about the square.

It drew Neville's eyes back to her, and he began to cry for her and for mankind, whom this morning he would be forced to condemn into eternal enslavement.

He cried for himself, as well, knowing that his failure would doom him to an eternal hell clasped within the brotherhood of the angels. He moaned most pitifully, and bent over, his clenched fists at his forehead. *Why couldn't he hand his soul to Margaret? Why? Sweet Jesu knew that he loved her. Oh, why? Why?*

The black glimmering ranks of the angels shifted, almost as if they had no solid foothold on the ground, and they drifted in the slight breeze that blew through the square.

You cannot choose Margaret, they whispered about Neville. *You know that . . . Beloved Brother among Us.*

Bolingbroke and his entourage had now reached the stand while the cart bearing Joan, Margaret still walking behind it, drew into the open space in front of the stake.

Joan, lost in some strange world of her own, stared unseeing about her.

Margaret shrank closer to the cart, one hand gripping its backboard, her eyes staring, terrified, at the angels about her.

Many of them hissed at her: *Demon. Bitch. Heretic imp.*

Bolingbroke dismounted from his horse, looked to make sure that Owen Tudor helped Catherine down from her mount, then shot Neville a smouldering glance of anger. *Choose Margaret. Hand her your soul. You have no choice.*

"I have no choice," whispered Neville, "at that you are right . . . but I cannot choose Margaret."

Bolingbroke's face shifted, his rage almost breaking through, then he swung away, and climbed into the stand.

Catherine sent Neville one brief, despairing look, then she, too, climbed into the stand, Owen Tudor close behind her. As Isabeau followed her daughter into the stand she glanced at Neville curiously. A dishevelled noble the worse for drink, she thought, and dismissed him from her mind.

Shaking, a hand clutching one of the wooden supports of the stand almost as hard as Margaret clutched at the cart, Neville turned back to look into the square.

The angels were now, quite literally, shaking. Their forms jiggered and danced about, the rims of their tightly drawn hoods fluttering and flapping, although they generally kept their places in the semicircle at the front of the crowd.

They were having fun, and it showed.

Another clarion of horns, and again Neville jumped.

Bolingbroke was in the stand now, and he moved to its front. He pointed down at Joan, now kneeling in her cage, still clinging to its bars.

"Witch and sorceress," he said in his clear, carrying voice. "Heretic and harlot, bloodletter and drinker . . . so has this Joan, so-called Maid of France, been condemned by our mother Church." Bolingbroke glanced at the stand containing the clerics, and they all nodded solemnly.

"People of France," Bolingbroke continued. "You think that Joan has worked for you, worked in your favour, but in reality she has been a harlot of the devil, working towards your eventual enslavement to the minions of hell. She is no earthly woman—for what earthly woman wears men's clothes, and armour, and wields a lance? What earthly woman refuses the embrace of a man, and refuses to bear his children? What earthly woman," his voice had risen now to a shout, "can fly from the tops of towers and land a mile away? She is a witch, a sorceress, and her contamination can be erased only by the purifying caress of the flames."

The crowd murmured, and shifted, disliking not so much Bolingbroke's words, but the vile manner in which he spoke them.

"Men of France—" Bolingbroke called out again, but was prevented from continuing by one of the angels, who now stepped forth, throwing his arms out wide.

Instantly, a great stillness fell upon the crowd, and Neville knew that the angel—Archangel Michael—had ensorcelled the ordinary men and women into a dream state. They might see, and might even remember, but it would be as a dream, not a reality.

Michael threw back his hood, revealing a bald cavernous skull only barely covered with dead white skin.

As the hood of his cloak dropped, so the obsidian crown vanished, then reappeared about the archangel's white-skinned skull as the hood folded about his shoulders.

Let us see who is the witch here, he hissed. *And let us finally decide this battle, once and for all.*

He turned slightly, holding out his hand, and Neville, sick to his stomach, his hands trembling with his dread, stumbled helplessly forth into the clear space.

Thomas Neville, the archangel said, and the ranks of the angels about him took up the refrain. *Thomas Neville! Thomas Neville! Thomas Neville!*

Neville wept, silent and despairing, not able to tear his eyes from Margaret, who was rigid with terror.

Beloved brother, said Michael, *one among us, now is the day, the time, and the hour towards which for so many years all of us have walked.*

Appalled, Neville realised that Michael was all but conducting a marriage ceremony: the marriage of Neville's soul, as well as those of all mankind's, back into the fold of the angels.

To whom will you present your soul, Beloved? To whom will you join forever and ever and for all eternity? Where is your whore, Thomas, who you love so deeply you will gift her your soul?

The archangel paused. *Not here?*

Not here? whispered the throng of angels. *Not anywhere?*

Will you admit to inevitability, Thomas, Michael continued, *and hand your soul back to us, to your brothers?*

The archangel grinned, and it was a horrifying thing. *But perhaps you would like to try Margaret, Thomas. Just in case we're wrong. Just in case there is a chance she's the right girl for you . . .*

One of the other archangels stepped forth and grabbed Margaret, who cried out. The archangel, Raphael, dragged her to stand close to where Michael and Neville stood.

Neville shuddered, feeling the weight of the angels about him, and the terrified eyes of Margaret upon him.

So, Thomas, Michael said, *whither goest your soul? To this Margaret—being all you have to hand—or to us?*

He stepped forward, so close now that Neville could feel the angel's cold breath on his cheek.

Michael leaned closer yet, and lifted a hand to stroke softly at Neville's cheek. *You are one of us, Beloved. Fight it no longer. Accept it. Join your soul with ours.*

"No," cried Neville, wrenching away from the archangel's touch.

You have no choice, Thomas. You are one of us, one with us—

"No!"

—and you must hand us your soul, and mankind with it.

He paused, and the ghastly rictus of a smile re-formed on his face. *But you want to try, don't you? Go on, then. Try and give Margaret your soul. Try it. Try and give this falsity your soul.*

Neville stared at Margaret, and took two stumbling paces towards her. She held out her arms, her face—her entire being—beseeching him, and he ran to her, and grabbed her from Raphael's grip, hoping that in touching her, something within him would give.

Give enough to enable him to hand her his soul.

She clung to him, wrapping her arms about him, sobbing almost uncontrollably, and Neville's heart broke.

"Margaret . . ." he whispered.

She lifted her tearstained face to his, and he bent to kiss her, and as he kissed her he tried, he tried with every part of him, every fibre of his being, every piece of want and desperation within him, to hand to her his soul . . .

And it would not budge. Every time he tried he felt as if he were being flung against a rockface, and that rockface was the dark irk that had grown within him ever since he'd learned of her trickery in making him love her.

He tried to shove it aside, tried to move about it, but he could not . . . he could not . . . he could not . . . again and again he dashed against it.

He broke down, weeping, and Margaret cried out again in terror, and slumped to the ground.

Neville was dimly aware that Bolingbroke was on his feet in the stand, his face horrified. He was shouting at Neville, but Neville could not make out the words.

About him the angels were closing in, laughing, gloating, knowing they had won.

You cannot deny our will, said Michael, *nor the path destined for you. Come join with us, Thomas, join the brotherhood. It is so easy . . . after all, you only have to do . . . nothing.*

Neville could feel their words pulling at him, feel their

effect within him. Michael was calling him home, and his soul was responding.

Michael screamed, and all the angels screamed with him, and Neville's soul screamed, too, terrified and jubilant at the same moment.

"No," Neville shouted, dropping to the ground beside Margaret and covering his ears with his hands. *"No!"*

There is no choice, Thomas. There never has been. Come home. Gift us your soul—

He could feel it within him, tearing loose, responding to the calls of the angels.

He screamed, but that only jerked his soul looser.

One more moment, and it would fly home . . .

"Tom."

EVERYTHING STOPPED, even, so it felt to Neville, the beating of his heart within his chest.

"Tom."

The voice came again. Deep. Calm. Loving.

And the voice of a woman.

Neville jerked, pressing his hands tighter to his ears, wondering what new trick this was.

"Tom."

The angels screamed, and it was the anger and fright contained in that sound that finally made Neville lower his hands from his ears and look about.

A woman stood at the edge of the crowd.

NO, roared Archangel Michael, and all the angels roared with him. *NO! NO! NO!*

A woman, James standing a pace behind her, looking tenderly at where both Margaret and Neville sat slumped on the ground.

Neville slowly rose to his feet, his eyes unable to move from this strange, compelling woman. She was tall, and wondrously striking in appearance. Her hair was very dark, bound in a crown about her brow. Her eyes were the deepest blue he had ever seen, almost violet, their colour accentuated by her pale, fine skin. Her body was exquisitely formed, slim and graceful, and with the round bulge of a five- or six-month pregnancy straining the front of her white robe. A sky-blue robe sat about her shoulders.

Her face . . . Neville blinked, knowing her face from . . . from . . . he gasped.

It was Mary. Mary Bohun . . . and yet not Mary Bohun. She was too tall, her hair and eye colour too wrong, her health too startlingly good.

And yet it *was* Mary. The Mary who *should* have been.

She smiled, her face full of pity, and Neville suddenly remembered where he had seen *this* face before.

It was the face of the woman who had knelt at the foot of the cross when Neville, on his way from Kenilworth to London, had been graced with a vision of Christ.

And then, suddenly, the third option, the third path, opened up before Thomas Neville.

No wonder the angels had attacked her. No wonder they had called her whore.

No wonder they were so afraid of her.

Neville took a slow step forwards, his eyes riveted on Mary's face.

She smiled, and moved a little, almost suggestively, as if she knew the power of her own body.

Mary . . . not Mary Bohun, but Mary Magdalene, the prostitute that Jesus had pitied, then befriended, and then loved.

The woman the angels feared before all others.

Mary Bohun . . . Mary Magdalene . . . one and the same woman.

The third path, the third choice. Mary, who he had loved and respected without reservation. Mary, who represented neither the angels nor the demons, for she was of neither, but mankind.

The woman who represented mankind's salvation and freedom . . . freedom both from the angels, and from the demons. Freedom for mankind . . . into their own destiny, whatever they might make of that.

The whore to whom he could hand his soul on a platter.

Neville took another step forward, then another, and then Mary laughed and she ran lightly to meet Neville. They met halfway across the square, their arms wrapping tight about each other, their bodies hugging close, and Neville spun her about, laughing and crying at the same time.

"Mary," he cried. *"Mary."*

ABOUT THEM the world erupted. The angels were screaming, Bolingbroke was screaming, and a sobbing Margaret still sprawled on the ground stared at Neville and Mary—but of none of this did either Neville or Mary take any note.

"Lady," Neville whispered, "I beg of you, will you accept my soul?"

"Gladly," she whispered.

Hesitating an instant, but only because at this moment his love seemed too overwhelming, Neville slowly bent his head to Mary's face, and kissed her.

Deeply and passionately, the kiss of a lover.

Her arms entwined about his shoulders, her hands buried deep in his hair, her body pressed tight against his, Mary took his kiss deep into her being.

And Thomas Neville's soul slid easily, gratefully, lovingly and with the utmost joy into her keeping.

He ended the kiss, and leaned back his head, and laughed with the sense of total freedom that enveloped him. Mary, still clinging tight to him, joined in his laughter, and together they spun about the cobbled square, laughing and dancing, surrounded by the throng of horrified black angels.

Finally, panting with both breathlessness and joy, they came to a halt.

"I had thought that my being would collapse when I

gifted my soul," Neville said. "Why is it then that I still breathe, and feel, and move?"

"Because," said Mary, "when you gift something wholly and completely and unhesitatingly it returns to you doublefold."

Then she leaned up to his face and kissed him again, softly, but not lingeringly. "Thank you, Tom. For your friendship, for your love, and, above all, for your gift."

Neville's smile suddenly dimmed. "Will I lose you?"

"I must return to my husband, and you to your wife," she said. "But we will not lose each other."

And with that she pulled out of his arms, paused, almost regretfully, then turned away and walked slowly back to where James waited for her.

Neville watched her go, his being equal parts of sadness and joy.

Mary reached James, kissed him, then took his hand and turned back to face Neville.

She nodded.

Neville himself turned back to those staring at him.

The angels, their entire beings still and silent as they watched.

Their eyes flat. Unbelieving.

Margaret, on her knees now, her own eyes wide, but with disbelief and relief combined.

Bolingbroke, still furious, his fists clenched at his sides.

Catherine, watching from her chair beside Bolingbroke, weeping with joy.

Neville looked back to Archangel Michael. "Enjoy your cold, bitter flowers for eternity, Michael," he said, "but enjoy them without me, and without mankind. I have made my choice, and I *deny* you."

And at that instant of denial, Neville felt the power of the angels flood through him.

I deny you, he whispered with his mind, and more power filled him.

Is this how Christ managed his miracles? he wondered

in a tiny, distant part of his mind as he stared unblinkingly, coldly, at Archangel Michael. *Because in denying the angels he gained their power?*

But now was not the time to ponder such things, for Neville understood that this power might not last long.

And so Thomas Neville smiled, cold and hard, knowing the vengeance he would exact on the angels.

On his brothers.

He opened his mouth, hesitated, then spoke the incantation of Opening, the incantation that all Keepers spoke when they wanted to open the cleft into Hell.

Michael's face opened in an horrific, but completely soundless, scream. He tried to tear himself away from Neville's smile, but he could not, for he was trapped by the incantation.

"I deny you, and all yours," Neville said. "Go forth to your own creation, Michael, the bitter fields of hell, and never trouble this mortal realm again."

There was a terrible grinding sound, and a fifty-foot-long rent appeared in the centre of the square. Stream and sulphur rose from it in great loathsome gouts, and flames flickered high into the air.

The angels screeched, twisting this way and that, but Thomas Neville, brother angel, was speaking again, completing the incantation.

When it was done, he spoke each of the angel's names, knowing them as part of their shared knowledge, and as he spoke each angel's name, so a tongue of flame twisted out of the Cleft and enveloped the shrieking angel, dragging him down into hell.

Neville left Michael to last. "Farewell, brother," Neville said. "I embrace mortality—may you embrace your new eternity. Farewell . . . Michael."

Michael surged forward towards Neville, his face twisting in his hatred and fury . . . but just as his hands reached for Neville, so the flame enveloped him, dragging Michael screaming into hell.

There was a moment left, only a moment, and Neville

knew what he had to do in that moment. He spoke one more word, and Wynkyn de Worde's Book of Incantations appeared in his hands.

Neville stepped forward, and, as the Cleft started to grind closed, threw the book down into hell.

There was a sudden surge of sulphurous flame, a shriek from beyond the Cleft as if this was, indeed, the final indignity, and then the ground closed, and there was nothing left to remind the watchers of what had just occurred save a faint odour of sulphur in the air.

There was a long moment, a long drawn-out gasp, an instant of silence, and in that instant several things happened.

All power seeped away from Neville, and he felt himself mortal, and vulnerable, and felt joyous in that mortality and vulnerability.

Free from the angels.

Bolingbroke strode to the front of the stand, shouting: "I *will* still have France, Neville. Nothing you have done here this morning can stop that."

And after France, the world, Neville thought. He began to say something, but was stopped by Mary, who had again walked forward.

This time, however, she did not look at Neville. She walked slowly and confidently to within ten or fifteen paces of the stand where Bolingbroke stood, looking furiously down.

"You did not love me," she said, "when that would have been the easiest thing in the world to have done." Her face softened into regret as she saw shock spread across Bolingbroke's face.

In that moment he had realised who she was and who she had been.

"France will *eat* you," she said, her voice soft yet carrying easily, then she swung about, and walked a little more slowly towards the cart which held the iron-caged Joan. Mary climbed agilely onto the large wheel, and from there took a firm grip on the iron bars of the cage.

"Joan?" she said. "Joan?"

Joan, whom everyone had forgotten in the past extraordinary minutes, crept forward towards the woman clinging to the side of her cage.

"I know you," she said. "You were the woman at the foot of Christ's cross. You were kind to me. And you were the Queen Mary, who was kind to me also."

"Aye," said Mary, "I was both those women. Come here, Joan, and kiss me."

Wondering that she should be so blessed, Joan moved to the side of the cage, and leaned close enough to Mary that their lips could briefly brush.

"Go home, Joan," said Mary, and smiled, suddenly and brilliantly.

Joan stared in amazement, and then her face went blank, and her eyes lifeless.

Her breast might still rise and fall with breath, but Joan was no longer there.

She had gone home to her father's sheep.

Mary smiled once more, soft and sad, then climbed down from the cart. She walked back to James, took his hand, and without a backward glance both of them faded into the crowd.

AND EVERYTHING woke up, and returned to the moment.

"BURN HER," screamed Bolingbroke, beside himself with rage and frustration. "Burn her."

The crowd murmured and shifted, knowing in their souls if not their minds that something extraordinary had just passed. A company of men-at-arms moved forward to drag an unresisting Joan from the cage.

No one noticed that the placard that hung about her neck had changed. No longer did it read *Sorceress*.

Now it simply read *Shepherdess*.

* * *

NEVILLE LEANED down and took Margaret's hands, helping her to her feet. She stared wordlessly at him, and he smiled, and pulled her gently against him.

"I have had enough of great doings, my love," he said. "Shall we go home, and watch over our children?"

"Mary . . ." she said.

Neville laughed, his hands circling Margaret's waist and lifting her high in the air in the full joy of the moment.

"Mary has given us back to each other," he said. "It is a precious gift that we should not waste."

Margaret's mouth trembled, and the tears in her eyes spilled over, but she finally managed a smile. "I had not known—"

"None of us did," Neville whispered, lowering her so he could kiss her. "None of us knew that Mary was our salvation." Then he grinned, and hugged her to him before gently moving her away from the square.

Behind them flames started to lick at the still figure tied to the stake.

"Let us go home," Neville said, "and to our lives."

ISABEAU DE Bavière savoured each lick of the flames, each spreading scorch of Joan's flesh. She watched as the flames enveloped Joan's feet and ankles, and shuddered in pleasure as the girl's skin bubbled and burst before it caught aflame. She leaned forward, her eyes bright, as the flesh of the girl's calves rippled then dissolved into blackened agony as they charred. She gasped with delight as Joan's shift suddenly roared into flame, obscuring the girl's face and turning her hair into a roaring inferno.

She moaned, triumphant, as the dying girl's tendons snapped in the heat and her limbs jerked as they cooked.

And finally, Isabeau de Bavière sighed, replete, as Joan's chains melted in the heat and her charred and unrecognisable body fell into the cauldron of flames in a scattering of sparks and a sudden, surprising, sizzle of melting body fat.

Isabeau's only disappointment—and it was indeed a profound one—was that the girl had not made one sound, not one moan, not one cry, not a single screech, as she had died her agonising death.

Joan's composure had not faltered for one instant.

JOAN SAT in the thick grass of the mountain meadow, half-dreaming in the warm embrace of the sunlight falling about her. Sheep ranged in a thick creamy crowd in every direction, and Joan thought she had never seen sheep looking so fat and so healthy.

She sighed, contented, although she knew there was yet one thing she needed to do. She rose, cast her eyes about the sheep once more to satisfy herself as to their safety, then walked down the meadow.

PART SEVEN

Christ Among Us

Saturday-night my wife did die,
I buried her on the Sunday,
I courted another a coming from church,
And married her on the Monday.
On Tuesday night I stole a horse,
On Wednesday was apprehended,
On Thursday I was tried and cast,
And on Friday I was hanged.

—Version two of a
traditional English nursery rhyme

Chapter I

Tuesday 10th September 1381

CONTINUED . . .

✠

CHARLES SLOUCHED IN his chair, listening to the lacklustre minstrel warble on and on and on about the beauty of the sun and the sky and the cursed green shaded meadows. The minstrel's playing was execrable, his voice worse, and the manner in which his Adam's apple bobbed up and down as though it were a ball on a string was quite repulsive.

But if the minstrel didn't sing and play, then Charles would be left alone with his thoughts. Worse would be the rising memory of his mother's twisted, bitter voice, reminding him of his constant failures. None of that did Charles want to think about at all. So he stared as if entranced at the damned minstrel, concentrating on the man's pitiful music, and using it to keep thoughts of his failures at bay.

He'd travelled with his entourage far enough south to reach one of Isabeau's castle outposts. It was a wretched place, full of draughts and crumbling walls and damp bedding and narrow, dark windows. Charles could not wait to move on to . . . to . . . well, to anywhere, most probably Avignon which was far enough away from everything nasty and problematical to be a safe haven. Charles was certain that Pope Clement would give him a sweet palace to live in, and trumpet mightily about how the dark English king had stolen Charles' throne (without actually making any move to force Charles to try to regain his lost realm), and entertain Charles once or twice a month at the papal table; more frequently, perhaps, if Clement entertained ambassadors or diplomats from far-flung places.

If Avignon proved too close to France for comfort (what if Bolingbroke decided *Avignon* was worth invading for its rich array of papal jewels and gold?), then there was always Constantinople. Charles had heard great stories of Constantinople's wealth and sophistication—even the streets were paved with gold and gems—and the quality of the minstrels and scholars there . . .

Bolingbroke would never, ever, surely, try to pursue Charles as far as Constantinople.

But even as hope waxed in Charles' thoughts, a niggling horror buried that hope so deep it brought instant tears to Charles' eyes.

Wasn't Constantinople packed, not only with wealth and sophistication, but also with the most fearful and skilled of assassins? Could not Bolingbroke—*or his own mother, more like!*—ensure with a hefty payment Charles' own death from poison? Or a well-placed knife? Or from the fangs of one of the hideous serpents that Charles had heard about?

He sobbed out loud, covering his mouth with a lace-trimmed neckerchief, and waved the minstrel away.

For some minutes Charles sat in pathetic despondency, weeping into his piece of lace, and wondering what terrifying end awaited him. Whatever it was, Charles knew it would be both painful and humiliating, and would be bound to involve his mother curling her lip in disgust at his inability to even die gracefully and courageously.

Then something—a noise, a movement—disturbed him, and Charles slowly raised his head.

Joan—*impossible, impossible*—stood in the doorway of his solar, wearing nothing but a simple robe and light hooded cloak . . . and, remarkably, carrying in her hands the crown of France.

Except this wasn't Joan, was it? It couldn't be, for the girl glowed with a gentle radiance and, as she stepped forward, Charles realised that Joan was diaphanous to the degree he could see straight through her.

Charles hiccupped in terror. This vision of Joan was most apparently a spectre—Joan's spirit come to torment him for abandoning her.

His sobbing increased as he cowered deeper into his chair. *Would the bitch never leave him alone?*

Was she going to pursue him into and beyond both their graves?

Joan glided forward, her expression becoming more gentle, more loving the nearer she came to the cowering, sobbing figure in the chair.

Strength, Charles, she said, her lips barely moving, *and courage and daring. These I finally bequeath you.*

And her spectral hands lowered the crown onto Charles' trembling head.

ISABEAU HAD just begun her descent of the steps to dismount the stand, the scent of charred flesh still lingering enjoyably in her nostrils, when the first agonising pain gripped her.

It felt as if a great hand had seized her heart and was slowly, inexorably, squeezing.

She stopped, one hand gripping the handrail of the steps, one hand buried deep in the folds of her gown above her chest, and stared goggle-eyed into the distance, as if her pain had opened to her a vision other than that of the rapidly emptying castle square of Rouen.

"No," she whispered, her hand twisting within the folds of her gown as another, stronger, pain tore through her. *"No."*

"NO," HE screamed.

Her hands let it go, and Charles felt the full weight of the crown rest on his head.

And something happened.

He blinked, and very slowly straightened in his chair. He blinked again, and stared into Joan's loving face. "What have I done?" he whispered, his tone completely altered from its normal, fretful whine.

It is not what you have done that matters, Joan replied, her lips again barely moving, *but what you* will *do. Gather your sheep, Your Grace, and make your meadow strong and safe.*

And then she was gone, in less than the blink of an eye. One second she was there, the next Charles was once more alone in the chamber, the only reminder of Joan's spectral visit the crown on his head.

"NO," ISABEAU said, her knees buckling, her chest and shoulders afire with the agony coursing through her, and she did not hear her daughter's anxious voice behind her, nor feel Catherine's hand on her arm.

"No," Isabeau said again, still staring before her at a scene that no one among her companions could see. "You are a peasant-born bastard . . . a *bastard*. You have no right to that crown. Take it off! Take it off!"

CHARLES SUDDENLY stopped just as he reached the door of the chamber. He stared back into the apparently empty room, and his face was terrifying in its might and purpose and utter contempt.

"I am the son of my father, Louis," he said. "But even

were I the son of some peasantish fellow, I would still do what I shall do now, and win back this kingdom from the foul grip of the English. Madam, your day is done, and *I* have done with your lies and curses. Begone."

And he turned and, striding from the chamber, slammed the door shut behind him.

ISABEAU JERKED in one last, dying breath, and twisted about on the steps to stare into Catherine's and Bolingbroke's faces directly behind her.

"Do you think to have killed her?" she gasped, and, crumpling into an untidy pile of grey silk and pale, bitter flesh, died.

Chapter II

Monday 16th September 1381

✝

"HOLY FATHER," THE secretary said, bowing deeply, "a man claiming to be the King of France awaits in the antechamber. He demands to see you. I have told him that—"

"The King of France?" Clement said. "John? No, no, John was murdered by England's boy-king, was he not? The one then murdered himself?" He sighed. "One finds it so tiresome to keep up with all these regicides."

Clement paused, affecting a frown as he glanced about the sumptuously appointed chamber within the papal palace at Avignon. So much more civilised than that mosquito-infested hall the peasant-pretender Urban inhabited in Rome . . .

"Ah, so this must be Charles, yes? The whore's son?" Clement gave a short laugh. "What is he here for? Protection from an imagined shadow? The last I heard of him the idiot had fled Paris and was seeking asylum in the south of France. And now he is here? I suppose he wants to beg a corner in which to cower."

"I am here to beg nothing," a voice said, and Clement jerked upright in his chair.

A man had pushed past the guards at the door (How? They had instructions to skewer anyone who tried to gain admittance without permission), and now strode towards the papal dais.

He did not look like the Charles that Clement remembered meeting some three or four years ago.

That boy had been a quivering mess of uncertainty and fear; this travel-stained man now approaching moved with the confidence, the courage and chilling murderousness of a warrior. This was a man who not only knew what he wanted, but who knew he was going to get it.

And, now that he'd halted only two paces from Clement's chair, the Avignonese pope could see quite plainly why the guards had allowed this man entrance: there shone a cold light from his dark eyes as if supernatural power burned within him.

Clement hastily crossed himself. "Charles—"

"I have no time for courtly politenesses," Charles said, stepping forward one pace.

Clement slid his shoulders up his throne, almost as if he thought to escape over the back of it. Around the chamber he could feel the breathless stillness that had gripped the score or so of attendants and clerics who stood about, and Clement was suddenly very well aware that whatever Charles chose to do in this chamber, not a hand would be lifted to halt him.

Sweet Virgin Mary, what had happened to change him?

"I have come," Charles continued, "to seal a bargain between us."

Words of a bargain reassured Clement. "How dare you enter my chamber in such a disrespectful manner? How dare you—?"

"I dare," Charles said, and took the final step between himself and Clement, leaning forward so that both his hands rested on the arms of Clement's throne, and his face hovered not a hand's span from the pope's, "because I have spent too much of my life playing the fool to have any time now to waste on fools. Clement, we could be good for each other. We can guarantee each other's safety and success and prosperity. Does this appear a bargain you could summon some interest in?"

Clement's eyes narrowed. "Indeed, Your Grace. But perhaps you would care to sit somewhere other than in my lap while we discuss it?"

Charles' mouth twitched, and he gave a brief nod, stepping back to sit in the chair that one of the attendants had scurried to place behind him.

"I need money to wage war," Charles said as soon as he had seated himself.

"Against?"

"Who else? The godforsaken English. I want my kingdom back, and I want to make it strong."

"And so you require me to make available the funds to allow you to do this. What assurance have I that you can—?"

The coldness in Charles' eyes intensified, and Clement fought to keep himself from again sliding back in his throne. *Sweet Virgin, this man has the power within him to accomplish his purpose by himself—he hardly has need of an army.*

"And when I have won back France," Charles continued, his voice low, his eyes not wavering from Clement's, "not if, *when*, then I will use France's power and wealth and influence to bolster your claim to the papal throne, and to extend your power throughout Christendom."

Even had not Clement so implicitly believed in Charles' ability to do just what he claimed, it would be worth backing a three-legged donkey if it stood half a chance of bringing the power of France behind the Avignonese claim to full papal authority.

Especially when the enemy threatened with destruction was the English king . . . and the English throne had always backed the Roman Urban's claim to the papacy.

"Would you not like to see the hope of England drown in the mud of France?" Charles said. "And would you not like to see your hopes take root and flower in that same soil?"

Clement smiled, the expression every bit as cold as that in Charles' eyes. "I think we can come to a ready arrangement," he said.

IN TWELVE hours Charles had his funds, in ten days he had a basic force behind him, in four weeks he had over-run Aquitaine and was advancing on Normandy. Before him Charles carried a banner of the Maid of France, de-picting her in full armour before the gates of Orleans, while behind him rode an army that swelled every day with thousands of Frenchmen who flocked to both Charles and the banner of the Maid.

Suddenly, France had found hope in the one man least likely to provide it.

Suddenly, France had found its soul and its heart and its courage.

Joan's work was done.

Chapter III

Thursday 17th October 1381

✠

BOLINGBROKE TOOK A breath, gasped, choked, then hacked a glob of black mucus—he refused to name it mud—into a cloth before bundling the stained material out of sight under the table where he sat with his commanders.

"The autumn is chill," he said by way of explanation, "and uncommonly damp."

The men grouped about the table—Warwick, Northumberland, Suffolk, Norbury and Tudor—all looked away: at their hands, at the maps and reports scattered before them on the table or at some distant anonymous point on a wall or through a window. None wanted to look at Bolingbroke.

In the past six weeks nothing had gone well, and much had gone decidedly ill. Bolingbroke had regrouped his forces in Rouen, but awaited reinforcements to arrive from England before he marched on Paris—which city had announced its loyalty to the ever-damned Charles and its intention to repel the English with everything they had. Bolingbroke hoped to be crowned king of France in Notre Dame by Christmastide, but this was now looking increasingly unlikely.

Not only was Paris loudly proclaiming its intention to

be as difficult as possible, and the reinforcing troops taking an inordinate time to arrive from England, but Bolingbroke's health had deteriorated alarmingly in the past weeks. His strange, hacking cough was taking such a hold within his lungs that scarcely a moment passed without him spitting or otherwise expelling the horrifying black substance from his lungs. His breath rattled and bubbled—anyone within ten paces could *hear* the mud of Agincourt welling within his lungs—and his entire face had sunken in upon itself. Bolingbroke's skin had turned ashen, his nose and eyebrows were gaunt ridges, his cheeks hollowed caricatures of health, his mouth a thin humourless line, and his eyes red-veined and swollen with both a constant fever and the effort of coughing.

In the past week his hands had taken to shaking ceaselessly.

Philip the Bad's curse had taken a fatal hold. Bolingbroke was a king dying, not a king about to insist on his right to take the French throne.

And on top of all this were the reports that had landed on the table this morning.

Disaster.

"I think we need not concern ourselves overmuch about these," Bolingbroke said, one trembling hand touching the parchments that lay before him.

"I think," Northumberland said, staring at the table, his own youthful, robust cheeks flushing, "that we need to concern ourselves *very* much about them."

"Charles is a walking jest," Bolingbroke shouted, shifting his chair backwards as if he meant to stand, and then subsiding, as if thinking better of it.

"If Charles is a walking jest," Warwick said, staring at Bolingbroke, "then he is a strange jest indeed. He heads an army of over thirty thousand men—"

"Where?" said Bolingbroke, thumping the table with a fist. "Where has he got these men?"

Warwick shrugged. "He's sold jewels, castles and lands, or promised them to those who aid him. He's managed to arrange a massive loan from Pope Clement in Avignon on the guarantee he'll push us out of France and then support Clement against Urban in Rome. He's called in favours and sent out threats. And with all this he had hired ten thousand of the best Swiss pikemen, five thousand of the best German mercenaries, and rounded up every knight and man-at-arms skulking about in central and southern France."

"As well," Norbury put in, "every city in France, *every one,* has promised him archers or the money to buy archers. By the time Charles draws near to us he will have close to fifty thousand behind him."

There was a silence.

"Fifty thousand," Suffolk whispered, "all led by a king who claims to have the support of the martyred Joan of Arc, returned from the dead with an army of ghosts to aid him." He hesitated, then made the sign against evil. "He carries before him a banner with her face and name on it, and it is said that her ghost rides a spectral horse in the clouds above him. With every murmur that ripples through Rouen, more of our men desert—none want to stand against such an ethereal army. We have barely two thousand men left, Your Grace. We hardly have an *escort* left to see us home, let alone an army."

"Charles is a jest," Bolingbroke said again. "A *jest,* I say. He cannot piss in a straight line, let alone lead an army into battle. You *know* this."

Every man who stood watching Bolingbroke thought the same thing. *If he cannot even piss in a straight line, then how is it he has overrun Aquitaine?*

Eventually Owen Tudor spoke into the long embarrassed silence. "Some say that this is not the same man," he said. "Some say that when Joan burned, her last action was to infuse his soul—and spine—with her courage and determination."

"These are the words of a fool," Bolingbroke said, finally managing to push back his chair and stand. He swayed, grabbing at the back of the chair to steady himself.

The eyes of all the other men in the room turned away, and Bolingbroke's temper finally snapped. "I am the King of France, and none can gainsay it."

"France gainsays it," Tudor said softly. "Philip cursed you, and now Joan's ghost haunts you. I think you will never be King of France."

"Get out of my presence," Bolingbroke shouted, his face mottling a dark red.

Tudor stood, but he did not immediately move off. "Let me repeat my Lord of Suffolk's words," he said, his eyes holding steady on Bolingbroke's furious glare. "We have two thousand men *only*, scattered in a line from Rouen to Harfleur, and every night more and more of those men desert, thinking it better to end their days before home fires and hearths than spitted on a saintly lance. You have an army of some fifty thousand marching towards you through a land that loathes you and which has cursed you. If you do not retreat to England, you will surely die, either on the point of the sword of France, or coughing your lungs out in your sickbed."

And with that he turned and left the room.

"He—" Bolingbroke began.

"Speaks nothing but sense," Warwick said. "We need to go home, Your Grace. You are too ill, and your army too small, to stay. And your queen, you tell us, is newly pregnant. You cannot risk either yourself or her or any one of your precious few remaining men in this hell hole of a country any longer. For Christ's sake, sire, think with your head, not your pride or your ambition."

"For Christ's sake?" Bolingbroke whispered, his face now white. "For *Christ's sake*? I think Christ has abandoned me."

He stared at his commanders a moment longer, then suddenly his shoulders slumped, and he sat down in the chair again.

"We will go home for the winter," he said. "Allow Charles his petty moment of triumph. But we will be back. Next summer." He looked up, his eyes bright with fever. "We will finish the job next summer."

If France has not eaten you first, Warwick thought, but he nodded agreeably enough, relieved that Bolingbroke had seen sense at last.

Chapter IV

Friday 18th October 1381

✛

"MADAM?"

Catherine turned, smiling gently at Owen Tudor as he walked to join her at the window. Then she returned her gaze to the hustle and bustle of the courtyard. "Will you be happy to be going home, my lord?" she said.

"I will be happy to see you safer," he said, looking not at the preparations below them but at her face. It was pale and thin, her eyes strained, her mouth humourless. Her black hair, so lustrous when Owen Tudor had brought her from Paris to Rouen, was now dull and lifeless, scraped back from her face without care to adornment.

"But," he added, dropping his voice lower so that the chamberlain directing the packing of Catherine and Bolingbroke's belongings in the chamber behind them could not hear, "that happiness will be tempered with sadness . . . knowing your sadness. England is a strange place to you. It is not your home."

"I have no home," she whispered, without self-pity. "The new man who rides at the head of a French army, and who once was my brother, will not want me—not pregnant. My mother has never wanted me. My husband . . ."

"Catherine, I—"

"You address me too familiarly, my lord. I am your king's wife."

"My king is dying," Tudor said, "and soon his wife will be widowed."

There was a long silence as Catherine stared unseeing through the window. Her mind pondered the fact that so much could be said with so few words. Eventually, she turned her eyes, and studied Tudor standing watching her.

He had such a kindly face. Gentle, but also strong. He was a courageous man. She remembered how he had chosen to stay and support her when, on her arrival in Rouen, Bolingbroke had ordered him from their chamber.

"Where is your home estate, my lord?"

"In eastern Wales, Catherine. It is a gentle and mild place. Peaceful."

As are you, she thought.

"Once I have given birth to my son," her hand strayed to cover her still-flat abdomen, "and once my husband is dead, I shall be more homeless than ever. My son shall be surrounded with regents, and I shall be a mere relic of glory now dead. Who shall want me?"

Tudor smiled, very slightly, his eyes warm.

Her own mouth curved in response, and she felt easier within herself than she had for . . . well, for years. Tudor might not be the great love of her life, but Catherine was tired of great loves.

"I think I should like to see this gentle and mild home of yours, my lord."

Chapter V

(8 MONTHS LATER)

✠

LORD THOMAS NEVILLE stood in the prow of the boat as it sailed up the Thames, his eyes half closed against both the sun and the breeze. He thought of the last time he and Margaret had come this way to London—then, Archangel Michael had appeared to them, spitting out his hatred.

Now? Now there was nothing but the sun and the lap of the waves and the scented breeze. Nothing but Margaret sitting further back in the boat, five months pregnant with what were apparently twins, and playing with Rosalind and Bohun, as Agnes, Robert Courtenay and Jocelyn Hawkins—now a part of Neville's household—chatted happily to one side.

The master of the boat shouted a curse at one of the men manning the sails, jerking Neville from his reverie. He turned from his spot at the front of the boat and made his way back to Margaret.

"You do not feel ill?" he asked, sitting down beside her and taking her hand.

"Nay. I shouldn't have worried about the water voyage so much." She smiled, and patted her abdomen with her free hand. "I think the gentle motion of the river has sent these two to sleep."

At that moment Rosalind shrieked as Bohun pulled at her plait.

"More's the pity," Margaret continued, her mouth twisting wryly, "that it hasn't subdued our older children in the same manner."

Neville smiled, but said nothing. He lifted a hand and tucked away a tendril of Margaret's hair that had escaped from beneath her simple lawn headdress. These past months since their return from France had been good for them.

The peace of Halstow Hall had been good for them.

They had settled down to a contented country life—overseeing the harvests and their tenants (Neville had freed every one of his peasants from the last vestiges of their feudal bonds on his return), listening to Thomas Tusser's increasingly execrable rhymes and Robert Courtenay's gentle laughter, watching their children grow in the sun and wind, making new children.

Making a life and a marriage for themselves without the ambitions and uncertainties and hatreds that had previously consumed them.

They never talked about what had happened in the square that day Joan had burned. They never talked of Mary, or of what Neville had given her.

To do that would have been to destroy everything they had managed to build over the past eight months.

WITHIN HALF an hour their boat had passed under London Bridge and was heading for the southern curve in the Thames that would take them to Westminster and the purpose of their visit to London.

Both a life and a death awaited them.

Catherine was due to give birth within the next week or so, and she had asked that Margaret be present. At that

Neville was not surprised—this would be the birthing of a new English monarch unlike any before.

And yet . . . yet . . . Neville had the faintest suspicion that since the events in the castle courtyard of Rouen the unusual powers and abilities of the angel-children were fading. A week or so ago Margaret had mentioned, so very casually as if it were of no matter, that she thought she would use the services of a local midwife to birth the twins.

A local midwife. A very normal, human woman.

It meant that Margaret was considering giving birth in her human form, not her angel form. Was she now more human than angel? Had the angel-children lost almost as badly as the angels on that day Neville had handed his soul to Mary, to mankind, rather than to either Margaret or the demons?

Was the cause of the angel-children dying with their king . . . dying with Hal Bolingbroke?

Bolingbroke's deteriorating condition was the other reason for Neville and Margaret's trip to London. As Catherine prepared to give birth, so Bolingbroke prepared to die, and Neville had come to see his once-friend for the last time. This was something he both wanted and had to do, and Neville suspected that Bolingbroke had been clinging to life for months waiting for Neville's visit.

Now, it was time to let go.

HAL AND Catherine had taken up residence in the guest quarters of the monastery attached to Westminster Abbey. This was due less to personal preference than to the wishes of the Privy Council and great lords of England. A king was dying, his heir was about to be born, and both events were to be conducted under the watchful eyes of those men who would make up the Council of Regents once Bolingbroke was dead.

At their head, virtual ruler of England ever since Bolingbroke's return from France, was Ralph Neville, Baron
of Raby and Earl of Westmorland, and now the most
powerful man in the country.

He had done well indeed from his connections with,
and loyalty to, the Lancastrian faction.

But, most powerful man in England or not, Raby was
still a family man, and when Neville's boat docked at
Westminster's wharf Raby was there to greet his nephew.
He stepped into the boat, impatient even for Neville to
disembark, and embraced him warmly.

Then he turned to Margaret, smiled, took her hand, and
kissed her in a brotherly fashion on her mouth. "The
queen has been asking for you, Margaret, desperate to
hear of news of your arrival. She went into labour early
this morning."

Margaret's eyes widened, and she allowed Neville to
help her from the boat where the palace chamberlain was
waiting to escort her to Catherine's side.

As she walked away, Raby turned back to Neville, his
eyes dark and sad. "And Hal has been asking for you,
Tom. He has not long to live."

THE CHAMBER was dark and cold, and stank of death
even though servants had set up sweet-scented braziers
and burners about the room.

Neville walked slowly to the great bed, and to the
gaunt and wheezing shape that lay upon it.

"Tom? Tom, is that you?"

Neville found it difficult to reply. Hal—or what had
once been Hal (*fair Prince Hal*)—had wasted to such an
extent he was now little more than skin-covered bone. His
hair, once so beautiful, lay patchy and grey across his
skull. His eyes had dulled so badly they were now virtually colourless. His skin was papery, so thin Neville could
see the irregular beating of the blood vessels beneath.

His condition, appallingly, reminded Neville of how Mary had died.

"Tom?" A note of panic crept into Hal's voice. "Tom, *is that you?*"

"Aye, Hal, it is me." Neville sat down on a stool by the bed and, with only the barest hesitation, laid his warm hand on Hal's cold fingers as they lay on the coverlet.

"You came." Tears slipped over Hal's lower eyelids and down his cheeks.

There was a long silence. Neville did not know what to say. All he could see, all he could remember, was how glorious Hal had been in his prime. How godlike he'd been when he seized power from Richard.

How beautiful . . .

"It has all come to this, then," Hal whispered, then jerked as he coughed.

Black mud ran from a corner of his mouth, and Neville took a cloth that lay by a bowl of rosewater on a table to one side and wiped it away.

Neville said nothing.

"I had not realised about Mary," Hal said once he had caught his breath. "I had not known."

"None of us did," Neville said.

"But you loved her."

"Aye. I loved her."

"Why? What was so special about Mary?"

You fool, thought Neville. *If you wanted an answer for why you now die, then it lies in that you still ask that question.* He did not speak.

"I should have loved," Hal said after a very long silence.

Neville's eyes filled with tears. "Aye. You should have loved."

There was another lengthy quiet between them, the only sound that of Hal's harsh breathing.

Then, eventually, Hal coughed again, cleared his throat of his accumulation of mud, and spoke once more. "Tom . . . is Christ among us?"

"Yes."

"Where? Why do I not see him? Why has he not come to me?"

"Because you did not love," Neville said, hating the fact that he had to say it.

Hal began to cry, great broken sobs that racked his weak body. "I tried so hard," he said.

"I know," Neville said, crying himself now.

"I wish I had loved."

"I know," Neville said . . . and then realised there was no one listening.

He sat there in the silence of death for what seemed a very long time.

THE DOOR to the chamber opened, and the palace chamberlain came in.

"My lord," he whispered, and Neville turned about.

"Yes?"

"The king has a son. Will you tell him?"

Neville hesitated a long moment. "The king is dead," he said eventually. "He no longer cares."

Then he stood, took one long look at the husk of the man he had once loved lying on the bed, then turned and left the room.

HE WALKED from Westminster to Cheapside in London—the distance taking him well over an hour.

By the time he'd walked past St Paul's the bells of the parish churches in London had begun to peal in mourning.

The city quietened under its pall of bells, and many shops closed for the day as working men and their wives thought to take themselves to church to pray for the dead king's soul.

But Neville knew that the door to one workshop at least would still be open.

* * *

HE FOUND the carpenter's workshop on the same laneway off Cheapside in which he had found it that day before they had left for Harfleur. The doorway stood open, as it had then, although now it opened under a newly painted sign: *James Emery, Carpenter.*

James had settled down, it seemed.

And, as the last time, a shadow lingered in the cool dimness of the shop.

Except this time the shadow was Mary, not the carpenter.

She smiled, a little sadly, as Neville hesitated under the lintel of the doorway.

"Hal is dead," she said, adjusting the weight of the infant wriggling in her arms.

"Aye," Neville said. He paused. "What happens now?" he whispered.

She walked forward, allowing some of the light from the doorway to spill over her face. Her black hair was wound about her head in a heavy rope under a trailing lawn veil, framing the translucent skin of her face and her deep blue eyes.

Neville's breath caught in his throat: this beautiful woman, this Mary.

How he loved her.

"I should not have come," he said.

"You are wrong," she said, and leaned forward to kiss him briefly on the mouth, "for it is good that you have come. James is waiting for us in the courtyard, and I have set out some bread and cheese and a jug of cider. Will you join us?"

Then she looked down to the child in her arms. "See my son? James and I have named him Christopher."

Neville glanced at the child, but the baby did not interest him.

"Mary—"

"Come to the courtyard, Tom." She turned, her movement lithe and unknowingly seductive, and led him through the workshop, the kitchen and storerooms behind it, and into the small, sunlit courtyard.

James was waiting there, and he stepped forward and embraced Neville.

Neville surprised himself at how fiercely he returned James' embrace. "I should have come earlier," he said as James finally stood back.

James nodded. "Aye, that you should have." His eyes, still as dark as Neville remembered them, were nonetheless very different. It took Neville a moment to realise what it was: James' eyes were soft and humorous, unburdened by the cares that had once tortured him.

"You are happy," Neville said.

"Aye, I am happy," James said, indicating that Neville should sit on the bench on the opposite side of the trestle table covered with food and drink. As James sat himself, Mary put their son into his arms, and James smiled at the baby, finally lifting his eyes back to Neville.

"How could I not be happy? I have my wife, and my son. Home with me. Finally."

Mary poured both her husband and Neville some cider, then sat herself and picked up a cup that she was already halfway through.

"No one hunts us now," she said softly. "Not the angels. Not the Roman soldiers. Not the priests. We can pick up our lives where once they had been interrupted."

Neville took a sip of cider, then allowed himself to relax in the sun, watching James play with the baby, and Mary watch her husband and son.

"You were killed, too," Neville suddenly said to Mary. "Soon after your husband died on the cross."

"Aye." Mary's face and body went very still as she remembered. "The soldiers, driven along by the hatred of the priests, came for me in the hour after they took down my husband's body."

She stopped, and Neville suddenly, horribly, knew what she was going to say.

"They stoned me to death, shattering every bone in my body."

"Mercy," whispered Neville, and looked down unseeing at the rough wood of the table as he remembered Mary Bohun's shattered, dying body. *They stoned her? They stoned the most wondrous woman the world had ever known? And then . . . then they dared to build a Church of lies about both Christ and his wife?*

"It is why Hal's Mary could not carry a child past six months," she continued. "I was six months gone with Christopher"—she nodded and smiled at the baby squirming happily in his father's arms— "when I died."

She turned her glorious eyes back to Neville. "And then my husband existed in torment within heaven, and I existed in torment without him" —her eyes filled with tears— "until this most remarkable of men loved me, and was my friend, and freed my husband."

"And now I think Tom more than half wishes he had not freed the husband," James said, his eyes crinkling humorously and his voice filled with laughter.

Neville stared at James, then at Mary, and then burst into laughter himself, all his sadness and regret gone.

"And you and Mary?" he said. "What now?"

They glanced at each other, and it was Mary who answered. "What now, Tom? Why, we raise our son, and any other children which bless us, and my husband works at his craft."

"We live and die as any, Tom," said James. "We are a husband and a wife, and that is *all* that we are."

"Then you are to be envied," Neville replied. He sampled some of the cheese that Mary had laid out, and discovered himself ravenous. "And the angel-children? Those such as Margaret, my wife?"

"Their link with the angels is broken, Tom," James said, passing his son back to Mary and helping himself to some of the bread and cheese that Neville was now munching down. "They will live out normal, mortal lives."

He paused, toying with some of the food, then continued. "You gave mankind control of his own destiny that day you kissed Mary. The link with the angels is completely broken asunder. They raven, trapped in hell, while mankind chooses his own path here on earth. What man chooses to do with his life—" He shrugged. "—is now his own burden to bear."

Neville relaxed even more. "Then we are all but husbands and wives, living out our lives."

James smiled gently. "Aye."

Neville nodded, feeling happier than he thought he had ever felt before. "Margaret is expecting twins," he said.

Mary and James grinned delightedly. "When you next come to visit," Mary said, "you must bring her."

Neville shot her a wry look. "I do not think she will come. But I will, if I may, and bring my children from time to time."

He looked up at the sky, realizing that the light had thinned. Dusk was not far off. "I should go," he said. "No doubt both my uncle and my wife wonder where I am."

They stood, and Mary and James escorted Neville back to the street door.

The bells were still ringing, and their sound made Neville turn one more time to James. "What of the Church?" he said. "It is useless—there is no God . . . while you . . ."

"No doubt it will continue for the time being," James said, clearly not very interested. "Too many men have too many ambitions tied up in it. But eventually it will fail and fall into irrelevance. Neither you nor I should worry overmuch about it, Tom."

Neville studied James' face, then he nodded. "And so I will not." He took his brother's hand, then kissed Mary on the cheek.

"I am glad you are both contented," he said, "and so shall I learn to be. I will go home to Halstow Hall, and raise my children, and learn to be a good husband for a wife who loves me very much."

He paused, introspective, then his mouth curved in a very small smile. "Somehow I do not think that her love will be a wasted thing."

"Love never is," Mary said. "Go home and tend your garden, Tom."

Glossary

For more information on characters and places, please visit:
www.saradouglass.com/crucibworld.html

AGINCOURT: Small village (approx. 180 kilometres) to the northwest of Paris.

AQUITAINE: a large and rich province covering much of the southwest of France. Aquitaine was not only independent of France, it was ruled by the English kings after Eleanor of Aquitaine brought the province, as part of her dowry, to her marriage with Henry II.

ARCHIBALD: fourth Earl of Douglas. His son is ARCHIBALD, Earl of Fife.

ARCHIBALD: Earl of Fife, son of the Earl of Douglas.

ARMOUR: the armouring of a knight was a complex affair, done in different ways in different countries and generations. Generally, knights wore either chain mail or plate armour or a combination of both, depending on fashion or the military activity involved. Chain mail was formed of thousands of tiny iron or steel rings riveted together to form a loose tunic (sometimes with arms); plate armour consisted of a series of metal plates fashioned to fit a knight's body and joints—the full suit of armour was rarely seen before the fifteenth century. Helmets (whether BASINETS or the full-visored helms), mail or plate gloves, and weapons completed the knight's outfitting.

ARUNDEL, WILLIAM: Archbishop of Canterbury.

AVIGNON: the French-controlled town which is the seat of the rebel popes.

BALLARD, AGNES: maid to MARGARET NEVILLE and nurse to ROSALIND.

BASINET: an open-faced helmet (although many knights wore them with a visor attached) that was either rounded (globular) or conical in shape. See also ARMOUR.

BAVIÈRE, ISABEAU DE: wife of LOUIS, mother of CHARLES and CATHERINE.

BEAUCHAMP, THOMAS: EARL OF WARWICK.

BEAUFORT, HENRY: illegitimate-born son of JOHN OF GAUNT and his third wife KATHERINE SWYNFORD, Henry is the Bishop of Winchester.

BEAUFORT, JOAN: illegitimate-born daughter of JOHN OF GAUNT and his third wife KATHERINE SWYNFORD. Now married to RALPH NEVILLE.

BEAUREVOIR: a castle north of Paris.

BLACK PRINCE: the now deceased first son of EDWARD III and his queen, PHILIPPA. The Black Prince was married to JOAN OF KENT, and was the father of RICHARD II.

BOHUN: Son of THOMAS NEVILLE and MARGARET NEVILLE. Named after MARY BOHUN.

BOHUN, MARY: heiress to the Hereford lands, titles and fortune, married to HAL BOLINGBROKE.

BOLINGBROKE, HENRY OF (HAL): King of England, son of JOHN OF GAUNT and his first wife, Blanche of Lancaster.

BORDEAUX: a port on the Garonne estuary in southwest France and capital of the duchy of AQUITAINE. Bordeaux was the BLACK PRINCE'S base in France (and in fact his son, RICHARD, was born there).

CATHERINE: daughter of Prince Louis of France and ISABEAU DE BAVIÈRE, younger sister to CHARLES.

CHARLES: King of France, grandson of his predecessor, the deceased KING JOHN, son of PRINCE LOUIS and ISABEAU DE BAVIÈRE. Older brother of CATHERINE.

CHARTRES, REGNAULT DE: Archbishop of RHEIMS.

CHATELLERAULT: a heavily fortified town some twenty miles north of Chauvigny.

CINQUE PORTS: the five (thus "cinque") important medieval southeastern ports of England: Dover, Hastings, Hythe, Romney and Sandwich. The barons of the Cinque Ports, as the Lord Warden of the Cinque Ports, were very powerful offices.

CLEMENT VII: the man elected by the breakaway cardinals to the papal throne after they declared the election of URBAN VI void due to the interference of the Roman mob. Clement rules from Avignon while Urban, who refuses to resign, continues to rule from Rome.

COOPER, WILL: apprentice physician to NICHOLAS CULPEPER.

COURTENAY, SIR ROBERT: squire to THOMAS NEVILLE. See also SQUIRE.

CULPEPER, NICHOLAS: physician to MARY BOHUN.

D'ALBERT, CONSTABLE: commander of PHILIP OF NAVARRE'S army.

D'ARC, JACQUES: sergeant of the village of Domremy, in the province of Lorraine, France.

D'ARC, JOAN (JEANNE, OR JEANNETTE): second daughter of JACQUES D'ARC. Known as the Maid of France for her visionary prophecies.

D'ARC, ZABILLET (ISABELLE): wife of JACQUES D'ARC and mother of JOAN D'ARC.

DATING: medieval Europeans almost never used calendar dates. Instead, they orientated themselves within the year by the religious cycle of Church festivals, holy days and saints' day. Although there were saints' days every day of the year, most regions observed only a few of them; the average holy days observed within the English year, for example, was between forty and sixty; in Florence it was as high as 120. Years tended to be dated by the length of a monarch's reign, each successive year starting on the date the monarch was crowned; EDWARD III was crowned on 1 February 1327, so, according to popular use, each new year during his reign would begin on 1st February. The legal year in England was calculated from Lady Day (25th March), so for legal purposes the new year began on 26th March. From the very late medieval period the government gradually instituted clock and calendar time as we know it. See my Web page on medieval time for a full explanation for calculating the medieval year: www.saradouglass.com/medtime.html

EDWARD III: king of England before RICHARD II. He died, mysteriously, during the Christmastide celebrations of 1378. Edward is the father of JOHN OF GAUNT and grandfather of HAL BOLINGBROKE.

EXETER, DUKE OF: See HOLLAND, JOHN.

FÉCAMP, ABBÉ DE: the cleric in charge of Joan of Arc's trial (see D'ARC, JOAN).

GABRIEL, SAINT: an archangel of heaven.

GASCONY: a province in the south of France famed for its wine and horses.

GILES, MASTER: BOLINGBROKE'S chief engineer at the siege of HARFLEUR.

GLOUCESTER, DUKE OF: see WOODSTOCK, THOMAS OF.

GLYNDWR, OWAIN: a prince of the Welsh.

GRAVENSTEEN, THE: the Count of Flanders' castle home in Ghent, capital of Flanders.

HALSTOW HALL: THOMAS NEVILLE'S home estate in Kent on the Hoo Peninsula near the Thames estuary.

HARFLEUR: town and garrison at the mouth of the Seine River, guarding the river and road approaches to Paris.

HARRISON, RICHARD: a London landlord.

HARWOOD, MARGERY: a London housewife. Her husband is William.

HAWKINS, EMMA: a London prostitute. Her daughter is JOCELYN HAWKINS.

HAWKINS, JOCELYN: daughter to EMMA HAWKINS.

HAWKINS, WILLIAM: captain of BOLINGBROKE'S castle guard in ROUEN. (No relation to Emma or Jocelyn.)

HOLLAND, JOHN: Duke of Exeter and Earl of Huntingdon, son of JOAN OF KENT and Sir Thomas Holland, half brother to the murdered RICHARD II.

HOTSPUR: see PERCY, HENRY.

HUNDRED YEARS' WAR: a period of intense war between France and England that lasted from roughly the mid-fourteenth to fifteenth centuries. It was caused by many factors, but primarily by the English King, EDWARD III's, insistence that he was the true heir to the French throne. The English and French royal families had intermarried for generations, and Edward was, in fact, the closest male heir. However, his claim was through his mother, who was the daughter of a French king, and French law did not recognise claims through the female line. The war was also the result of hundreds of years of tension over the amount of land the English held in France (often over a third of the realm).

HUNGERFORD, LORD: one of BOLINGBROKE's commanders in France.

ISABEAU DE BAVIÈRE: see BAVIÈRE, ISABEAU DE.

JOAN OF ARC: see D'ARC, JOAN.

JOAN OF KENT: wife of the BLACK PRINCE, and a famed beauty in her youth. Mother of RICHARD II.

JOHN, KING: deceased king of France.

JOHN OF GAUNT: DUKE OF LANCASTER and Aquitaine, Earl of Richmond, King of Castile, and prince of the Plantagenet dynasty; the deceased son of EDWARD III (Edward Plantagenet) and his queen, PHILIPPA, John of Gaunt was the most powerful and wealthy English nobleman of the medieval period. The name Gaunt (his popular nickname) derived from Ghent, where he was born. Married first to Blanche of Lancaster, then to Constance of Castile; both dead. By Blanche he had a son, HENRY (HAL) BOLINGBROKE; by Constance two daughters (who became the queens of Castile and Portugal); and by his longtime mistress, KATHERINE SWYNFORD, two legitimised children, HENRY and JOAN

BEAUFORT. John of Gaunt died during the burning of the SAVOY by the peasant rebels.

JUSTICIAR: the chief political and legal representative of the King of England, acting as regent in his absence.

LAMBETH PALACE: the London residence of the arch-bishops of Canterbury, Lambeth Palace sits on the eastern bank of the Thames almost directly across from WESTMINSTER.

LANCASTER, DUKE OF: see JOHN OF GAUNT.

LEMAISTRE, JEAN: Dominican Vicar of the Holy Office of the Inquisition in ROUEN.

LOLLARDS: the popular name given to followers of JOHN WYCLIFFE. It is a derisory name, taken from the fourteenth-century word "lolling," which means mumbling.

LONDON BRIDGE: for centuries there was only one bridge crossing the Thames. It crosses from South-wark on the southern bank into London itself, linking up with Watling Street, one of the great Roman roads in England. As with most bridges in medieval Europe, the bridge is built over with tenement buildings and shops.

LOUIS: only son of KING JOHN of France. Louis suffered an unfortunate encounter with a peacock which drove him insane, and now his son, CHARLES, has succeeded Louis' father, King John.

LYNLEY, LADY ALICIA: one of MARY's ladies.

MARCEL, ETIENNE: a rich and influential Parisian cloth merchant and Provost of the Merchants of Paris, an of-fice somewhat like that of a Lord Mayor. He died dur-ing the French uprising (known as the Jacquerie) some three years before the events of *The Crippled Angel*.

MARIE: a midwife, and companion to JOAN D'ARC.

MICHAEL, SAINT: an archangel of heaven.

MONTAGU, JOHN: Earl of Salisbury.

MONTGIES, ALAIN: Mayor of ROUEN.

MOWBRAY, THOMAS: Earl of Nottingham and Duke of Norfolk and a boyhood friend of RICHARD's.

NAVARRE: a rich kingdom in the extreme northwest of Spain, it has been in the control of French nobles and kings for generations. Until the early fourteenth century the King of France had also held the title King of Navarre, but a complicated succession crisis witnessed the separation of the two kingdoms into separate branches of the same family. Currently it is ruled by PHILIP, known as Philip the Bad.

NEVILLE, MARGARET: wife of THOMAS NEVILLE. They have a daughter, ROSALIND, and a son, BOHUN.

NEVILLE, RALPH: Baron of Raby and Earl of Westmorland; a powerful noble from the north of England. Uncle to THOMAS NEVILLE.

NEVILLE, THOMAS: a senior member of the powerful Neville family. Nephew to RALPH NEVILLE. Married to MARGARET with whom he has two children. Neville was once a Dominican friar.

NORBURY, SIR JOHN: a member of BOLINGBROKE'S household.

NORTHUMBERLAND, EARL OF: See PERCY, HENRY.

NOYES, SIR GILLES DE: a French nobleman.

PERCY, HENRY: the EARL OF NORTHUMBERLAND and the most powerful nobleman in England behind LANCASTER. Northumberland has long been rivals with the Lancastrian faction which includes RALPH NEVILLE and THOMAS NEVILLE.

PERCY, HENRY (HOTSPUR): son and heir of the EARL OF NORTHUMBERLAND, and a powerful nobleman in his own right.

PERCY, THOMAS: Earl of Worcester, brother to the EARL OF NORTHUMBERLAND and uncle to HOTSPUR.

PHILIP THE BAD: King of Navarre and Count of Evreux, cousin to KING JOHN and a powerful figure in French politics. As well as ruling NAVARRE, Philip holds extensive lands in the west of France.

PHILIPPA: a now-dead Queen of England, wife to the deceased EDWARD III, and mother of LANCASTER. She died some years previous to the events of *The Crucible*.

POITIERS: a town in central France, and site of one of the BLACK PRINCE's greatest victories during the HUNDRED YEARS' WAR.

POLE, MICHAEL DE LA: EARL OF SUFFOLK, commander in BOLINGBROKE's army.

RABY: see NEVILLE, RALPH.

RHEIMS: cathedral city approximately 200 kilometers to the northeast of Paris. Also spelt Reims.

RICHARD II: King of England, son of the BLACK PRINCE (deceased) and JOAN OF KENT. Deposed and murdered at BOLINGBROKE's hand.

ROSALIND: daughter of THOMAS NEVILLE and MARGARET NEVILLE.

ROUEN: a city on the River Seine, partway between HARFLEUR and Paris.

SAVOY PALACE: the DUKE OF LANCASTER's residence on THE STRAND just outside London's western walls. It was burned down during the peasant rebellion.

SCARLE, JOHN: BOLINGBROKE's chancellor.

SHERIFF HUTTON: RALPH NEVILLE's main castle and residence some ten miles northeast of York.

SMITHFIELD (or Smoothfield):   a large open space or field in London's northern suburbs, just beyond Aldersgate. For many centuries it has been the site of games, tournaments, and trading, craft and pleasure fairs. East Smithfield is a similarly large field to the east of London.

SQUIRE: in the late fourteenth century the social status and meaning of squire is much different to the earlier chivalric perception of a squire as a "knight-in-training." The late fourteenth century squire is just as likely to be referred to as a valet or even a sergeant. He was generally of noble blood, but he might not be a "knight-in-training" as such.

STRAND, THE: an important street running from London along the northern bank of the Thames down to WESTMINSTER, lined with palaces of the nobles.

STURRY, SIR RICHARD: a councillor of BOLINGBROKE's.

SUFFOLK, EARL OF: see POLE, MICHAEL DE LA.

Swynford, lady katherine: dowager Duchess of Lancaster, widow of john of gaunt, Duke of Lancaster. By John of Gaunt she has two children, henry and joan beaufort.

Thorseby, richard: the Prior General of England, administering all Dominicans and their friaries in the realm of England.

Tonsure: a round, shaved patch on the crown of a cleric's head.

Tudor, lord owen: a member of bolingbroke's household.

Tusser, thomas: steward to thomas neville.

Umfraville, sir gilbert: one of bolingbroke's commanders at harfleur.

Urban vi: the man elected by the College of Cardinals to the papal throne after the death of Gregory XI in 1378.

Vere, robert de: deceased Earl of Oxford, and close friend of richard's.

Warwick, earl of: see beauchamp, thomas.

Westminster: in medieval England Westminster was an important municipality in its own right, and separate from London, although both were inextricably linked. Most of medieval Westminster was destroyed by fire in the early nineteenth century, but it consisted of a large palace complex boasting three halls (only one of which still stands) as well as the abbey.

Whittington, richard (dick): former mercer and alderman of Broad Street ward, now Lord Mayor of London.

Williamson, jack: apprentice engineer to master giles.

Windsor: royal castle to the west of London.

Woodstock, thomas of: the now deceased Earl of Buckingham and duke of gloucester, seventh and youngest son of edward iii of England; Constable of England.

Worde, wynkyn de: the last of the Dominican friars who worked the archangels' will on earth.

Wycliffe, john: an eccentric English cleric and master of Balliol College, Oxford.

Look for

DRUID'S SWORD

BOOK SIX OF THE
WAYFARER REDEMPTION

by Sara Douglass

Now available.

Waterloo Station, London

Saturday, 2 September 1939

✠

"MAJOR? MAJOR? I'M sorry to wake you, sir, but the train has arrived at Waterloo and you'll have to disembark."

Jack Skelton jerked too fast from deep sleep into wakefulness, and for several disorienting moments stared into the face of the conductor leaning over him, his mind unable to let go the dream images that skidded through it.

Frank Bentley and his insipid wife, Violet, Stella Wentworth, standing beautiful and untouchable under the embankment light. Matilda and Ecub, suburban housewives in dressing gowns. Asterion—Weyland Orr—taking him to Pen Hill. Faerie Hill Manor, and both the Lord of the Faerie and the king of England, George VI, waiting for him.

Grace—everyone's doom.

"Sir, I must ask you to—"

"Yes, yes. I'm awake." Jack Skelton struggled to his feet, one hand clutching at the overhead luggage rack for support as his head reeled.

The conductor stepped back. "It's been a bad few days, sir," he said, watching the American major curiously as he straightened his tie and uniform jacket, then lifted his greatcoat down from the rack. He wondered why the

American was here, and hoped that it might be some indication that the Yanks wouldn't leave it as long to help out in this war as they had left it the last. "We've heard news on the wireless that the PM has sent an ultimatum to the Nazis. Get out of Poland or we'll go to war."

The conductor paused, his face glum. "No chance that the Germans will back off, d'you think, major?"

Finally fully awake and oriented, Jack studied the man, knowing there was no chance for peace, and wondering if the man wanted false reassurances or the truth.

"It is too late now," he said. "I'm sorry."

The conductor's face tightened, and he gave a small nod. "Let me help you with your bag, sir."

ONCE ON the platform, Jack tipped the conductor then stood motionless, looking about. Because he'd been so deeply asleep when the train had pulled in, and had probably then slept for fifteen minutes or more before the conductor woke him up, most of the other passengers had departed, and how the great cavernous space of Waterloo Station was all but deserted. He shivered, and tried to put it down to the cold night air.

The conductor had got back on the train, and now the platform was empty save for himself and several baggage handlers at the far end of the train, standing about an empty trolley, smoking and talking.

About the forthcoming war, no doubt. The Germans had invaded Poland earlier today, and war was inevitable. Jack could *feel* it seeping over the vast stretches of land and water between where he stood and where the Poles battled desperately. It was only a matter of time before it reached London.

He shivered again, and hunched deeper into his greatcoat, lighting his own cigarette then flicking the match away. He drew a deep breath; taking comfort in the smoke. Jack had first come to this land almost three and a half thousand years ago as Brutus, the exiled Trojan prince. With Genvissa he'd thought to resurrect the ancient Troy Game, but everything had fallen apart when his then-wife, Cornelia, had murdered Genvissa before they could complete the game. For three and a half thousand years Jack had—as Brutus, then as William, Duke of Normandy, and subsequently Louis de Silva—fought to finish what he had started so long ago. But always events and people (and that mostly Cornelia in her rebirth as Caela and then Noah) conspired to prevent him.

God, how long had it been since he'd last been in England? Almost three hundred years, give or take a decade or two. Oh, he'd come back briefly now and then, stepping through the realm of the Faerie, to meet with either Coel, the Lord of the Faerie, or with his father, Silvius, but apart from those fleeting visits ... nothing. He'd walked away from the smoking ruins of London in 1666, walked away from the disaster of his hopes and dreams.

Walked away from Noah, who had abandoned her love for him to live with Asterion, and give him a child.

Walked away from the Troy Game.

Walked away from it all.

To roam.

He'd wandered first in the form of Louis de Silva. He'd gone back to his father's estates in France, and from there, desperate, restless, angry beyond knowing, he'd drifted through the forests and fields and pleasure halls of Europe. Then, as the years passed, he assumed the form of a priest, because in his anger that amused him, and desecrated his way through Egypt and Arabia. From there, to India, and then even farther east, and as the decades spun by and his resentment and bewilderment at what had happened deepened, he became a sailor in a Portuguese man-of-war that had berthed in the Philippines, and fought and squandered his way across the oceans of the world.

Then he'd landed in America—new and brash and uncaring—and here Jack had found a home. He settled in the Appalachian mountains, finding solace in their high mountain lakes and dark forests. He lived there for a hundred years or more, spending more and more time not as a man but as Ringwalker, the name he took when he assumed the mantle of the ancient Stag God, roaming the wild paths and tracks through the wilderness.

He found peace, and a renewed purpose. It was about this time, perhaps almost two hundred years after the Great Fire of London, that Jack made contact with the Lord of the Faerie again. Just a touch, a glimmer of friendship sent through the Faerie, but it was enough to begin rebuilding the bonds between them. From that point they'd met once every five or six years, sometimes in the forests of America, sometimes in the Faerie. These meetings lasted only a short while, less than an hour, and they rarely talked. They just spent time together.

About forty years ago, when they'd met in a lonely spot of the Faerie, the Lord of the Faerie had put his hand on Ringwalker's shoulders, and said, "My friend, John Thornton is back, a prince of the realm now. Loth is back also, and as wedded to the Christian church as he was when last he walked."

Ringwalker had tensed. "The others?"

"None of the rest of us had to be reborn. We have all done much as you have for the past few hundred years— moved in and out of the Faerie and in and out of mortal form as it suited us. Apart from John and Loth, we've all gone too far to be trapped by birth and death now."

We're all way too powerful. Too fey.

"And *her*? Is she still with *him*?"

"Noah? With Weyland? Of course, for they love each other deeply. Ringwalker, please, the land needs you back. We need you back. All of us."

"I don't think I can—"

"You must," the Lord of the Faerie had said quietly, and Ringwalker had bowed his head in acceptance.

Five months ago dreams began to pervade Jack's sleep. Each night, over and over, he dreamed of arriving in London, meeting with a nervous man called Frank Bentley, then walking about London, meeting in turn each of the people who had become caught up in the Troy Game.

Everyone save Noah.

Jack never met Noah in his dreams.

He knew what the dreams meant. It was time to go back. Time to *move*.

Time to find Noah.